Advance Pr~~~~ ~~~~ ~~~~ Gulf

"A smart, funny, and hugely entertai ~~~~ ta-
tion and reality, integrity and profit,

...~~~ Evison

"A new work by Belle Boggs is a cause for celebration. In *The Gulf*, she leaps across perspectives with ease, bridging America's political divide with compassion and comedy, clarity and insight. *The Gulf* is a hilarious and healing novel for these polarized times. Reading it consumed my nights, and gave me hope." —Tania James

"Belle Boggs takes the term 'high concept' to a whole new level in her brilliant comic novel, *The Gulf*. A satirical send-up of the whole business of commercialized Christianity and also for-profit 'creative writing' workshops, *The Gulf* is literally a DIVINE read—it's also smart, profound, very funny, and finally redemptive." —Lee Smith

"Belle Boggs puts her keen eye on the writing workshop as a kind of lab for examining differing parts of America, and the result is a wildly engaging exploration of characters finding their way through connection, and through language." —Aimee Bender

"The brilliant humor in Belle Boggs's *The Gulf* comes from a kind of clarity that only the best writers possess, an ability to look so closely at the world that you can see the absurdity without getting lost in it. These characters, because Boggs takes such care with them, feel so real, so wholly unique. And then there is the story itself, moment after moment, that took my breath away. It's an amazing novel. You have to read it." —Kevin Wilson

"Wit and humor abound in *The Gulf*, and so do great wisdom and compassion. With her wonderful short stories and essays, Belle Boggs has established herself as both a stellar writer of fiction and a brilliant voice on important issues within our society; in this fine novel, her many talents come together, delivering a community of memorable characters and a compelling story as suspenseful in its emotional twists and turns as the approaching hurricane." —Jill McCorkle

Praise for *The Art of Waiting*

"Boggs has done something quite lovely and laudable with *The Art of Waiting*: She's given a cold, clinical topic some much-needed warmth and soul. The miracle of life, you might even say." —*The New York Times*

"An eye-opening, gorgeously written blend of memoir, reportage, and cultural analysis." —*The Boston Globe*

"Boggs joins the ranks of great American essayists, writing fearlessly about the personal and the political and where they intersect." —*O, The Oprah Magazine*, Top 10 Books of 2016

Praise for *Mattaponi Queen*

"Boggs has a knack for capturing both the comedy and the absurdity in all levels of human relationships." —*The Millions*

"[An] impressive debut collection. . . . These linked stories reach toward hope when they aren't heading for heartbreak." —*Elle*

"Belle Boggs has created funny, but understated, characters and her sharp, clear voice seems suited to stories relatives swap on slightly rickety wooden lawn furniture. . . . A bewitching debut." —*Chicago Tribune*

"Boggs knows her landscape—how the mildew smells, what the frost looks like on a badly tended garden, how trees around an old house look different from one decade to the next. Reading these stories is satisfying, like going to a concert in which the musicians, you can just tell, have given everything for the moment: your unforgettable evening." —*Los Angeles Times*

The Gulf

Also by Belle Boggs

Mattaponi Queen
The Art of Waiting

The Gulf

A Novel

Belle Boggs

Graywolf Press

This publication is made possible, in part, by the voters of Minnesota through a Minnesota State Arts Board Operating Support grant, thanks to a legislative appropriation from the arts and cultural heritage fund, and a grant from the Wells Fargo Foundation. Significant support has also been provided by Target, the McKnight Foundation, the Lannan Foundation, the Amazon Literary Partnership, and other generous contributions from foundations, corporations, and individuals. To these organizations and individuals we offer our heartfelt thanks.

This is a work of fiction. Names, characters, businesses, places, events, locales, and incidents are either the products of the author's imagination or are used in a fictitious manner. Any resemblance to actual persons, living or dead, or actual events is purely coincidental.

Published by Graywolf Press
250 Third Avenue North, Suite 600
Minneapolis, Minnesota 55401

www.graywolfpress.org

Published in the United States of America

ISBN 978-1-55597-834-1

2 4 6 8 9 7 5 3 1
First Graywolf Printing, 2019

Library of Congress Control Number: 2018947086

Cover design and illustration: Kimberly Glyder

For Richard

And beside all this, between us and you there is a great gulf fixed: so that they which would pass from hence to you cannot; neither can they pass to us, that would come from thence.

Luke 16:26

The Gulf

Part One

1

The applications arrived, first in a trickle that Marianne could have read in an afternoon, then all at once, in alarming, mailbox-stuffing sheaves. She spent all day avoiding them, swimming in the Gulf of Mexico instead, or reading the stubby, water-damaged Judith Krantz and Stephen King novels she borrowed from the paneled-wood study. The applications covered every horizontal surface in her room: the oak-veneer bureau, the top of the boxy, old-fashioned television, the round Formica dinette table. They splayed across the second double bed's glossy navy-and-orange bedspread, and blocked the heating and air vents that jutted out below the heavy floral curtains.

They were Christian poems and stories and novels, or rather the novels and stories and poems of Christians, and Marianne could hardly bear to look at them, much less read more than a page or two at a time. First off, a good number of them had been printed on pastel paper, pinks and blues and yellows and creams. Easter egg colors, baby blanket colors, three-pack-of-panties colors, clashing, in their ever-growing stacks, with her room's dark-and-bright seventies decor, the grainy wood furniture and the demented cabbage roses on the upholstery. And they *smelled*, some like talcum powder and others like a cloying, familiar perfume, many like menthol cigarettes. Together the smells blended into a noxious, headache-inducing sweetness that drove Marianne outside, into the hazy light of Florida's late summer.

The Genesis Inspirational Writing Ranch—or the *Ranch*, for short, suggestive of a mix of industry and ease, Republicans and wealth—was a collection of white stucco buildings set back from the road and obscured by a stand of live oaks with twisted gray trunks and dusty, rubbery leaves. It had two long rows of guest rooms, perpendicular to the beach, behind a central building, which had since been turned into the common areas: a room for pool and darts, a library, a caterer's kitchen. These would comprise the school's office and dining hall, its spaces for readings and public functions. There were two large rooms in a single building, and a smaller cabana near the water, that would serve as classrooms. The grounds included a kidney-shaped pool, a sliver of beach, a garden—but groundskeeping, or any other kind of upkeep, had not been a recent priority. Broken things—the pool filter, some of the air-conditioning units, most of the minifridges—had gone unfixed, while everything else took on an air of seaside decay. Screen doors made an uneven seal with the rooms. Giant bugs lurked in corners. Almost every room had a spreading stain on the ceiling, marking the many places where the roof shingles had dislodged. Outside, vicious sand burrs crept onto every footpath, and the statues in the garden, a collection of half-naked nymphs and satyrs thoroughly unsuitable for a Christian writing ranch, groped each other in long tufts of switchgrass.

"This was a bad idea," she told Eric over Skype, her laptop screen angled to show a recently scrubbed fridge and a towering pile of manuscripts. "Here is what you should do: sell this place for the land, then refund all these application fees."

Eric Osborne—her best friend, ex-fiancé, and business partner—had recently abandoned her for the United Arab Emirates, where he had a semester-long gig teaching fiction. Marianne pictured him lazily eating figs and pomegranates, sunning himself next to a pool uncontaminated by algae or raccoons.

Skype's slight delay, made worse by the way the internet here cut in and out, gave Eric's normally calm and reassuring voice an annoyed and impatient edge. "Everything is mortgaged, we need to make money with what we have. Plus." The screen froze for a moment. "Where will you go?"

"Maybe Dubai," she said, squinting at the screen. The room behind Eric's head glowed with an opulent golden light. She could see a bookcase filled with leather-bound volumes, and a sparkling chandelier. What kind of a fool did Eric think she was? "Do you know what I found in that minifridge behind me?"

"Trust me," he said, and the screen froze again. "You wouldn't. Like it here."

"A condom," she said. "Full of sand. I thought it was a penis, and I screamed, and there was no one here to hear me. Also: the applications," she said, putting her eye up close to the camera so that all he could see of her was a big, staring eye. "They are crazy."

"How many?"

"One hundred and twenty-three," she said. "But I haven't gotten the mail today. Or yesterday." She groaned and lay back on the bed, remembering the last time she'd neglected the mail. The mailman had simply left a stack of envelopes on the ground.

"There are bound to be some good ones," he said. "In a sample that large. Some. Interesting ones. Have you read. Them all?"

"Yes," she said. "No." The day before she'd tried to read a few, but stopped after coming across a series of poems that had been conceived, both in manuscript length and creativity of the punishments inflicted upon sinners, as a contemporary *Inferno*.

"Don't worry about cleaning fridges or fixing stuff. Mark is working on getting some people out for that. Just read, interview the teachers, and I'll be there in December to help you make the final decisions."

"Tell him to get the pool fixed," she said. Eric was never able to talk long, and she pictured him logging off to take his students—demure, kohl-eyed women—on coffee dates where they asked him about their manuscripts, which he would have mistaken for good because they described a world so foreign, and because the women themselves were so pretty. While Marianne scrubbed odiferous minifridges and took notes on poems (poems!) about serial killers.

Just a month ago, Marianne had her own place in Brooklyn, a miraculously cheap railroad apartment on the top floor of a four-story walk-up in the treeless and newly trendy neighborhood of Greenpoint. Not that she cared about trends (and she would have preferred some trees), just the cost of things, which needed to be bargain-basement low. Marianne wasn't cheap; she was just a poet. Really? she thought each year at tax time, totaling the measly grant or teaching payments she'd collected. She felt like someone on a calorie-restricted diet, looking over a list of what she'd eaten in a week: shock and a little pride that she was even still alive.

It was, in its way, the life she'd imagined for herself, growing up in rural Virginia: the sparsely furnished apartment, the neighborhood buzzing with unfamiliar languages (Polish, mostly, but also Russian and Spanish), the clacking of grocery and laundry carts along the street. A job she didn't have to go to every day. Time, hers alone, for writing.

Her mother, an art teacher at the local high school, had fed Marianne this vision when she was very young, with books like *This Is New York* and *Eloise* and later with stories of her own time at the New School, studying painting. "Every artist requires a New York experience," Theresa used to say, her soft coastal Virginia accent mixing with a slight Yankee nasality. For Marianne's fifth birthday, she'd given her a heavy glass snow globe with a pewter cityscape, and had pointed out the crowded-together landmarks: the Chrysler Building, the Empire State Building, Central Park. Though Marianne couldn't draw or paint or act or sing, she had loved books and words even before she could read, and was relieved to learn that writing, too, was an art that could provide you some entrance to that fabled city, some reasons for being there.

But those reasons, in her thirty-fourth year, were beginning to dry up like the slowly evaporating water in her snow globe. Her mother died before Marianne made it to the city, and she was no longer so sure she was honoring her memory by living there. Yes, she'd been the recipient of various grants, had published a chapbook, and was working on a full-length manuscript of poems, but her career had not exactly taken off. She took her turns reading to dispiritingly small crowds at coffee shops; at the post–high school level, she could only get hired to teach remedial composition at vocational schools. Unlike her mother, who met Marianne's father, in town for an academic conference, in a seedy East Village bar, she had not found love. Or else—and maybe this was worse—she'd found it and had thrown it away.

Even her neighborhood, never the bustling, glittering, taxi-crowded place of her childhood imagination, was not what it had been when she moved there. She watched its best features disappear: the brutal but effective Russian aestheticians, the Italian bakeries where everything tasted of amaretto, the bocce courts with shuffling men in guayaberas and straw hats. Now androgynous twentysomethings walked their dogs across the bocce courts, whimsical boutiques lined even the dingiest blocks, and you were lucky to get a tepid facial for less than a hundred bucks. And yet the harshness of New York—heavy winter snows, hot summers, human feces on the subway—felt unabated to Marianne. But as long as she had her apartment, she told herself, she could stay.

Then one afternoon, in early August, she got the letter from her landlord that she'd long feared was coming. Her building was being turned into condos, which the current tenants could buy instead of rent. The landlord referred to the condo sales as an exciting opportunity, except in his haste or lack of English fluency, he'd written *exiting opportunity*. Which, given the anticipated cost of the condos (not mentioned in the letter), Marianne supposed it was.

On this very same day—at the very same *moment*, in fact, that she was learning of her impending homelessness—Eric called Marianne with his news. She'd come in from a walk in one hundred–degree heat, ripped open and read the letter, and heard the strident, old-fashioned ring of her telephone, four floors above. She ran to get it in case it was her landlord, calling to say that she could stay. She was breathing hard, holding the torn envelope and badly spelled letter in her hands, as she told Eric what it said.

"That's terrible," he agreed. "But you had to have known it was coming." He'd moved away from the city years ago, back to Charlotte, where he'd planned to make the advance on his two-book deal last as long as possible. But he'd gotten married instead—not to Marianne—and bought a ring and a house and had then gotten divorced and found himself teaching English at a high school hard up enough to hire someone without a license. The things that happened to him there—insults hurled like chairs, followed sometimes by actual chairs—eventually led him to sign on to the job in Dubai. He had yet to write the second book.

"I thought I had another year, at least," she said, scanning the letter again. She turned on the box fan in her kitchen window and took in a great, vibrating lungful of air. Would she ever find another apartment with a window that so perfectly fit a box fan? "It says I have to move out by September 15. That's fifteen days into my new lease. I already signed it. I was about to send it back. Doesn't that count—that I signed it?"

"This is perfect, actually," Eric was saying over the roar. "Perfect timing." "Thanks for your concern."

"No, really," he said. He explained things slowly, savoring the story like a person talking himself into something.

In July, a large brown envelope had come in the mail for him. Inside, Eric found a long, handwritten letter rubber-banded atop a thick stack of papers—the deed to a seaside Florida motel his great-aunt Frances closed down years ago.

Eric began to read from his aunt's letter, in a quavering drawl: "*I always thought the property could be used for something more creative than a place for beach bums to watch television, which was all the imagination my late husband could muster. I'm too old to take this on, but I can finance it.*"

"Don't do the voice, Eric. The voice is weird."

He continued: "*It would bring me the greatest pleasure to help my nephews begin what I'm sure would be a successful and personally rewarding business venture.* She wants us to start a school, Marianne. A school for writing."

"Well, congratulations," Marianne said, peering again at the letter in her own hands. "I don't see how you turn a motel into a school, or what any of this has to do with my situation. Or, for that matter, how you and your brother will possibly run a school together."

Eric's brother, Mark, was an investment banker who'd moved from Charlotte to an apartment downtown, just a few blocks from Ground Zero. Marianne had met him exactly once, at a trader's bar with bras hanging from the ceiling.

"That's the thing, he's just helping with the business side. I told Frances I need help, obviously—teachers and an administrator to start off—and she's willing to invest." He paused. "She's willing to pay your salary. To run it."

"My salary? To run a school?"

"There are some details we have to work out—she wants it to be a place for Christian writers, but that's perfect, isn't it? It's what we always talked about."

"Eric, it's what we always *joked* about. There's a difference."

"I told her that you had this exact same idea years ago," he said. "That's why she wants you to be the administrator. The *director*."

This was the business they'd imagined together in grad school, after too many scotches for Eric and too many mojitos for Marianne: a low-residency master of fine arts program for evangelical Christians.

The idea first came to her after she'd gotten a scholarship to a workshop on formal poetry at a little college in Pennsylvania. Tuition was over two thousand dollars, and the workshop had attracted more than a few Christian poets, who'd flown in from all over the country. They'd been good workshop participants, polite and deferential, dutifully taking copious notes about their poems. Though they were better dressed and more formally educated than the evangelical Christians Marianne had grown up with, she recognized the same placid countenances: self-satisfaction masquerading as serenity. During a discussion of process, Marianne had been surprised and a little horrified to discover that many of them wrote more than one poem a day.

That was years ago, and the evangelicals, it seemed, had more and more to say. In Marianne's hometown, religious signs, haphazardly stenciled onto primer-painted plywood, began to appear by the roadside, along with political messages, mostly veiled threats against President Obama. Letters to the editor, which frequently invoked God, now took up two whole pages of their tiny weekly paper. In many parts of the country, it was okay now to question anything put forth by science—evolution, climate change, black holes—as an attack on God. And they had money: you could turn on any television set to see as much.

The motel was on the gulf, Eric was telling her, with a pool and a sculpture garden designed by his aunt. It was near Sarasota, a haven for artists of all kinds. What could be more inspirational to a community of inspirational writers?

"But that was a joke," Marianne said, twisting the coiled black phone cord around her arm. "A joke about taking money from Christians. Which I'm all about, but it was a *joke*."

"Think about it," Eric said. "You're getting kicked out of your apartment—where else will you go? You wouldn't have to teach."

"I'd have to teach Christians."

"For two weeks at a time!" he said. "And it wouldn't be Christians, necessarily. We could sell it as a place to work on inspirational writing."

"Inspirational writing." Marianne scraped a kitchen chair across the linoleum and sat down near the fan. She'd found the chair on the street and always meant to fix it up—paint the rusty legs a cheerful color, replace the cracked vinyl seat. It was absurd to think that someone with so little follow-through, someone who couldn't even do minor DIY projects or pay her bills on time, would be successful at running a school.

"Right," said Eric, apparently taking her silence for interest. "It's really popular right now, it has been for years. Especially the Christian market. And no one is capitalizing on that. We would be the first."

"Listen to you," she said. "Capitalize. Selling. We didn't go to school to learn to sell our work. I didn't, anyway. Clearly."

"I went to school because it was the best way to avoid ever having a real job, or so I thought," said Eric. "And so did you. You could finish 'The Ugly Bear List'—think about the inspiration you'd have."

Marianne felt a little electrical jolt at hearing her book-in-progress named, this book hardly anyone knew about but Eric. It had been in progress for a couple of years now, since the earliest days of the Tea Party, but wasn't close to done. The title came from a private saying, passed down from her grandmother to her mother—you wouldn't want to be on *her* ugly bear list—and referenced all the people and movements and decisions that made Marianne's blood pressure rise. Climate change deniers, racists and gun nuts and abortion foes. The NRA as a whole. Big Tobacco. Republican legislators back home who sold out the coast, stingy school board members who wouldn't take government money for a free school breakfast program, members of her own extended family who still loved that spunky former governor from Alaska. A shit list, a first-against-the-wall list, an accounting of all the people who'd one day have to pay, but also an examination of the incomprehensibility of those people's minds and the fear it created, the bears gnawing away inside your mind. The way its existence changed you, made you vigilant and suspicious.

She'd barely worked on it since starting her new job, a teaching gig at P.S. 150 in Brownsville, where she tutored kids in writing and sometimes taught poetry. Last school year she'd taught three days a week, and summer school wasn't full time, either—but the long commute and the intensity of routinely performing her own incompetence had left her little energy or motivation to write, which had come to feel like a private admission of defeat.

"You're still working on it, right? Wouldn't this be the perfect place to finish?"

Marianne lifted the sticky hair off her neck and knotted it loosely into a bun. Three of her students lived in homeless shelters all year, and her baby sister was a registered Republican.

"Yeah," she said, "still working. How old is your aunt? Does she have all her . . . faculties?"

"Great-aunt," Eric said. "Somewhere north of eighty. But sharp as a tack! Really, you should see—"

"Would she be looking over our shoulders all the time?"

"No, she's got a full life, over at the retirement home," he said. "She said in her letter that she *trusts my good judgment about teaching and writing*. She's getting older. She wants a legacy. We send her some of the students' work, invite her to a few readings . . ."

"What if the students aren't any good?" Marianne said. "What if they're terrible—unteachable?"

"Of course they won't all be good! Were all your classmates at NYU good?"

"No," she admitted, thinking of a beautiful heiress with an exceptional coat wardrobe who shrugged off the table's harsh criticism each week, leaving the bar they convened in after class for dates with various washed-up celebrities. Marianne had liked reading her poems mostly for the experience of looking into a rich person's life and point of view, but she had agreed with the class consensus that they were probably not publishable. There was a whole series, for example, written from the perspective of a variety of interchangeable Filipina maids. "I guess not. Did that make it right, though, for NYU to take their money? *Our* money?"

"That's a very paternalistic attitude, Marianne. I'm surprised," Eric scolded. "We could find the next Manny Abrams."

"Who?"

"Manny Abrams, the Holocaust survivor who wrote the best-selling memoir about having a heart attack and meeting Jesus, Muhammad, and the Buddha, and how they all agreed that Jesus was the one? He was on the *Today* show. Frances told me about him—she read him in her book club."

"That sounds terrible," Marianne said. "Was it written well?"

"Of course not! That's the point," Eric said. "This stuff doesn't have to be written well, or be believable. People don't care about that. It's like television. Frances has this idea that these people—these undiscovered, raw talents—are everywhere."

"But I thought you were going to Dubai. I thought you were waiting on your passport. Why don't you have a passport, anyway?" Even Marianne had a passport, obtained after a solid day of line-standing on Jay Street. She'd gotten it in case the law professor she'd been half-heartedly dating wanted to take her on an elaborate, spur-of-the-moment trip.

"I am going," he said. "That's the thing. It's four months. You could go now, get situated, sit on the beach, read applications, meet with Frances, then we could start in the spring. Or the summer."

"*Applications?*" Marianne said. The phone cord made a tourniquet around her purpled arm. "We don't even have something for people to apply to. Also, I have a lease."

"I put an ad up two weeks ago, and we already have thirty-five applications, forty dollars each. My brother is taking care of the business licenses and tax stuff."

"Your *brother?*"

"We went over the plan, and he thinks it's a winner. He even talked Frances into giving each of us a profit share in the school. He wants to take you to dinner, go over some things."

"I have a lease, I said." She thought that maybe she could fight for her apartment, deny the existence of the impending condos.

"I'm sorry to tell you this, Marianne, but your apartment is a dump. And they're not going to honor your lease."

"I'm sorry to tell you this, Eric, but your brother is a stockbroker. And your great-aunt is crazy."

He was silent for a while, and Marianne regretted what her voice implied. He was touchy about his brother and his success, and maybe he was sensitive about Frances too. She turned off the box fan to hear whether

Eric was still on the line. As its rotation slowed, she saw that the blades were gray with city grime. Eric was right: her apartment was a dump.

"What about my sister?" she said finally. "I invited her to New York for Thanksgiving."

"Thanksgiving is four months away," Eric said. Marianne didn't point out how early she had to make invitations, now that Ruth was married. "Did she say she was coming?"

"No," she admitted. Her sister hadn't made any promises.

"Invite her to Florida," Eric said. "Where would she rather be, anyway—Brooklyn, or a Christian writing school in Florida?"

"I don't know," she said.

"You do know," Eric said softly. His voice on the telephone, a gentle drawl, had always been irresistible to her. "What's keeping you there?"

Marianne thought of her things—what would she take with her, fleeing the city? Some poetry books, her clothes and shoes, the small framed watercolors by her mother. The snow globe. A brown pottery mug that once held her mother's brushes. Ten years in the city, and almost everything of value she had was something she'd brought with her, something from home. She'd thought, years ago, that she could bring Ruth too.

"You said your aunt was an artist—a sculptor?"

"You'll love her," Eric said. "And your sister can visit you in Florida. She'll love it," Eric said, with so much certainty that Marianne believed him.

"Tell me more," she said. "About my salary."

She should have stayed, defended the apartment, piled her sparse furniture at its doorway. If her landlord kicked her out, put her belongings on the street, she could have dragged a sleeping bag and her few belongings down to Zuccotti Park, started some new poems, put her middle finger up if Mark walked by. In Florida she watched CNN's mocking footage of the Occupy protesters in their zombie face paint and Uncle Sam drag, then found an internet livestream that told a different story: marches and daily meetings, vegetarian meals, people who spoke eloquently of the debt that broke them, their families. She imagined herself as one of them: organizing the books in the People's Library, donating her own. If anyone asked, she could tell her story: forty-two thousand dollars in student loan debt, part-time work in a high-poverty school, newly homeless.

Join us! the protesters chanted at an open-air tour bus plastered with *Lion King* advertising. The tourists leaned over the railing, snapping photos. No one got off the bus.

Would Marianne have disembarked from her own comfortable perch? Would she have camped in a public park, shared food, brushed her teeth in a water fountain? Maybe not, she thought, but she kept the livestream rolling.

Meanwhile the applications continued to pile up, in high, wavering towers. Besides, she had run out of Krantz and King—her own book collection, mailed from Brooklyn, had not yet arrived—and watching grainy protest footage in an abandoned motel made her feel guilty, and also like a squatter. She turned the sound off on her laptop and began to read applications seriously. Choosing the first one was hardest—a slim packet of poems, clipped together with a paper clip in the shape of a heart—and the process reminded her of the struggle she sometimes had with writing. The physical part, what novelists called "butt in chair," was the hardest, but after a little while you forgot that you were doing it.

Soon the piles began to take on a sort of order. A small subset of the writing was, as she had told Eric, truly crazy, and this was the work that was most recognizably religious. A few pieces were preoccupied with the Rapture and seemed concerned with actually bringing it about, if such a thing could be accomplished through punctuation and spelling errors. Marianne collected these applications with a thick rubber band and placed them inside one of the dresser drawers. But most of the work was not overtly religious at all.

If the applications had been organized into a pie chart, semiliterate novels about chaste vampires and insatiable werewolves would have been represented by a healthy slice. These pieces, along with other writing with obvious technical or taste problems, made a tall stack by the door. A second, somewhat smaller pile that sat on the dresser was made up of writing that seemed to have been done for the sake of the act itself— she could see the authors, identifying themselves to family members as *novelists* and *poets*. The novels in this group tended to have boring car chases and a lot of hard-boiled talk, but the periods and quotation marks, the exposition and the action, were all where they should be. The poems were worse, in their way: obvious metaphors unfurled in careful, unbroken meter. Sonnet after fucking sonnet, she told Eric in an email.

She gathered a third pile, much smaller, made up of work that seemed, if not promising or publishable, at least like something she could not easily toss into the other two piles. There were several stories about cults, and in each one, the abuse scene—there was always an abuse scene—was the most vivid and terrifying part. There was a memoir called "Baby Dust," written by a preacher's wife who'd had eight miscarriages. There was a novel from a washed-up R&B singer, about a washed-up R&B singer's triumphant return to the stage. There was a series of poems whose speaker was the late Terri Schiavo, establishing the preoccupations of her locked-in mind. She braced herself for the experience of finding a story like Ruth's and hers, a story of sisters separated by faith, but so far the closest she'd come was an application from a young woman, not yet out of college, who said a Christian writing program was the only one her dad would allow her to apply for.

Marianne kept this pile in the room next door to hers. She visited them to reread the Terri Schiavo poems or add a novel excerpt describing a woman's strained relationship with her gay adult son. Sometimes she separated them into their individual submissions and made up two workshop groups, one for prose and one for poetry. She sat the manuscripts in a circle on each of the two double beds, like a doll's tea party, and imagined each of the writers, the conversations they could have.

It was a delicate thing, putting a workshop together, and she thought of writing a letter of appreciation to the chair of her department, who in the winter carried a tote bag filled with applications everywhere she went. She knew that her professor, a reserved and elegant woman who liked things just so, had considered not only the work but also the personalities of each of the workshop members she invited. Even then there were misapprehensions of character, risks that did not deliver reward. There was a very young woman who dropped out in the first week, and in Eric's workshop, a hot-tempered Cormac McCarthy acolyte whose tantrums scared the rest of them.

That would not do here. It was easy to picture the pastor's wife crying on the phone to her husband, the Schiavo poet going postal.

So she went back to read and reread the personal statements. All Eric's form had directed was "Tell us something about yourself." They went on and on about hobbies, a love of animals, a feeling that Jesus walked next to them, strange anxieties about their families. There was an essay by a woman who had been in jail for embezzlement. Marianne had placed her unremarkable memoir in the literate-but-no pile, but after reading her statement, which described coming home to find that her husband had left her and taken the children, she decided to move her, with equal parts sympathy and nosiness, into the maybe pile. It had grown to twenty manuscripts.

When the personal statements were too vague, Marianne took to sniffing the pages, holding them up to her face and breathing deeply. She got a vague scent of cigarettes and suntan lotion, but that may have been the room. She closed her eyes, tried to imagine her professor, whose commitment to poetry was so stately and impressive that she had served *two* terms as U.S. poet laureate, doing the same. An earnest whiff of Harvard grad, a faint perfume of granddaughter-of-a-South-American-oligarch. Marianne envisioned herself at the university's holiday party, describing her new role as the Oral Roberts of the MFA world.

Driving Eric's un-air-conditioned Jetta to the supermarket, its radio stuck on a staticky AM talk station, she suddenly found herself remembering a line from a poem or trying to picture the faces of the participants. Shopping for lettuce and oranges and avocados, she peered at the other customers, retired, pleasant-looking people, wondering if perhaps one of them might in fact be an applicant. It now seemed possible, after reading poems and stories from hairdressers and prison wardens, singers and preachers' wives, for anyone to be an undercover Christian writer, a Manny Abrams in disguise.

For example, this woman in the line in front of her, with her grocery cart full of bottled water, Wonder Bread, and peanut butter. She could be one of those apocalyptic types.

"That's a lot of peanut butter," Marianne said. Something compelled her to be friendly all the time here.

The woman turned to her and smiled, an act that never seemed to happen in the small, crowded C-Town in Brooklyn. She had crazy Florida hair—poet hair—coarse and long and unconfined, and her batik tunic, decorated with fish, came down just to the tops of her tan, wrinkled knees. "It's a big storm that's coming," she said, looking with concern at the measly contents of Marianne's cart. "You're not going to ride it out?"

"Oh," said Marianne. "I guess I am." She hadn't turned on the TV in more than a week. The sky was blue and cloudless, and the gulf was calm this morning.

"Thursday," the woman said, loading her provisions onto the conveyor belt. "Just a tropical storm. This place'll be packed tomorrow, better get what you need now. Faye's the name."

"Oh," Marianne said. "Nice to meet you, Faye."

"The *storm*, honey. The storm is Faye."

Marianne thanked the woman, then turned her cart around to shop for something more substantial and nonperishable. Living most of her adult life in Brooklyn had not prepared her for this kind of shopping; she never bought more than what she could carry.

She wound up selecting the exact same provisions as Faye, and was pleasantly surprised by the low total in the checkout line. It took Marianne a while to find her car—she had not learned to mark the spot where she'd parked—and, wandering the lot with her cart, she surveyed the atmosphere. The ratty palm fronds lining the edge of the parking lot were completely still. Marianne hauled the flats of water into the trunk, nestled the bread on top.

Some say it's God's judgment, a deep radio voice intoned as she turned the key. Then laughter. Nah, said another voice. You sound like one of those climate crazies. It's just fall in Florida, same as always. Marianne turned up the radio, wondering if she'd hear news about the storm, but the hosts moved on to other concerns.

Back home, she made herself a fat peanut-butter-and-white-bread sandwich and ate it on the beach next to a stack of manuscripts. A slim stack, compared to the noes, but rich with promise: not of publication and esteem, perhaps, but of a kind of legitimacy, steady work, and—yes—tuition. Nine thousand dollars a year for two years.

Marianne had been using hardship deferments (surprisingly easy to obtain) to avoid her own debts and had managed to pay very little principal on loans that had somehow continued to grow. She'd lately imagined that she would never pay them off. She'd just defer and defer, one hardship after another; wasn't that how life went?

But now she saw another possibility. Doing rough math on the back of an application, Marianne figured that two and a half students paying full fare was all it took to make forty-five thousand dollars. It was simple addition: take this long-winded missionary memoirist, add this evangelical poet, throw in half a writer of an ill-conceived Christian bodice ripper starring a hot Jewish carpenter stud, and she'd be back to where she started. They planned to admit thirty students in the first class; in a single year, not counting application fees, that was more than a quarter-million dollars. For once in her life Marianne could imagine coming out ahead.

Just follow any major religion on the planet Earth, a white-bearded man toting a red flag explained on the Occupy livestream. *Greed is not a virtue.*

But this was not greed; it was perfectly fair. Eighteen thousand dollars was a bargain compared to her tuition, and didn't they have the same chances that she had? Better, maybe—the most popular books in America, after all, were Mormon vampire romances and pious, Pollyanna-ish collections of poetry by cancer-stricken children.

The sky had taken on a slight greenish haze, and far out, Marianne could see whitecaps on the choppy water. The creamy peanut butter and soft bread was the perfect food to eat while reading, Marianne thought. Easy, cheap, elemental. She smelled the salt of the sea, inhaled it deeply. She would sit here and watch the storm come in.

Across the gulf, Janine Gray unlocked the file cabinet where she stored ten years of lessons—on nutrition, setting up a bank account, planning a budget—and checked the folder where she'd collected her photocopied submission materials. She reviewed the order of poems, the personal statement, even her own address, neatly hand-lettered on the information page, which she'd also photocopied. Janine did not often apply for things—not credit cards (she did not believe in them), not mortgage applications (her husband had filled out the paperwork), and certainly not creative writing programs. How long would she have to wait before she heard something back? She had no idea. It was an extraordinarily personal and uncharacteristic thing she'd done, writing the statement and sending in the poems. If they—whoever they were—did not like her poems, would they write to her anyway? Would they respond to the something Janine had tried to say with the poems?

She wished for a cup of coffee and a cigarette, an early-afternoon-break routine she'd established when the girls were little, before she'd started teaching. But she didn't smoke anymore, and hardly any of the other teachers at the high school did either. The ones who couldn't quit had to walk all the way to the teachers' parking lot to sit in their cars, and while Janine *occasionally* felt like joining them—say someone set a fire in the kitchen, or she suspected a student may have called her a bad name in his native language—she resisted. How would it look for the *life skills* teacher to demonstrate such a nasty addiction?

Life skills. When Janine was in high school, they'd called it home economics. The curriculum had hardly changed—some sewing, some cooking (really the preparation of prepackaged convenience foods), and a little math—but home ec, the principal said, had a girly and old-fashioned ring to it, and the students were no longer the same perky future housewives who had been Janine's classmates. No, Janine's students were bored, gum-snapping girls, delinquent boys who needed one more class to graduate, tenth-graders who could not read or pronounce the word *ingredients*. These were students bound for work in fast food restaurants and big box stores, some of them bound for deportation. And every year, more of them: twenty-eight in a classroom meant to hold twenty-two, thirty sometimes. Janine knew the word *whore* in several languages and kept a stack of detention slips signed and filled out on her desk. "Gross disrespect" she'd written under "reason" on every one.

One day last fall, the principal came to speak to her about the frequency of her detention referrals—didn't she think it would be better to work on her relationships with the students? He was a reasonable, maddeningly patient man who had taught for exactly one year.

"You mean," Janine said, "I should let them—"

"Not *let them*," the principal said. "Work with them."

That was when Janine started writing the poems. At first, she'd simply flipped the detention slips over and started writing. Someone used the smooth green jersey intended for frog-shaped pillows to make a pot leaf? She wrote a poem. Someone used the hot dogs, meant to be baked into pigs in blankets, for lewd gestures? Poem. Someone cussed, talked over her lessons, texted, or passed notes? Poem.

The students had thought she was writing detention slips, and they would wait for her to hand them over so they could suck their teeth and roll their eyes at her. But she'd merely stuffed the slips into her top desk drawer and continued with the lesson: this is how to remove a seam, this is how to season a pan, this is how to extinguish a grease fire.

"What you doin' with them slips, Ms. Gray?" asked a boy who had spent most of Life Skills I in detention. He had passed—that seemed to be the point of life skills, everyone passed—and was back for more, as two of the classes made one math credit. He eyed her desk nervously. "You savin' 'em up or something?"

Janine had shrugged. "Just writing something to myself," she said.

He held out his hand. "If I'm gonna have detention, I'll take it now," he said.

"But I haven't given you detention," Janine said. "I was only writing."

"Not 'cause of me?"

"I didn't say that," Janine said.

They went back and forth for a while. None of the students was able to confirm that Janine was not hoarding a trove of detentions, to be formed, in the distant future, into a megadetention—and there was significant argument about that strategy's feasibility—but they were also not able to dispel the worry. One day's detention, served on the spot: that was one thing, that was survivable. But facing a desk drawer crammed with them? That was another thing entirely.

And for Janine, the poems helped. At first they were about the students themselves, and their strange, unknowable, ridiculous choices: Why would someone choose to ruin perfectly good food? Why not spend a class period sewing a cute stuffed animal or a pair of boxer shorts instead of clowning around and breaking expensive sewing machines? Why would someone take another student's homework and ruin it?

But then she grew bored with those questions, and her mind drifted to larger concerns. She'd always been an avid letter writer, mostly to her local newspaper. She did not for the life of her understand why a student prayer group could not pray before assemblies and football games. She questioned teaching sex ed to middle schoolers. She thought that parents should take more responsibility for their own children, instead of expecting the schools to feed them breakfast, lunch, and snack and teach them things that were once learned in church or at home. Soon she was no longer writing letters at all but drafting everything she had to say about the world in lines and stanzas.

Janine returned the folder to its place and locked the file cabinet. Her classroom had one measly window, and she could see that the storm her daughter warned her about was churning the sky with dark-gray clouds. Her students had spent the morning debating the possibility of school cancellation. Just a little bitty storm, one of them said dismissively.

When she got home, there would be more to do: taking down awnings and bird feeders, folding up the lawn chairs left out after her daughters' afternoon tanning sessions. It would be nearly six o'clock before she finished, no time to write or even sit down for a moment. She unlocked and opened her cabinet again and rummaged beneath the folders for the familiar, crinkly package: a stale pack of menthols she was saving for such a day as this. She closed her fingers around the package, then let go. She had a stack of papers to grade, and surely Rick was not taking a break at his job. He didn't believe in breaks and would work straight through a twelve-hour, hot-sun day, just to set an example for his crew. Everything in Rick's world was done according to a predictable schedule and for a purpose; he didn't believe in anything as wasteful as a smoke break. Janine imagined what the cigarette would taste like, outside, with the wind whipping and the air taking on a sudden sharpness.

In the early years of their marriage, Janine had stayed home, and even then she had written—stories for the girls, letters to her sister, then to the editors of various North Florida newspapers. She had never written poetry, not until this year, and she couldn't explain it well to anyone except Rick, who had been her truest confidant ever since they'd started dating, way back in high school. "I don't know how it happened," she told him. "It's like I'm suddenly talking in a new language."

She'd shyly handed the poems over one morning in bed, and Rick had handled them reverently, then excused himself for his morning BM. After spending an entire hour with them, in the bathroom, he confessed that he did not understand the new language she was speaking, but he believed whatever it was must be coming from God. Rick believed firmly in the intervening hand of God; he was like one of those biblical men who built boats and temples on command, the kind of man, strong and certain, that the world didn't make anymore. Janine sometimes felt an acute pain for her daughters, knowing they'd never find a man like their father.

"Why do you need to go someplace else to write?" Rick had asked her early this morning when she showed him the application to the Ranch, which she did not tell him she'd mailed two weeks ago.

At the beginning of the summer, he'd built Janine a solarium, an octagonal room with glass walls and smooth white oak floors. He'd set her desk in the center of the room, facing out at the various staked finch feeders in their yard, and when Beth, their older daughter, had wanted to use the space for her elliptical trainer, Rick had told her no, her mother needed that room to write.

It was hard to explain that the room itself, along with the application, seemed to be interfering with her writing, with the hand of God that had once guided her poems. It was embarrassing to think about one of her neighbors seeing her in the act of writing—though imagining some professor at the school reading the twelve short poems she'd enclosed with her application was not any easier.

"I want to be around other poets," Janine had tried to explain.

"Oh," he'd said, and she could tell that he was a little hurt.

"Also, I want a teacher. Someone to help me make the poems better," she'd said, though it was hard to imagine how one went about changing a poem.

"Okay," Rick had said, kissing her forehead. He took his lunch from the counter—three ham and cheese sandwiches and an apple in a paper sack—and left for work, same as always. Janine followed him to the door and watched him haul his heavy frame into the cab of his truck, adjust the mirror, and wave good-bye.

"Will you be home early, if the storm comes?" she'd called after him.

He'd ducked his head out of the window and looked up at the tranquil sky. "It won't storm today," he'd told her. He did not seem to be thinking anymore about the school. That was the thing about Rick: he never held on to emotions for long.

Perhaps if the room had not been glass, she thought now. Because he had nothing to hide, Rick believed in absolute transparency. None of the bedroom doors in their house locked, and Rick and Janine had shared the same email account for more than ten years. How could she explain that poems needed privacy? That it would have been better for her if he'd simply cleared out a closet?

Janine checked her application folder one last time, then closed and relocked the drawer. It was likely she wouldn't get in anyway. What did she know about poetry? And who cared anymore about her subject, poor Terri Schiavo, who'd starved to death years ago?

Marianne turned over the manuscript in her lap—yet another end-times piece—and thought of Ruth, who'd once confessed to reading the first of the Left Behind books. "Did you like it?" Marianne had asked, trying not to let her alarm show.

"It was okay," Ruth said, in that way she once had about most everything. She could take it or leave it, her tone seemed to imply, but Marianne thought what she was really saying was that she wasn't sure what she was *supposed* to like. Marianne had been that way herself, as a teenager, and for many years she'd seen the process of becoming an adult as about replacing that uncertainty with strong, unyielding opinions. About music. About politics. About books. About art. In that way she was not so different from her sister.

Marianne did not believe in God and had suspected that He did not exist as soon as she noticed how much other people insisted on His existence. In high school Ruth had become one of those people, attending a Baptist church three times a week and eventually dating and becoming engaged to the youth minister there. Their father, a community college philosophy professor who liked conflict on paper but not in real life, insisted that it was a phase, provoked by postponed grief. He'd rebuffed Marianne's offers to come home, to get involved, and she hadn't pushed it. "You know how she is," he'd said.

"That's the problem with people like you, you don't believe in anything," Ruth later claimed, full of certainty, when Marianne tried to talk her out of teenage marriage while their father despaired in his study. "Not God. Not God's love. Not even *love*."

Ruth was wrong to say that Marianne didn't believe in anything. She believed in things you could see or prove. She believed in science, believed in abortions, believed in the miracle of stem cells. She believed in population control and drug legalization, gun control and public transportation. She believed in generous arts grants and taxes for the rich. She thought everyone should be an organ donor and should have no say in the matter. She thought cats and dogs should be spayed and neutered, and that no one should have children before the age of thirty. She believed in climate change and the electric car, in NPR and PBS, in free speech and online privacy and free lunch and Medicaid. She believed in gay marriage and no marriage. She had no business starting a school for people equally passionate about their own opposing opinions, people who clearly believed in God. Her father said as much, when she told him she was moving to Florida to start an inspirational writing ranch for evangelical Christians.

"That doesn't sound like you," was actually what he said.

But at least she was doing *something*: participating in this world, instead of letting it run over her or leave her behind. Bending it to her needs instead of the opposite.

The storm was taking its time. It seemed that she'd been watching the sky's gradual darkening, the gathering clouds, for hours now. Above the smoothness of sand worn down by surf, there was a thick stratum of black, papery-skinned mussels, each one broken open and picked clean by a seabird.

Oh, I'm as happy as a clam, Marianne remembered telling Ruth once, when her sister asked over the phone how she was doing. It was maybe a year after their mother died, and every call from home was still a shock.

It was her mother she wanted—to tell about her classes, her friends, the problems of dorm life. Any other voice, even her baby sister's, left her with a hollow feeling in her stomach.

Just how happy are clams anyway? Ruth had asked. In her youth and her earnestness, she'd been serious, though for a moment she'd sounded just like their mother, had brought her back to life, performed a miracle.

Sometimes it made Marianne angry, not believing in God.

2

The storm arrived on Thursday, as the woman in the supermarket predicted, but aside from a brief loss of power and general strewing of detritus—brown rafts of seaweed, torn palm fronds, the contents of an unsecured trash can—there was little damage. Marianne spent the storm in what Eric later told her, during their weekly check-in, was the least advisable part of the Ranch—the big rec room with its plate glass window, which could have easily shattered into a thousand flying shards. Marianne said he might have told her that *before* the storm, but Eric said everybody knew that you should stay away from big windows during storms. "Do not assume I know what everybody knows!" Marianne had shouted into her computer. "I do not have that sort of knowledge!"

But she had not felt threatened sitting in the chintz-cushioned wicker armchair she'd dragged near the window, a plate of peanut butter sandwiches and a flat of bottled water at the ready. Even after the power flickered off in the late afternoon, the room felt cozy and familiar and safe, with its shelf of ravaged board games and terrible novels. The gulf disappeared behind rain that splashed in gray sheets, but other than a brief screeching of wind that happened at full dark, there was little to send one running for cover. The next day everything sparkled with raindrops, even the plastic cups and bottles and grocery bags that littered the beach.

On Monday, workers arrived to do some of the work she'd requested: a crew to fix the roofs, a crew to repaint the buildings and outbuildings, landscapers to weed-whack the sculpture garden and clear away overgrown brush. Though she was glad to see things getting done, Marianne felt crowded by their vehicles and paint cans and coolers and half-empty bottles of Gatorade. She felt even more crowded by their general busyness, which was measurable and obvious, while she sorted piles of paper into different stacks in an air-conditioned motel room with daytime television on mute.

She found a bicycle in one of the tool sheds, powder blue, with rusty fenders and fat, deflated tires she managed to mostly inflate with a small hand pump. It had been years since she had been on a bike, though her Brooklyn neighbors tootled around helmetlessly, the soles of their flip-flopped feet black with dirt. This bike had a wide seat and graceful handlebars that didn't require you to hunch over. It was the perfect vehicle for cruising the neighborhood. Marianne waved good-bye to the roofers as she rode past the front entrance.

Across from the Ranch was a Kangaroo gas station where Marianne sometimes bought snacks and tampons. A few miles to the north was a stretch of identical T-shirt-and-beach-towel warehouses, dimly lit shell shops, the Publix—but turning right, then left, she could ride through a development of new houses that sat on the east side of the beach road. Even before she made the turn, past the elaborate pale-brick entrance, she could see that they were still under construction, the plywood a garish orange against the cloudless sky, the shingled roofs draped with tarps. On closer inspection, she realized none of the houses had workers hanging Sheetrock or laying flooring. They were all large, empty, half-finished shells. The tarps held standing water. Sun-faded trash littered the short weedy drives.

Marianne's crews worked until dusk, then packed up with the speed of a television home-improvement show. They picked up all the bottles and coolers before they left, and Marianne noticed that things were looking neater, less abandoned. She figured they were glad to have the work. "Back tomorrow, miss," the landscape boss called to her cheerfully. Marianne waved good-bye.

"How'd it go?" Mark asked on Skype later. It was his custom to pace around with a headset, doing other things while she struggled to keep his attention. The computer's camera faced an empty chair, and through his window Marianne could see the early-evening skyline.

"I guess it went fine," Marianne said. She told him about the empty development.

"Yeah," he said. "That developer ran out of money—too bad. Someone else will come along. Look how close it is to the water."

"How much is our renovation costing?"

"Don't worry about that," he said. "You just take care of whatever you have to take care of on the school side. Finding students and teachers. That's really the priority here. The school stuff."

"The school stuff." Marianne wondered, watching the window behind Mark's chair, if she missed New York. She thought she could make out the graceful arches of the Brooklyn Bridge, but it may have been a trick of the light. How much time had she spent on the Brooklyn Bridge anyway? Maybe once she'd walked across its wide pedestrian walkway. Most of her transriver experiences involved the subway or the ugly Manhattan Bridge, or the absolutely ordinary Pulaski Bridge, which crossed only a greenish creek.

"*Yes*," Mark said after a long pause. "Eric thinks you should stay in more of an administrative role. You know, hire someone else to teach the first poetry workshop."

"Oh," Marianne said. "Could you sit down, please? In front of your computer?"

"You can, you know, focus on your writing." His voice was still faraway and tinny. What was he doing? Tidying up? Most likely, she realized, he was working on a desktop in another part of his office. She strained to hear the decisive tap-tap-tap of number typing, which was what she assumed he did all day.

"My writing is not going well," Marianne said, rather loudly, so she could not take it back. (She hoped that if she announced it often, like a recovering alcoholic, it might help.) "What does an administrative role entail? Could you move over to your computer, please?"

"You know," said Mark. "Interacting with the students on a personal level, making sure things go well. Mediating between the interests of the students and the teachers, who may not be used to some of the same . . . thought processes? Of the students."

"So, like a religious concierge," she said. "Or an activities director on a religious cruise ship. Or an admissions director at a religious college."

"*Yes*," Mark said happily. She could definitely hear a keyboard's busy clacking. "Like that."

The Ranch was not accredited. It did not have an endowment. It did not have a beautiful campus or a quad, though the gardens and pathways were less treacherous after a week of landscaping. It did not have classrooms or a photocopier. And yet the applications, mostly generated by a few well-placed advertisements, continued to roll in. Marianne added a few more applications to the *yes?* pile—a memoir from a remorseful maker of slasher films, a speculative novel from a 9/11 truther, poems by an escaped Scientologist who'd moved to Hollywood to write a screenplay about being an excommunicated Mormon. Although she maintained, to Eric, an outward hurt at being asked not to teach, on the inside Marianne was deeply relieved.

She began contacting possible poetry professors from an old email list she'd saved from graduate school. *Ha ha,* wrote some of her old classmates, who'd remembered her drunken thought experiments. Marianne did not try to prove anything to these people, who had their own problems. A tiny minority had teaching jobs, mostly in small, Midwestern towns with winters that were beginning already. Others had moved on to real jobs: lawyer, accountant, graphic designer. A great many had gotten married, had children, and taken up fake jobs: cupcake baker, jewelry maker, graphic designer.

It was one of this latter set, a beautiful girl whose family owned wineries in California and who had married the scion of a Kentucky horse-breeding family, who suggested that they were barking up the wrong tree. Her poems and workshop comments always had something of the bluntness afforded to people of her class. *This is a job for the desperate,* she wrote. *You need to find someone experienced, but who has made some career mistakes. Someone always on the visiting circuit. What about Lorraine?*

Lorraine Kominski had spent a semester teaching at their school. Her first book had won the Yale Younger Poets prize, but that was a very long time ago, before Marianne was even born. Years of low-grade alcoholism and erratic workshop behavior had bumped her several rungs down the teaching ladder, from an Ivy League college to a SUNY school to the occasional visiting writer post offered by a sympathetic friend. She showed up late to class and was occasionally threatening or belligerent with her students. Sometimes she disliked a student's poem so much that she would place it on the floor, cross her arms, and shake her head at it. Every now and then she published a poem about one of her cats in the *New Yorker*.

"No," Eric said. "I don't think she would be right. For our students."

"She's a very good writer," Marianne said. "*Landlord Death Chants* was a great book. And I like those cat poems. I always cut them out and put them on my fridge."

"*Marianne.*"

"And I think her teaching style might be what the students are looking for," she continued. "Like fantasy baseball. Or space camp. You don't go to space camp expecting *not* to throw up at some point."

"You think these applicants are expecting to throw up? You think they want to be told how bad they are?"

Marianne thought for a minute. "Yes," she said. "They want to wear a space suit, but they also want to throw up. They want to be nurtured, but they also want to be abused. Haven't you ever been to church? Lorraine would be poetry's holy roller."

"Well, who even knows if she's available?"

"She is," Marianne said. "As a matter of fact."

OKAY, Lorraine Kominski had typed back, four minutes after Marianne's email, like she was waiting for exactly such an invitation. She'd detailed her modest salary requirements and the airport and flight times she most preferred. I LIKE TO FLY DELTA FOR THE DELTA MILES. NICE TO HEAR FROM YOU. HOPE YOUR WRITING IS GOING BETTER.

A few days later, Eric had warmed up to the idea of Lorraine as poetry teacher, or at least accepted it, and Marianne, for her part, felt more and more relieved to be in an administrative role, to avoid the actual teaching.

Can't wait to get to FL with you, he texted her. *This is really going to work out.*

Excited to see you too, she wrote back, laboring over the buttons on her flip phone, which Eric said looked like something an old lady might use to call an ambulance. *I hope so.*

She wasn't sure what they were talking about—the school, or living in proximity again—and guessed that Eric wasn't either, but it was better, easier, than clarifying.

He was still in love with Marianne. She knew this and had encouraged it in small, mean ways: wearing certain dresses (low-cut, shoulder-baring) when he visited her in New York, brushing against him in the narrow aisles of the Strand, reaching across restaurant tables to take food from his plate like a girlfriend. And sometimes she was in love with parts of him too—the sound of his voice on the telephone on Sunday nights, the funny emails he sent her from work about his students, memories of lying in bed with him in his tiny Astoria walk-up, her head on his chest, his fingers in her hair.

Marianne was good at the early stages of a relationship—dressing up for dates, flirting, doing thoughtful things that required only a small, unintimidating, spontaneous kind of effort. She was not good at the things required by a long-term relationship (visiting other people's families, planning trips or holidays or extravagant surprises), but this was something that was difficult to make someone else understand; they had to see for themselves, over time. Early on, when she told Eric that she had never lived with a man and never intended to, he wasn't dissuaded. "A Woody/Mia thing then," he'd said gamely.

"Sure," she said. "That turned out great."

Love. It wasn't much, but in the absence of other options she counted on it to get her through, like a tax refund. From Eric, it came to her automatically, unearned. Why her? she sometimes wondered. It was true they had some things in common, it was true she was often available, and, yes, her looks were what some people called striking. She had a heart-shaped face, green eyes, cupid's-bow lips. Her nearly black hair had started turning gray when she was eighteen years old and moved away from home—gray with relief, she always said. She'd hoped that she would grow a thick white feminist streak, like Susan Sontag's, but instead it came in evenly, forming a kind of veil over the rest of her hair when she pulled it back. She liked the way her graying hair contrasted with her young face, but knew that one day her face would catch up and she would just be old.

"You're a poet," Eric accused on the night she first met him. He reminded her of someone—she couldn't remember who—but the question nagged at her. They were at a university-sponsored mixer, and Eric was standing by what passed for the bar, alternating between cheap tequila and cheaper beer. There was a bowl of nuts and a bowl of Chex Mix with the liquor on the folding table: that's what twenty thousand a year got you, party-wise. "I can tell by your hair."

She wasn't sure then if he was gay or drunk, but she liked both drunk guys and gay guys, so she let him monopolize her for the rest of the night. She'd been surprised when, at the West Fourth Street subway entrance, he'd pulled her in for a kiss. "Get a room," she'd heard someone walking by say to them, not angrily but casually, as if it were a helpful suggestion. "What a good idea," Eric said into her ear. He was never that bold sober, but Marianne didn't know that then.

The next morning, she realized who he reminded her of—a fictional character in a computer game she played in her college French class. "À la rencontre de Philippe!" she announced, in bed.

"Qu'est-ce que c'est?" Eric asked. "That's actually the only French I know."

"A game I used to play," she explained. "In the language lab. You remind me of Philippe. He was a depressed journalist, and you were supposed to help him with his problems."

Eric frowned. "A depressed French journalist. Very flattering."

"Oh, Philippe was very handsome! But he really was a jackass."

What kind of problems did he have? Eric wanted to know. So many, Marianne explained: his girlfriend had kicked him out because he was au chomage—unemployed—and on the aide sociale. He needed a new job and a new apartment, but all he wanted to do was go to cafés and smoke cigarettes. You were supposed to help him by looking in the petites annonces.

"He was animated?"

"No, a real person—an actor. You watched videos and typed in these . . . exhortations. Demands? Encouragements? In French." Marianne sat up and looked around at Eric's tiny apartment, the single bedroom window that opened to a dim air shaft. "Maybe it's your apartment that reminds me of the place I finally found for him: 11 rue Saint-Honoré."

"You remember the address? I hardly remember anything from college."

Marianne leaned back in bed and thought—why did she remember it so well? She was no longer close to fluent in French. But she could recall the maddening café conversations with Philippe almost word by word. She understood now that Philippe probably dismissed every French II player's advice with the same prerecorded, *café*-swilling disdain, but at the time it felt like he was actually her friend, and it was strangely comforting to have a friend who was such a fuckup. "I remember sitting in the language lab after Philippe blew off this job interview I'd gotten him, and just cracking up. Everyone looked at me but I couldn't stop. It was the first time I laughed, like really laughed, after my mother died."

Eric sat up and looked down at her, gentleness and sorrow on his face. "How did your mother die?"

"Cancer." She took a long breath and blew it out. "I'm not over it."

"Of course not," he said. "I'm sorry."

Telling him about her mother felt like a bigger intimacy than sex or sleeping side by side. It was in some ways the truest thing she knew about herself—that she had not recovered, did not expect to recover. This was behind all her choices—living in an unsustainable city, on unsustainable loans, in pursuit of an unsustainable career. Immediately, she regretted telling a near stranger this truth she could barely admit. Had she thought he was like Philippe, someone she could just abandon in a café?

She found herself arguing with him as they decided what to do next—where to get brunch, whether they needed to shower before brunch, whether they should keep their dalliance a secret from their fellow students. When she said good-bye to him at the entrance to the L train, Marianne figured they would be awkward and silent the next time they saw each other.

But that wasn't how it went. "Marianne!" Eric called across the next MFA gathering, his southern lilt splitting her name into the more familiar *Mary-Anne*. Her name in his mouth was urgent and delighted. Like she was special, remarkable, someone to scan the room for.

They went home together again, to Eric's apartment, where instead of falling into bed (to Marianne's slight disappointment), they talked: about workshop, their hometowns, living in New York as southerners. It started to get dark, and Eric began making dinner, referring disconcertingly often to a recipe in a cookbook. "The way people won't even wait for a less-crowded train!" Marianne insisted. "They'll just cram themselves in. Elevators too—the hurry to do everything, shoveling snow as soon as it falls!" Eric agreed with her; at least, he didn't argue, just looked at her slyly, slightly adoringly, waiting for the next pronouncement. "Not that I'd want to go back," she clarified.

"Not eventually?"

No, she insisted: she loved New York, and feared living the life her mother lived, putting her art second, or third—really last of all the things she had to do in a day, in a week, in a year.

"But if she hadn't moved to Virginia," Eric said. "If she hadn't met your father."

"I know," Marianne said. "You can appreciate something without wanting it for yourself. Don't you ever go home and feel—at the grocery store, or wherever—*proud* of living here?"

"Sure," he said, plating the pasta.

"You would give that up? And go back to being—what?"

"Myself?" And there was something about the way he said that, the essential simplicity and honesty on his face—why would he want to be anything else?—along with the pasta, which was surprisingly good in its lemony cream sauce. It was comforting. Unchallenging. It was, at the moment, exactly what she'd wanted without knowing.

All spring and all the next year they did New York things: went to concerts, readings, museums, out to dinner. They got bronchitis and nursed each other with Gatorade and deli-bought soup. They took long subway rides to Coney Island and the botanical garden in the Bronx; they rented a car and got sunburns and a parking citation at Rockaway Beach. Eric read and marked up (with checks and exclamation points) Marianne's thesis, mostly poems about people in her hometown; she read his novel, about a family of moonshiners, and did not complain that not a single character resembled her. As graduation loomed, they never talked about leaving, about what they would do next. What was wrong with life as it was? Why did there have to be a next?

But then it happened, the inevitable *next* they never again mentioned, though sometimes, even over the telephone, Marianne could feel Eric thinking about it. Why had she said yes, only to say no the very next morning? Why had she led him on? She found herself thinking about it too: Why had he even asked her, when he knew how she felt about marriage? For twelve whole hours following a celebratory dinner (he'd just signed with an agent), the half-carat ring he'd presented her sparkled bluely on her hand, and he'd insisted on calling both of their families. His mother had cried and congratulated them and asked when the wedding would be. Even her father had gotten unexpectedly emotional. "You know," he said, "your mother and I were engaged in New York."

Of course Marianne knew. Wasn't that what she'd been thinking of when Eric ambushed her in the restaurant?—the sort of place that Marianne's mother would have loved, with its small rickety tables, mismatched chairs, candles flickering in glass jars. And Eric, he was someone her mother would have loved too: artistic but steady, handsome, a good conversationalist. Her father had said as much when he came up for Marianne's graduate reading and they'd all gone to dinner: Your mother would have liked him.

Mom would want this for me, Marianne thought. And she'd nodded yes, teary-eyed, just like someone in the movies.

All night she lay awake, looking at the ring and thinking about her life with Eric. He wanted to move somewhere cheaper, he'd said on the way back to his apartment. Like Flushing? Marianne said. Or Long Island City?

No—he actually laughed at her—like North Carolina. Or Virginia. And then, his arm around her on the N train, he'd launched into all the other things he wanted: a yard, kids, good schools. Marianne felt her heart racing—*good schools?*—but she didn't say much, just looked at the ring on her finger and thought about her mother, who'd wound up trying to interest untalented high schoolers in modern art while they sketched loving portraits of pickup trucks and deer antlers. By the next morning she had convinced herself that her mother would have wanted something different for her entirely.

Eric said he knew she didn't really mean it when she said yes. Then why did you even ask me? Marianne wanted to know. They had a long argument about whether it would be possible for Eric to get his money back. Marianne thought if he just made the situation sad enough, the jeweler might feel sorry for him.

"That's exactly what I want right now," Eric said, holding his head in his hands at her kitchen table. "Thank you!"

"Tell him I died," Marianne suggested, and Eric looked at her, just for a moment, as if maybe that were a possibility. "Never mind," she said quickly. "Tell him you caught me cheating."

The ring was not returnable, it turned out, and Marianne wasn't sure what he ever did with it. Six months later Eric moved back home, and soon he married someone else, a girl he'd known in high school. Who gets engaged after three months of dating? They had been going out for almost two years when Eric asked *her*. Who leaves New York to go back to *Charlotte*?

It was just as well, she told herself, falling into her own rash commitment: a subscription to match.com, where she browsed painters and installation artists, spoken-word performers and trust funders. Eric was too nice and too normal, too much the kind of guy you would take home to meet your parents; he belonged with someone who actually *had* parents, not just a still-grieving father. "My boyfriend?" she told people, when they asked what happened to Eric. "He came down with male pattern blandness."

That didn't mean she didn't think of him on those online dates: Eric would hate this movie as much as I do, Eric would never wear a keffiyeh, Eric would hold the door for me, ask me if I was cold, offer to pay for the cab. Eric would understand—not pretend to understand—when I talked about my family. Then she'd go home early, work on a poem, and send it to Eric.

It was October, a month still warm enough for shorts, when Marianne began to get inquiries from the applicants. (And from her sister, in response to a long handwritten letter: a brief email declining her invitation to visit and expressing mild interest in the Ranch.) She'd set up a temporary office by then, a space in a corner of the large rec room, with a desk for storing application checks, which she bundled and sent to Mark once a week. Determined not to miss another storm warning, she kept her radio tuned to the local NPR station. On her laptop, a small window displayed the Occupy livestream, where things were already falling apart: she never would have lasted there. It contrasted strangely with the conservative talk station she found herself listening to in the Jetta, another kind of stream where men went on about the decline of the country: No more Christmas tinsel in America's grammar-school hallways. No more cursive in the classroom. But plenty of room on the cafeteria lunch line, they howled, for *tacos y fajitas.*

She obsessively refreshed the liberal sites that delivered news about the disturbing fleet of candidates vying for the Republican presidential nomination. Each revelation brought a rush of adrenaline and despair. One wanted to give embryos personhood status, another to make "In God We Trust" *larger* on money. They all agreed that gay marriage was an abomination. The governor from Texas said that schools *oughta be* teaching creationism.

She cringed a little when the applicants, surely the intended recipients of this posturing, got in touch, though they were polite, even deferential. Each week a letter or two, an email, and several phone calls: Sorry to bother her, but when would decisions get made? When would the applicant hear something? The check had not been cashed—was the application complete?

"We have to let people know," Marianne told Eric. "We can't wait until December."

"Most programs don't notify until January or February. At the earliest," he said.

"The first session starts in March. We told them it was rolling admissions. Besides, they might move on to something else by then. Woodworking, pottery. Missionary trips. These are not regular applicants."

"Okay," he said. "Decide, then."

"No!" Marianne said. She did not want to be responsible for the groups that sat around the long tables Mark had ordered. "That wasn't what I meant. You have to help me. Or maybe Frances should help. It was her idea."

She still hadn't met Eric's great-aunt, though she'd twice driven by her ranch-style retirement community. Rest home, Marianne remembered her mother calling the one where her grandmother lived, though inside it seemed more like a depressing hospital, a place where no one expected to get better. This was why she hadn't stopped and inquired—what would she do if she found a woman as diminished as her granny, who spent entire days gazing out the window at an empty parking lot?

"She trusts us," Eric said.

So Marianne bought a scanner and emailed him the promising applications. It took more than a week to hash out their favorites over Skype. It turned into a series of trades and compromises, and by the end Marianne wondered if she might have been better off making the decisions herself.

Insisting on the R&B singer, she had to concede the pastor's wife with her many miscarriages, a woman she feared might be too fragile for workshop. They agreed on the strange *something* expressed by the Schiavo poet but disagreed about the teenage girl whose father had found the Ranch online—Eric thought she was too young. They both had questions about a poet with a pseudonym.

In early November they accepted a tentative first round: ten fiction writers, twelve memoirists, and twelve poets, mostly from the Southeast but also as far away as Vermont and Oregon. There were twenty women and fourteen men. There was a veteran of the first Gulf War (female) and a ninety-year-old sod farmer (male). Two applicants indicated that they were in recovery from homosexual impulses, and Marianne liked to imagine them falling off the wagon together.

She made each of the phone calls, delivered to family answering machines and cell phone voicemails, and, occasionally, to a live voice.

"Hello," she said late one afternoon, then faltered. It was the last call of the day and she was tired. She began again. "Hello. May I please speak to Janine Gray?"

There were voices in the background, the sound of kitchen work. "This is Janine."

"My name is Marianne Stuart, and I'm calling from the Genesis Ranch. We'd like to admit you to our first class of poets."

The background voices got quieter, but the woman did not speak. For a moment Marianne thought they'd been disconnected, then she caught the sound of her breathing, a heavy door closing behind her.

"I'm sorry, please say that again."

Marianne repeated herself and stated the dates for the first session, which would take place over two weeks. She told her when to expect paperwork and talked up Lorraine's gifts as a workshop leader.

"I don't know if I should cry or jump up and down," the woman said, but did neither, just breathed rapidly into the phone. She did not ask to hear Lorraine's name repeated.

"Your poems are … different," Marianne said. "But we like them. They're very moving."

"Thank you," said the woman. "My husband thinks they come from God."

"Is that where you think they come from?"

"I don't know," said the woman. "Sometimes I think so. They seem to just come out of me."

"Well," said Marianne, picturing her wildest, youngest classes at P.S. 150, the way the children careened about the room, stopping now and then to write a word, a syllable, on the pulpy gray paper she arranged across their desks. She was overcome by a sudden doubt about the Ranch, something that happened every afternoon around this time. What if this woman said such a thing to Lorraine?

But this conversation was about the delivery of praise, which she recognized from long experience as the food of poets. "The committee was unanimous about your work," Marianne told her.

"Thank you," the woman said again. "That means a lot to me. I didn't have any expectations about this. I didn't know what I'd hear back."

Marianne made a check mark next to Janine's name.

Janine closed the front door softly, then walked back into the kitchen, her breath held tightly in her lungs. Chrissy was sitting at the table doing homework while Beth tended the dinner her mother had walked away from—pork chops and mashed potatoes, a pot of green beans, a salad. Rick sat at his usual spot in the family room, his boots on the coffee table, watching the evening news.

"They want me," Janine said, exhaling. She clasped the phone lightly against her chest, like a kitten or a baby. "The writing school. It was unanimous."

Chrissy looked up from her algebra textbook and smiled. "That's great, Mom."

"Congratulations," Beth said, mashing potatoes with a fork. Janine took only the mildest notice that she'd used soy instead of regular milk. "That's awesome."

Rick got up from his chair and came over to kiss her forehead. "I knew they would," he said. Janine told herself that he was merely expressing confidence in her abilities, but she could not help feeling a little let down by his reaction.

At dinner, conversation moved on to other topics: an upcoming church mission trip Chrissy wanted to take, a problem Beth was having with one of her professors and her plans for her upcoming twenty-first birthday, which she hoped to spend in Daytona Beach. On her eighteenth birthday she'd come home with a small Chinese character tattooed in black on her shoulder blade. The character meant "freedom," she'd explained, but it was easy to cover up for job interviews. (What about her *wedding*? Janine had despaired.)

As Beth entered her third year of community college, Janine and Rick had wondered to each other when she would want to move out, but they liked having her home, where they could keep up with her increasingly confusing career aspirations and stay vigilant against cohabitation or any further tattooing. Janine thought it was strange the way rebellion and the desire to please could coexist in Beth, but from her friends and her sister she understood that this was the way of this generation. They wanted to sin, then confess their sins to their parents, who acted more like friends than parents. Janine never would have told her own mother some of the things she'd had to hear.

"And next semester I have to take Communications *III*," Beth was saying.

Rick chewed his pork chop, which had gotten tough in the oven while Janine took her phone call. He was a thorough chewer and a patient listener. Janine had once worried that he might miss being a father to sons—quiet, stalwart builders and fishermen, like all the men in his family—but Rick was perfectly content to be the father of these girls, with their pretty smiles and constant chatter. In fact, he seemed to want little more than what he had: a house, a wife who did not bring work problems home with her, daughters around his table telling him things about the world he had given them. Sometimes he expressed the desire for a bigger fishing boat or some hunting property. Sometimes he mentioned a recipe from the early days of their marriage, something too fatty or caloric for Janine to make in good conscience. But mostly he was content, perhaps *more so* as each year passed.

"But the final grade is based on a project, not an exam," Beth continued, tossing back her hair and pushing aside the healthy mound of potatoes her mother had served her. "Which I hope is not a *group* project, because I really work better on my own."

For a long time Janine had not wanted anything more either. Now she was having a hard time following what her daughter was saying. What did Rick think would become of them when—very soon—their daughters left them? Janine wondered what surprise Chrissy had in store for *her* eighteenth birthday. Perhaps a piercing, but more likely something more inconvenient and self-sacrificing: a trip to Africa or South America, an allegiance to a sect of the church that took her away from her family to somewhere dusty and unhygienic and dangerous.

Janine let her mind drift above the table, above the conversation anchored by Rick's attention and the girls' self-involvement, which she herself had cultivated over twenty-one years of care. She floated over them, through the family room and into the solarium, above the desk and the folder that contained her poems. During these months of anxious waiting, she'd felt something separate and strange growing inside her—not confidence or certainty, exactly, but promise. She felt full of promise, in a way she hadn't since she was pregnant.

The tattoo appeared in one of her poems, a reference to the way your children's bodies escaped you as they got older. How tenderly she had bandaged it as it blistered and seeped a yellowish fluid a week into Beth's nineteenth year. How relieved she'd felt when the blistering and seeping was over and the tattoo itself appeared, black edges clean and sharp, almost shiny with health. She had marveled, removing the last bandage, at the way her daughter's skin had regenerated and healed. "Hallelujah," Beth had said, twisting around to check herself in the bathroom mirror. It was how their family always greeted good news, though at the time Janine wondered if it was appropriately applied to good news delivered, in a foreign tongue, via tattoo.

Now she thought, eating mashed potatoes gummy and gray with soy milk: Hallelujah!

Forking up salty beans and gristly meat: Hallelujah!

Watching her younger daughter slouch over her plate, watching the older talk with her hands in that new way she had, spying a glistening green bean seed caught in her husband's mustache: Hallelujah!

Praise Him! she thought, and in that moment, three weeks from Thanksgiving, an hour past sunset, in the imperfection of her forty-third year, she loved everything.

3

A week after Marianne finished notifying accepted students, Eric called to say he'd been offered a longer teaching contract. He didn't want to stay in Dubai—he'd much rather be in Florida, with her—but there was a bonus to consider, plus he thought that he would finally make some headway with his novel.

"I'll be able to put all my attention into the Ranch when I get home," he told her.

"When?" Marianne wanted to know, but he must not have heard her because now he was going on about the way an international experience helped him see America more clearly, which was of some use to his new book. "When, Eric? When are you coming back?"

"Oh," he said, as if surprised to be interrupted. "Early March. I'll fly straight to Tampa."

"Classes start in March," she said. "And I still haven't met your aunt."

"That's a good sign—a sign she trusts us," he said. "Have you been getting paychecks?"

"Yes, but that's not the point." She wasn't sure what the point was— that she wanted, needed supervision? At her school in Brooklyn, every time the classroom teacher would duck out to get coffee or go to the copier or the bathroom, she'd get nervous and sweaty, which was a little like how she felt now, all the time. But, she remembered, the teacher's return hardly improved things. "And you're coming in March?"

"Yeah," he said, his voice now muffled and indistinct, as if he were cradling the phone between his shoulder and neck so he could do something else. She hated this, though it wasn't as bad as being put on speakerphone—both practices made things easier for the people on the other end, while you had to strain to understand them. It was like what her mother always said about call waiting; what did it take to be someone's first priority? "Late March. I'll be there in plenty of time to read manuscripts and help you out. But I know you have things under control. Mark is really happy with your management of everything."

She didn't know how to tell him that his brother's approval meant far less to her than it did to him—it had almost a negative quality, in fact—so instead she said she had to go, they could talk again next week.

"Okay," he said. "I really am sorry I won't be there sooner. I was looking forward to being with you."

"Do you have seasons in Dubai?" she asked, suddenly anxious to stay on the line. "Without them, I feel like time moves indiscriminately. Like a cartoon clock. Every week is the same as the last. Before we know it—"

"We don't have seasons here either, if by seasons you mean leaves falling from deciduous trees," he said. Marianne noticed, jealously, the way he included himself among the Emirates. Dubaians? He must be doing well there, she realized, to have been offered a second contract. What if he was offered a third? What if he never came back, what if he left her alone with the Ranch? "You have to tune in to subtler signs. You have to get out—are you getting out?"

"I have a date," she said. "Later this week."

"A date!"

She was pleased by Eric's slight alarm, but she clarified anyway. "With a woman. An older woman. Drinks on the lanai, probably something with pineapple and rum."

"Pineapple and rum," Eric said fondly, and then repeated his wish to be in Florida, maybe one too many times. Marianne got off the phone before she could gauge his sincerity, and began missing him at once.

Though Sophie LaTour, proprietress of the Manatee Inn, was practically Marianne's next-door neighbor, they'd met in the birdwatching section of a used-book store in Sarasota, ten miles away. There were no bookstores or coffee shops near the Ranch, or anywhere else you might meet someone new. The beach was always full of people, but they were usually paired off or obviously busy with something solitary—speed walking, shell collecting, metal detecting. But in the birdwatching section—labeled, on a yellowing index card, *ornithology*—she thought she recognized one of the early-morning shell collectors. A fifty-something shell collector who sat in the narrow aisle of a used-book store, her lap stacked with bird books—that was her best option, and she'd seized it.

After a brief discussion of their island and the hazards of innkeeping, Sophie invited her over for drinks. "Just casual," she'd said from under her pile of books, though Marianne bought the wine she would bring at a shop in Sarasota rather than in the Publix spirits section, with its cheap and vulgar-sounding bottles. Marianne dressed up, too, though she had to take off her strappy sandals for the beach walk. In Brooklyn, she'd avoided her neighbors' parties, with their talk of international travel and community gardens, but it had been months since she'd been invited anywhere.

"Hello!" Sophie called from the elevated deck that stretched from the inn to the beach, as if Marianne could have missed the weathered, manatee-shaped sign. Sophie wore the same paint-spattered overalls and white T-shirt she'd had on when they met, but her short blond hair was pulled back from her face with a twisted silk scarf and mascara stiffened her lashes. With her light hair and her delicate features, she looked a bit like Sissy Spacek, if Sissy Spacek had spent a good deal of time in the sun. She held a glass of wine and was leaning against the railing, facing the inn. "I'm trying to decide if I should repaint the whole thing. Do you think I should?"

Marianne climbed the steep steps and scuffed on her sandals. The Manatee Inn was closer to the beach than the Ranch, but the steel-gray color made it appear to recede behind the palms. "A different color? Maybe. Gray is sort of—"

"Blah," said Sophie. "I know. But it's the color of manatees. Poor things. Propeller bait. I bought this place for the name, if you can believe it. I was just divorced and sort of *identifying* with the manatees, their sweet, dumb helplessness. Now I know that was a trick—neither one of us is as sweet or dumb as we look."

Marianne was never sure what to say when people announced their divorces: I'm sorry? What if the divorce was something they really wanted, or the correction—as with Eric—of a mistake?

"It was already gray then," Sophie continued. "Sort of a dispiriting color for a resort. It looks prison-like, doesn't it?" She produced a bottle from an ice bucket and poured a glass for Marianne, sat down on the built-in bench. The Manatee's decking was gray too, the boards worn and softened like driftwood. "I've got some guests at the pool. We'll stay here until they tromp out for the sunset, okay?"

Marianne handed her the bottle she'd brought, which Sophie plunged into the bucket—no saving for later. "What about a lighter blue-gray?"

Sophie tilted her head. "Maybe, but it's a lot of expense for a small change. I was thinking a yellow"—she pointed to a blotch of sunflower paint on her overalls—"like this. You've been doing a lot of work at your place; it's nice to see. It had been going downhill for a long time. Are you set to reopen soon?"

"In March. We still have a lot to do."

"March! Too bad you'll miss the holiday traffic. Well, more for me." Sophie stretched her legs in front of her. "I take it you're new to the exciting world of hotel ownership."

"I'm not the owner," Marianne said, surprised by how happy that made her. "I'm just the caretaker, I guess." She took a long sip of wine before admitting: "It's not really a hotel, either."

"Even better!" Marianne wasn't sure if it was novelty or lack of competition that made Sophie happy. "What is it then?"

"More of a school and . . . a retreat, for writers. When we open in March, that's when our students arrive."

"Brilliant! What's it called?"

Marianne hesitated, remembering the bumper stickers—Coexist, Marriage Equality, NOW—she'd happily spotted on the back of Sophie's Subaru. "Genesis Inspirational Writing Ranch."

"Huh. Genesis, like in the Bible?"

"Like the genesis of an idea," Marianne said. "But also like the Bible. We're marketing to Christians, mostly. It's a niche market."

Sophie cocked an eyebrow.

Marianne turned her face toward the water, where the sun was sinking, fiery orange. "It wasn't my idea. Well, it was my idea, originally, but I didn't mean it."

Sophie raised the other eyebrow.

"I moved here from New York. Basically, I had nowhere else to go. My apartment was being turned into condos, and I didn't have steady work, and the owner of the motel invited me to be the administrator. Hired me. I guess you could say I missed certain boats—relationship boats, career boats—and I wound up here."

"It's not the worst place to land," Sophie said, pouring more wine for them both. "Those boats can leak. They can sink." She told Marianne about her divorce: a cheating husband, a cross-country move, the new financial reality of going it alone. "You're not married?"

Marianne shook her head.

"No significant other?"

"Not exactly."

Sophie nodded, as if this answer satisfied her. "It gets lonely, but that's when you make your discoveries, right in the middle of your loneliness. People these days can't be lonely for a second. I see it with my guests—every one of them wants to know about Wi-Fi, or the cell reception on the beach. They can't bear to be with their thoughts. Also the repeat offenders—people married again and again. What are they looking for?"

"Wasn't Frances—the owner of my inn—married a few times?"

"More than a few," Sophie said. "Five? Six? She outlived them all, and good for her, but that didn't mean she wasn't lonely. I mean, she always had some project. Like the school, I guess. I haven't seen her since she moved into the old folks' home."

"Did you know her?"

"A little. Her inn was getting a little crumbly when I bought the Manatee, and her last husband had died by then. She started a walking group, and I went once or twice. She had a Christmas cookie exchange. Then she had a book club, and I thought, well, that's nice to see. But the books got weirder and weirder—she picked all of them herself. That was maybe two years ago? After that she moved. I assumed she'd sold. It's not an easy business to keep up as you get older."

It was a relief to hear Frances identified as a reader, though Marianne wondered about the strangeness of her choices—she hadn't seen Sophie's own bookshelf, so it was hard to know what she meant. "I've been thinking about visiting her," she said. "But Eric says she wants everything to be hands off. He says she's busy."

"She loved being busy, that's what I remember. Eric—he's the not-exactly significant other?"

"He's my business partner. We used to date."

Sophie turned away to look at something happening down the beach, and Marianne felt the sudden desire tell to her the whole Eric story—how they met, their engagement, his marriage and divorce. How now she got anxious before she Skyped with him, a nervousness that stretched hours before the appointed call. Suddenly she remembered her first boyfriend, a soccer-playing stoner, and how her desire to talk about him was constantly at war with her other desire, to keep everything about him private.

"I've been here since September," she said, drawing her knees up to her chest. "And it is lonely, but I expected that. New York was lonely too. I thought if it felt more like I was choosing the loneliness, if it was deliberate, it wouldn't be so bad. It would feel heroic, maybe. That's what I'm waiting for."

"I can tell you this: being lonely is a lot better than pretending to be someone you're not," said Sophie. "Though I guess you'll have that problem once your Christian soldiers get here."

"I'm a poet," Marianne said. "The idea is that I'll write, when the students aren't here, and do the administrative stuff. I get paid, but I don't pay rent. It's like a retreat for me, too." She took another sip of wine. "It's really a great situation."

"I figured you were some sort of artist. There's a community of us here, you know," said Sophie. "I paint. For a long time just ocean mammals, especially manatees, but lately I've been doing the birds of Florida."

Whenever people told her they were artists, Marianne used to say that her mother was an artist too, but invariably this involved telling them about her mother's work, and then the fact that she was no longer alive, and then accepting the requisite sympathy or ignoring the clueless "she's in a better place" comments. So she'd fallen back on "I wish I could paint," which was not exactly true. What she wished was that she could watch her mother paint again, could sit in the studio breathing the earthy smell of linseed oil, listening to the *scratch-scratch-scratch* of her brush.

"I show every spring at the art fair in Sarasota, and getting time away from here is hard," said Sophie. The guests had begun their trek to the sunset, slowly toting beach chairs and surreptitious drinks across the sand. "These guys take a lot out of me. Some of them have been coming since before I even owned the Manatee. I never thought of having them here for just a short time. Genius idea if you can make it work. Hey, want to see my paintings?"

There was no way for Marianne to say no, so she poured another glass and followed Sophie. The boards made a hollow, uncertain sound under her sandals, and she wondered about insurance and liability. The Ranch had plenty of similar threats, and she was never sure what to do about them. You couldn't eliminate risk entirely.

"Here it is," said Sophie, leading Marianne down a path that tinkled with wind chimes. "My home, office, and studio."

Unlike Marianne, she had a cottage apartment, small and separated from the main inn by a garden planted with hostas and ferns. Just inside the door was a pale-yellow room filled with paintings in various stages of completion, abstract and figural at once, and the strong smell of turpentine. The ones hanging on the walls were clearly manatees, purplish-gray shapes bending and twisting underwater. You had to look to see it, but there were the eyes, plaintive and sorrowful as marbles, and in some of the pieces, near the top, there was the suggestion of a boat's menacing propeller or careless hull. Propped against the walls and on easels were incomplete canvases, with still more lumpish, oily creatures, but instead of underwater things she recognized tree limbs, sky. These were the birds, Marianne understood, but they looked like manatees too.

She murmured what she hoped sounded like appreciation as Sophie crouched and rotated some canvases to the front of a large stack. "Birds are harder," she said. "Birds are the hardest thing I've painted." She turned to Marianne. "Now it's your turn."

"My turn?"

"Give me a poem! You can't tell me you don't know any of your own poems by heart."

"Oh," said Marianne, feeling her face go hot. "I really don't."

"You do!" said Sophie. "You must!"

"I really don't. I'm not that kind of poet."

Sophie pushed until Marianne finally relented, with a poem she remembered from a six-year-old at her school in Brooklyn: "Swimmy lives / in the corner / like a scared / cloud." The boy, in a class for the emotionally disturbed, had accompanied his poem with a drawing of the class pet. It looked like an M&M with six legs, but it was supposed to be a hamster. She had told him how to write the words *corner* and *scared*, and she had helped him make the spaces between the words by placing one finger there to hold the words apart. She had not asked, as she wanted to, why is your class hamster named Swimmy? She had concentrated on reading the words as he wrote them, knowing them rather than guessing them, and when she read it out loud to him, with a poet's pausing, he had nodded, satisfied, then bitten her on the wrist.

Sophie repeated the poem to herself. "I like it. Simple, but haunting." The sun had set, and they could hear the guests coming back from the beach, like sea turtles in reverse. "I better go. I set out cookies and wine— cheap stuff, not this—after sunset." She drained her glass, pointed at Marianne, who felt a little lightheaded from the wine or the paint thinner. "That's the boat that'll take you somewhere."

"I'm sorry?"

"Art," Sophie pronounced, shaking a bag of dry-looking cookies onto a platter, Marianne's wine bottle tucked under her arm. "What else is there?"

The beach was empty for the short walk home, and she passed the Ranch, quiet and lightless, in favor of the busy hotels down the strand. It was the time of day—after sunset, before dinner—that she reserved for thinking about Eric. He'd sent her an email earlier with a funny story about his students, and a promise that he'd send her new chapters from his book. *As soon as they're done,* he'd written. *I just have some polishing left to do.* She'd sent back a photograph of one of the naked statues, two MoveOn petitions about climate change, and a promise to send work in return.

But she had no new poems to send. She'd been making tiny changes to the same old drafts every day. Lately she'd been on a deletion kick, carving her poems into their sparest forms yet, as if she hoped they might disappear.

She found a padded chaise that had been left out at the White Sands Resort, the nicest hotel on the beach, and sat down. The padding was thick and springy, covered with smooth navy cotton. She stretched out and reclined the chaise so that it was almost flat. The stars were just visible, and she wondered what time it was in Dubai; she could never keep track. Very late, she thought, or very early.

Eric knew the time where she was—even in his sleep, she felt sure he was tuned in to her life. When she started teaching at P.S. 150, he knew her schedule better than she did, remembered the names of her students. From Charlotte he sent them little gifts: erasers and pencils and pocket-sized notebooks with glittery covers. Mr. Eric, her students called him when they wrote the thank-you note together.

"Ma'am," said a voice behind her. "Ma'am?"

Marianne sat up, then turned around to see a teenager in a White Sands windbreaker. The windbreaker suddenly reminded her that she was cold.

"You can't sleep here," he said. The apologetic tone in his voice made it worse.

"I *know*," she told him. "I wasn't."

In her room, Marianne turned on her laptop and refreshed her political news sites while a frozen bean burrito rotated in the microwave. Not much had happened today, but still the alarms sounded: some dumb things said by a couple of dumb governors, legislation moving forward in Marianne's home state that would require every abortion seeker to have an ultrasound (their governor, too, had higher ambitions). One of the more popular candidates for president owned a chain of pizza restaurants, and each outlandish statement he made increased his popularity, according to polls. Every hour or so there was something to make your heart pound with anxiety and disbelief—it was addictive, that sickening, stomach-dropping feeling. Checking email was the same: who knew what could be in there? Maybe a prize, the kind you earned without knowing it. Maybe a missive, or the promised chapter, from Eric.

No prizes today, only a dozen or so email petitions, which she dutifully signed and forwarded, and new profiles, still New York–based, selected by match.com. She switched to another tab on her browser, an online version of *À la Rencontre de Philippe*, which she'd found and begun playing again. Philippe looked the same—she was repeating the same series of grainy videos she'd seen in the language lab more than a dozen years ago—but she found helping him more frustrating. He didn't think the apartment she found was close enough to the Metro. He didn't like only a standing shower; he preferred a bath. He didn't want to work on Saturdays. Her French was no longer convincing; they'd been sitting at the same café for days.

She checked her voicemail, where there was a message from her father. "Marianne, it's Dad. Hello?" Someday she would have to tell him that she knew he was familiar with answering machines and voicemail; there was no reason to pretend otherwise. "I'm just calling to see if you've made any plans for, ah, Thanksgiving. You are of course very welcome here. Your sister is having one of her church things, and we could stop by there. Or we could just have dinner here, and see her on Friday. That might be best. Let me know, okay? It's Dad."

Thanksgiving was two weeks away. A plane ticket would be expensive, the drive more than twelve hours without traffic. She thought of calling, explaining this to him, and having to listen to the faint notes of hurt and disappointment in his voice.

Dad, she wrote instead, in an email. *I wish I could come for Thanksgiving, but it looks like travel will be too difficult. I'll be there for Christmas, and I can stay longer then. Does that sound good? Hope your semester is going well.*

The microwave dinged. In Brooklyn, Marianne hadn't even owned a microwave, but here at the Ranch she didn't have many other options. She could drive to Sarasota and pay too much, or go nearby and take her chances. Instead she cooked food in an appliance that looked, as her mother would have said, like a television, rolled it onto a plastic plate, and watched a reality show while she ate. The plot tonight was the same as last night: something about switching families. It always involved the same two kinds: a rigid, God-fearing, paternalistic one in a large, clean house, and a free-spirited, undisciplined Wiccan or feminist one in a smaller house where no one made the beds. The mothers each spent a week trying to cajole the other's family into her preferred lifestyle, but in the end, after tears and hugs, all agreed that their own way was best.

In the morning, an email from her father: *Dear Marianne, I'm sorry you can't come but a long visit at Christmas sounds good too.*

The semester goes along, better now than at the beginning. Each of my online classes was overfilled, but then people drop or withdraw, usually by about a third, and that helps. They lose their money after the first week, which as an ethics professor makes me uncomfortable, this wishing for a third (or more) of them to back out. Does it cause me to make the first of their assignments tougher, the readings longer, more daunting? But they tell me I'm not supposed to teach ethics anymore anyway, so I should put it out of my mind. I hope you won't have to contend with these issues in your school, Marianne.

Please tell Eric he's welcome also at Christmas—will he be back by then? I would be interested to hear about teaching in the U.A.E. Are the students better there? More focused? Does the school take a more serious approach? I am guessing not.

It's bad all over, but that doesn't mean that you have to participate. I've got five years to retirement, so I'm holding on.

Probably it's not better or more serious, she wrote back. *But that's how our school was too—it's up to you to make something out of it. I imagine it's the same for your students. You shouldn't feel guilty.*

I'm getting used to Florida—actually, I think I like it, this extended summerfall, the blazing sunsets. I have a friend who owns a hotel down the road from me. We take walks in the morning sometimes. She's your age, an artist (not as good as Mom). Maybe if you visit sometime you could meet her.

Eric will be in Dubai until spring, but I'll tell him he was invited. He'll appreciate it.

Marianne spent Thanksgiving at a seafood restaurant with Sophie, drinking margaritas, trying to shake off the dread feeling of familial truancy, and, later, flirting with Eric over Skype. Santas, crèches, reindeer, and snowmen appeared at the entrances to all the condos and hotels by early December; it was seventy-five degrees outside, still sunny, but lighted icicles hung from dormers and windowsills all along Gulf Drive. In mid-December, a check arrived inside a thick Christmas card printed with an image of the Chrysler Building in silver. You're doing a great job, Mark had scrawled inside the card. Just a token of our appreciation!

What did he mean by *our* appreciation, she wondered? Mark and Eric's? The patronizing tone bothered her until she realized she'd never gotten a bonus check before, and began thinking of how to spend it. It was more than enough to pay for a flight home, saving her the drive. Or she could pay her student loans—three months of principal plus interest. But after years without a car, she liked driving, the freedom to pack up and leave exactly when you liked, and it felt wrong to spend bonus money, an amount she earned from doing a great job, on something so intangible as debt.

Instead she splurged on presents for her family. Usually she gave them cheap, last-minute gifts—used books for her father, a T-shirt from a literary festival for her sister—and suffered through thank-yous too effusive to be more than pity. But this year she could prove that she was doing fine, that leaving her life in New York had been a choice, and a good one.

She made the long drive in a single day. Then she spent a week sleeping in, taking long walks with her father, and avoiding the questions of what-was-the-point-of-her-school-exactly? And how-were-they-paying-for-it? A pot of coffee warmed continuously in the kitchen; Howard shuffled around the house with a mug in his hands and a book under his arm. Marianne wondered what Sophie would think of him. Too old, probably: her last boyfriend had been a thirtysomething chef from Ecuador.

Ruth was preoccupied and wan-looking, with an amateur haircut, baggy sweaters, and a phone that beeped reminders to her: who was expecting a comfort visit, who needed a phone tree started, a casserole delivered. Only her shoes were something Marianne recognized: Ruth had always favored neon-bright sneakers, and she wore them still, though Marianne could tell these were new. Good, she thought. At least she can buy something she likes.

On Christmas afternoon they exchanged gifts at home. Marianne presented each gift with a theatrical flourish, and their faces registered surprise at the gleaming, professionally wrapped packages. For her father, a titanium fishing reel and a book about morality and war. For Darryl, a cashmere watch cap and leather gloves. She saved Ruth's present for last.

"Dangly," said Darryl, as Ruth held up the earrings.

"I thought they looked like water," said Marianne. "They match your eyes."

"I'll have to find somewhere nice to take you so you can wear them," said Darryl, though it sounded less like an offer than like an obligation.

"Thank you," Ruth said, tucking them back into their tissue-lined box. "Our presents aren't fancy, but they are handmade." She nudged two identical-looking packages shyly across the coffee table toward her father and Marianne.

"A notebook!" said Marianne, turning the lumpy blank pages. "Thank you; I'm always needing these. I didn't know you were into bookbinding."

"One of our congregants," said Darryl. "She makes the paper and sews the books herself." He patted Ruth's knee. "Ruth here is too busy taking care of people for stuff like that."

Ruth smiled at her husband as if he'd paid her a compliment. "If you plant it when you're done, it'll grow wildflowers," said Ruth.

"Probably a good use for whatever I put in there," said Marianne, running her fingers over the embedded seeds. "Bury it."

"Not your writing," said her father, getting up for more coffee. He was sensitive to any suggestion that one of his daughters might feel slighted by the other, but that didn't mean he wanted to have it out. "Mine very probably though. It takes the pressure off—thank you, Ruth!"

Darryl's and Ruth's phones beeped simultaneously; a reminder that they had to go to the next place on their list.

"That's what this house is to them," Marianne said, after they left. "Just one stop among many."

"That's what it is to everyone except for me," Howard said. "She's got a busy life. Is it the life I would have chosen for her? That your mother would have chosen? No. But it's the life she's chosen, so there you go."

"Remember how Mom and I always thought she'd be a performer? An actress or a comedian?" Ruth had liked to dance and put on shows every night after dinner. She'd memorize jokes and recite them on the way to school. "Where is she? I don't recognize my sister at all."

Howard poured out the coffee to make another pot. He had the reel propped up on the counter and had been reading the instructions. "How much do any of us recognize each other? Or ourselves?"

"Thanks, Dad. Very helpful," said Marianne. Later, she tried writing in her new notebook; she had to press hard on the uneven pages to form the words, which looked like they'd been set down by someone writing with the wrong hand. She'd been thinking of the yellow Tea Party signs, stenciled sloppily in black, which appeared now at regular roadside intervals on the way to her father's house. The poem, even incomplete, was longer than anything she'd written in months. She took photographs of the pages she'd composed and tried to text them to Eric, but her phone had only one bar of service, and the messages failed.

In the new year, driving south with a half-written poem in her bag, things looked better to Marianne. It was satisfying to note the way the landscape gradually became green again, as if she were fast-forwarding into spring. The squat palmetto trees and stalky palms looked familiar now, the pro-life billboards and stark messages from God (Where Would You Spend Eternity if You Died Today?) merely an editing problem (wouldn't "If You Died Today, Where Would You Spend Eternity?" be more gripping?).

In Georgia she stopped at a rest stop and finished her poem, a memory of seeing a bald eagle flying, a long black snake writhing in its talons, which turned into a reflection about the unnaturally coiled Don't Tread on Me snake she'd seen on so many flags at home.

She felt shaky, getting out of the car in the humid January air. Part of her wanted to keep writing in her lumpy notebook, but she had hours more driving ahead. Instead she went inside, fed wrinkled dollars into a snack machine that spat out bags of chips and cookies. Driving again, she ate them ravenously.

She considered stopping in to see Frances—in four months she still had not met her, mostly out of fear. It had occurred to her that Eric had not seen his aunt in some time. What if Frances was diminished or impaired? How would they feel about following the Christian-commercial whims of someone out of her right mind? The way Sophie described her, she didn't sound like someone who would want to start an inspirational writing school.

But perhaps they would get along great—maybe Frances would be just as Eric described, funny and sharp and generous. Maybe she'd have some pointers for dealing with the students. Relationship advice? She'd settle for gardening tips. It would be great to have another Florida associate, someone to run ideas by, to reassure her—Sophie was too appraising, and Marianne thought she was perhaps a little eager for the students to show up. Maybe she imagined them fleeing—for the Manatee Inn! Maybe she just wanted some entertainment, a way to pass the time. Frances, on the other hand, was certainly rooting for its success.

Just before the turn off 75, Marianne lost her nerve. Her hair was greasy, her clothes rumpled, her fingers orange with Doritos dust. She'd been listening, with morbid curiosity, to a program on the radio: *Talking to Tad*, a call-in show whose host, Tad Tucker, was a state representative with a penchant for baseball metaphors, alliteration, and defense of the unborn, which for him stretched all the way back to conception. "Our president recently gave a speech in which he said that the lives of people in the poorest countries on God's Earth are no less valuable than those of Americans. Even all the people in countries at war with us since 9/11, every one of them. Wonderful sentiment. Right? Wonderful words. How wonderful would it be if the president would someday say those wonderful words in reference to the lives of unborn children?"

Marianne had found herself starting to argue aloud with Tad—*it's a fetus, you asshole . . .*—but Tad's argument was already pivoting beyond her grasp.

"How wonderful would it be if our president said those wonderful words in reference to the elderly advancing in their sunset years?" he intoned. "Do you believe the most proabortion president in U.S. history thinks everyone in our land of liberty has—even the most *elderly* and *fragile* and *vulnerable* and *small*—has an *equal* right to life? I sure haven't heard him *say* so recently, have you? Caller, you're talking to Tad."

"Cluster of cells, you racist asshole, not a child," Marianne muttered, unprepared to argue that the president could in fact be trusted not to euthanize the citizenry.

Clearly Ruth's godliness hadn't rubbed off on her. She'd barely seen her sister, and hadn't had a chance to ask her about what she liked to read, what her congregation liked to read. She was certain that she would not appear credible as the director of an inspirational writing program.

But the Ranch looked better than when she left, and she was heartened, and a little surprised, to find that turning into the drive felt like coming home. Landscapers had worked through the holidays, widening the path to the beach and taming the overgrown mangroves. The interiors of all the rooms had been aired out, the worst of the furniture (broken lamps, humidity-swollen dressers) carted away. The common spaces had been painted a tasteful pale blue, the walls lined with new bookshelves, the catering kitchen scrubbed. The classrooms were next.

"It's not bad," Sophie said, when Marianne invited her for a tour. "I'd say you could get one-fifty a night in peak season, one-sixty with breakfast."

"How about if I add in top-quality inspirational writing instructors, flown in from across the country?"

"Probably need to do something about your sculpture garden," Sophie said, nudging a naked nymph with her foot.

Sophie lifted a statue off its pedestal, leaving only the stout wooden post where she'd been anchored. "Better let me take these. I'll paint some fig leaves on them, file off the nipples."

Marianne pictured the statues returning in manatee drag, but that would be better than the current situation. "Well, thank you. But I can pay you. I insist on paying."

"It'll be a challenge for me, artistically," said Sophie. "Let's see what I come up with before you make any commitments on the monetary front. Hey, could I hang a snake from a tree, something like that?"

"A *snake*?" Her mind went to the poem in her notebook.

"Like in the Garden of Eden? To go with Genesis?" Sophie laughed. "I could give this naughty gal an apple."

"Oh," Marianne said. She'd forgotten about the name, and the fact that there would soon be a sign out front, announcing it. "Right."

"You better bone up on your Bible stories before March rolls around," said Sophie. "I'll bring my truck for the rest."

In the beginning God created the heaven and the earth.

She knew that part, but had to read on for the specifics: the division of night and day, the creation of the firmament, the stars, the division of water and sky and dry land, the thoughtful addition of fish and fowl and cattle for man to dominate and eat. And then, the creation of the garden, where He set man like a doll and named some rivers and put him in charge (sort of). But dominion wasn't enough for man: God saw that he was lonely, and it wasn't right to be lonely, especially with all that gardening to do.

She knew the whole pissy, woman-blaming rest, and so she went back to day one. She read aloud, the words beautiful and strange in her mouth: *And the earth was without form, and void; and darkness was upon the face of the deep. And the Spirit of God moved upon the face of the waters. And God said, Let there be light: and there was light. And God saw the light, that it was good: and God divided the light from the darkness.*

That was the best part of any project, when everything was new and formless and possible. The spark of an idea. The smell of fresh paint, oven cleaner. Carpets with vacuum lines. Microwaves with no food smells or spatters. A blank page.

She was lonely for Eric, felt it each night on her walks, or at dinner, or lying in bed with the orange safety lights burning through the curtains. She thought of his teasing, Skype-halted voice, the physicality of him—long-limbed, smooth-skinned, just the right amount of muscle.

It would have been nice to have him there beside her. A helpmeet. Naked and unashamed, both of them.

Maybe just as the Ranch could be rehabilitated, turned into something new, their relationship could be revived. It would be something else. They wouldn't bicker. She wouldn't judge his conventionality and he, in turn, would be less conventional.

With the energy of new love, she devoted herself to making the Ranch better each day—she got recommendations from Sophie on daily housekeepers, what sort of toiletries to put in the bathrooms, and how to order labels printed with the Ranch's name. Marianne had no plan to provide lotions or shampoos, or to adhere personalized labels to the bottles, but Sophie said this was a must, otherwise she'd have people asking to borrow hers. "And toothbrushes, get a drawerful," she said. Sophie had been working on a whole Genesis-themed garden: Adam and Eve in fig leaves, Eve being tempted by the serpent, Cain slaying Abel. It was less sordid than before. Slightly.

"Great!" Eric said, every time they Skyped and she reported something new. She'd sent a welcome letter to the students; she'd been in touch with the teachers; she'd organized and added to the small library. She'd learned Excel while watching the first Republican primary debates, and had kept her cool when the libertarian doctor said it was okay to let the uninsured die, just kept adding columns and formulas. *She'd learned Excel.*

And she'd written: three new poems, which after all was the point of being here, wasn't it? To write, if not alongside the students then on some parallel track of interest and productivity.

"I think I need to meet Frances," she told Eric in February. "I think it's time."

Eric hesitated so long she was afraid her internet had failed and she'd have to redial. Finally he said he'd never heard Marianne so confident, so productive, so—happy? Was she happy there, in Florida?

Was she? It wasn't happiness so much as having a purpose. Doing for others—those mysterious and hopeful others who would soon fill the rooms of Genesis Ranch, who would fill the pages of their notebooks and files of their computers, perhaps even the shelves of bookstores and libraries, with their inspirational writing. This was what Frances had asked of her *and she'd done it*, she was thinking each time she called the Largo Shores Club and asked to be connected with Mrs. Ketterling. But it was hard to reach her. The first time she called, Frances was playing tennis; the next time, she was shopping. There was a weekend trip to Orlando. Finally they spoke by phone. In an unbroken monologue Marianne told her what she'd done.

"Wonderful," Frances said briskly. Her voice was strong and assured, the consonants sharp. "It sounds remarkable, exactly like my nephew described."

Before Marianne could thank her, she continued: "And you are pleased with the students you selected?"

"It's hard to say," she began, before correcting her uncertainty. "I'm happy with the students. I think we have a good group."

"Because the mix of students, that's what will make the school," Frances began.

"I agree completely. In graduate school—"

"They are pioneers, these students," Frances said, and then she began her own monologue: how she and Eric and Mark and Marianne were all pioneers too, in this important and generous work they were doing. They would make a space for Christian writers to be taken seriously, to learn and grow and thrive. Anyone could open the kind of writing school that had been opened a thousand times already—what they were doing was new. It could become a model. It would be remembered. Did Marianne know what it was like to be taken not-seriously?

A rhetorical question, apparently, because when Marianne tried to answer Frances kept going. Of course she knew! The school was her idea, after all—the idea of someone who could be mistaken as crazy but was in fact a visionary. She did not answer when Marianne tried to confirm, or reiterate, or otherwise get on the record that the school was *Frances's* idea, but kept on going, until suddenly she ran out of words and said she had to go.

A visionary, she'd called her.

Hanging up, Marianne had the unsettled feeling of having just ordered something she wasn't sure of—a meal from a foreign menu, a large piece of furniture, an expensive trip.

She walked outside into sunshine that felt like it would go on forever. Blue sky reflected on smooth clear water, a tidy pea-gravel path that led from the pool to the guest lodging to the classrooms.

A truck had pulled up with a load of folding chairs—where did she want them? the exhausted-looking driver was asking. He'd already opened the back door, and she could see the cheap but matching chairs—white plastic seats, white metal legs—waiting on the truck bed. She pulled herself onto the truck—she'd learned to do counts and quality control inspections before accepting any order.

"Let's take them inside," she said, grabbing four. How small they all were! How light! There were sixty chairs, more than enough for the students and faculty, but it never hurt to have too many chairs, did it? In her Brooklyn apartment she'd only had one. "I'll show you."

She carried the first set to the doorway of the library, leaned them against the wall while she fished in her pocket for the keys.

"This a new wedding spot?" the driver asked, waiting with his own armload.

"A school," she said, surprising herself—just a little—with the confidence and brevity of her answer. Just a month ago she would have hesitated before launching into the whole complicated story: Eric, Mark, Frances, her own writing and teaching career. She found her keys and unlocked the door. "Over here," she said, walking with her chairs to the far side of the room.

"Right on," he said, following her. "Education is the most important thing in the world. They can't take your education away from you, that's what I tell my son."

Marianne surveyed the room, took in its fresh-paint-and-paper smell, its stocked shelves, its gleaming new windows. Its stack of slightly used, suitable-for-a-wedding-venue chairs. Its partial gulf view. Its wood-veneer podium and mounted wireless microphone.

"The most important thing," he repeated. "I'm in school myself. Police academy. Six more weeks!" Just mentioning school—its promise of a different, better life—had brightened the man, who started back for another armload. Marianne began arranging the chairs, making two neat columns that faced the podium.

"You're a teacher?" he asked when he returned.

"No," she said, sitting down in a chair she'd just unfolded, leaning back. "I'm in charge."

Part
Two

4

Donald Goldston, known to his fans as Davonte Gold, settled into his room at a little after one o'clock on an overcast Sunday in March. Even when he was still an opening act, he'd stayed in nicer places than this, a small room with badly patched wall cracks, mismatched wood-veneer furniture, and a window that looked out over some dusty bushes. Craning his neck, he could barely see the water. One of the lamps didn't work, and the dresser drawers had to be yanked open, revealing pyramidal mounds of fine wood shavings that Davonte gathered with a tissue. What made those little mounds? Was it termites? Could termites eat your clothes? Those were some questions Davonte had never had to ask himself before.

It seemed like only yesterday he had a whole suite of rooms at the Bellagio in Vegas, with a view of the dancing fountains. He'd headlined for a week, then gone on to Los Angeles, San Diego, then back to Vegas and up to Oakland. Along with the band, the sound technician, the lighting people, the roadies, and the dancing girls, he'd traveled with a posse that included a personal trainer, a bodyguard, a personal assistant, and his best friend since third grade, Avis Conway, who'd signed onto the payroll after receiving a dishonorable discharge from the Coast Guard. How fucking hard was it to stay in the Coast Guard? Davonte still wanted to know. Back then there were very few questions that Davonte didn't have answers for—or people ready to answer them.

But in this room he was alone—there was no space for anyone else— and his life coach, who dropped him off without a car or any access to spending money, had said it was time for Davonte to start asking the questions himself and figuring out the answers on his own. Coach Harris (that was what they'd decided Davonte would call him, after Davonte recollected that his high school football coach was the last person he listened to reliably) had this way of throwing things back at you that made Davonte want to hit him.

How am I supposed to get around without no car?

How do you think you'll get around?

What'll I do if I need money? Like, really need it?

What do you think you should do?

How am I supposed to write this book by myself? I never wrote a book before.

Where would be a good place to start?

Davonte hired Harris with some of the last of his tour money, and together they'd formulated a new plan: disappear for a while, lose fifty pounds, write some new songs, and pen a best-selling book. Davonte had made his mark on the world as a sex object, possessed of a smooth golden voice and six-pack abs. A certain scandal involving unpaid taxes (really his manager's fault), a follow-up record that didn't sell, and several years of daily pot smoking and delivery pizza had eroded the appeal. Except in his hometown, where people seemed to look at him with pity (like they had ever headlined in Vegas!), Davonte didn't even get recognized anymore.

You couldn't make money these days except from touring and making appearances, so now was the perfect time to create a new Davonte Gold. He was going to have a Christian focus and the same six-pack abs. Look-but-don't-touch, Coach Harris had explained. Ladies dig that, he said, because it meant that no one else would have him either.

Coach was the one to find this place, a writing ranch that would help him get started on his manuscript, a novel about the life of a strayed artist who found the Lord and made a comeback. He had it on good authority that Davonte needed only fifty pages—tops!—to sell the whole thing for a healthy six figures, which would lead to media appearances and opportunities to perform. He'd bought Davonte a handheld voice recorder and a laptop. He'd rented an apartment not far away (its address still undisclosed to Davonte), and he was taking meetings with reality show producers (not one of those celebrity rehab shows, he'd promised, but something more in keeping with Davonte's talents). How much was all this costing? Davonte asked, and Coach had replied, as usual, with his own question: How much is your comeback worth to you?

Davonte checked himself in the mirror. He'd never hidden his body with baggy T-shirts and sagging jeans, but now he had no choice, as none of the slim-fitting clothes he liked to wear fit him anymore. He still wore a one-carat stud in each ear and kept his hair in neat cornrows, but the weight had softened his once-sharp jawline. "I know you better this way, Donald," his mother told him after he put on the weight. She lived in the same brick rancher he'd bought her after his first big paycheck, but she'd never liked his new name, and she used every opportunity to call him by the one she'd given him. She refused to watch the video the girls had gone crazy over, in which the camera had focused on Davonte's naked, sweaty, slowly gyrating abdominals, and seemed to prefer the sweetly smiling, decidedly chubby Donald of the school photos that decorated the hall table and the long-unused upright piano. He'd moved back in with his mother after meeting Coach, who knew that Davonte couldn't be trusted to live alone. Coach had given her a low-carb cookbook and a stack of Lean Cuisines for the deep freezer, but after a half hour of study she said the whole business was confusing and went back to the same meat-and-potato meals she'd always cooked.

Davonte stood over his suitcase, which he'd opened on the ugly bedspread, and considered where to put his clothes. He started unfolding and shaking out the T-shirts and polo shirts on top. The closet was only two steps away, a narrow space enclosed by flimsy folding doors. On the wooden bar were three measly hangers.

Davonte's temper was shorter since he'd gone off weed and gluten, and he stalked outside and squinted into the white, overcast afternoon. He was about to go give that woman in the office a piece of his damn mind when his neighbor, a trim white man in running clothes, appeared in his own doorway.

He was the kind of person, Davonte could tell, who was raised on friendliness. He put his hand out right away and introduced himself as Pete. Pete the poet, here from St. Augustine, home of the fountain of youth. Davonte hesitated before giving his own name—should he go by Donald? Or Davonte?—and finally decided on no name at all.

"Nice to meet you," he said. "Looks like I'm a little scarce on supplies."

"Oh really?" Pete said. "Like what?"

Davonte told him about the hanger situation and the problem with his dresser.

"And I have an abundance of them!" Pete said, like it was the luckiest thing in the world that their two rooms, one with too many hangers, and one with too few, happened to be side by side. He motioned for Davonte to follow him, but Davonte hung back in the doorway, confirming, at least, that his room was no worse than this one. Pete returned with a jumbled armful. Davonte thanked him and took them back to his own room, where he was surprised to find that Pete had followed him. He busied himself arranging the hangers, hoping he would go away.

"Somebody sure loves you!" Pete announced.

Startled, Davonte turned around. "What?"

"A care package," he said. "Already."

He pointed, and Davonte saw that nestled into one corner of the suitcase was a package of cookies his mother had baked and packed inside a Ziploc bag, along with a note: *In case you get hungry. Love, Mom.*

He felt a sudden surge of pride for his mother, a woman who raised him all alone, working a straight forty-hour week as a clerk for the city, and still had time to bake and keep the house neat. Every drawer in her house had a different, specific purpose, and none of them were heaped with wood shavings.

"My mama," Davonte said, peeling off the note. He unzipped the bag and inhaled: chocolate chip, none of that oatmealy rabbit food shit Coach tried to feed him. "You want one?"

"Oh, no thank you," Pete said, patting his flat stomach. Davonte could see that he was older than he seemed at first, with a generous sprinkling of gray in his hair and a ropy, strained look about his neck and arms. "I'm about to go for a run. Want to come with?"

In another bag were the unworn running shoes and workout clothes Coach bought him, tags still attached. But there was no way he could keep up with this guy, who looked like he could run a marathon and maybe even win. "I might meet you on the way," he said.

"Okay," Pete said. He stood there for a minute, and Davonte could feel himself being recognized: the little hairs on his arms stood up, and a tingly warmth spread from his neck to his earlobes. "I didn't catch your name. And are you a poet? Or a fiction writer?"

"Donald," said Davonte. "Fiction. Looking for somebody to help me get my story into shape."

"Aren't we all!" said Pete, and turned and jogged away.

A ghostwriter: that was what he was really looking for. Somebody to take his idea—about a handsome but down on his luck, supertalented singer who makes some honest mistakes, then finds God and makes a worldwide comeback—and put it down on paper. Davonte was a big-picture guy, that was what he always said, wasn't it? He wanted to find this person as soon as possible. Coach hadn't specifically mentioned ghostwriters, but Davonte was sure that was why he'd brought him here.

He considered the cookies, which had been folded into waxed paper before being tucked into their bag. The chips were a little gooey from riding in the trunk of the car for so many hours. But then he asked himself, as he'd been instructed: Will these cookies taste as good as success feels?

No, he told himself, they won't, and he dumped the cookies into the same trash can where he'd thrown away the wood shavings.

Feeling lighter already, he picked up his itinerary from the nightstand and checked the schedule. Four o'clock: welcome reception. Five o'clock: dinner. Six thirty: opening reading. He looked at the laptop in its black case, waiting on the dresser. But he knew if he turned it on he'd just wind up googling old articles about himself, and it would only be a matter of time before that little mouse made its way to porn sites. He'd be better off going for a run along the beach.

Lacing up his new running shoes, avoiding prideful habits, and abstaining from pornography made him feel virtuous. And if I'm going to run, I can surely have a cookie, he thought, and fished one, then a second, out of the trash can. It was strange the things you were willing to do when you knew you were completely alone.

In the office, Marianne scanned her list of students and tried matching names with the many faces that had stood expectantly before her desk today. There had been a lot of drop-offs by strangely tearful family members, and that had confused things. Oh well, she thought. She'd have name tags for them later on anyway. Most everyone had arrived early enough to stroll along the beach, tour the sculpture Garden of Eden, and complain about the rooms.

"I don't mean to complain," the complaints always began.

Lorraine Kominski had been the worst offender, arriving by taxi in a floppy straw hat, giant sunglasses, and trailing caftan and installing herself next to the telephone in her room, which she used to request a series of things: a different brand of toilet paper, that the television be removed from her room, that the televisions be removed from all the rooms. She wanted to send out for Bloody Mary mix and a copy of Amiri Baraka's *Hard Facts* ("I could order it," Eric suggested, his hand held over the receiver. "*No,*" hissed Marianne). Lorraine didn't know how to work the internet. She wanted a nonsmoking room that she could smoke in.

Eric was tending to her while Marianne waited for the last students and for Tom Marshall, their nonfiction instructor. He'd been a tough, last-minute hire after their other teacher won a grant (she sounded rather relieved, Marianne thought, to turn down the position). Tom had written a memoir about his years as a war reporter but had been fired from his last job as writer-in-residence at a boys' boarding school. ("Total bullshit," he explained during the phone interview.) Marianne had not checked his references but had accommodated his request for a room that could be locked from the outside ("Parasomnia," he said. "Look it up.").

From her window she could see out across the mangroves to the beach, where Davonte Gold had been occupied in an elaborate stretching routine for the past half hour. She still had *Hurt Songs*, his first album, on CD, had played it on her stereo the one night the law professor had come over to her place, votive candles flickering on her windowsill.

"*This guy,*" the professor had said. "I thought he was in jail."

"No," she'd said. Davonte Gold was from Newport News, and Marianne felt obligated to defend him. "It was mismanagement, which happens to a lot of artists. The IRS is really unfair sometimes."

"Wasn't there a sex tape too? A perverted video?"

The professor had once had Marianne pee on him, and liked other vaguely scatological things done to him with the lights off. They'd gotten into an argument then about the meaning of the word *perverted*, and whether it could apply to something that was natural, biologically speaking. It was about social norms, the professor had insisted, and Marianne had remembered how hard it had been to make herself pee on him. Rather as Marianne had expected, even from the moment she lit the candles, the evening had not ended romantically.

Davonte did not *look* like a pervert, but rather like an overgrown child with his cornrows and baggy T-shirt, the shiny gym shorts that hung to the middle of his tattooed calves. She wondered what all of this stretching—the futile attempts to touch his toes, the unlimber side lunges—was in service of. It was hard to picture him jogging, but then, to her surprise, that is exactly what he did. He turned away and started running, arms held in tight L shapes at his side, tennis shoes kicking up sand, and he did not stop for as long as she could keep him in her sight.

"Like watching a sunset" was how Marianne described it later to Eric. He had returned from examining the cavernous spaces underneath Lorraine's beds and killing several palmetto bugs. "The way something so big could just disappear."

"One was the size of a shoe," he said. "It was bloody."

"I mean, he must weigh three hundred pounds?"

"He doesn't weigh *three hundred pounds*, Marianne."

"Well, I've never been good at estimating. And he just *ran*, all the way up the beach."

"Lorraine is still a chain smoker," Eric said.

He'd come back tanned and spoiled from Dubai, Marianne thought. Everything overwhelmed him, and he needed to be talked down from negative thinking. But then, Marianne had to admit, so did she. It seemed that negativity and pessimism were necessary, essential, but heavy and unhealthy, like a bucket of third-world water, which they passed back and forth between them. This was not how Marianne had imagined their reunion, or even the beginning of their partnership in the school.

"I am trying to say something *positive* here. I am trying to talk about potential. It's been a hard day. I thought we could keep the bad stuff to ourselves for once."

"Sorry," Eric said, holding up his hands in a gesture of surrender. "You think anyone here recognizes him?"

Marianne frowned at the now-empty beach, trying to conjure Davonte. She'd been somewhat flustered when he checked in, and he'd seemed irritated by how long it had taken her to find his keys. "No, probably not. Do you think it would be a problem if they did?"

"Maybe. Probably. I doubt we have too many Davonte Gold fans here anyway."

"He's going by Donald," Marianne said. "So don't call him Davonte."

They still had so much to do—find their nonfiction instructor, set up for the evening's welcome reception, make tropical punches (with alcohol and without). Marianne kept getting the urge to drive off, maybe to the Keys, where it would be warm enough to swim. It was a feeling she'd gotten at every job she'd ever had, even as a child at school, sent on an errand—*I could just escape*—and the only way she knew to fight it was to focus on small tasks, like tracking down Tom Marshall's cell number.

"His *novel*." Eric shook his head as if trying to unsee something. "I don't know how I let you sneak this one by me."

"Positive things," Marianne reminded him, paging through her nonfiction hiring folder. "Keep the negative ones to yourself."

"If people like you are still reading and writing, then we do not have to worry about books becoming obsolete," the woman at the podium was saying. This was Janine's teacher, a famous poet who had won prize after prize, back in the seventies. You could google her name and get thousands of hits, and Janine, in the first blush of excitement over her acceptance, had clicked on nearly all of them. She had also ordered her first, most widely praised book and dutifully read it, marking lines and stanzas she did not understand with sticky notes. The slim book, stiffly ruffled with pink and blue notes, peeked out of Janine's tote bag, which vibrated now and then with texts from her daughters. She was trying very hard to ignore the texts and focus on her teacher. She thought texts should be reserved for important communications—things too immediate to chance losing to the black hole of voicemail—but realized that her daughters felt exactly the opposite.

Janine, who had long been sensitive to slights, wondered what the woman, her teacher, meant by *people like you*. She had witchy gray hair that flowed over her shoulders, round glasses pushed on top of her head, and a way of looking out and over the audience instead of at them. In her author photo she'd worn her hair in the same tumbling, frizzy mass, though it was darker then, and she'd stared right at the camera in an unsettling way. Janine craned her neck to see if there was a very tall or standing person that Lorraine Kominski might be addressing, but all she saw were the same attentive, mostly middle-aged students, seated on folding chairs that rested unevenly on the ground, and the sculpture garden behind them. She was talking about the state of poetry today, and Janine felt, despite the woman's imperious air and fast way of speaking, a kind of kinship forming across the rows of students. The gist of her speech was this: she had seen things change, and she did not feel hopeful about the direction of these changes. That was exactly how Janine felt in her own most trying moments, and she found herself nodding with each pronouncement. After a few more minutes Lorraine Kominski paused abruptly and looked out at the audience as if she were surprised to find them still in their seats, then set her glasses down on the end of her nose and began to read from a stack of poems.

The woman on Janine's right was sitting with perfect posture, her hands folded neatly in her lap, her eyes trained on the poet. Her hair was so thick and dark that it looked like a doll's hair, so smooth that Janine wondered if it might in fact be a wig. Her bag, neater than Janine's floppy tote but also set on the ground, glowed every few minutes with messages arriving to her iPhone. Janine watched the phone and watched the woman, who did not turn her head or otherwise acknowledge her messages other than a brief squinting and raising of her chin, that extra effort of ignoring the distraction. She might have been Janine's age or she might have been ten years younger; it was hard to tell in the same way that it was hard to tell the ages of people on television.

Lorraine was reading a poem about the ocean, one of Janine's favorites because it was so clear, compared to the others. It always appeared on the poetry websites that would offer you two or three examples from the poet's work, so perhaps its clarity came from the fact that Janine had read it many times. Lorraine had never had children—Janine knew this from the biographical notes—and this fact was reflected in the poem, which was about feeling powerless and insignificant in the face of nature. She had read this poem many times, Janine could tell, and so its emotional significance was hard to gauge. Janine wondered if she felt the same way now, if it would help her to know that children had their own ways of making you feel powerless and insignificant.

Soon the reading was over, and everyone was milling about with cups of sparkling punch. Janine was suddenly shy of Lorraine Kominski, who was standing behind the punch table, tipping a cup to her lips.

"Wasn't it a wonderful reading?" Janine asked the woman with the perfect posture. Janine was not used to being around so many strangers, and their proximity during the reading suggested a greater intimacy than she would have ordinarily felt with such a pulled-together woman. "I'm studying with her."

"Yes, wonderful," the woman said, though she offered nothing else about the reading. She hitched her purse over her shoulder and smiled broadly at Janine. "Are you a student here?"

"Oh, yes. I'm here for poetry," she said. It was still difficult to say *I'm a poet* and not feel foolish, but *I'm here for poetry* sounded wrong too—like she was in line for a movie. "And you? Are you a student also?"

The woman shook her head apologetically. "No, my talents are not in the writing arena. How I wish I could write! You are very lucky. Tell me, how did you find out about the Ranch?" She took an electronic tablet from her bag and tapped lightly at the screen, which cast a pale glow on her poreless skin. "You don't mind if I take notes, do you?"

"I found out about the Ranch in a magazine. I just applied," Janine said slowly. The woman's swiping and tapping made her self-conscious. Was she a reporter? Some kind of agent? Janine had heard from someone at church that agents were the way to get a book published. She thought perhaps she could keep talking. "I'm a teacher. I have two children. Two daughters. Almost grown. And a very supportive husband."

Everything that came out of her mouth sounded so boring, so utterly ordinary, but the woman nodded eagerly, tapping the screen as though she could barely keep up with Janine's brilliance. "How fascinating!" she said. "And what attracted you to the school? Was it the Ranch's Christian mission, or the convenience of the schedule?"

Janine had to take all of her spring break, plus four accumulated sick days, to cover the time at the Ranch. Her daughters had complained—wouldn't she rather spend her time off with them?—and her principal had only grudgingly signed her paperwork. But it was true that a more traditional school—the kind where you had to be in class all semester, and move, maybe to another state, wouldn't have worked at all.

"I guess both things?" she tried. "I mean, I never thought I would go back to school at this age—I'm forty-three—and so of course it made a difference that I could come here for a couple of weeks at a time and then go home again, you know, because I have a family, because I have a job. But I *am* a Christian, and my work has a Christian purpose, so I felt more comfortable applying to a school that embraced those same ideas. I felt like, maybe this school could help me get where I want to go with my writing, like it wouldn't be a selfish choice? And I wanted to meet other writers, but especially other Christian writers." Janine looked down at her cup of punch, which was almost empty. "I'm sorry, I'm just going on and on."

"*No*," the woman cooed, still looking down at the glowing screen. Maybe she really was an agent, Janine thought. Should she tell her about the book she was writing? Should she ask for her card? "This is *wonderful*. So helpful."

"My name is Janine. Janine Gray."

"Regina Somers," the woman said, tucking her tablet under her arm and gripping the ends of Janine's fingers as if she might lead her to a dance floor. "Such an *honor* to meet you. I'm sure I'll see more of you around the school and—hopefully—in the marketplace."

Janine took a last sip of punch, and when she looked up again Regina Somers had sidled over to speak to someone else, her tablet in hand again. So she had not asked for the probably-an-agent's card, had not told her about her sense that something very powerful could be said—needed to be said—about the life of Terri Schiavo. She had at least introduced herself, which was a start.

It was growing dark. Paper lanterns hung from the eaves of the main building and Christmas lights twinkled around the outdoor reading area. Pea gravel crunched under Janine's sandals as she walked the perimeter of the sculpture garden, which had probably seen better days. Some of the sculptures were missing from their pedestals, while others leaned lumpily against the boxwoods. Some of them appeared to be fleeing rape, though they also looked like they were enjoying it. Marianne was the first person Janine had spoken to about the Ranch, a pretty girl gone rather thin and harried, she could tell, with taking care of everyone's needs. She had a young face, long salt-and-pepper hair that she twisted into a bun. Janine wondered if she should grow her own hair long again. She'd cut it when the girls were little.

Janine's phone buzzed, and she fished it out of her bag to read the string of text messages, which she'd ignored over the past hour, from Beth and Chrissy. Beth got an A minus on a paper she was sure was an A paper; should she complain? Chrissy wanted to know where the recipe for tamale pie was kept. Beth thought Chrissy was trying to compromise her diet; would Janine please speak to her? And yes she was definitely going to complain about her paper. Chrissy said she missed her, things weren't the same when she was gone. Chrissy signed her texts Luv u!!! Beth signed her texts with <3 <3 <3. It had taken Janine a while to understand that those were symbols of hearts. For some reason they looked a little vulgar to her.

She thought about the difficulty of communication between generations, how it all came down to an interpretation of signs and symbols, and then she thought of Bob and Mary Schindler, the wide expanse of understanding they crossed to be closer to Terri, and then she was grateful, so grateful, for her own daughters' sweet, mildly complaining texts. She texted back: LOVE U GIRLS! XOXO MOM.

Then she turned back to the party, where in short order she met a farmer, a preacher's wife, a Gulf War veteran, and a singer. She drank one cup of punch, and then another, and she thought about writing a poem.

At midnight, some of the students were still awake, loudly talking and laughing in a cluster of folding chairs they'd dragged near the pool. The punch, studded with rum-soaked pineapple, was sweet and easy to drink, and it cheered Marianne to think of the drinkers' impending hangovers. She was making photocopies of last-minute handouts Lorraine requested—the copier Mark had ordered jammed after every third copy—and Eric was dozing in a chair.

"Tell your brother that *used* is not a good choice for copiers," Marianne said. She'd been talking to Eric in a quiet, firm voice, the way she used to imagine herself talking to the chain-smoking Philippe. Opening the side door, she wrenched out a copy of Galway Kinnell's "Flower Herding on Mount Monadnock," pleated into the shape of a fan, and tossed it onto the floor. "You have to ask yourself, why did someone get rid of a perfectly good copier?"

Eric shifted in his chair but did not open his eyes, and Marianne remembered, from grad school, that he could sleep just about anywhere, on subway benches or in movie theaters, like an old man or a homeless person.

"The answer is, they wouldn't," Marianne said, banging each drawer and door shut a final time. Treating the machine roughly seemed to improve its performance. "This is not a perfectly good copier. I'd be better off copying this by hand, like a monk. I'd be better off photographing the pages and developing the prints in a darkroom."

Opening a writing school turned out to be more expensive than Mark and Eric reckoned, she'd learned in these last few weeks. The city had its hand out, demanding various fees, applications that required lawyers, and inspections they never passed on the first go. Converting the kitchen into something a caterer could use hadn't been cheap, nor had the roof repairs, the painting, the landscaping, or the housekeeping services. Marianne told them not to worry, quoting Frances—it was *remarkable* and *important*, this work they were doing—but Eric and Mark felt it was better to protect their aunt from the extra expense. *Shield her*, was the phrase Mark used. In the end, Mark had used his connections to secure venture capital, which provided for the copier and office equipment and unexpected bills. Before the venture capital arrived, Marianne had taken on the reading of the next batch of applications alone while Eric supplemented the school's income with odd jobs, offering online critiques of college application essays and handling the Twitter accounts for several Mars brand candies. "It'll come back to you a thousand percent," Mark had assured them both, when Marianne complained.

"Who knows what he even meant by that," Marianne muttered. "Effort? Karma? I don't know what your brother got us into, Eric."

"Mfff," said Eric, shutting his eyes more tightly. It embarrassed Marianne to think now of all the ways she'd fantasized about his return: jumping into his arms; running into the shallow waves of the gulf; tumbling, salty-skinned, into bed in Marianne's shade-drawn room. None of those active, romantic, cinematic sequences had come true, not so far—they'd been too busy, too tense, she told herself. Best to wait until these twelve days were done, then they could start over. Twelve days! It would go by in no time.

His mouth was slightly open; he may have been drooling. He was certainly snoring, though very softly. Marianne looked away.

Over the copier's slow, high-pitched whine came a rumbling sound, and Eric startled. "What's that?" he said, sitting up and blinking. The rumble settled into the recognizable sound of a motorcycle, and as the motor stalled, then stopped, Marianne could hear the group near the pool go quiet.

"Let's hope it's Tom." Marianne had given up trying to locate him hours ago and had prepared to teach his first class herself. This had involved reading chapter one of two memoirs—the first from the Desert Storm veteran, the second from the preacher's wife. They'd encouraged the students to send new work—not the same material they'd used in their applications, and maybe that accounted for the awkwardness on the page. Both memoirs, oddly, had been written in the third person. They had also been written oddly.

Tom Marshall stood in the screen doorway, holding his helmet in one hand and running the other through thinning hair. He opened the door, then stepped through, blinking in the fluorescent light.

"Thank God," Marianne said. She'd met him at a conference years ago, and he looked mostly the same: rumpled, unshaven, cowboy booted, surprised to be here. Part of his shtick was never dressing appropriately, which Marianne had not connected, at the time, to a penchant for motorcycle riding. "Where were you? Why didn't you answer your phone?"

"Got lost," he said, then made a show of finding his cell phone in his pocket. "You can't hear these things on a hog. Maybe your little Suzuki, but not a Harley."

"Probably shouldn't answer them either," Eric said. "On a hog. How's it going?"

Ignoring Eric's outstretched hand, Tom seemed to blink Marianne into his vision. He strode over to her and picked her up as if they were long-lost friends.

"Mary-Ellen," he said, kissing her ear wetly through her hair. They'd sat together on a panel—"Life after the MFA: Alternatives in Employment Opportunities"—and had joked about the alternatives. Marianne knew someone who penned greeting cards. Tom, before grad school, had made some money doing medical research (*being* medical research, Marianne had corrected him). "Little Mary-Ellen the poet. How's it going?"

"Marianne," Eric corrected him.

"Oh," she said, set down again and turning back to the copier. "I'm happy as a clam."

"I can show you your room," Eric suggested. "Where's your luggage?"

"Just this," he said, hefting a knapsack. "The Sandinistas taught me to travel light."

Marianne rolled her eyes at the copier, then remembered the manuscripts.

She handed him the two thick packets. "These are up for discussion tomorrow. Ten o'clock. A.M. Breakfast is at eight."

Tom looked wearily at the pages.

"Point of view problems," she offered. "Among other things."

He sighed and flipped through the manuscript on top, turning the pages so fast they fanned air into his face. "I used to work at Princeton," he said.

"Well," she said. "This is not Princeton."

"What's this?" he asked, pointing to the "GWGW" logo on the manuscript's cover page. The logo had been printed on pale blue card stock, according to Mark's instructions, and added to each manuscript. It was this card stock, mottled like old paper money, that originally jammed the copier.

"That's one of our funders," Marianne said, fitting a fresh copy of "Flower Herding" into the feeder. "Don't worry about it."

"It's *the* funder," Eric said. "Other than tuition. God's World God's Word. They pay your salary."

"Such as it is," Tom said.

"Right," said Marianne. "And for all of this wonderful office equipment."

"Say," Tom said, peering at the logo, which featured a globe with a cross planted at the North Pole like a moon flag. It cast a shadow across North America. "This isn't some right-wing organization you're fronting?"

"Do you really want to know?"

"God's World God's Word is a faith-based organization involved in education and outreach efforts," Eric explained. "They've been very generous."

"No, I suppose I don't want to know," Tom said. "I'm beat. Where'd you say my room was?"

"This way," Eric said, opening the screen door.

"Needs to lock from the *outside*," Marianne heard Tom instructing him as they rounded the corner toward the dormitories.

After locking Tom into his room, Eric helped Marianne copy and bind the last of the packets, then walked her to her own room, deliberately sited all the way on the other side of the Ranch, just across from his. Sitting across from each other on her two beds, they shared the last of the punch, which seemed to have gone through an additional fermentation process since Marianne had funneled it into her thermos.

"To a successful opening night," Eric said, raising his paper cup.

"To no one getting permanently lost," Marianne said. "Or into any fights."

"That's true," Eric said, pouring himself another. "Though I wanted to deck Tom when he picked you up and kissed you."

"Me too," Marianne said. "Yuck. Why didn't you?"

Eric shrugged. "I didn't think you wanted to teach nonfiction. Also, I think he would have knocked me out."

"That's probably true," she said. The punch in her cup was down to its syrupy dregs, and she stretched her tongue to reach a maraschino cherry stuck to the bottom. Dislodged, it exploded alcohol into her mouth. "Anyway, you did a good job of evangelizing GWGW to him."

"I didn't evangelize," he said. "I wouldn't know how."

"You did! You called it a *faith-based organization involved in education and outreach.*"

"But that's what they say they are," Eric said. "I was just repeating—"

"What the hell do you think evangelizing is?" she asked. "I'd really like to know where your brother met these people. And I thought Frances paid our salaries."

"It was getting expensive. With the property taxes, and all the fees—"

"But when we talked it seemed like she was happy to pay for it all! Like it made her proud!"

Eric stood slowly and moved to her bed. He sat very close and poured more punch into her cup. "Frances is eighty-two years old," he said. "Largo Shores is almost four thousand a month. And that's in the independent-living section. She can't spend all her savings on our project—"

"Her project," Marianne said. "This was her idea."

"Her project," Eric agreed.

Marianne suddenly felt very sleepy. She rested her head on Eric's shoulder. "Does she know about them? GWGW? I mean, she didn't seem like someone who would appreciate some corporate group coming in and taking over everything."

"They're not. And she doesn't know much—she doesn't need to. GWGW is Mark's thing, a supplement. You know that."

"I feel so reassured. So supported!" She sat up.

"I'm going to talk to him," Eric said. "About the copier. Okay?"

"That would be helpful," she admitted. "But I don't like the idea of them. God's Word God's World. God's World God's Word. It's hard to keep straight. Plus, what the fuck are we doing? I think that, all day long. What the fuck are we doing?"

"Probably best *not* to think about it," Eric said.

"Best not to think about what?"

"About what we're doing, or about GWGW. We're doing it. It's going okay. It's going *great*, considering."

"But God's World—"

"They're a Christian organization, just like us."

"Not just like us," Marianne said. She lowered her voice to a whisper. "We're not serious about what we're doing. We're . . . taking advantage of certain expectations. We're exploiting certain ideas."

Eric laughed. "What do you think they're doing?"

"Fuck," she said. She hadn't thought of it that way—there were so many ways to be cynical and exploitative. It didn't seem so bad, when the profits were keeping her own friends afloat, paying back student loans. But a corporation? "I guess you're right. As long as they're just paying for copiers and card stock. Just promise you won't let things go too far, okay? Promise it'll still be us in charge?"

"Yeah," he said. "Of course."

"Promise?"

"I promise," Eric said. He stared into his cup, turning the viscous liquid around the edges. "I think this is my last chance, Marianne," he said after a while, his voice quiet and pleading. "I need this to work."

"Last chance," she scoffed. "You're an internationally published, internationally traveling novelist and teacher. This isn't about *last chances*."

"I sold fifty e-books in New Zealand. I didn't finish my novel in Dubai. I need *this* to work."

"Your book came out two years ago," Marianne said. "There's no rush. It's not a race." This was something she often told herself when she was notified, via email, of publication news from their program.

"Three years ago," he said.

"What?"

"It came out three years ago. And I'm on the hook for another one."

"Oh," she said. No real money exchanged hands to mark the publication of poetry, no promises of a second book made to eager publishers. At the end of each of her grants, Marianne had typed up reports to the funding organizations, but had heard very little back other than reminders that they were one-time grants. It was hard for her to imagine herself in Eric's situation. But she did not want this idea, which she'd dreamed up in her twenties, to be a career maker for either of them.

"You can always teach—"

"I want this to work," he said. He set his cup on the nightstand and lay back, on top of the bedspread, and closed his eyes. Suddenly she saw him as he must have seen himself: a washed-up, divorced novelist who'd quit the only job he'd ever had that offered benefits. A financial failure who desperately wanted to impress his older brother in a get-rich-quick scheme. A jealous ex-boyfriend who backed away from confrontations with pushy older men.

Marianne put a tentative hand on Eric's shoulder, and he didn't stir. She knelt on the bed next to him, gently shaking him until his eyes opened.

"Hey," he said sleepily. He reached up to brush a strand of hair away from Marianne's face and let his hand come to rest on her bare shoulder, where it felt solid and reassuring. For a moment she wanted nothing more than to lie next to him, in the comfortable curve of his arm, and let him stroke her hair and her face, tell her that she was beautiful. It would be easy to reach for the lamp and turn it off, to concede to whatever might happen in the dark.

But this moment, drunken and confused and slightly pitiful, wasn't the right one. It was too much like their first time, and nothing at all like what she'd imagined in his absence. They couldn't fall back into old patterns, not now, anyway—it would be better, more fulfilling, to wait. Wasn't that what the Christians told themselves? Twelve days, that was all. "You have to get up," she said briskly, moving away from him on the bed. His hand dropped to his side. "You can't stay here."

"But I'm comfortable," he said, closing his eyes again. She turned on the overhead light.

"If you want this to work, you can't have people here thinking we're cohabiting."

"Cohabiting?"

"*Fornicating*," she said.

"Ah," he said, slowly sitting up and squinting. He took his cup, smoothed his shirt and hair, and made his way to the door. "It's been a long time since we did that."

From her window Marianne watched him walk, in a slow and dignified zigzag, back to his room, and resisted the urge to call him back. She was right to send him home, she told herself. They had a big day ahead, no time for distractions. There would be plenty of time to figure out where they stood after the students left.

Eric fumbled his door open and turned on the lamp next to his bed. Marianne waited for him to pull the curtains closed, but he left them open. She wasn't sure if the open curtains were a gesture of innocence or a rebuke, but eventually she grew tired of watching and climbed into her own bed, alone.

5

Janine's mind had always compulsively imagined terrible things happening to whomever she most treasured. It started when she was young and her parents would leave her with a babysitter. Waiting for the sound of tires crunching gravel, the splay of headlights through the curtains, she'd played unending games of Monopoly with her sister while she visualized car crashes, abductions, murder, even though she'd grown up in a town where hardly anything like that ever happened. In fifth grade, her good friend Cindy's mother had died of a brain aneurysm, and suddenly that was what Janine thought of, when she worried—a narrowing and bursting in each of her parents' brains, her own self, small and helpless, finding them slumped over in the garden or on the kitchen floor. She never told anyone about this compulsion—truly, it felt like something her brain was *doing* to her—not even Rick, whom she married just a year out of high school.

It grew worse when she became, at twenty-two, a mother. For the first two years of Beth's life Janine would not allow anyone to drive her except Rick—not even herself. It got a little better with Chrissy—she was too busy with a three-year-old and an infant to do much imagining—but her anxiety increased when Beth entered kindergarten and she had all day long to think about perverts lurking in the schoolyard, someone posing as an uncle and signing her out of school. Beth was an open, trusting child, and the secretary at the primary school was nearly seventy years old, half-blind, and it wasn't hard to see how such a thing—a terrible thing—could happen.

So Janine confessed. Told Rick about the visions, worse than any nightmare, admitted the sickness of a mind that could picture such awful things. She'd held her breath, expecting Rick to scold her or accuse her of willing evil into their life. Instead he told her, in a sorrowful voice that was much older than his twenty-seven years, "It's not your mind, it's the wicked world we live in." After performing some calculations on the pad of yellow legal paper he kept next to the phone, he allowed Janine to pull Beth out of kindergarten and enroll her in the Christian day school down the street, where Janine and Chrissy could stroller the sidewalked half mile to meet her for lunches Janine made at home. Janine admired the tiny schoolyard's high wooden security fence, the small size of Beth's class. Strolling home again, she'd think of Rick, who poured concrete six days a week to make sure his family had everything they needed. He was her rock, she told people, assuaging her fears without writing them off as silly. Though Janine questioned the workings of her own mind—why did the images have to be so disturbing? why couldn't she imagine something nice?—Rick had never suggested she see a therapist or that in any way she was sick, and for that she was grateful.

They got through soccer camp and swimming lessons, a vacation Bible school instructor who seemed a little too eager to take the children to the church basement arts and crafts room. They endured the transition to a public middle school, with its nighttime dances and questionable curriculum, survived even Janine's transition to the workplace. They lived through Britney Spears and Christina Aguilera, the fashion for bare midriffs and jailbait music videos. They made it through 9/11, the anthrax mail scare, the D.C. snipers, and various child abductions. Because Rick did the instructing, she even got through Beth's first tentative driving lessons, which Janine thought were given earlier than necessary.

Beth was fourteen years old and in her first year at the public high school, a long-legged blond girl just beginning to receive phone calls from boys who already seemed to anticipate her turning sixteen, an age Rick and Janine (too long ago! what were they thinking?) had deemed old enough to date. That was when Janine first heard about Terri Schiavo, a woman who, at the age of twenty-six, the very flower of her life, collapsed in the hallway of her St. Petersburg home and was rushed by ambulance to the hospital, where she was intubated and ventilated and pronounced comatose. Janine did not know about this woman until she had been in a coma for more than a decade, when the fight between her parents and her husband made national news. Her husband had not wanted to take her off life support (she could breathe on her own), but to remove her feeding and hydration tube, essentially starving and dehydrating her to death. Her parents, devout Catholics who believed it was wrong to interfere with God's will, opposed him.

Michael Schiavo, Terri's husband, and the lawyers and politicians and even the doctors, who stood against Terri's parents and against God, seemed to represent something about the world Janine's daughters would be growing into. A world in which, instead of praising God for sparing his wife's life and giving him the opportunity to care for her alongside her devoted parents, a man might kill her with the full participation and support of a hospital staff and court of law. A world in which a life only counted if it looked, on the outside, like everyone else's. Janine could not imagine releasing either of her sweet girls, still as tender and uncertain as kittens, into such a world.

Janine had never been a political person. She voted in presidential elections and kept the evening news on while she made dinner, but she was aware that most of her ideas about politics came from other people, namely Rick. The Schiavo case was different. Unlike taxes or gun control or war or even abortion, issues that were merely theoretical in Janine's life, this seemed wholly within her realm of experience and power of imagination. It was a case that struck at the very heart of what people meant when they told you that you were a mother for your child's entire life, that you would protect them always, no matter what. Terri's open-mouthed, beatific smile (*was it a smile?*), her head lolling against a wheelchair's cushioned neck support, was an image that flashed across every television screen while the likes of Jesse Jackson and Jeb Bush and lawyers from the ACLU talked on and on in the background.

Janine could do little but pray for her and put her name in the church bulletin's prayer list, but her prayers felt like an occupation. She prayed when the feeding tube was removed, and when it was reinserted under Governor Bush's orders. She prayed when Terri left the hospice for the rehabilitation center, and prayed when she was returned to the hospice again. She prayed for Terri's parents, held at arm's length by the courts, and prayed for Jesse Jackson to please go back to Chicago and mind his own business. She prayed when the tube was removed again, prayed when Terri was given something called a swallow test, and for the efficacy of a therapy called VitalStim, which was supposed to help Terri swallow on her own. She prayed on her knees, after making each of the beds in the morning, prayed in the car on the way to the supermarket, prayed in the produce aisle, while pondering the phrase "persistent vegetative state," which did not seem to touch the miracle and mystery of a human life lived without communication or the expression of need.

Then the president came back from a round of golf or a bike ride to sign emergency papers (Janine did not trust grown men who rode bicycles or vacationed at odd times of year) and the Florida memo surfaced, describing Terri's case as a "great political issue" for firing up the "base"—people, she assumed, like herself, dumb fools who went to church and voted as they were told. Terri became an issue, not a person, and Janine could hardly pray at all. She fell into her own vegetative state, a state of spiritual entropy, and as she moved through the routines of her day, she imagined that her brain would show the same blank expanse of inactivity as Terri's own CT scans. Food was dull as ash on her tongue, her body a sluggish piece of meat, her daughters' voices, asking for this or that, as grating and needy as animals' cries. Chrissy wanted to know what was wrong, Beth heedlessly answered calls from some boy, Rick patted her good-bye each morning with sympathy that did not communicate understanding.

Janine did not start praying again until the final standoff, which began on a cool rainy day in March and lasted for thirteen days. She prayed for the police officers who had to stand guard against intervention, prayed for the nurses forced to deny Terri the comfort of a sip of water or an ice cube held against her lips, prayed for an understanding of God, who let such a thing happen. She prayed for forgiveness for the days when she had withheld her prayers, and she prayed in gratitude for the ability to pray again.

Sometimes, in the years that followed, someone would bring up the Schiavo case in the service of some other cause—disability rights, euthanasia, abortion, even animal rights—and Janine had the strange feeling that she, in her years of praying and wondering, had come to an understanding that others had missed. They—the fighters on both sides—were looking for something that was recognizable, something that looked like them, as if it was some kind of test Terri could pass. Could she feel? Could she hear? Could she respond? Not long after that, the poems started. The first one was about the brain's experience of electrotherapy, the influence of a monstrous medicine on the slow, godly letting go of neurons, the holy withering of synapses.

A terrified sadness. That was how one of the police officers described the look on Terri's face before she died. It was the best description Janine could think of for her own helpless imaginings of the things that might or might not happen to the people she loved best. Chrissy was now a high school junior, and Beth was studying meteorology at the community college. Both girls had hundreds of friends on Facebook (Janine was one of them), but seemed to spend their time exclusively with on-and-off boyfriends whom Janine suspected, in her worst moments, of murderous impulses.

She found that the poems helped, like a drug that does not eliminate pain but allows a coexistence with it. And like a drug it only worked to the extent that she could look forward to writing another one. If she had been truly honest with Rick, she would have said that she thought she'd developed an addiction to writing the poems, and she was afraid that she might run out.

Despite her headache, Janine was the first to arrive Monday morning to workshop, in a musty, wood-paneled room with two smallish windows overlooking the gulf. It had been furnished with a long antique table and mismatched chairs. Janine chose the one closest to what she assumed would be the head of the table, then switched for a more comfortable, padded chair. She hadn't seen Lorraine at breakfast. Concerned about things she might have said—exuberance brought on by too much punch—she had avoided the other students she knew were poets, forking dry eggs and greasy hash browns into her mouth while examining the poems they had to discuss.

Right at ten, the room began to fill with the other poets, carrying their lucky coffee mugs, their day planners, their laptops and carefully tabbed binders. Janine had only a spiral notebook, two pencils, and the packet they'd passed out at the reception. She smiled at each new student, said hello, and ruffled the edges of the packet with her fingers to soothe her nervousness.

It was 10:05. It was 10:10.

"In college," offered one woman, wearing a helmet of expensive-looking silver hair and a sweater tied around her shoulders, "we would leave after fifteen minutes of waiting. That meant class was canceled. It was a rule."

Janine remembered Beth telling her something similar, but did not imagine such a rule applied here.

"That seems sort of different," said another woman Janine vaguely remembered meeting last night. She smiled kindly and tried to explain: "College courses last twelve or fifteen weeks, and we have less than two weeks. Plus," she said, looking around the table. "We are all adults."

"It was a way of keeping the professors in check," insisted the first woman. "So they couldn't just breeze in whenever they felt like it."

"I'm sure that isn't—" began the second, more reasonable woman.

"She can leave if she wants to," said a man with small, puffy eyes, scraggly hair, and a large gold watch fastened around his bony wrist. He spoke with a slow drawl. "Don't let the door hit you in the ass, sweetheart."

"Maybe we should introduce ourselves," said Janine. Her own poem was one of the pieces selected for the first workshop, and she did not want to waste time on formalities. "I'm Janine. From near Panama City. I'm married and have two daughters. I'm a high school life skills teacher and this is my first poetry workshop."

"We'll just have to do introductions all over again," complained the woman who, moments ago, had wanted to leave. "Once Lorraine gets here."

"I'm Manfred Collins," said the man with the small eyes and the gold watch. "Though I write under the pen name Wilhemina Drexel. For family reasons."

They had gone all the way around the table, as Janine considered the possibility and wisdom of a pen name, and the possible significance of Manfred's, when Lorraine arrived, carrying a thin sheaf of photocopies. "Oh good," she said. "You've introduced yourselves." She did not ask them to repeat their names, nor did she bring up any of the poems selected for workshop. Instead, she wordlessly passed around Lawrence Ferlinghetti's "Poetry as Insurgent Art." Lorraine had each member of the workshop read it aloud, going in a circle around the table. The woman who had wanted to leave—her name was Barbara—struggled over the pronunciation of *apocalyptic* and *Mayakovsky*, and Janine worried that she might struggle as well (or worse, be asked to identify some of the poets), but Manfred read the poem with such a flourish that she was confident by the time it was her turn.

"'I am signaling you through the flames,'" Janine began, her heart beating fast. She had already heard the poem a dozen times. Though the poem had seemed strange at first—it was so plain, and not particularly *poetic*, and what did he mean about the North Pole being in a different place?—by now she felt as if *she* were being signaled, as if she were reading a letter or missive written just for her.

"'Civilization self-destructs,'" she read. "'Nemesis is knocking at the door.'" How true that was—you could see it on every television or computer screen or newscast, the lying face of every lying politician. She paused and looked up to see if the poem was making the same impact on her classmates. Some of them were doodling on the page, like the high schoolers who would intently decorate her handouts as if they were trying to turn a useful thing—instructions for preparing a casserole or sewing on a button—into something else entirely. Manfred nodded at her, encouragingly.

"'What are poets for, in such an age? What is the use of poetry?'" she continued, louder. By the time she got to "you can conquer the conquerors with words," she was practically shouting.

She had been the last to go. She set the poem down—the paper was wrinkled where she had been clutching it—and looked at her teacher. Lorraine, slumped in her chair, took a minute before straightening up. "Well," she said, in her smoker's voice. "I don't know that any of you are Whitman."

Janine waited for Lorraine to ask questions of them, but instead she stared at them, her eyes glassy and rimmed with red—not, Janine could tell, from crying. With her wild gray hair, her loose, purplish clothes, and her unnerving stare, she reminded Janine a little of the bag lady who used to beg for quarters outside the liquor store next to Publix. It was always quarters she wanted, as if she had never considered that someone might give her a dollar. The girls, when they were little, called her the purple lady for her clothes—she even had purple-tinted eyeglasses—and Janine always let them give her a quarter, though she told them never to tell their father.

There was some silence and some uncomfortable shifting.

"I am not here to do the work of thinking for you," Lorraine warned.

"Lawrence Ferlinghetti," offered Manfred. "He was a Beat poet?" Lorraine didn't nod or correct him.

"I believe he was a socialist—"

"The poem," she snapped. "Stick to the damn poem."

No one said anything for a while. Janine looked back at the poem, and wondered if Manfred was right. But the poem said "you are an American." It also said "or a non-American," but that didn't necessarily mean *socialist*.

"I like it," Janine said before she could stop herself. Everyone looked at her as if she should have more to say, so she continued. "I mean, I've never read this poem before. And I didn't like it at first. But I like it. I agree with it."

"You agree with it," Lorraine repeated.

"The part about conquering the conquerors," Janine said bravely.

"Ah," said Lorraine, putting a finger in her ear. "You were shouting that part."

"Well," said Janine. That was what she said sometimes, to keep herself from apologizing. *Well.*

"But you didn't like it at first," Lorraine said.

"No," Janine said. "I thought it was too simple, and also at the same time confusing. And I didn't like the word *insurgent*, in the title," she said. Across from her, a young woman, whose name she remembered as Laura, nodded. Janine saw that she was holding something white and fuzzy in her lap. A kitten? "I also didn't know every one of the names."

The woman shifted her gaze to the fuzzy white mass, and Janine could see that she was knitting a sweater. Was that allowed? She reminded herself that it was not her job to keep order here—even where it was her job, she was not very good at it.

"Whitman—" began Manfred, helpfully.

"Not Whitman," Janine began. "I know him. And Edna St. Vincent Millay."

"Neruda, then," he said.

"Everyone here is responsible for correcting their own ignorance *on their own time,*" Lorraine said. "Back to the idea of insurgency. What didn't you like about it?"

"Not the idea, the word," Janine said. "It made me think of terrorists. And the flames. And the phrase 'apocalyptic times.' It sounded . . . awful." She was now afraid to ask when the poem was written, but she imagined that it was some time ago, before things were even half as bad. Beth, who had recently begun an internship at the local television station, said that for every terrible thing you heard on the news—a mother backing a carful of children into the water, apartment fires set by jealous boy-friends, robberies committed by idiot thieves—there were several more that they did not even have time to shoot. That had been a revelation.

Lorraine stared at her with such intensity she thought she had better keep speaking. "But then I realized that he was right. Things are bad. They're getting worse. That a poem could be a voice against the conquer-ors, that words could be conquerors . . . I liked that idea. Even the line about the North Pole, which was confusing at first. I realized it made me think of Santa Claus. Last year I was in line to do my Christmas shopping and I heard a little boy—he must have been six or seven—tell his mother Santa Claus was a load of crap. That's what he said!"

"I don't remember ever believing in Santa myself," said Manfred.

That started a long argument that veered rather significantly away from the poem.

"Apocalyptic times," concluded Lorraine. She passed out a stack of new poems. Janine flipped through them quickly; not one of them was by a student in the class. "We'll discuss these others tomorrow. Let us try to stay closer to the poem being discussed. If there is something you don't know, *look it up.*" She scowled at the room, stuffed the poems back into her dingy tote bag, and disappeared through the door, ending class twenty minutes early.

I am signaling you through the flames, Janine thought, walking to lunch be-hind a group of her classmates. She'd waited, gathering and organizing her papers, until most people left, embarrassed by the way she'd monopo-lized class discussion. But what a perfect metaphor—that's what it was, wasn't it?—for the kind of work she had tried to do with her life, with her writing. Each poem a flag, not of surrender but of contact. Look, pay attention. That's what she should have said, instead of mentioning the kid at the mall and Santa Claus—what was she thinking? She should have talked about the *idea* of the signal, the challenge posed by apocalyptic times and the radical idea that poetry could make a difference.

Though the media machine that thought it knew Janine's mind imagined an apocalypse of city streets and technology run amok—gray, looming buildings, lurching robots, public transportation decorated with uninviting graffiti—the end times she imagined took place right near Panama City, in its flat expanses of strip malls and stoplights. In its tattoo parlors, check cashing places, signs for Lotto and for off-track betting. In its lurid billboards: for fast food and for megachurches, for motels and for pro-life counseling centers. In gas station crowds of dark-skinned men waiting to be carried off in trucks to work that lasted only a day. In windows rolled up and doors kept closed and locked, even in the daytime. In the listlessness of its teenagers and the accommodating gestures of their parents, who accompanied them—her own students told her—for the application of their first tattoo.

"Wait, sweetheart," said Manfred. Janine turned around and saw that he was the last to leave their classroom. He did not seem to be in a hurry but walked with a deliberate and almost stately slowness, as if he expected her to wait as long as it took him to catch up. She had been slightly annoyed by the way he'd prompted her during class discussion, but she did not want to eat alone. Manfred seemed to study the uneven pea gravel path before each footfall. Janine noticed his yellow socks and wondered about his pen name.

"Thank you," Manfred said when he finally caught up. "Good discussion."

"I wish I hadn't brought up that kid at the mall," Janine said. "That wasn't useful."

"You're paying good money to be here," said Manfred. "And no one else was saying much of anything, to tell the truth. What do you think of Ms. Kominski?"

"Oh, I don't know yet," said Janine. "I liked the poem she brought us. But she was a little . . . intense, maybe?"

Manfred laughed. "You should have seen her in her prime."

"You know her?"

"I took my first workshop with her at a conference in Key West, back in the eighties. On the first day she kicked three people out because she didn't like their poems. Insipid, she called them. On the second day she kicked a fourth person out for taking up space. This is *mellow*, post-treatment Lorraine. I've taken three other workshops with her." He paused at the place the pathway forked, between the dormitories and the dining hall, and said, somewhat ruefully, "She doesn't remember me."

Janine wondered what he meant by post-treatment. "Maybe when we talk about your poem," she suggested. "Perhaps the pen name confused her?"

"She may not learn any of our names, to be honest," Manfred said. "But she's a good teacher if you listen to the right things. She once crossed out every other line in a poem I wrote. I was mad, but when I typed the damn thing up again, it was a better poem. I published it."

Janine tried to imagine how she would feel about that happening to one of her poems. At school, they'd recently implemented a policy of no-writing-on-student-work, after the assistant principals went together to some conference in Orlando. Everything—*you didn't finish this, please check your spelling*, even grades (B or better for work that was basically complete and reasonably on time, C minus for what was unintelligible or barely begun)—was communicated through sticky notes, which inevitably fell off the page and littered the hallways, making a yellow path of gentle chiding. *Disney World shit*, the other life skills teacher called the pads of sticky notes delivered to their department, and continued writing—in black Sharpie, which bled through one student's work and onto the next—on the weekly worksheets she collected.

Perhaps Lorraine's tough love approach would be refreshing. Surely the knitting woman's days were numbered. Manfred pointed himself in the direction of the dormitories. He reminded Janine of an alcoholic turtle.

"You're not going to lunch?" Janine asked.

"Oh no," he said, taking out a pack of cigarettes. "*Chili mac*. Do I need to say more?"

That was something too old-fashioned and caloric even for Janine's life skills classes, but she had not brought anything from home. She felt a cigarette urge tugging at her, but Manfred didn't even light his own cigarette, just fiddled with the pack.

"Maybe I'll see you later," said Janine. "Will you be at the beach for sunset?"

"I didn't take you for one of those sunset worshippers," Manfred said. He sounded disappointed.

"It was beautiful, last night," said Janine. "I thought I saw the green flash. But I could have been wrong."

"The green flash is a myth," said Manfred. "Though I'm pretty sure I've seen it too."

Inside the dining hall she spooned out a portion of chili mac—a scoop, rounded, like meat-noodle ice cream—and penitentially filled the rest of her plate with salad. She found two women from her class seated in a far corner. They hadn't said much in workshop, and perhaps they thought Janine said too much. But it was better, wasn't it, to stick with those you knew? Janine had always felt loyal to whatever group she was assigned, and she only had to stand for a moment with her tray before they waved her over. She was pleased that she remembered their names and where they were from. Maggie, a woman about Janine's age, was a nurse from Tennessee, and Lilian, a little older, was from Sarasota. Apparently, she wasn't staying at the ranch; Janine had seen her steer her broad silver Mercedes into the parking lot this morning.

They were in the midst of a conversation about husbands. Both women were leaving theirs. Janine had the momentary thought that she should excuse herself—what would she have to contribute, other than sympathy?—but decided it would be equally awkward to get up again.

"Hopeless," Maggie was saying about her situation. "We tried counseling at church. Then we went on a special couples retreat where we didn't speak at all, just communicated nonverbally. But that was hardly any different than what we already had going on at home. Then we tried a special journal we wrote in every night, to say what we appreciated about the other person. Litotes—remember that word, from English class? It means saying something positive in a negative way. *She's not a terrible cook. He hasn't lost as much hair as I thought he would.* That's what our journal was full of. I actually wrote a bunch of them down, in a poem, and put it in my application here."

Janine thought she had seen it in the packet, but wasn't sure if she should mention it.

"The director, Marianne? She told me it was her favorite one. Isn't that the pits? I'm not even a talented poet. I just have a poetic divorce journal."

"It doesn't mean that," Janine insisted. She instinctively liked all insecure women: perennial dieters, remorseful child-spankers, closet smokers and binge drinkers and stress eaters. It gave her a role to play. She had a talent, she thought, for building people up—her own daughters, quite ordinary girls in many respects, anticipated extraordinary futures, Beth as a weather-forecasting television personality, Christine as a humanitarian leader of some sort. "When I write a poem, I don't even remember having written it. Something just takes over. How can I take credit for something I don't remember doing? Not that my poems are necessarily something to take credit for, but still. We're all here, aren't we, for a reason? You never know if someone else reading that poem will take comfort from it. Perhaps it will help them in their own marriages."

"That's nice of you to say," admitted Maggie. "Maybe they'll realize things could be worse."

"Things could definitely be worse," pronounced Lilian, smiling as if she had found just the right moment to tell them something terrible. She took two bites of chili mac, made a face like someone taking medicine, then chewed for an appropriately long time. Janine braced herself for what this woman might say. Finally she dabbed her napkin at her mouth, which glistened with grease even after she had wiped it. "I discovered that my husband was shopping for a new wife, online. Not a mistress, but a wife."

"Oh no," Maggie said. "On a dating site?"

"On a mail-order bride site," said Lilian, pushing her plate away from her.

"They still have those?" Maggie asked. "Yikes."

Janine was pretty sure that her colleague in the life skills department had found her husband through that sort of site. He was from

Syria—directly, before the wedding, from Syria—and Gladys had never mentioned going on any trips to Syria. He was much shorter than Gladys, who returned from their Pensacola honeymoon wearing a hijab. They seemed quite happy. Janine thought she would not mention their story here.

"They are a booming, multinational business in legal prostitution," Lilian told them. "I found the sites bookmarked on his laptop, and large funds mysteriously withdrawn from our accounts. Chinalove.com and Russianbride.com. He was still deciding. Apparently he didn't have much of a preference, Russian or Chinese, so long as she didn't speak English, was under the age of thirty, and wasn't me."

"I'm sure that's not—" Janine began.

"I'm taking him for everything," Lilian said. "I hope a double-wide in Bradenton suits her vision of the American dream. I hope she likes franks and beans."

"Ha," Maggie said. "That's a slant rhyme."

"Maybe I should jot it down," Lilian said, though she made no effort to do so. "I'm writing a collection of poems about the experience. It's called 'Mail-Order Bride,' though I suppose that term is outdated. But 'Internet-Order Bride' doesn't have the same ring to it."

"'Online Bride,'" Maggie suggested.

"That's good," Lilian said, though again she did not write it down. "I wake up and write a new poem each day. I switch off. Half are about the Chinese woman," she said. "And half are about the Russian."

"Catharsis," Maggie said. "From the same root as *catheter*. I read that in a story somewhere."

"What suits you at one point in life may be unacceptable later," Lilian advised. "Jerome was quite kinky, early on."

"How did you wind up . . . here?" Janine asked tentatively.

"You mean at a Christian writing program?" Lilian said. "I'm Episcopalian. We believe in the suffering of Christ, but also in the cunning of lawyers, and my lawyer advised channeling my rage somewhere more wholesome than Facebook. I can drive here during the day, and keep an eye on our condo at night. So here I am." She shrugged. "How about you? Marriage woes?"

It took Janine a moment to realize that Lilian was talking to her. She blushed. "No, I mean, my husband did not exactly understand why I needed to come here to study something I was already doing on my own. He thinks poetry is like hooking rugs, or needlecraft, something you just pick up. He built me a room for it, at our house. Like a sewing room."

Lilian got up from the table, evidently bored with the relatively small gaps of understanding that characterized Janine's marriage. "I must take a nap."

"Do you want to borrow my room?" Maggie asked. "I only slept in one bed."

"Oh, I have a room," Lilian said. "They told me I could have a discount because I'm staying at my own home, but I wanted the full experience." She waved her hand to encompass the ranch: its crowded dining hall, with hardly enough room to walk between tables, its unmanicured view of the gulf. "Besides, I'm spending as much money as I can before the divorce is final. Just in case."

"I wish it could be like hooking a rug," Maggie said, after Lilian was gone. "Writing poetry, I mean. I'm not sure Lorraine will be the easiest teacher to learn from. Your husband sounds sweet, though."

"He believes in my work," Janine said, glad to have the chance to say something nice. "He believes in its message, about the sanctity and value of life."

"Wait," Maggie said. "Your poems are the ones about that woman who died? Terri Schiavo?"

Janine nodded.

"Those were very sad. Very sad."

"Thank you," Janine said.

"But Lilian told me something you should know. We were reading through the packet, at the beginning of lunch, which is how our divorces came up. Her husband consulted on that case."

"What?"

"On the Schiavo case. He was one of the doctors who declared her brain-dead. I don't think she realized it was you. Maybe I shouldn't have told you."

Janine was suddenly very dizzy. She gripped the sides of her chair to steady herself.

"I shouldn't have told you. I'm sorry."

"No," Janine said. "You should have. It's amazing, what God puts in front of us."

6

By the end of the first full day Marianne had listened to a long parade of complaints from the students, many of whom were new to the workshop process. The complainers made a continuous and ever-changing line, sometimes three and four people deep, outside her door, and Marianne would apologetically but carefully close it in the hope that she could contain the complaints. Putting out fires, Mark called it. Marianne always pictured his businessman clichés in literal terms—her own feet stamping out actual fires, two people standing on the same giant page, a dinner plate overflowing with things to do.

Tom thought one of his students was a neo-Nazi. Eric was ten minutes late for class. Lorraine ended class twenty minutes early. Lorraine did not discuss any of the poems by the students. The chili mac was too spicy, too greasy, too salty. Tom had already mixed up two young blond students' names, repeatedly. Tom said what the hell did twentysomethings have to write about anyway? The salad bar's sneeze guard had been sneezed on. Eric had misunderstood a short story's central biblical allusion. Lorraine had never asked anyone their name.

All day Marianne had looked for Eric. She had left the door to her office open, in between complaints, in case he might happen by. She'd felt immediately sorry after kicking him out of her room—sorry for the look of disappointment on his face, sorry too for the emptiness of her room, the loneliness she'd felt after he was gone. But he did not walk by, not even once, and she had to settle instead for disparaging scraps of him delivered by the students.

"You're right," she said, to the woman who complained about Eric's punctuality. "I'm sure he'll be on time tomorrow." "I don't know how he could have missed that allusion," she told another student. "I'm sure he's reading about it now."

To the students whose names Tom kept mixing up, she repeated their names with each apology. She read and praised a strange and bloody poem about childbirth. She agreed with several students that punctuality was a way of showing respect ("Punctuation," Tom said later, "that would show some respect"). She made tea for a woman who began crying in her office for no apparent reason. "Of course," she said to each of them. "You're right."

By five o'clock her neck was sore from nodding. Each complainer left her office placated and soothed, while Marianne felt more and more exhausted, her feet burned from all the fires, her dinner plate smeared with remnants of unappetizing dishes. And how would they fare tomorrow? Marianne had once been in workshop with a young woman who had contradicted Lorraine on the reading of her poem. Lorraine had slid the violently marked up page across the table at the woman, who'd suddenly looked stricken with fear. "Let us agree then," said Lorraine, "that it's a subtle fucking masterpiece." Marianne had not exactly warned her against such performances here.

By supper time, Marianne was hungry for chili mac, something cheesy and starchy, a gummy sauce thickened over Sterno. She had given up vegetarianism weeks ago, after Mark warned her it was anti-Christian. She still had not had a glimpse of Eric, and she looked forward to scolding him playfully for being late (she'd been impressed, if not surprised, that a slight tardiness and mild biblical ignorance were the only complaints levied against him). Maybe they could take a walk later, she thought, and she could let him know that there would be plenty of time to work out their relationship—whatever it was—after the students left. There were only eleven more days of workshops, after all. She had already crossed out today on her calendar, a fat black X.

She got up to draw the blinds and lock the door, but saw, approaching the office, another petitioner—another complainer—clutching a composition book to her side. Marianne snapped the blinds shut and retreated to the back of the office but the woman wasn't deterred. She rapped on the door's glass panes and peered through a gap in the blinds. "Hello?" she called. "Hello?"

"Office hours ended half an hour ago," Marianne said, opening the door but blocking the woman's entrance. She was, to Marianne, indistinguishable from many of the other students: ordinary, middle-aged, unremarkable in appearance. She had a thick middle hidden by a T-shirt, stick-like legs in capri pants, a girlish, sandy-brown bob. "Dinner is being served. Is it possible for me to see you in the morning?"

"Oh," said the woman, clutching her notebook more tightly to her side. "I just saw someone leaving, so I thought . . ."

Sighing, Marianne let the woman enter. She sat down on the sofa and reached in a practiced way for the Kleenex, like someone used to being consoled in other people's offices. She had an incoherent story about a woman in her workshop whose husband had two mail-order wives, and somehow this connected to her desire to be transferred to another poetry class. There was no other poetry class.

"So your problem is with . . . polygamy?" Marianne guessed. She stood behind her desk, packing applications for the next round of students into her tote bag.

No, the woman said: it wasn't that. The content of the writing, she explained between tissues.

"She's writing about polygamy?"

"My writing," she insisted, sitting up straighter. "*My* writing connects to things in her life. Powerful, terrible things. I think God has brought me here for a reason."

Marianne had heard versions of this search for meaning in randomness all day long: God brought me here for this reason or that reason, to battle with my peers or teach my professor about the finer points of Habakkuk. But this woman had no conflict; she'd just come here to share. Ruth had a similar story about the first time she met Darryl at a youth group gathering, and Marianne had tried her sisterly best only to listen, not judge, as Ruth went on and on about the divinely inspired nature of their meeting. Why couldn't people see that it was unreasonable— arrogant, even—to picture a god placing them on Earth like chess pieces? Why couldn't they see that the connections they made were very highly correlated to their personal, individual, deeply insignificant and often foolish *choices*?

"That's a lot of folders. Student work?"

"What?" Marianne said. She looked down at her tote, now stuffed to overflowing with paper. "No, just applications. Many, many applications."

"For next year?"

"For next round," Marianne said. "Two hundred so far, just in poetry."

"That's incredible—so few of us are chosen," said the woman. She sounded awed and pleased. "You read them all?"

"Yes," said Marianne. She wanted to cry, looking at the papers and thinking about their probable contents. "I should just close my eyes and reach in, like a card trick." She demonstrated, reaching in and pulling out a submission bound in a cumbersome plastic claw binding. With a flourish, she held it up as two other packets fell to the floor. "Ta-da!"

The woman picked up the two manuscripts that had fallen to her feet and set them carefully on Marianne's desk.

"Not that that's what we do," Marianne added quickly, gathering the submissions and putting them back in her bag. "We have a very rigorous selection process."

But it was too late. The woman, whose name she still did not know, neatly deposited her Kleenex in Marianne's trash bin and thanked her for her time. Marianne knew she should run after her, apologize, but instead she waited until the woman was safely on her way before sneaking out of the office. Hadn't her own professors guarded their time? Marianne was pretty sure she'd once seen Phil Levine, in his seventies, *sprinting* away from one of her more careerist peers.

In the dining hall, the buffet line was long but not discontented; writers chatted amiably, passed tongs and plates and napkins. And the food looked unexpectedly promising—blackened grouper with some kind of fresh salsa, salad greens, stuffed peppers. Spooning salsa onto her fish, Marianne overheard the words "tough" and "challenging" and "different" but not "crazy" or "mean" or "I want my money back." The office complainer was already seated with other students. Maybe she'd forget about Marianne's slip. Maybe she hadn't noticed—though Marianne thought that was unlikely.

Eric was sitting at a round table near the window, leafing impatiently through a pile of papers. His plate rested off to the side, untouched, and he didn't look up as Marianne approached. She took the seat across from him and reached for his plastic cup of Coke.

"Do you ever forget where you are?" she asked, taking a sip through the straw. "Like, you wake up in the morning and have no idea how you got here? Or you space out and forget who you're talking to?"

Eric frowned, marking one of the papers with a red pen. Marianne knew he wasn't listening to her—he was unable to pay attention to anything when he was reading. Back when they were dating, she used to make up nonsense sentences to see if she could get his attention. She thought she'd better not do that now. He looked as if he'd been up all night. His hair and clothes were rumpled, his shirtsleeves were rolled up to his elbows. A walk, she thought, would do them both good.

"I wouldn't be too hard on them," she suggested. "Maybe start with the positives. Tom made a student cry today."

"These aren't manuscripts," Eric said finally. "It's a business plan. Projected expenses, projected income." He lowered his voice. "We're in the red, Marianne."

"I don't see how that's possible," she said. "I did the math too, and—"

"The repairs, the permits. Insurance." He went back to paging through the document. "Frances's endowment is spent."

"I thought we had new . . . funders? Investors? Can't we send the bills to them?"

Eric shook his head. "That isn't how it works. We have to show them that we can make a profit, that this idea is scalable, or we'll lose their interest. Mark says he has some ideas. I'm gonna talk to him tonight."

"Why didn't he send any of this to me? I thought I was the administrator."

"You work with the students, Marianne," he said. "That's plenty. You'll be brought in for big decisions. Don't worry."

The way he said that—don't worry—made Marianne suddenly feel very small and petty and in the way. Don't worry! she thought. Hadn't she given up everything—her apartment, her whole life—to come here? To live in a single room (no matter that it was roughly the same size as the apartment she gave up) and listen to people complain all day?

"I don't know who decided I was the one who was good with people," she said, spearing the dry fish angrily with her fork. "I don't know whose brilliant fucking brainstorm that was."

Eric eyed her warningly over his papers; they'd agreed on a cussing prohibition for the two-week residency.

"Brilliant *freaking* brainstorm."

"You're great with people," he said. "Better than Tom, apparently. Didn't you used to cry at every workshop?"

"Not *in* workshop," she insisted. "After. It was cathartic. Sometimes. And crying is good for the skin."

"Oh, look out," Eric said. "Davonte wants something. I bet you can help him."

Two tables over, the former R&B star was signaling for their attention. "I think he wants you," Marianne said. "You're his teacher."

Eric closed his eyes. "I think you're better with him. Please."

"Fine," Marianne said. She took Eric's Coke with her and walked over to Davonte's table, where he was sitting alone.

"Hi, Donald!" she said, pleased to remember the name he wanted to be called. "What's up?"

"This food," he said, gesturing at his plate: two stuffed peppers, two fish fillets, a tall mound of rice topped with salsa. He had already eaten some of it, and he resumed eating while Marianne stood next to him, as if he was proving something. "It's too salty," he said between bites. "And unhealthy."

"Oh," Marianne said. "But it's fish! It isn't fried."

"For lunch . . . were you here for lunch?"

Marianne suggested the salad bar. But Davonte said he did not like cold food that other people had messed with, and could not be counted on, if she wanted to know the truth of it, to control himself in the face of ranch dressing. But he had a solution—his life coach, who was staying nearby, would bring him supper, and he would eat Lean Cuisine for lunch, if only Marianne could microwave it for him and have it ready on a plate.

"On a plate," Marianne repeated.

"Yeah," he said. "I can't eat from a fucking tray. Excuse me." He closed his eyes and mouthed something to himself. "I can't eat from a *tray.*"

He had been so handsome, ten or fifteen years ago, the star of more than a few shameful sexual fantasies for Marianne. The shame wasn't from the sex she imagined, but the inadequacy of her own body, soft and dimpled where Davonte's was hard and chiseled. Now everything about him was slack and soft: his face was round, his biceps undefined. Who knew what his famous abdominals looked like now?

"I'm trying to get everything right with God," Davonte explained. "The words I say. This book I'm writing. The food I put in His temple."

"Okay," said Marianne. Who knows, she thought. Maybe she would see him get back to his old self, fit and muscled. Maybe she would see him that way, in a swimsuit. "So. Lean Cuisine. Heated up. On a plate."

"Yes," he said. "Not too hot. It dries out."

"Any particular time?"

"You think I'm being arrogant," he said. He stood—he wasn't much taller than she was—and pulled out a chair for her. Marianne's mostly unsuccessful dating history had left her helpless against even the smallest expressions of chivalry. Open a door for her, and she'd walk through it. She sat.

"You know who I am," he said.

Marianne nodded. His eyes were two deep, velvety pools; she couldn't move. I will never move again, she thought. This was what it was like to be looked at by a famous person.

"Well, after *Hurt Songs* blew up, I got . . . a lot of attention. From girls," he said. "From women. Hell, from grandmas."

"Yikes," Marianne said. "That was a good video, though. I liked it, I mean. I don't think my grandma ever saw it."

Davonte laughed and shook his head. "That video ruined my career. Do you know I couldn't leave the house after it came out without somebody throwing herself at me? Couldn't go to the grocery store, the 7-Eleven, nothing."

"I bet a lot of guys would like that," Marianne said. "The attention."

"They might think they like it," Davonte said. "But it gets old. It wasn't for me. I lost who I was. I had some legal troubles. I started ordering in: pizzas, sub sandwiches. Weed. That was all I did, eat and smoke, and in a year I'd gained a hundred pounds, and nobody looked at me like that anymore.

"But it was a bad solution. It messed up my voice and my confidence. I am borderline *diabetic*, Mary-Anne. This is not what God wanted for me.

So I am learning to ask for people's help. And I am asking you to microwave my Lean Cuisines."

She nodded; it felt like she was under a powerful, paralyzing spell. She would microwave his Lean Cuisines, she would put them on a special plate at a special time. If he needed it, she would lace up his running shoes for him. She would strain to hold his feet while he did sit-ups.

He turned back to his meal as if it was some unfinished, unpleasant work. She thought of asking him if he wanted her to take it away, but didn't know how to offer. She got up and walked slowly back to her table.

"Want to take a walk?" she asked Eric, who was still hunched over his papers. "It's nice out. Breezy."

Eric looked at his watch and frowned. "I've gotta call Mark soon. You go," he said, and she had the feeling, again, that she was being indulged and discounted, pushed to the side.

"Should I join you?"

"Nah," he said. "I'll fill you in later."

"Okay," she said. "Fine. Have fun."

"*You* have fun," Eric said.

She leaned in close. "None of this is fun."

Avoiding entreating expressions from several tables, Marianne walked quickly outside, letting the door slap closed behind her, and jogged down the path to the beach. Her heart was still thudding angrily by the time she reached the fine white sand. Eric had seemed upset too, his shoulders hunched tightly, his voice clipped and angry. Mark would find them more money, just as he had before, or else they would shut the place down and not have to worry about it. After the day she'd had, Marianne would not exactly mind saying good-bye to the lot of them, these sentimental poets, these apocalyptic whiners.

But hadn't Eric insisted, last night, *I want this to work*?

And hadn't he also touched her shoulder, and held his hand there until she moved away? Hadn't he said "ah" so sadly when she'd kicked him out, and mentioned how long it had been since they were together?

After an old woman confessed a strange whim, he had built an entire school for her, the school Marianne had joked about for years. It was cruel, what Eric had done, like presenting someone who said "I could eat a horse" with a giant horsemeat steak.

She turned around and faced it—she could see the fiction classroom near the beach, the dining hall up the hill, the garden and swimming pool near the dormitories. Marianne turned back to the water, the late-afternoon sun glimmering off a light sea chop, a few pristine sailboats in the distance. As a child she'd realized that, for adults, the real charm of a beach vacation was not the smell of suntan lotion or the sound of the surf or the feeling of warm sand between their toes. It was not the possible glimpse of porpoises or seabirds or the brief dips they took in the water. What mattered most was sitting with your back to everything else.

The last time Marianne spent any real time at the beach was the summer Ruth turned thirteen, when they'd gone as a family. Her father had a girlfriend then, a woman named Noreen who answered phones at the elementary school and had known their mother vaguely. Marianne could never understand what the two of them had in common, but figured that Virginia's Middle Peninsula offered slim pickings when it came to dating. Noreen was the one who extended the invitation, calling Marianne at home on a Friday evening in May. "Oh," she'd said, surprised-sounding, when Marianne answered the phone. "I just meant to leave a message."

"What is that *noise*?" Noreen asked, after telling her about the house—four bedrooms, oceanfront.

"What noise?" Marianne said, walking away from the window, as far as the phone would stretch. She thought about the space, the wall-to-wall carpeting of silence that would be her family's beach vacation. The phone cord stretched all the way to her bed—three big steps. "I would love to see Ruth, too. Girl time."

"Yes," Noreen—a woman who kept a menagerie of Beanie Babies arranged around her school system name plate—said warmly. "Girl time!"

Marianne flew down from New York, a choppy flight on a commuter plane to Richmond. Heaving her lumpy duffel bag into the used book-lined trunk of her father's Chrysler, still shaken by the turbulence she should have left thousands of feet above her, she felt old. But somehow over the six-hour drive, riding in the backseat next to Ruth, she turned into a teenager again. She asked how long until they got there, she slept with her head against the window and her mouth falling open, she bought Cheetos and Dr Pepper at rest area vending machines. She listened to her iPod, a time capsule of the year she bought it. Occasionally Ruth passed her an earbud, and she obligingly bobbed her head before passing it back.

They arrived at dusk, the sun setting over the sound. It must have been the last long stretch of time they spent together: six days of late sleeping, lazy swimming, ineffectual tanning, and bad television. Marianne liked the swimming best, the waves no more than gentle hills in the water, lifting them lightly from the sandy bottom, then setting them down again. No surfers to distract Ruth. No surfers to distract Marianne.

Marianne taught Ruth to scuff her toes along the bottom for sand dollars, which they lined up on the beach house's balcony railing to dry and bleach in the sun. Ruth told Marianne about her favorite bands and painted Marianne's nails purplish-black. They gorged themselves on pizza and watched scary movies. When Howard and Noreen went out for seafood one night, Marianne drank a bottle of sweet, five-dollar wine and dyed Ruth's bangs pink.

"I can't believe you did that, I can't believe you did it," Ruth kept saying, after they'd rinsed and dried her hair, but she couldn't stop looking at herself in the mirror. Her ears weren't even pierced. "Dad is going to kill you."

"I've been killed by Dad before," said Marianne. She wondered, sleepily, if she should dye her own hair pink. "I always resurrect myself. I'm like Jesus."

"You shouldn't say that." Ruth could become instantly serious and stuffy, whenever religion came up. She was that age, Marianne figured, that wanted to please and rebel at the same time, an age when pink bangs and black fingernails were little more than innocuous signals to other kids her age. She'd asked Marianne to take her to an all-ages show the next night, but Marianne was sure she'd tell their father all about it the following morning, even recounting the boys she'd flirted with.

"I was just kidding," Marianne said, pulling the undyed portion of Ruth's dirty-blond hair into a ponytail with one hand. "I should French-braid the back; you'll look like a punk cheerleader."

"I mean it, Mare," Ruth said. That was her childhood name for her sister—Mare, like a horse. She found Marianne's eyes in the wide, spotless bathroom mirror. Ruth's were blue and as wide set and earnest as a cartoon character's. "It isn't something to kid about, another person's religion."

"Okay," said Marianne, sectioning out the crown of Ruth's hair into three pieces. She began to twine them together, pulling neat sections of hair from the side. "But no one else is here, right? Just us?"

Ruth crossed her arms over her chest. "I've been to youth group. I've been to church."

"I've been to youth group too," Marianne said. "It was boring." The braid was starting to veer away from the center, and Marianne had to loosen two sections and start again. In high school chemistry class, she'd sat behind a girl who wore a different, impeccably neat French braid each day—sometimes straight, sometimes diagonal or even zigzagged—and Marianne had studied the back of her head intently for an entire school year. She pulled more hair from the other side and carefully worked to correct things. "But you liked it."

After a long time, Ruth said, "I guess I thought it would be helpful. I like to think about heaven. You know, to picture Mom there, like a place I could see her again."

"Oh," said Marianne. At twenty-seven, and a poet, she didn't have any words of solace or wisdom, nothing that would not sound false or hollow. "Is it something you've talked to Dad about?"

Ruth shook her head. "Do you miss Mom?"

Marianne sighed; the braid looked nothing like the girl's from chemistry class. "Every day. Then sometimes I think what I'm missing is the idea of her. I miss the things I imagine us doing, things we spent, like, a tiny percent of our life together doing."

"Like what?"

"Like, if I see a mom and daughter in a museum, I'll miss her, even though we went to the Virginia Museum or the Smithsonian maybe once a year. Or a mom and daughter in a sushi restaurant. Mom never ate sushi with me. There wasn't any sushi around when I was growing up."

"Now there's a place next to Food Lion. It's a teriyaki place, but they have sushi too."

"Yeah." Marianne took the elastic band holding her own hair in a ponytail and secured the end of Ruth's braid, doubling the elastic many times. It had turned out okay—lumpy in some places and not exactly straight, but it wasn't falling apart. "There," Marianne said. "Punk cheerleader, French-braided by her drunk mom."

Ruth patted her head. "You might be drunk, Mare, but you're not my mom."

"I know," said Marianne.

"I don't have a mom."

"You do," Marianne said. "You did, I mean. You'll always have a mom, even if it's just a mom you remember."

Ruth slipped her fingers into the braid and undid it, setting Marianne's elastic band on the edge of the sink. "Thanks. Dad is still going to kill you."

Except, of course, he didn't. The next morning at breakfast, Ruth waited for him to say something, her hot pink bangs combed in front of a black velvet headband, but he kept his eyes in a John Grisham paperback while Noreen, unsure of her role, nervously smiled. Marianne, on a walk at the time, came home to find her sister loading the dishwasher, her father on the deck with Noreen.

"You look intact. What did he say?"

Ruth shrugged, clacking bowls into the rack. "Didn't notice."

The Ranch kept a stack of lightweight beach chairs near the end of the walkway to the beach. Marianne lifted one from the top of the stack and carried it near the water's edge and set it down, then dragged it a little north of the Ranch, in front of the mangroves that separated their property from the homes and hotels on either side. Where she was sitting, she could be from anywhere—a guest of one of the nicer hotels or even a homeowner, taking a break at the end of a long day. The tide was going out, and she concentrated on marking where each wave lapped the sand.

Just a week ago, she'd been able to come down here, alone or with Eric, every night. Now there were students scattered everywhere, their dark silhouettes facing the still-shining water.

"Beautiful," said a voice nearby. Marianne looked to her left and saw that it belonged to the woman who'd most recently cried in her office. She had a spiral notebook in her lap, a pencil sheathed in the metal coil.

Had she told Marianne her name? Marianne was bad with names; it seemed that she was always thinking of something else when people announced theirs.

"Thanks," Marianne said, then realized it sounded like she was taking credit for God's creation. The sun's orange light was quickly draining over the gulf's horizon. "I mean," she said, "thank you for watching it with me."

"Last night I was sure I saw the green light," said the woman. "But now I'm not so sure. My friend Manfred said it was a myth."

"I haven't seen it yet, and I come here almost every day," said Marianne. "But I don't think it's a myth. A lot of other people have seen it. I think it's a scientific thing, actually." Perhaps it was a good sign—a tolerant and open-minded sign, at least—that this woman counted Manfred Collins as a friend. Marianne had met him, a chain-smoking, bourbon-swilling serial workshopper, years ago. His great-grandfather had made so much money refining sugar, Manfred once told her, that no Collins had ever been useful to the world since.

"Good," the woman said. "I didn't want to think it was my imagination. It's terrible, when people try to talk you out of something harmless, like the green light. Who would want to do that, Marianne?"

"I don't know," Marianne said. "I'm sorry, I'm terrible with names."

"Janine," the woman said. "I'm sorry I barged in on you at the end of the day, when you were trying to leave. I hate it when my students do that."

"No, you were fine. I'm sorry, it was a long day. It must seem long to you too—I forget that."

Janine considered. "Yes and no. It's been six months since we got in. We've been here two days now. That seems pretty short."

"Good!" Marianne said. "I mean, right? I wouldn't want this to be the longest workshop of your life."

"It's the only workshop of my life. So far."

"That's right," said Marianne, suddenly remembering their phone conversation in the fall, the woman's shock, her heavy breathing. Then further back, to the poems themselves: modest but tightly packed, wounded. "I loved your poems, actually. About Terri Schiavo. You said you'd only shared them so far with your husband."

"Thank you for remembering them," Janine said. Marianne looked over and saw that she was smiling, but she did not ask, as Marianne would have, which ones she had liked best, did not search Marianne's face for clues about her sincerity.

"Is that what you're still working on?"

"I don't know," Janine said. "I thought I was done with them, but then I had an experience today that made me think I'm not. I think God brought me here for a reason."

Marianne made her face as plain as it would go.

"I mean, to have certain experiences. To push me. In workshop today, we read this poem, 'Poetry as Insurgent Art.' Do you know it?"

"I am signaling you through the flames," Marianne said, dramatically.

Janine got up and dragged her chair closer. The sky was a deep lavender now. "Right, that's it. I had this feeling that Lorraine—Ms. Kominski—chose the poem just for me. I know that's crazy, but that's how it felt. My husband would say it was Jesus walking next to me, then picking me up and carrying me before I even knew it. Because I felt so weighed down, just before we read it. I kept getting texts from my girls, and I was missing them and missing Rick and thinking, what am I doing here? Do you know I never got an A in an English class in my life? Always Bs, B pluses. And I look around and see all these other people and think, what am I doing here? They must have a reason, they must have talent, but I do not."

Marianne had in fact always gotten As, and had even been awarded a prestigious scholarship in her first year of graduate school. But where had it gotten her, all that promise? Not much further than Janine, a self-taught poet from Panama City. "Self-doubt," she said. "I know it well."

"But then," said Janine, putting her hand on the armrest of Marianne's chair. "Lorraine came in, and she passed out the poem and I read it and it just spoke to me. I've read that poem so many times today I could recite it for you," Janine said, and then she recited it.

"That was very good," Marianne said, when she was finished.

"So I got filled up with this powerful poem," Janine said. "And I talked too much in class, which embarrassed me, and I was almost going to lie down during lunch but something made me go into the dining hall."

"Not the food, I imagine." Marianne was about to apologize when Janine continued, urgently.

"So I went into the dining hall and I sat with these two ladies, from workshop, Maggie and Lilian. They hadn't talked much in class and I was afraid they'd think I was hogging the conversation, or showing off. But I sat down and they told me these horrible stories." In the dimming light Marianne could see Janine frowning, as if remembering the stories pained her. She lowered her voice. "About divorce. And I felt so bad for both of them. And then Lilian left and Maggie told me something that just shook me to my core."

She sat back, as if satisfied and exhausted to have said this much.

"What was it?" Marianne asked. "Do I want to know?"

"Her husband," said Janine, "who is a cheater—he was also one of Terri's doctors. He consulted on her case. I went to the computer room and I looked him up. He wrote a report that said they should stop feeding her. He testified to that, in one of the court cases."

Marianne could see Janine closing her eyes. She tried to think what she should say—it was like trying to do something delicate while looking into a mirror: you had to remember that everything was backwards. You had to go slowly. She didn't say anything.

"I have nothing against Lilian," Janine said. "It wasn't her. But what are the chances that I would meet her here, and she would tell me a story like she told me?"

"Very small," guessed Marianne.

"I think so," Janine said. "I thought at first, I have to take these poems out of workshop. I even went to Ms. Kominski's room and I was about to knock on the door, but then I thought, why? Lilian is obviously parting ways with her husband, but even if she wasn't—even if she thought he was God—which apparently *he* thought he was—even then, why should I not write what I came here to write? *The state of the world calls out for poetry to save it,*" she recited. "That's what today taught me. That's what I think now."

"Civilization self-destructs," Marianne said. It was nearly dark now. "Nemesis is knocking at the door."

"Yes," Janine said. "Yes."

It was a remarkable thing, Marianne thought, to deliver someone to her purpose, especially if that purpose was not quite what you intended, or even believed in. When she thought of Terri Schiavo, which until reading Janine's poems had not been very much at all, she mostly thought the opposite of what Janine thought. She saw an empty shell of a person, an empty, grasping, brain-dead—or at least brain-compromised— vegetable person. She saw a suffering and emptiness so deep that the only answer was an end to that suffering through death. She thought the doctors had made the best choice in a difficult situation, and that Terri's husband, chosen in adulthood, had more of a right to determine what happened to Terri than her parents had.

But that wasn't how Janine saw things at all: Janine saw Terri's parents as the rightful and righteous guardians of a life worth guarding, a life they had after all created. She saw a flickering of something in Terri's brown, hollow-looking eyes; she saw smiles where Marianne saw accidental grimaces. The sacrifices being made on Terri's behalf were not, in Janine's mind, a loss of freedom or agency but instead the representation of a higher calling. She saw not base suffering, but noble struggle, in all of it, and truly believed she'd been sent here to write about it.

How much better, or at least easier—happier?—might Marianne's life be if she could think the same way Janine did? If she could think, here I am, alive, and be happy for it?

The sun seemed to flatten before it disappeared entirely, and Marianne could hear gasps and appreciative murmuring. But there was no green light, no flash, just an ordinary sunset. Janine stood and folded her chair. "Eleven more chances," she said, and didn't sound displeased or worried about the clock ticking down. "Though I guess you get to see them all the time. Do you live here full time, Marianne?"

"Yes and no," said Marianne, who suddenly realized how strange that sounded. "I used to live in Brooklyn."

"With Eric," said Janine.

"Not *with* Eric," Marianne corrected her. She'd wondered, if they did get back together, whether Eric would push to move in. But that was the beauty of the Ranch, wasn't it? They could live together and apart at the same time. "He lived in Queens, actually. Then he moved back to Charlotte."

"I just meant, you went to school together? And were writers together, in the city? With agents, and publishers?"

"That's not really how it works," said Marianne. "Not for poets, anyway."

"I think I met an agent the other night, or maybe a publisher," said Janine. "At the opening night party? Her name was Regina Somers."

Marianne was fairly sure there hadn't been any agents at the party. Maybe Mark had paid someone to pretend to be one? That would be low, even for him.

"You must know her." Janine waved her hand dismissively. "I just meant to say, this is all new to me. Completely new. And also that it must be nice to have a partner who understands what you do. My husband— he's a contractor—he's very supportive of my work, but I don't think he understands it. Poetry. You must have a lot of readers, since you're published."

Marianne thought about divulging the print run of her chapbook— two hundred and fifty slim copies, circulating mostly with friends and classmates—but decided against it. "It's good to have a first reader who's close to you. I actually send my poems to Eric first. I have since we were in school."

"That's beautiful," Janine said. "To have someone you trust, another writer, a partner . . ."

"Novel writing is probably closer to contracting than you'd guess," Marianne said. "And Eric and I, we're good friends, that's all." She felt Janine looking at her in the near dark, and her face grew warm.

"Okay," Janine said. "I should go call Rick and the girls. See you to-morrow." She hoisted her chair under her arm and began the trip back to her room. Marianne wanted to call her back, to explain that they really were just complicated friends, but she knew that would only make the opposite case. She turned back to the gulf, where just a faint line of pink hovered over the horizon, and wished that someone would join her.

7

In the first year after *Copper Creek's* publication, Eric Osborne could not enter a bookstore without looking for it. Spotting its handsome sepia-toned cover among the primary-colored jumble and clutter of other titles was like spotting a fellow fan of your college's basketball team in some far-away locale. Or it was like seeing a long-lost family member who shared a feature you were glad to have inherited, the same straight nose or square jawline or enviable height. He looked forward to that moment of recognition and even, in a way that he could not explain, felt that it was mutual, felt that the book recognized him. Because he liked to shop for few things other than books, Eric experienced these moments often, both in large, impersonal chain bookstores and small, charming independent ones; for a short time, when he was traveling long distances to read to tiny audiences, he even had them in airport bookstores, with their rotating kiosks of neck pillows and clip-on book lights, their gilded bookmarks and pillow-sized bags of trail mix. Sometimes he'd find copies in a promising stack among the front tables, but more often, especially as that first year approached its end, he'd find a single copy of *Copper Creek* shelved alone, along with more successful writers' paperbacks: between Vladimir Nabokov and Cynthia Ozick, or, in less literary bookstores, in the airport ones staffed by neck-tattooed teens with little concept of alphabetical order, between Ozzy and Sharon Osbourne. For a while Eric would quietly remove the book from its rightful or wrongful home and reshelve it on a "staff favorites" table, or even with the "coming soon to a theater near you" titles. He felt like it was his duty to the book, and even to the publishers, with whom he was still on good and familiar terms. It felt like introducing a shy but very worthy and witty friend around at a party: how could you not?

But now, three years out, *Copper Creek's* very presence in a bookstore embarrassed him. Not because he thought it wasn't a good book—that hardly seemed to matter, somehow—but because he was pretty sure, whenever he did see it, that it was one of the same copies he'd seen the first time he'd looked. He was pretty sure he'd seen the same two or three thousand copies, and according to his royalty statements was seeing them still. *Copper Creek* was remaindered in hardcover, and its paperback release—a small run—had not been reprinted. So it was now like going home and seeing some high school friend who used to brag about big plans hanging around at a Sheetz gas station, or watching a graying hometown band play the same seedy bar. He felt like hiding the book now, or buying it at whatever discounted cost it was offered, taking it home, and peeling off the discount sticker. Sobering it up, like a drunken, bawdy aunt, among the O'Connors and Orwells and O'Haras on his own shelves. Sometimes he did this, and he wondered if he could deduct the cost of ashamedly buying his own novel from his taxes as a professional expense.

Occasionally—very occasionally—a bookstore clerk would notice that the name on his credit card and the name on *Copper Creek*'s spine matched, and would make a comment. "They don't give you extra copies? Damn," one particularly observant airport clerk had remarked. The worst and most common comment went something like this: "I gotta write a book one of these days" or, head-shakingly, "Man, if I ever write my book . . ." as if whatever book the clerk might write would obliterate every other existing book, as if Eric's book—the handsome, remaindered *Copper Creek*—was actively interfering with the clerk's book writing. If only the clerk didn't have to sit around putting sale stickers on *Copper Creek* all day, he or she might actually get some writing done. Eric was always tempted to say, "Well, why don't you just write the goddamn book?" or "No one cares why you got a neck tattoo!" But, being the mild-mannered book author he was, he would instead say thank you, no he did not need a bag, and yes he would like a receipt.

This feeling of outrage and disappointment was not something he could confess to anyone at the Ranch, not even Marianne, who had diligently worked on the same manuscript for years, without expecting anything in return. It was not a feeling he could share with people whose only goal was to write their one book and have it published. They would have to find out for themselves how each goal opened up into a bigger one, like hideously distorted nesting dolls, how ever-elusive publication became ever-elusive praise, prizes, more publications, bigger advances, a movie deal.

Eric worried, most of all, that *Copper Creek*, meant to be his auspicious debut, might become his one and only book, when it was not what he had to say about life at all. He was beginning to realize that this was the same fear he had about his marriage, which, embarked upon in the year after his book's release, had essentially the same shelf life. One could compare the engagement to the period of prepublication—both had lasted about six months, felt exciting, and involved the design and selection of a number of glossy publicity materials. The marriage itself, beset with unsatisfying travel, ever-present anxiety, and attacks on his self-esteem, was like the first year of publication.

He had rushed into things, had been too eager to prove that he was a real adult and a real writer. He had competed with other people, had noticed, on Facebook and in his own mailbox, that other people were blissfully (smugly) getting married and publishing novels. He had developed a preoccupation with the ages of people who were marking milestones in their lives—book, marriage, child—and calculating how far behind he was falling. He had signed on with an agent before his novel was really finished, and had felt obligated to turn it over to her quickly.

Likewise, he had proposed to Christine after only three months of dating, without a ring or any real forethought. They had been to a concert by a popular nouveau bluegrass band. The band had returned to the stage for a ten-minute encore, and everyone in the audience had sung along:

Baby take off your apron I'll get my hat
Come on, it's just as simple as that
We're going to townnnn

Accustomed to standing motionless at interminable experimental performances, or vaguely keening at indie rock shows, or crossing his arms across his chest at rap concerts, Eric had been stirred by the band's easy, welcoming harmonies, by how good it felt to like something that everyone else agreed was worth liking, worth going out of your way for and even looking a little silly for (the band members, guys in their twenties, all wore straw hats and suspenders, but no shoes). He resolved then and there that he was through with things that were pointlessly difficult, unreasonable, hostile. How could he mark this moment? he wondered. Several of the band's songs were about weddings, and the idea of proposing came to him as they were walking back to their car with a large, jolly crowd of fellow concertgoers. He'd gotten down on one knee in a patch of gravel spotlit by an amber streetlight, and the crowd had slowed to watch him deliver his proposal, which even now he remembered as powerful and sincere. They clapped when Christine said yes, and did not seem to notice the lack of a ring.

It was not the first time he'd proposed.

Or even the second.

"You're a serial proposer," his brother accused, around the time he started thinking about married life—not with Christine, but with Marianne. By then Eric had already asked two women to marry him— the first time was in college, the second a confused, underemployed time just before he moved to New York. Both said no right away, though both times he'd been prepared, with romantic evenings out and specially selected engagement rings: a lumpy silver Claddagh for Denise, the shocked college girl, and a half-carat diamond in a white gold Tiffany setting for practical, pharmacy-school Julie, who forcefully told him that she needed to get her own career started before she settled down.

He'd kept Julie's ring in its black velvet box at the back of his sock drawer. A few years later, it was perfect for Marianne—pretty and elegant, exactly what he would have chosen for her—and he didn't see any reason to buy a new one. "Thrift," said Mark, when Eric told him of his plans. "Probably a good habit in an artist."

Looking back, Eric saw that the ring was part of the problem. If he hadn't had a ring ready to go, he might have thought things through a little more. He remembered holding his breath after he asked her, in a dim corner of their favorite Brooklyn restaurant, the familiar, slightly terrified look on her face.

"Please," he'd whispered, holding his breath. "Say yes."

Marianne had not said yes but had nodded, laughing and even crying a little, and held out her hand—the wrong one, he remembered—and he'd gently taken the correct one and had slid the ring onto her finger, where it was a perfect fit, as if the ring as much as Eric had simply been looking for the right person. It was just like in the movies: fumbling and sudden and joyful, patrons around them breaking into cheers and applause. Their waiter brought them their favorite dessert, crème brûlée, and two spoons to crack the caramelized sugar.

Mark called him from work the next afternoon. "How'd it go? I was waiting for you to tell me."

"She said yes," Eric slurred, halfway through a fifth of whiskey. Marianne had left hours ago. "But then she changed her mind."

His brother—the asshole—reminded him that at least he hadn't bought a whole new ring. "You're better off anyway," he'd told Eric, before taking another call.

Eric wondered what he meant—was he better off not getting married, or better off without Marianne? At that moment, only hours after celebrating, then ending, their engagement, Eric could not imagine life without her. Beautiful, crazy, capricious Marianne. Every annoying habit was suddenly endearing and precious—the way she underdressed for the weather, in filmy dresses and ridiculous shoes, her terribly decorated apartment, her foul mouth and open atheism. Eric rooted through his CDs and found *The Essential Leonard Cohen* and played "So Long, Marianne" on repeat until Mark showed up after work.

"I'm no English major, but listen to the song, dumbass," Mark said, turning it up. "The fucker was glad to be rid of her."

What other choices did she have? Did she really want to wind up alone, in some crummy fourth-floor walk-up? What were her goals, her prospects? She did not seem to want any of the things he wanted so desperately, not publication or marriage or a permanent address, or at least did not expect them. Perhaps she knew something that he did not—he was too good for her, maybe that was it. Eric began to catalog Marianne's faults obsessively. Aside from part-time teaching, she hardly even worked, while Eric had taught, temped for a medical supply company, answered phones for an escort service, and worked in social media consulting. Marianne never had any decent furniture and spent her discretionary funds on psychoanalysis and vitamins instead of health insurance. She was a connoisseur of the pointlessly difficult—long readings held at inconvenient hours, meals so spicy you could only bear to take two bites, exhibits of ephemeral art—and everything she wanted to do was far away, so that what you remembered, instead of the actual experience, was how hard it had been to get there. She canceled plans, she was self-absorbed and argumentative and petulant. She was pretty in a way that he told himself would not last—her hair would grow frizzy and coarse; her pale, freckled skin would wrinkle early.

For almost two months, they hardly talked. At the end of the summer, he moved to Charlotte, and soon they were dating other people. They began their Sunday-night phone call ritual, and Eric thought, *so this is how we're meant to be.* Then Eric was married—he had pictured Marianne at the country club wedding, tearfully but powerfully reading a poem composed just for him and his bride, but she didn't show.

Now, of course, he understood that it had all been a mistake—proposing to Denise and Julie and Marianne, marrying Christine. He worried that the rest of his life would be lived in the wake of these mistakes, that they would influence his future chances at happiness, the same way his poor novel sales would influence the sale and marketing of a new book. He did not want to look back on another *Copper Creek,* another failed marriage. He was done with serial proposing.

Dimly, he was aware that all of his efforts—pursuing a writing career, getting engaged and married and even buying the house in Charlotte—had been, in some ways, about succeeding in areas his older brother overlooked. Mark didn't care about art, he didn't care about relationships—money was his muse and his wife and his children. "Mark does very well for himself": that was how Eric's mother put it, when someone complimented a bracelet or noticed the cruise line brochures on her coffee table. Of course she'd been proud of Eric too—both of his parents had dutifully come to readings, and dragged cousins and neighbors and friends along too. But *Copper Creek* had never provided anything tangible to his family, no tennis bracelets or winter vacations. After he took the high school teaching job, they studiously avoided talk about his career.

And so Eric wanted the next book, the next relationship, the next *thing*, whatever it was, to be about something bigger and truer than what he'd done so far. He wanted something that would last at least as long as Mark's portfolio. Longer.

He still had Marianne's diamond solitaire (Christine, after their impromptu engagement, wanted to design her own ring). Just the other night, after Marianne kicked him out, he'd rummaged for it in the pocket of his suitcase, pulling out a lint-covered black velvet box, which traveled with him everywhere, even to Dubai. It opened with a familiar snap, and he was relieved to see that inside, everything was pristine. The white gold band had not been nicked or scratched, and the ring still had a satisfying heft in his hand. Long ago, a jeweler told him that the diamond quality was exceptional, but who could really tell? Eric turned the ring this way and that, watching as the stone caught and reflected light.

Eric sat grimly in the Ranch's office, his laptop on Marianne's desk, the door locked and the bank of fluorescent lights turned off. In the small Skype box that showed his own image, he saw a tired-looking, sallow-skinned, slump-shouldered man. Next to his laptop, a cardboard box spilled its contents across the desk: two large black smartphones and their various chargers, headphones, and GWGW-themed accessories—blue cross-embossed cases and blue styluses and microfiber screen cleaners.

"So I'm gonna give it to you straight," Mark told him. Mark believed in bad news first, let's-get-this-over-with, no sugarcoating. Nothing to cut the sting. Mark *liked* the sting, the risk of teetering, then toppling failure. It was what allowed him to do what he did, Eric assumed, all that financial roulette playing. But Eric didn't like things straight—couldn't Mark remember that much, at least, from childhood? His medicine had to be hidden in yogurt, the bad news of pet deaths or new schools or sick grandparents softened with ice cream or merry-go-rounds.

"Things are not looking good, bro," Mark continued, leaning toward the screen. He looked healthy, ruddy, as if he'd just come back from tennis or a beach vacation. "You are way over budget. Way over."

Eric picked up one of the smartphones—he supposed it was meant as a kind of softening-up, a toy to distract him, but its expensive heft gave him a sick feeling. He set the phone down again. "We can cut back on photocopying. We can advertise more, get more applicants. Getting more applicants would be great—"

"That doesn't touch the kind of deficit I'm talking about," Mark said. "We're gonna have to think bigger here. Leveraging what we do have."

"Okay," Eric said, straightening and blinking. "I can go see Frances. She believes in our—"

"It's beyond her means. Way beyond. "

"How can we be so behind? I mean, I know we went over budget on some things, but looking through all the paperwork, I just don't get—"

Mark leaned forward and lowered his voice. "Eric, you've uprooted your whole life, right? You quit your job, you moved to a shitty motel. In Florida."

"It's not that bad."

"Sure, but sometimes opportunity knocks, and you get a chance to make up for all that effort. I'm talking about the chance to make real money here. It's like payback—like karma."

"Karma," Eric repeated.

"Right, but first we have to show that this thing is scalable, a good return on investment for GWGW."

"Yeah, about them."

"About who?" Mark had turned away from the screen and was clicking away at another computer.

"GWGW," Eric said, louder. "I don't know that they fit the mission Marianne and I have for the school. Our instructors are asking questions."

"The mission you have for the school, hmm, let's see if I can remember it," Mark said, turning theatrically back to the screen in his rolling chair. Eric wished he had another computer to be busy with, or even a chair on wheels. "Was it, let's see, exploiting the Christian literary market?"

"Mark—"

"Was it also financing the renovation of our great-aunt's busted hotel so that she doesn't lose it in foreclosure? Something like that? Rescuing yourself from total financial meltdown? Getting ahead, for once in your life?" Mark said. "Also, your instructors: they are your employees. You ask the fucking questions. Not them."

"Got it," Eric said. It was pointless to argue with Mark when he got all *Glengarry Glen Ross.*

"Eric," Mark said, looking directly at his laptop's camera. "This was your idea. Christian creative writing program. Remember? Taking money from religious nuts? Remember that?"

"It was Frances's idea, actually."

"Frances's idea was a fucking bookstore with readings. You talked her into this school idea. To impress Marianne, your ex-fiancée, the woman you're still in love with?" Mark said. Eric watched himself wince on-screen. "Look, bro. These are the richest Christians I could find for you, and frankly, I'm hurt that you are rejecting them. They are a growing regional company, with international interests and holdings, overseeing campuses in three states. They have the resources to completely remodel the Ranch, get it out of hock, plus pay tidy bonuses to you, Marianne, and whatever literary snake-oil salesmen you want to hire. You're telling me you don't want to take their money?"

"Wait, are we really in trouble, or are you just trying to make more money? What do you mean by 'overseeing campuses'?" Eric picked up the phone, snapped it into its GWGW case, and held it up to the screen. "I mean, what the hell is this—some sort of tracking device?"

Mark shook his head, laughing. "All smartphones are tracking devices, bro. And what's wrong with more money? So they spread their logo around, they advertise, they bring you students. Maybe they do a little training of your instructors. They add legitimacy to the idea that you *are* a Christian creative writing program, and not a scam."

"Right," Eric said. "But is that just an idea, or is it true?"

"Don't ask me," said Mark, turning back to his other keyboard. "I went to business school."

This was the real problem, he told Marianne, after finding her down by the beach. They hadn't decided where they stood, exactly, relative to the students.

It was dark and damp and chilly, but Marianne was still wearing a sundress, no sweater, and was curled up on a beach chair. He handed her his jacket, which held the phone meant for Marianne in one of its pockets.

"Let's walk," he said, gesturing up the beach, where the hotel workers were stacking chaises. Far down the beach, lights twinkled from a fishing pier.

"So do we hate them?" he asked. "Do we just want to take their money?"

"No," she said. "Yes? Can't we not hate them and want to take their money too?"

"But how do we feel about them, and what they're supposed to get out of this? Are we really teaching them to write Christian novels and poems and memoirs? Do we expect them to publish them?"

"Oh God," Marianne said, hugging his jacket to her body. "You don't know how to teach them that. Lorraine doesn't know how to teach them that. *Tom*—"

"Right," said Eric. "So if that was the case, why didn't we just run their credit reports instead of spending weeks arguing about this one or that one? Why didn't we just pick the richest vampire novelist and get it over with?"

"Damn," Marianne said. "Running a credit check would have been a lot easier."

"I'm serious."

"I know, I'm sorry. Let me think." Marianne had a serpentine walking pattern—she'd walk away from you, then suddenly, her hip would be bumping against yours. Eric put his arm around her, and she leaned into him.

"When we started out, you told me I'd get inspiration for my book. A whole ugly bear list to choose from—homophobes and anti-environmentalists and pro-lifers and self-righteous bootstrappers. So when I read the applications, everyone was on my list. But there was so much of it, I started sorting it, and some of the pieces, they stood out. They weren't good, maybe, not in the sense that you could publish them—"

"But they were interesting."

"Yeah, they were." Marianne broke away, walking diagonally into the shallow tide. "The personal stories of the writers, they were interesting too. I mean, Davonte Gold—he's different than I expected. He's a pain in the ass but, I don't know, he's also completely honest. I guess the list changed."

"It wasn't a shit list."

"No. Tonight when I came down here, I was mad at you," she said. "I felt like you were pushing me away from running the school, like you were dismissing me. Then one of the students—Janine Gray—she was here. The Terri Schiavo poet. Earlier today, I was rude to her. Okay, I was very rude—I didn't know who she was, you know I'm bad with names."

Marianne looked up at him, as if seeking his forgiveness, or maybe an admission that he'd done the same with someone else. He'd actually been gentle with his class, though twice already he'd had to intervene in an argument between Davonte and another student who seemed determined to provoke him. Eric could picture things escalating to fisticuffs before the session ended. "It happens," he said. "She probably didn't notice."

Marianne crossed her arms and shook her head. "She noticed. But then she came down here and we talked about—poetry, I guess, and relationships, and her family. She has a job teaching home ec, and two daughters, and her husband doesn't really get her poetry, even though it's religious."

"That doesn't sound so strange."

"That's what I mean! She's a totally normal person. Do you know she told me that she met an agent at the welcome party? Was there an agent here?"

Mark had told him that some people from GWGW might stop by, incognito, but he didn't say they'd be posing as agents. It wasn't such a bad idea, really—it could make the students more hopeful, even confident, to think they had attracted an agent's attention just by being here (at least, until they had the inevitable misfortune of being ignored by one). But he decided, absent confirmation from Mark, to keep that to himself. "Agents? I don't remember any agents."

"Because I'm just thinking that the manipulation, the game playing, is just not right for this crowd. I should have picked the worst ones, or just the richest ones, but I was alone and I didn't, and now we're stuck with these people, and I don't think I can take advantage of them. I don't think I can screw them over while I'm living with them."

"Nobody said we had to screw anybody over."

"You said, when you told me about this, that it would be good for everybody. We'd make money, your aunt's hotel would get fixed up, we'd finish our books, and the students would have a chance to feel like writers. I thought I wouldn't care about the students—I thought I just cared about our needs—but I don't know that I can do it if they wind up hating us, if they find out we've invited in an organization that is clearly problematic."

"How is GWGW—"

"*Averse to our values*, Eric. Just a scheme. Promise me that won't happen."

Eric stopped walking and turned to Marianne. Without her heels—she wore flip-flops all the time now—she was a whole head shorter than him, and she was appealingly small, even frail, in his jacket. He put his hands on her shoulders and bent down to look into her eyes. "Marianne, I promise we can do this right, okay?" he said. "Can you just trust me on that?"

She shook her head but did not remove his hands. "No, Eric, I cannot just trust you. I have to be involved. You can't just go having meetings with your brother and leave me out. This was partly my idea, and I feel responsible."

Your idea was taking money from Christians, he almost said but didn't. He knew this wasn't the way to convince her. He took a breath, let go of Marianne's shoulders, and started walking. "Okay, so, going back to the goals of the students and how they connect with, say, the expertise of our faculty. We have a problem there, right?"

"Ugh," she said. "We have a big problem there."

"And operating expenses—we need those for copiers and paper and keeping the students in electricity and toilet paper and chili mac, right? All GWGW is talking about doing is taking a tour, meeting some of our students, and suggesting—just suggesting—some techniques and strategies that might help us. That might help our students. That doesn't sound so bad, does it?"

"I guess not."

"Then, let's just try it, okay?" he said. "We're doing something completely new here, and people are gonna want to help us. They're gonna want to get involved. We have the power to say yes or no. It's up to us." He told her what Mark told him—that some investors and curricular experts from GWGW would be there in a day or two, touring the campus and assessing how they might help—without mentioning his suspicion that Mark was just profiteering. He made their visit sound the way Mark made it sound to him—like an honor and a favor both—and the more he talked about it, the more he believed it.

They turned back without reaching the pier. As they made their way up the path to school, Eric felt Marianne leaning into him. The heavy phone bumped against his side, but she didn't mention it. She stopped before they reached the end of the mangroves, while they were still—promisingly—alone.

"I should give you your jacket back."

"Keep it. It looks good on you," he said, though it was his only nice jacket and far too big on her. She shrugged her arms out of the sleeves so it hung loosely on her, like a cape. Eric felt the awkwardness before a first kiss, the magnetic pull of two faces, the anxiety of possible rejection. It was his favorite part—one of his favorite parts, anyway—of a relationship, something he'd missed out on, in his drunken, grad-student boldness, with Marianne. Maybe that had been their problem.

He cupped the back of Marianne's head and stroked her long neck with his thumb. He was about to kiss her when they were interrupted by a loud splash and hooting, far up the darkened path.

"We should go before someone spots us," she whispered. "You should check on them."

"What could they be doing that needs checking? It's not like we told them not to use the pool."

"People already think we're a thing." She was still whispering. "A couple."

"So? It's not like the Bible says people can't date each other."

"What do you know about the Bible?" Marianne slid out of his jacket and folded it over his arm. She held her hand there a moment, and Eric felt its warmth through the scratchy tweed. Then she reached inside the pocket and pulled out the smartphone. "I didn't know you had one of these."

"Mark sent it. There's one for each of us, to make work easier—emailing and stuff." He didn't mention the GWGW accessories in the office.

"To make work more ever-present," she said, handing it back. "If that's even possible."

"We'll have time soon," he said. "Just us. I promise."

"I should go. I want to write something before bed, and I'm getting tired. But we can take another walk tomorrow?"

So that's how it would be, he thought: a rewinding, a return to the courtship they should have had. He could do that. He knew all about romance: it was just a story, after all, with a beginning, a middle, and an end. He and Marianne, they were back to the beginning.

8

To: RuthandDarrylBoyette@healingwaters.org
From: MarianneStuart@gmail.com
Subject: Dear RUTH

(Darryl, this is an email between sisters, so please give Ruth some privacy.
Thank you for understanding!)

It is really kind of absurd that you share an email address with Darryl. You
should get your own—you had one in high school, remember? Superrgirl15@
gmail.com? When I type someone's address that starts with *S* into my email,
that one still comes up.

Anyway, I've already started off on the wrong foot, which is becoming a pattern for me. I guess I could go back and delete all of that, but I want you to
see: I recognize that I'm being a jerk. The school I would have told you
all about at Christmas, if you'd had more time (or Thanksgiving, when you
were invited to see it for yourself), is in full swing and I am beat—look, two
clichés in a single paragraph, "wrong foot" and "full swing." But what are
clichés if not tired metaphors? That's the only kind I have to offer right now,
I'm afraid.

It's a school for inspirational writing. Dad says he told you about it. I know
writing wasn't your favorite subject—you were better at reports, projects,
being in charge of a presentation. But I still think you would like it here,
Ruth. Being with our students reminds me a little of going to events at your
church—all these middle-aged, earnest people, everybody so community-
minded. At the opening-night gathering, people didn't just stand there waiting for their beverages to be refilled (well, I guess some did)—they actually

went on ice runs for me without being asked. At NYU, that never would have happened on the first night. We all would have been too busy checking our own reflections in the available shiny surfaces, or thinking about what pretensions to lead our conversations with.

Not that these people are angels (ha, another metaphor). They are, after all, the reason I'm so exhausted—I think I talked to every single one of them today about some problem or fear or complaint. But that's just it, I realized, talking to a woman at the beach tonight (you'd like her, she's working on this series of poems about the fight to keep a brain-dead woman alive, I guess you'd say it's pro-life?). They're coming to me, instead of keeping everything hidden. They're not afraid (as I always was) of being judged. There's something honest and on the surface about them and the fact that they know everyone is here for the same purpose. But also, they're different: we have a preacher's wife, an R&B singer (I won't say who, but he's pretty famous), a veteran, former teachers, housewives, moms, dads, grandparents, a few younger people (no one as young as you).

It's my job to take care of their needs while they're here, though I'm not teaching them. I suppose I'm a little like you in that way, a behind-the-scenes preparer and organizer—that hadn't occurred to me until tonight, when I sat down to write. I meant to write a poem—I had an idea about the green light, this flash of light that appears green as the sun goes down—but wound up with more things to say to you. Starting with: I know I haven't tried very hard to understand you or your recent choices, you as an adult. I am working on it. I promise. I think this place may help.

I spent a lot of time alone this winter. Eric (no, we are not getting married, so please don't ask) was still in Dubai, so I was by myself. I know, I lived in New York by myself but this felt different. Like being in a monastery. I went days— days, Ruth!—without talking to anyone. The news was horrible most of the time. (We may have different definitions of horrible and different sources for our news but I think we'd both agree that things are not good.) Sometimes I'd call Dad, and he'd tell me about whatever new indignity he was suffering in his department, thanks to budget cuts and overcrowding. Do you know he's teaching five classes this semester? Three of them are intro, with a writing requirement, so all he does is grade papers. I remember when he had three classes in the spring—he grew asparagus and zinnias and built bookshelves for all our neighbors, because he was worried people weren't reading books anymore (like the lack of a place to put them was the cause). Anyway, I think he's lonely, overworked. Maybe you and Darryl could take him supper one night? One of those casseroles you specialize in? Or maybe you already do that. He hasn't mentioned it, though.

But I wanted to talk about us, that's why I'm writing. When you got married, Ruth, it was like a gut punch to me. Not because I'm not married, but because you were so young. There was so much out there—going to college, living on your own, dating—that you hadn't experienced, that I know Mom would have wanted for you. That I wanted for you. I mean, your first apartment! Being completely alone and free to do whatever you want—to eat ice cream sandwiches for dinner, lie on the floor and think, sleep as late as you want or not at all. I know I moved away, didn't come home enough. I know I didn't call enough. I know I wasn't the sister Mom wanted me to be to you, and I'm sorry.

So I'm asking now: what was it like, living at home with just Dad? Was it okay? It's seemed for a while now like you're mad at both of us, but Dad really did his best. I could have done better. You don't have to let me off the hook (another cliché). Reel me in. Rake me over the coals. Let me have it.

Love,
Marianne

P.S. Sarasota really is a pleasant place to be. We're a little north of Sarasota, but it's still pretty, maybe a little down-at-the-heels. The weather is almost always better than it is everywhere else (I watch the Weather Channel when the news stresses me out too much), and there's a beach just a short walk from my doorstep. No waves, just gentle lapping water, white smooth sand. And the green light. I've never seen it, but maybe you'd get lucky. You should visit.

To: MarianneStuart@gmail.com
From: RuthandDarrylBoyette@healingwaters.org
Subject: Re: Dear RUTH

Dear Marianne,

You asked what it was like, living with Dad. You can probably imagine it. We had frozen dinners when he remembered to stock the freezer, and peanut butter and jelly when he didn't. It was quiet. Dad was in his study a lot, grading papers or reading. There was that time he was dating Noreen and went out more, but other than that it was quiet. We talked twice a day, in the morning before school and at night while we ate our sandwiches or our reheated burritos or pizza from Sal's. I asked him if I should get some cookbooks and learn to cook. He said no. He said he liked this just fine. One time I asked him if he was one of those people who'd take a pill instead of eating, and he looked at me like I had two heads. Of course, he told me.

That's what I fell in love with about the church. I love feeling needed and necessary and part of a community. I think that's what Mom loved about teaching. You're more like Dad, you don't need other people. But I do.

All those things you say I missed out on? You make them sound really great, Marianne. ("Living in a monastery"? Lying on the floor and thinking—about what? Not sleeping? Waiting for some weird green light?) You said not to ask about Eric, but I liked him. You can't wait forever to get married, Marianne. That isn't what Mom would have wanted for *you* either.

Darryl doesn't even check this account. He's too busy for email. If something comes to him, I just print it out and give it to him.

Your sister,
Ruth

P.S. Dad did tell me about your school. And I saw that you're run by a group that helps us with fund-raisers, GWGW?

To: RuthandDarrylBoyette@healingwaters.org
From: MarianneStuart@gmail.com
Subject: Re: Dear RUTH

That wasn't exactly a raking over the coals.
Can you send me the link to the story you found, about us and GWGW? They
don't run us, by the way. They're funders.
xMarianne
P.S. Mom didn't love teaching. She loved art.

To: MarianneStuart@gmail.com
From: RuthandDarrylBoyette@healingwaters.org
Subject: Re: Dear RUTH

It wasn't a story, just a newsletter in my email. It wasn't just about your school,
but about a lot of different campuses. They're expanding pretty quickly. Can't
find it now.
About Mom: what's the difference?

Though the omission worried Eric, Marianne decided not to warn the
other workshop leaders before GWGW's visit, just three days into the
residency. She remembered the stern warnings about visitors from her
school's administrators in Brownsville, and the flurry of bad feelings and
recriminations kicked down the line from principal to teacher to student, especially those students—the biters and scratchers and Tourette's
swearers—who were corralled in the assistant principal's office. There
was so little you could control, after all—nothing she could say would
keep Manfred from drinking or Lorraine from passing out poems by
Amiri Baraka or Tom from forgetting his students' names. To warn them
would only make it more likely that they would exhibit their troublesome
behaviors, she reasoned. And besides, hadn't Eric agreed that the tour
was up to her to coordinate?

He acquiesced, grateful that Marianne was willing to lead the tour. He didn't comment on her last-minute preparations—straightening the office, removing one or two nymphs from the sculpture garden, ironing her clothes, and gathering her hair in a neat, low chignon. Probably he didn't notice.

The visitors arrived in a black SUV, like Secret Service agents or the FBI, and emerged wearing identical pale blue polo shirts, the GWGW logo emblazoned on their chests. There were three of them, two identical tall men and a woman, attractive but hard-faced and a little frightening, like a politician, or a politician's wife. They introduced themselves and offered firm handshakes and a tote bag full of tchotchkes.

"Thank you," said Marianne, peering inside the bag. There were note-pads and bumper stickers, water bottles and pens. She escorted them to her newly straightened office, which felt somewhat too small for the four of them. Marianne offered chairs, but no one wanted to sit.

"We have shirts for you in the car, too," said the woman brightly. Her name, *Regina*, was spelled out in cursive above the logo on her polo shirt, which she'd tucked in to a trim pencil skirt. Despite the casual quality of her shirt, she wore nylons and heels. "Different sizes and colors. White *and* pale blue."

"Oh good," Marianne said, pulling a pale blue and white Rubik's-style cube out of the bag. It was printed, on one face, with GWGW's logo, but along the side it also read "School of Law."

"That's from one of our partners," said Regina. "We're partnered with a law school."

"And a nursing school," said Matt, the taller of the two tall men. "And a library science school, a digital arts school, an academy for hairstylists and aestheticians, and a school for social work." He ticked them off across his fingers cheerfully.

"And a school for medical billing," said the other guy, who had intro-duced himself as Christopher. "That's in development."

"A Christian medical billing school?" Marianne asked, spinning the cube into disarray. Now it read S_oGl df WL_w.

"We've found that our students—" began Christopher.

"Our *clients*," Regina corrected.

"Our clients prefer a Christian learning environment," he said. "They want to know that their peers and teachers are also Christian."

"They want to know that what they are learning strengthens their values," Regina added, "instead of damages them. They want to feel comfortable in a learning environment that is part of their faith journey."

"Wow," said Marianne. She rotated the cube three times, then held it up. "This Rubik's Cube is very easy to solve."

"You are a quick study, I can tell," Regina said. She winked at Marianne. "I understand the Ranch was all your idea."

"Well, yes, I suppose it was," Marianne said, still examining the cube. How could a Rubik's Cube be only two colors? And why did the two colors mean it would be so easy to put back together, especially if many of the squares were marked with letters? But it was true—she scrambled the cube again, making five quick twists, and was able to return it to the start again in no time.

"Mark tells me that you were dismayed by your own fine arts training," she said.

"There was dismay," said Marianne, still studying the cube. "And it was also difficult to get a job once it was over."

"The value you are bringing to these writers is immeasurable," said Regina. "Giving them a place to express themselves without judgment."

Marianne looked up. "Not entirely without judgment," she said. "It is, after all, a place to learn."

"Of course," said Regina. "A place of supportive learning that will help them refine their talents. And part of it online, yes?"

"Yes," confirmed Marianne. From beneath a stack of new manuscripts, she unearthed the schedule for the current cohort. "They have twelve days here in session, with a half-day optional field trip tomorrow. Then they return in August. In between, they're in email contact with their professors, working on drafts and revisions."

"This is an essential part of our strategy," said Regina, tapping the page. "Our clients want a Christian experience, and they also want part of it to be online."

"They're busy folks," Matt said. "Moms and dads, working people.

They have church responsibilities, family responsibilities. They are soccer coaches and baseball coaches and Sunday school teachers."

"They don't have time to mess around," Christopher said, somewhat angrily, as if Marianne herself were trying to rob these hardworking Christians of their civic and family-minded time.

"They want a school experience that fits into their faith *and* their life," Regina said, more gently.

"Like the Rubik's Cube," Marianne said, holding it aloft, like an evil queen with an apple. "They don't want it to be too hard."

"Exactly," said Regina. "I think we understand each other exactly."

The tour went less than well. All three workshops met concurrently, and with so little else to see—they dispensed quickly with the pool, the beach, the dining hall, and the common spaces, though all three visitors dutifully admired the sculpture garden—they had no choice but to open the door on each classroom, where the business of education was taking place.

In Tom's workshop, Patty Connor, author of a six-hundred-page manuscript about her eight miscarriages, was pressing tissues underneath her eyes and shaking her head vigorously. "But that's exactly how it happened," she was saying, or rather sobbing, while someone patted her arm and another woman handed her tissue after tissue, pulling them from the box one after the other as if that would somehow stop her crying. At the head of the long workshop table, Tom, dressed in his usual jeans, T-shirt, and safari jacket, leaned back in his chair. He looked helpless and stricken.

"Memoir," whispered Marianne to Regina, backing them out of the room. "It brings up a lot of feelings."

In their classroom, the poets were doing some kind of exercise, all of them bent over their notebooks in the obedient posture of schoolchildren. Lorraine had not devoted any class time to workshopping the students' poems yet, but had introduced the idea of the "generative workshop," in which the goal was to collect not praise or suggestions but ideas and material. Now they were each sketching something intently. On the board, there were two stick figures locked in some sort of combat, one labeled "T.K.," the other "L.K." Lorraine was smoking. She had propped a small fan, facing outward, in the open window, and was considerately blowing her smoke in its direction. "Your worst sexual memory," she was saying, between puffs. "Any age."

Marianne held her breath and looked at the ceiling while Regina made notes with a stylus on a black, shiny tablet. Marianne wondered where else they could find investors. She wondered if she'd have to give her phone back—already she'd gotten used to sending emails and reading the news on its small, glowing screen. Matt and Christopher, who did not have tablets to hold, circled the room, peeking rudely at the students' open pages, their faces registering expressions of confusion, concern, and disgust.

"Professor Kominski won the Yale Younger Poets prize," Marianne offered as they left. "She is really an inspiring teacher. She's been through a lot," she added.

"Kominski," Regina mused. "Is that a Polish name?"

Thinking that Eric had the best control over his students and likely the most conventional teaching style, Marianne had saved his class for last. When planning the Ranch, months ago, she'd given him the best classroom, too: a cabana and game room steps from the beach. Though the seating was cramped—eleven people fit snugly, elbow to elbow, around the small table—the gulf views were incredible, and Marianne thought the ocean smell, the sounds of the waves and the gulls, would be invigorating and inspiring. But she could hear voices arguing even over the sound of the waves as they approached. She thought of turning around, heading back to the office to dial up Mark on speakerphone, but Regina stepped powerfully ahead, her heels crunching into the sand.

Davonte leaned forward across the table, obviously exercised, his forearms propped up on a pile of papers. "Why don't you just say his name? Come on. Don't play dumb with us. We all know who you're talking about."

The author of the work, a placid-looking retiree with a snow-white beard and snow-white sneakers, was reddening slightly around the temples.

"As I stated before, this is a work of speculative fiction. None of the characters are intended to resemble any individual living person."

"Oh, come on," Davonte groaned. "America's first president of Lebanese descent . . . everyone votes for him because of his one-word slogan, 'Trust' . . . he negotiates a global arms control treaty and brings about world peace . . . and then in chapter five it turns out he's the Antichrist."

"Again, this is not a work of political commentary. My novel clearly takes place in the future, as indicated by its title, '2016: The Final Battle.'"

The other students looked uncomfortable. "Help me out here, Eric," Davonte said.

Marianne willed Eric to say something diplomatic, to soothe with vague praise and move on, but it was too late.

"I understand that this is speculative fiction, Louis, but in order for those of us still living in the present to relate to it, your premise has to be believable."

Matt snorted, apparently finding Louis's premise quite believable.

"So, in the year 2016," Eric continued. "A world peace treaty is a *bad* thing?"

"It is when it leads to one-world government."

"And just playing devil's advocate here, ha-ha, but *that* is a bad thing because . . ."

"Because once the Antichrist controls all of the governments of the world, he will be able to turn their power against the Church. The Church is his ultimate adversary. You'll understand once you reach chapter fourteen . . . or once you reread your Book of Revelation."

This answer seemed to mollify Davonte. "Well, I do remember that in Revelation, the mark of the beast and such." He shuffled his papers, his voice softening. "All I'm asking is why it's gotta be Obama, though."

"Young man, I do not intend to state or imply that President Obama is the Antichrist," Louis offered.

Davonte lifted one of his forearms off the table.

"Only that we must remain vigilant *in case* he is the Antichrist. You see, it's far too early to tell."

"President Obama is *not the Antichrist*," Eric snapped.

"Goddamn right about that," muttered Davonte.

"How do you know? None of us can know for certain," said a woman at the end of the table.

"*Oh, please,*" someone else moaned.

"Again, President Oliver Hussain is a composite of various . . ."

Eric was already rounding the table on his way to show Marianne and her visitors the door.

"That was one of our more challenging pieces," he said, once they reached the hallway. "I firmly believe workshop can be a place where we all learn about each other's views and treat them with respect, where we can learn not only about writing, but also about other people. Other people are so fascinating!"

"Thanks, Eric!" Marianne said, turning away with her GWGW guests— she was certain they would be on their way soon, never to return, taking their polo shirts and tote bags and Frisbees with them. Marianne wondered how they could make up for the money they'd be losing—maybe enroll more students, solicit more applications? She hoped they would let her keep the Rubik's Cube.

"There are some tweaks to be made, for sure," Regina said, as they made their way back to the office. She was still tapping things into her tablet; the screen reflected the Florida sun in such a way that Marianne had no idea what she could be noting. Perhaps she was texting her boyfriend or ordering shoes online. "Some adjustments. But there always are. You should have seen the school of cosmetology when we got there!"

"Goth city," Matt said.

"*Stripper* city," Christopher said.

"We've found that a set of guidelines helps," explained Regina, waving her hand in a gesture that said, to Matt and Christopher: shut up. "About conduct, appearance, and expectations. It sets the tone for the students."

"Right," Marianne said. "Wait—you're not leaving? You're still . . . *interested* in us?"

"It's a process," Regina said. "We are prepared to help you in this time of growth and transition. That's why we're here."

"We're not exactly talking about beauty school students here," Marianne said. "And I can't really see Tom in a polo shirt. No offense."

"None taken!" Regina said, though Matt and Christopher both looked down at their shirts, perplexed, as if they were part of their own poly-cotton skins. The four of them reached the office and stood for a moment at its cracked cement steps. Marianne was reminded of the awkwardness after a bad first date, how much you wanted it to be over so you could have your regular self back.

Regina carefully set down her tablet on one of the steps and held her hand above her eyes, scanning the campus like she was sizing the place up for demolition. She bent down and made another tap or two with her stylus, then smiled brightly at Marianne. "We'll be talking about becoming publicity-ready, and also market-ready."

"Market-ready?"

"Remember what you said, about not being able to find a job?" Regina didn't wait for Marianne to answer. "What if you didn't *have to* find a job? Can you imagine selling enough books that you could support yourself, your family?"

"No," said Marianne. The idea of a collection of poetry supporting a family sounded like a kind of suspicious trickery. Like stone soup.

Regina held up her tablet, made two taps with her stylus, and angled the screen for Marianne to see. "Do you know what that is?"

"A spreadsheet?" Marianne guessed.

"It's a spreadsheet of *best sellers*," Regina said, in a pleased, teaching tone that was at once impersonal and intimate. She tapped to show Marianne the way it was organized, a basket weave of numbers. "Organized by year." *Tap.* "By genre." *Tap.* "By sales region."

Marianne squinted at the screen. "I have a mental block for charts and graphs," she admitted. "It's one of the intelligences. I was born without it. Sorry."

"Well, to summarize," Regina said patiently, "four years ago, the Christian share of the best seller market was six percent, averaged across genres, though it's slightly higher in memoir. Two years ago it was nine percent. Last year it was twelve and a half. If you look back ten years, you see the same thing." On the screen, she opened a graph that made a staircase pattern on the screen, the steps getting steeper at the end.

"What do you mean by Christian share, though?" Marianne asked. "I mean, couldn't those Mormon vampire books count?"

"We did not count books by writers who happened to be Christian," said Regina. "We counted only *specifically*, deliberately Christian-themed,

Christian-messaged books, bought by Christians. Like the Resurrection series, or the WWJD novels."

Marianne remembered seeing the author of the WWJD novel series on the *Today Show*. She had been a wild-eyed, unkempt woman who had come from somewhere Marianne had never been: Nebraska? Oklahoma? The premise was brilliantly boring: a choose-your-own adventure series for middle grade readers. At the end of each chapter, you were supposed to ask yourself What would Jesus do? then choose that option, but reading the books, choosing the less Jesus-y path, and guessing its outcome had also become a popular teenage drinking game. One teenager had died, and another was hospitalized—this was the reason Matt Lauer interviewed the author, and the reason Marianne knew the series.

"Half of these books start out as self-published," said Regina, opening another screen, this time pie charts. "Until they get market share, your average New York City editor doesn't want anything to do with them. Typical, right?" She looked at Christopher and Matt.

"Typical," said Matt.

"Completely," said Christopher, with more venom. "It makes me sick—"

But Regina had turned back to her screen. "We're thinking GWGW can find the great ideas first. Or," she said, lowering her voice conspiratorially, "grow the ideas, right here. We, at GWGW, can train your educators to work on the kind of exercises and programs that will help your students achieve this type of success. Or we can help you find new educators . . . you look sort of pale, Marianne. Do you need some water? Christopher, Matt, please get Marianne some water."

"No, I'm okay," Marianne said. She was trying to imagine holding such a workshop with Tom and Lorraine. "My head hurts a little, that's all."

"It's the sun!" Regina said, as Christopher handed Marianne a bottle of water branded with the GWGW logo. "Also, this must be a lot to think about. Why don't you let me email you with some of this information, and we'll formulate a plan of attack?"

Marianne nodded, chugging GWGW water like a teenager in a drinking game.

• • •

Some of the students were hosting an after-dinner reading in the dining hall, offering snacks they'd frugally saved from the salad bar. Apple slices browned next to bowls of toppings and vegetables: fried ramen and clumped golden raisins and sliced carrots and broccoli florets. The meager snacks, the atmosphere of expectation and nerves reminded Marianne of her first NYU readings, but something was different here. Though she had always searched the crowd at school functions for her professors, the Ranch's poets and memoirists and novelists did not appear to mind that half the school's tiny faculty ducked out of their reading before it even began. Lorraine and Tom, sitting helplessly near the back, looked pleadingly at her as she dragged Eric by his shirtsleeve toward the door. *Stay,* she mouthed, like they were dogs.

"Maybe they're onto us," Marianne suggested, when no one asked her where they were going. "The students know we can't really help them."

She opened the office door with one of the keys she now wore all the time, on a lanyard around her neck, though weeks ago she'd discovered that it was openable just by turning and yanking the knob. It was important to keep up appearances, to preserve the idea that everything was as it should be. Doors closed and locked properly. Writers were learning *something.*

"I don't know," Eric said. "I thought my class had a pretty good discussion going today—not the part you saw, of course, that was sort of a mess. But after you left, I think we got Louis to understand something about the power of subtlety."

"The power of subtlety," Marianne repeated, peeling, from her computer screen, some of the sticky notes she'd left for herself, mostly phone messages she'd forgotten to deliver. "Well. I hope Manfred remembered to take his medicine. Also: I think we're back to square one."

"Didn't you talk to Mark? They loved the tour. They think there's a lot they can do for us. So, good job. Really, I'm proud of you."

"This was not what you or your brother said it would be," she said. "These people had *charts*, and *graphs*, and a *plan of attack.* They had facts and figures. They had promotional materials." She scrambled the Rubik's Cube and handed it to Eric.

"They're businesspeople," Eric explained. He turned the cube this way and that, then set it down again on the desk, as if it were an *objet d'art* rather than a puzzle he was meant to solve. "They have an interest in the bottom line. They also oversee six or seven other campuses—"

"They have a Christian cosmetology school, Eric," said Marianne. "That's where they were headed next, after they were done with our tour. Doesn't that strike you as strange? Shouldn't a Christian cosmetology school be, like, soap and washcloths?"

"Ha," said Eric. That was the most he was contributing these days, in terms of laughter. He'd been this way, serious and preoccupied, right before his divorce. Marianne had worked overtime to be amusing and distracting, sending dirty postcards and performing her famous Bill Clinton impression over the phone, but all he'd give her was a wan *ha*, or maybe ha-*ha*, if something was really funny. When it was over—next Friday, when the students left—he'd be able to relax.

"And they have a Christian medical billing school, and a Christian law school, devoted, I'm guessing, to the replacement of the Bill of Rights with the Ten Commandments," Marianne went on. "None of this bothers you?"

"Marianne," Eric said quietly. "What do you want me to do—fire Tom and Lorraine? Cut their pay? Send everybody home?"

"I don't know. Maybe."

"Did you see that reading the students were having? The bowls of raisins and cookies? Their manuscripts under their chairs? Nothing GWGW wants to do is gonna change that spirit they have."

"A Christian medical billing school," Marianne said again. "You can't tell me our students won't see through an organization like that. You can't tell me they won't smell a rat." She didn't want someone like Janine to think—to *realize*—that she was a scam artist, but neither did she want to fire her teachers, who'd made and canceled various complex plans just to come here. "They want to train you and Tom and Lorraine to teach people how to write YA best sellers."

Eric truly laughed at that one, doubling over in his chair: "Ha-ha-ha-*ha*! Best sellers! The nerve!" he said. "That doesn't sound like knowledge that's going to hurt anyone. In fact, maybe it could help all of us. But if it makes you feel better, I'll take a meeting with them, okay? I'll listen—I'll listen *critically*—to their whole spiel. Okay?"

"Maybe," Marianne said.

He nodded, satisfied. "That's what Mark and I thought. I've got a meeting scheduled Saturday night. With Regina and Davonte." He patted Marianne on the wrist. "Sound good?"

"Okay," she said, though she wondered why and how he'd already scheduled a meeting. "Why are you taking Davonte?"

"He's our most high-profile student," Eric said. "Mark looked it up, and his first album went platinum—"

"I *told* you. "

"Well, you were right. You were right, Marianne, and the GWGW folks think his comeback story could be big. Apparently Regina is also a fan of his."

"A Davonte Gold fan? Really?"

"She thinks that getting the student perspective, from someone with market potential but limited writing experience, someone like Davonte, will help us understand something about where the school needs to grow."

"Okay," said Marianne. She was glad, at least, that Eric wasn't going to dinner alone with Regina.

"Listen to that," he said, cocking his head toward the unlockable door. From across campus came the sound of applause, beginning as a faint patter, then growing stronger, like a rainstorm.

The next afternoon, while the students took an "inspiration-gathering" field trip to the Ringling Museum (the tall, air-conditioned bus was hastily chartered by their friends at GWGW), Marianne met with Tom, Eric, and Lorraine to go over some of the charts and graphs Regina sent her. Marianne hoped that Tom and Lorraine might express their concerns to Eric, but they were less resistant than she had imagined, dutifully reading the numbers and charts projected onto the wall. Tom even whistled appreciatively at some of the sales figures.

"I didn't know *anyone* was selling that much these days," he said. "What did you say that book was about?"

"It's a young adult choose-your-own-adventure series," Marianne said.

"Young adult choose-your-own-adventure," Tom repeated slowly.

"It was in the news a lot?" Eric suggested. "You really never heard of it?"

"I hate the news," Tom said vehemently. Lorraine shrugged.

"Well, that's one thing GWGW is suggesting," said Marianne, clicking through to another PowerPoint slide. "Awareness of current events, current trends, can make something more likely to catch an editor's eye, though I don't know if it does anything for a book's longevity. GWGW thinks they can also help us choose our next writers more carefully, so that we're looking for people who are already producing work that is likely to be successful. For example, young adult and middle grade fiction—it's a huge market right now."

"Middle grade," Lorraine mused. They looked at her expectantly, but she did not continue.

"Like Harry Potter," Eric said. Lorraine looked confused but unperturbed by her confusion.

"I just don't like the look of that cross," Tom said, shaking his head at the GWGW logo at the bottom corner of the screen. "It creeps me out, that big shadow."

Marianne nodded encouragingly. "You are resistant to some of their corporate imagery. What about you, Lorraine?"

"A curriculum would be helpful, on the other hand," Tom continued. "I mean, it's hard to know what to do with some of the submissions. I'll be honest with you; I've got a lot of criers in my group. I don't think photocopying Norman Mailer is gonna do much to turn that around."

"I'm meeting Regina Somers for dinner tonight," Eric said. "I can talk to her about our curricular needs."

"Was she the hot one on the tour yesterday?" Tom asked. "With the updo and the fuck-me heels?"

Eric reddened. "She's one of the specialists."

The hot one? The fuck-me heels? Marianne thought, looking down at her flip-flops and chipped blue pedicure. "Davonte's going too," she said.

"Davonte Gold?" Tom said. "Freaky."

"My workshop was going quite well, I thought," Lorraine said finally, turning over the GWGW water bottle Marianne gave her as if calculating exactly how much vodka-and-cranberry it could store. "We started from scratch and have been accessing primal memories. Productive work, in writing and in life. But of course I agree with Thomas that I want my students to be successful in whatever . . . *arenas* seem most compelling to them. They are not readers of *Poetry* magazine. They are not *readers*."

"Yeah," said Tom. "I agree with Lorena. At first I thought, 'What if this gets out and people think I was working for right-wingers? How will this affect my teaching career?' But then I realized, how will this get out? And also, who am I kidding?"

"Okay then," Marianne said, a bit hesitantly. She was surprised by their compliance, by how easily they gave up. Then she recognized the conversation. It was the same one actual teachers of actual students had everywhere, from university composition programs to elementary school faculty lounges. Let's make the best of what we have to work with, the line went. Also: this isn't my fault, it was going on long before I got here. And finally: if we can't solve the problems we set out to solve, can't we at least be relevant? She'd once heard a sixth-grade teacher explain, in exasperation, that fractions had *many* uses. Drug dealers needed to understand fractions, after all . . .

"And bonuses," Lorraine said. "Those are very motivating."

Marianne turned off the projector. "I guess that ends our meeting."

She wanted to talk to Eric again, but Tom had already overtaken him. "Did I ever tell you about covering the whole Jim and Tammy Faye Bakker scandal back in the eighties, the women I met at PTL? Their supporters? Their *secretaries*?" He lowered his voice obscenely. "I mean, I was drowning in it."

Marianne excused herself, saying she had to speak to the caterers. She walked purposefully across campus to the dining hall, which was never locked. It was empty, as she knew it would be—there was no lunch service because of the field trip, and the caterers weren't due until late afternoon. The hall's big windows faced west, so this time of day, late morning, the whole place was church-dim and shadowed, even though outside it was bright and sunny, eighty degrees. Marianne was glad she'd decided to keep the room's wood paneling and Frances's kitschy gilt-framed prints of manatees and alligators and herons. Though she'd complained to Eric about living in a motel, there were times when she was filled with the deepest kind of affection for this place, like fondness for the face of a homely child or an ungainly animal.

Near the door, on a collapsible metal table, someone had left the things they must have borrowed for last night's reading's refreshments: a white tablecloth, unevenly folded, and cups and bowls they'd washed and stacked. A cut-glass punch bowl and a thin metal ladle. Marianne picked up the lumpy tablecloth and shook it out, then folded it, bringing the corners precisely together, then together again, into a neat square. After their mother died, her father had left all the laundry, especially the sheets and towels, crumpled in baskets near the washer and dryer until he needed them, and when Marianne was home she ironed and folded them, set the linen closet back to rights.

She was good at repetitive, precise tasks, and she could fold anything, even a fitted sheet, as smoothly as paper. It was something her mother taught her—if you're going to have a lot of stuff, you have to learn how to put it away properly. The family linen closet was given over to Marianne to arrange when she was only eight or nine, and Marianne announced that she'd like to be a professional organizer. This was before such a job existed, or was widely known. "You mean a maid?" her mother laughed.

Now she supposed that was only the first in a long line of inappropriate ambitions that practical reality revealed to be less desirable than she'd imagined. A professional organizer was really a maid. A poet was actually just a teacher of other poets. Director of an inspirational writing program? Try coconspirator with modern-day Jims and Tammy Fayes.

Marianne took out her phone and typed a hasty message.

To: RuthandDarrylBoyette@healingwaters.org
From: MarianneStuart@gmail.com
Subject: Question for RUTH

Hey, did those GWGW people actually help you with fund-raising? Did it all work out?

Immediately, the phone pinged.

To: MarianneStuart@gmail.com
From: RuthandDarrylBoyette@healingwaters.org
Subject: Re: Question for RUTH

Thank you for your email! Darryl and Ruth Boyette are on retreat with Healing Waters Baptist Church, with limited access to email. Please be patient, and they'll get back to you soon. Peace and blessings, R&D

9

Davonte would have preferred to stay back at the Ranch, but he boarded the bus with everybody else, all the racists and crybabies and rich old ladies he'd been avoiding at meals. He was sure that his time here, limited as it was, would be better spent exercising or working on his manuscript—on Eric's advice, he'd started telling the story into his digital voice recorder—or checking in with his life coach. He didn't care much for museums, the hushed snootiness of them, the way you were expected to file through, looking at one painting, then the next, reading from a tiny plaque on the wall and nodding your head as if the dates and names meant something to you. And a circus museum sounded even worse. Davonte hated clowns, acrobats, tall men. Painted faces spoke to him of hidden agendas, deviance. Cirque du Soleil, which his agent made him see in Vegas, had given him weeks of nightmares.

"No, trust me, you'll love it," Marianne told him at breakfast, when he said he thought the trip was optional. That was the other thing—he hated to have his plans changed, and there was also the matter, arranged yesterday, of some kind of special dinner tonight. "It won't be all day," she promised. "I think you'll love it." It was true that Marianne had been good to him so far, accommodating. The special dinner suggested that finally, they saw him for the talent he was, though he'd been warned about these kinds of—what did Coach call them?—*self-aggrandizing* thoughts. Plus she seemed a little stressed, and Davonte figured it wouldn't cost him much to go along with the group. That's what Coach was teaching him to do, measure things in terms of costs and benefits, which basically meant pretending things weren't all about you, just so you could get what you want. He spends a morning ambling around a museum? In return, he gets more attention for his admittedly significant needs.

So here he was, sitting next to a plump woman who looked happy to be going anywhere. She had a little girl's haircut and wore a T-shirt and green shorts that showed her pale, veiny legs. As soon as the bus got moving she was digging through her purse for a book of poems, all underlined and highlighted and marked with ragged sticky notes. Reading in moving vehicles made Davonte so sick he couldn't stand the sight of anyone else reading, and he considered how to ask her to please put the book away.

She didn't read long before she wanted to talk. "The house—the Ca' d'Zan Mansion," she pronounced the name slowly. "I've heard it's incredible. But I think our tickets are just for the museum. Too bad. My name is Janine, I think I heard you read last night? From a memoir?" She took out a tin of candies from her purse and offered one.

"Donald Goldston," he said, shaking her hand and refusing the candy. If he ate so much as a mint he had to write it down and look up the calories later. Too much trouble. "It was fiction, actually. A novel."

"Sorry. It must have seemed very realistic to me."

Davonte got that response often enough—a resistance to fiction, like it might be the same as lying—that he sometimes thought he might be better off writing a memoir. But the plot of his book, about a dissolute R&B singer who turns his back on old ways and returns to the stage reformed, and newly adored, was still in process, as far as real life went. That was what was exciting about the book, he'd told Coach: the chance to envision life as it should be. As it *could* be, Coach reminded him. It made him want to sit down and write every word—almost.

He wondered if this woman knew who he was, but guessed against it. If she did, she probably would have taken another seat. He waited for her to say something about his reading—he'd felt compelled to read from one of his favorite scenes, when Damian is tempted by a groupie who is a dead ringer for a young Vivica Fox—but she didn't mention it again.

"I think it's good to shake things up," she said cheerfully. "You know, to experience another art form. Paintings, sculptures. Maybe it'll help our work. I think that's the idea."

"You write about paintings?"

"No," she admitted. "But I do write about God, our relationship to Him. I think that a lot of the paintings are very old, religious paintings."

"Not circus art?"

"I think there's a wing devoted to that, but it's mostly baroque paintings that they collected. European art." She pointed at her copy of the pamphlet Davonte had already lost, back at the Ranch.

"I'll skip the circus art," he said. "But I don't get that—the idea that just because you're writing, you should be looking at paintings or sculpture or whatever. My mother thought that. Used to drag me around to art museums, got to where I dreaded Saturdays."

"She wanted you to be cultured," said the woman.

"She read this book about raising gifted children. She checked it out from the library and carried it around so everybody could see what she was going through, having to raise someone gifted. Sometimes people acted like because she had only one child, her life was easier. The book told her that if you were gifted in one area, you were likely to have gifts in another. So she had me taking piano, going to museums, stuff like that."

"That's what mothers do," she said. "My mother didn't, of course—I don't think it would have occurred to her, but I've tried to encourage my daughters in all of their gifts. Your mother saw your writing talent when you were a child?"

"Not writing," he said. "Singing. I used to sing in church. Solos, even, before I was in kindergarten."

"So the book was true! Singing and writing, all for God. That's wonderful."

Davonte wasn't sure writing was, in fact, among his talents—unlike making music, it went very slowly and didn't usually turn out the way he'd imagined it. But he had ideas, and that was the important part, wasn't it?

They pulled up in front of a great house. Disembarking, he was separated from the talkative woman, but that was okay. He had a strange shameful feeling, new to him but frequent, since he'd come to the Ranch, that he had said too much. Why had he told a stranger about those museum visits with his mother? It was none of her business. He edged away from the rest of his classmates in line.

• • •

They met up again in one of the galleries. By then Davonte was impressed with John Ringling—the museum was like a big empty house, with polished wood floors and plush carpets and gold wallpaper and painting after enormous painting. Passing through the open terraces between galleries, you could see elaborate gardens, marble sculptures, a distant, turreted building that must have been the mansion. No tents or clowns or funhouse mirrors.

The woman was sitting on a narrow bench before a large painting of the Christ Child. Mary was holding back a sheet to show him off, and he was being admired by a cherub and a couple of old men. His skin, and Mary's skin, glowed white as the moon.

Janine—that was her name—was bent over a notebook, furiously scribbling, when suddenly she began gasping and heaving. Afraid she might be crying or struck by some sort of religious feeling, Davonte started edging toward the next room, but then she stood and pointed to her throat. She was choking.

Shit, he thought. He looked for someone to help, but the adjacent galleries were empty. Her face was turning purplish-blue.

He stood behind her and whacked her back, but she continued heaving and gasping in a terrible, airless way. He conjured an image from a poster he'd seen, positioned himself behind her, and wrapped his arms around her waist, just below her ribs. He clasped one hand over his other fist and thrust upward once, twice, and she was suddenly sputtering and wheezing, her hands on her knees.

"Are you okay?"

"Candy," she gasped. Her eyes were shining with tears, and she still looked terrified. Her voice was scratchy and raw. "I was sucking on a candy, and it went down the wrong way. If you hadn't been here—"

"Everything all right?" A guard came in, worriedly checking the big paintings but not Janine, who was still gasping. The guard was short and slow, an older woman. Davonte thought she probably wouldn't have been able to help, even if he'd called her.

"I'm okay. This man did the Heimlich on me." Janine put a hand on Davonte's arm and squeezed. "He saved my life."

A small crowd was forming and the guard retrieved a butterscotch candy from the corner of the painting, where it had landed and stuck at Jesus's pale, curled feet. "Why we don't allow food in here," she said, frowning as she handed it over in a tissue. Janine accepted the candy as if it were a relic or work of art, some sacred or holy thing.

"I almost died," she kept saying, and for the rest of the tour, Davonte kept overhearing her tell and retell the story. He wondered if he could work it into his book somehow—except in his book the threat should be more dramatic than a butterscotch. Maybe Damian saves someone from drowning? Or rescues her from a fire? Or pulls her from a wreck? A Halle Berry type, he thought. She was a terrible driver.

"You are meant for big things," his mother used to say to him, on the way to piano lessons or the ballet—she even took him to the ballet! She would look at him as she said it, but with a stern expression, as if to say: Don't mess it up, son. Giftedness, in her world, was the same as a limp or a bad eye or some other affliction—something that had nothing to do with you. It was how you dealt with it that showed who you were.

10

Eric called his brother while he got ready for dinner, shaking out his rumpled button-downs one by one and hanging them in the shower. He didn't have a tie, or even an iron. He should have taken a polo shirt while he had the chance.

"I just want to make sure, Mark, that the expectations are clear," Eric said, when his brother finally answered. He set the phone on the vanity while he got out shaving soap and his badger brush and a razor and filled the sink; he could at least be clean-shaven. "The deal we're entering into—Frances is still going to be the majority owner of the school, right?"

"Frances has never been an owner of the school, per se. She owns something better." Mark's voice, echoing off the bathroom walls, sounded distant and tinny; he was probably doing something else too.

"Which is what?"

"A significant equity interest in the offshore LLC that now owns the hotel property, and that we believe will soon be party to a very lucrative ten-year commercial lease with the school as sole tenant."

"Mark. *Who owns the school at this point*? At least tell me you still own it."

"We have something better: lucrative consulting contracts with a separate offshore LLC I set up to manage the school's intellectual property assets, which it's leasing back from another offshore LLC, giving us a massive tax advantage for a for-profit institution. I've already entered into mine, and soon you'll have one too. The lawyers are drawing it up."

"Who owns the school, Mark?" Eric's razor wasn't sharp enough; he rinsed it in the sink.

"The school isn't one thing, and it never was. There's a parcel of real estate. There are tables, chairs, a stack of smartphones, a couple of tablets. And the intellectual property: the curriculum, the marketing data, but more importantly, the trademarks, the overall concept, the accrued goodwill, the word of mouth, the *brand*. That's the important thing. We still control that. Our contracts say so. And the last major asset is the accounts payable: our contracts with the students."

"And who owns those?" Eric kept his voice calm, low: it was necessary for the close work of dragging a blade across your skin.

"A consortium of investors, mostly in the greater New York area. I'm not sure I'm at liberty to say more than that. But if you heard their names, you'd probably recognize—"

"Jesus Christ." He nicked himself just below his right nostril.

"Not him."

A watery droplet of blood ran over Eric's upper lip and into his mouth. It tasted like soap.

"So as soon as you could, Mark, without explaining it to us, you sold the school to the Illuminati. To a bunch of snake-people." He leaned in closer to the mirror, trying not to cut himself under his other nostril.

"You don't *want* to own companies like these. You want to be a vendor. You want to be a creditor. You consult: you agree to give them whatever bright ideas you have and you get paid for them on long-term contracts. Or you're their landlord. Better yet, both. If you own equity, stock, whatever, when the whole thing goes belly-up, the value of what you own evaporates. If you're a creditor, you at least get to participate in the bankruptcy."

"*When* the whole thing goes belly-up?"

"You always have to anticipate failure. For-profit education is a volatile sector of the economy. Fads come and go. You have to expect there will be economic downturns, government investi—anyway, things happen."

"Goddamnit, Mark, are we breaking the law?" Another nick.

"Education laws, lending laws, they change all the time."

"Of course," Eric groaned. "And so do tax laws . . . probably campaign finance laws . . ."

"You can break the law without *knowing* it, Eric. Most educational institutions do at one time or another, with no way to predict how much it's going to cost, and no way to stop the bleeding. Tuition hikes are unpopular. Even if the balance sheet is in the red for a decade, they just have to . . . keep educating people."

"Whereas the moment our school starts losing money, it can fold up like a Halloween store on the first of November. Nobody ever finds out who the investors were, Marianne and I can slip away in the night, and everyone can pretend the place never existed. Everyone except the students who paid thousands of dollars toward a certificate—not even a degree, a certificate!—that will never be issued, unless the laser printer happens to still have some ink in the drum on our last day."

"That's not going to happen, bro. Your school—our school—is going to succeed! And even if it doesn't, our students are positive-minded, resilient, optimistic people. With generally good credit."

"*Our* students! We don't have students. We don't actually *have* anything—it's all in your snake-people's hands. GWGW has a sack of hamsters. That's it."

Mark didn't reply.

"And that's why people like you are so eager to sell things to people like them. You see them as easy marks. To you they're a bunch of suckers."

"Eric, listen to me," Mark said evenly. "They *are* a bunch of suckers."

"I know," Eric sighed. "I know."

"I mean, there are studies on it."

"At least now I understand what they teach you in business school. How to use studies to find suckers." He splashed his face with cold water, closed his eyes. Marianne had warned him, hadn't she? But this was beyond the limits of her considerable paranoia. How would he explain it?

He looked in the mirror. His cheeks and chin were speckled with blood.

"Look, I have to take this other call," Mark said. "Let's do more on this another time."

A hero, Regina called Davonte at dinner, beaming at him across the basket of rolls the waiter had been asked not to bring. She wore her hair down, in loose and shining waves she tucked behind one ear, and had on a dress that managed to be modest and snug at the same time. She wore simple pearl earrings, the same high, glossy pumps she'd worn on the tour. Eric wished *he* had saved someone today. He wished he had on a tie. He wished most of all that he'd never talked to Mark.

"I knew there was something about you," Regina said. "When we stopped by Eric's classroom and you were so passionately engaged in discussion."

Davonte shredded his roll into fine crumbs, making a mess of his plate and the tablecloth. He was clearly uncomfortable talking about the rescue, which had been widely discussed around campus. Louis, the one-world-government novelist, had even given Davonte a gruff handshake.

"She probably would have been okay," Davonte said. "The candy probably would have melted in her throat. Butterscotch is kind of soft."

"Some butterscotch is hard!" Regina insisted. "We are lucky to have you as a member of the GWGW community. In more ways than one! I understand from Eric that you are a talented novelist."

Eric had said no such thing.

"Yeah," said Davonte. "I'm working on a book."

"That is wonderful," said Regina. "Novels have the best sales potential."

"That's what I heard," he said. "That's what I was thinking when I decided to go with a novel. I always had a good imagination."

"They don't always reach their potential, of course," said Regina. She looked at Eric, then looked away, as if embarrassed by his lack of success. He grabbed one of the last rolls before Davonte could mangle it, and stuffed it in his mouth. It was consolingly delicious—rich with butter and yeast, warm from the oven. He signaled the waiter for another basket.

"We think the inspirational market—that's a little broader than Christian, though I know you have a Christian background, Davonte—is taking off. Is it Donald? Or Davonte? I want to use the name you prefer."

"Davonte is fine," he said. "I go by Donald in an academic setting."

Regina nodded. "Donald is your Christian name."

"It's the name my mother gave me."

"Though your book will probably sell better with the name Davonte Gold attached," she said. He agreed. They talked about all the various ways Davonte's unwritten book could sell and sell. On *Oprah* and *Dr. Phil*. On Amazon and the *Today* show. To teens and moms and old ladies. To blacks and whites and Latinos—there was a marketing angle for everyone. Eric would have loved to be on *Dr. Phil* or the *Today* show, but the most he'd done, in terms of TV, was a brief segment on a public-access program in Charlotte. There hadn't even been hair and makeup.

Eric carefully swallowed the big gob of bread he'd been chewing—he didn't want to necessitate the Heimlich himself—and leaned forward. "So how are you doing," he said, "in terms of word length?"

"I'm keeping the long words to a minimum," said Davonte. "Like Regina said, this is a book for everyone."

Regina smiled warmly, forgivingly. Silly Eric, her smile said. Trying to trip up an international star. "And how long is the book? The word count?"

"Oh," he said. The waiter arrived with their plates—pasta for Eric and Regina, poached fish for Davonte. He frowned at his food like it wasn't what he ordered. "I haven't counted them. But not that many, to be honest with you. It's hard, writing a novel."

"It is," agreed Eric, the only bona fide novelist at the table. A novelist, and a teacher! Not a businessman, after all. "Has using the digital voice recorder helped?"

"A little."

"What about what I said in class—writing to the heat?"

"What's that?" Regina asked.

Eric turned to her, glad for a chance to play the expert, even if it wasn't a suggestion he personally believed in. He was often giving advice, in his classes, that he didn't use himself—but that didn't mean it wasn't useful to his students. Hadn't he had glowing reviews from his students in Dubai? Hadn't they wanted him to stay another term? "Basically, if you're stuck, you write the more exciting parts—the climax, or just the intense scenes of conflict—first. Then you fill in the rest later. It can be motivating for new writers."

"I tried that, but I kept writing the temptation scenes, because that was the part I connect with the most with this character." Davonte put his hand over his heart. "I think Damian has got too many women in his life now. Honestly, I'm not sure I'm a good novelist on my own. When my life coach found this opportunity, he kind of led me to believe I'd get some help."

"The classes aren't helpful?" Regina asked. She pushed her plate aside and took out a tablet, wiped her hands on her napkin, and began typing.

"A ghostwriter," he explained. "I was hoping to find a ghostwriter. Like

Jay-Z. You know he didn't write that book himself. Three hundred and fifty pages? I don't fucking think so. Excuse me, *I don't think so.* I mean, I would supply the ideas—I've got the ideas—but someone else would do the rest."

Regina nodded. Eric wondered how she'd handle the dispiriting news that a novel wasn't the same thing as a celebrity tell-all, and Davonte would have to write it himself—just like Joyce, like Hemingway, like Terry McMillan. Like Eric.

"That's a marvelous idea," said Regina. She turned to Eric. "Don't you think?"

"Um," said Eric, setting down his fork. "No?"

"At GWGW, we believe that our students need to be given the tools to access success—on their terms. It's one of our founding philosophies," she said, tapping a screen on her tablet and holding it up for Eric and Davonte to see. "That's one of the things we like so well about the Ranch. You are built to honor the students' needs for a flexible schedule."

"The low-residency model is pretty well established, actually," said Eric.

"But combined with your focus on faith—that's what makes the school unique. Plus a flexible schedule and availability to the students' needs. I think what Davonte needs is someone to help him, to get him started. Would that be useful to you, Davonte?"

"Definitely," he said. "It would also be great if the Ranch had a gym."

Regina typed that into her tablet, too. "I just know that with my marketing contacts, and Eric's talent, we can help you make a *big* splash in the publishing world."

"Have you read my book?" Eric asked suddenly. He couldn't help it— it was a question that seemed to ask itself.

"Have I read *Copper Creek*?" Regina hefted her formidable handbag from the floor and plucked a copy—hardcover—from the side pocket. It was like a glimpse of lacy bra, a flash of panties. He was helpless. She shyly slid his novel toward him. "I was hoping to get your autograph."

In her room, Marianne waited for the sound of Eric's door opening and closing, and kept peeking through her window to see lamplight in his window. But his window was dark when she peeked, and dark when she peeked again, five minutes later. This was the time of day when Marianne was supposed to be writing poems; her black notebook was waiting on the bureau. She had not opened it in days; her only recent writing, other than work emails and memos, had been unreturned texts and emails to Ruth.

She wanted to talk to him about his date—that's what she would call it, teasingly—with the prim, capitalist Regina. Where had they gone, and what had they talked about? Had Davonte stuck to his diet? No carbs, she'd specified, though Regina had invited them to an Italian place. No carbs and no dessert. Nothing fried. Eric had seemed preoccupied, changing his shirt twice until he finally decided on a pale blue button-down, khaki pants, and the blazer he'd let her borrow on the beach. You look like your brother, she'd said, reaching to brush a scrap of bloody tissue from his face. He'd looked at her like she'd slapped him.

She'd make it up to him, when he got back. She would walk right across the courtyard and knock on his door; she'd lounge across one of the beds in Eric's room and ask him to tell her about his whole day—the afternoon workshop, the dinner, the drive back from the restaurant with Davonte. She wouldn't say, as she often did, hurry up, get on with it. She'd *listen*.

Marianne put on her favorite dress, wispy silk in flattering peacock blue, and dangling silver earrings. She put up her hair the same way Regina wore hers, but it wouldn't stay, so she took it down again, dabbed on lip gloss and powder. On the beach trip, with Ruth, they'd found a 1970s marriage guide called *Loving Him Best*, and they'd cracked each other up with the sexist advice, taking turns reading to each other in serious voices. "Look as attractive as possible when he comes home," Ruth intoned. "What if this is the best I can do?" Marianne had said, clutching her beach-frazzled locks in mock despair. "What if this is all I've got?" And Ruth had howled.

She checked his window again. Still dark, though they'd left hours ago. He must have gone to the office, she decided, where he was probably intently reading terrible manuscripts, making good suggestions that their authors would not heed. Marianne put on a pair of heels, low sandals, and walked across the garden. She could see the light inside, the door propped open.

But it was Tom she found, not Eric, standing helplessly next to the copier. All its doors were opened, and there was a burning smell in the room.

"Mary-Anne," he said. "Thank God."

In her heels and her dress, she knelt beside the copier, pulling levers and turning knobs, extracting torn bits of paper that smeared her fingers with ink. He backed away, not even bothering to pay attention to how to do it. Finally the copier made the sighing noise that indicated you could try again.

"Okay," she said. "All yours. Just try one at a time. Have you seen Eric?"

"Not my day to watch him," Tom said. He set his book on the glass and pressed the copy button without closing the lid, though she'd warned him that it wasted ink and made the machine more likely to jam. Turning his face from the copier's green flash, he gave her the once-over. "Hey, you look really nice. You and Eric going somewhere?"

Marianne looked down at her wrinkled, toner-smeared dress. "No, I guess not."

Tom turned the page in his book, then set it down on the glass again. "I forgot, he's out with that Republican babe, right?"

"And Davonte. It's a business meeting," said Marianne. "Why would you be into a Republican, Tom? It doesn't seem like your thing."

He shrugged. "People have a lot of things. Sometimes you want to be with a woman you hate. Sometimes you want to feel *bad*. Guilty. It's some kind of potent Oedipal shit."

"Eric isn't like that."

"Yeah, probably not." The copier jammed again. "Forget it. I'll deal with this in the morning."

"Great," she said, yanking the paper drawer open again. "*You'll* deal with it. Thanks a lot, Tom."

She looked behind her and saw that Tom was already gone, and she was alone. She sank down to the grubby tiled floor and leaned against the exhausted copier, which should have been leaching chemicals into a landfill by now. It occurred to her to go by Janine's room—it was only ten o'clock—and see if she wanted to take a walk.

She looked up her room number, then went back to her own room and changed into her only pair of shorts and a sweatshirt. She scuffed on her comfortable flip-flops and took out her heavy earrings.

Janine's light was off—she was probably already asleep, after Skyping with her family and writing three poems and saying her prayers. Marianne wondered if she'd prayed for her—what would she have prayed for? It was not a thing you could ask someone, the way you hinted around at Christmas or birthday presents. But she could guess at what it would be: for Marianne to find peace, comfort, solace. For her school to thrive. She was probably not praying for anything as mundane and insubstantial as Marianne's love life.

11

"Ghostwriter?" Marianne coughed at breakfast, after Eric told her about his new assignment. He motioned for her to lower her voice, though the dining hall was full and lively. She'd slept badly and was on her second cup of watery Ranch coffee, which left her both jittery and distant. She spotted Janine with two other women at her favorite spot by the big, gulf-facing window, and waved, then turned back to Eric and hissed, "How is that even ethical? Or possible?"

"I was skeptical too," he said, calmly spearing the pale cantaloupe and watery melon left on his plate. "I was resistant. But Regina pointed out, for someone like me, this is really a no-brainer."

"A no-brainer meaning an obvious decision?" she asked. "Or like an idea to which you have devoted very little brain power?"

"Look, Davonte is obviously a big star," Eric explained. "His work is going to sell, he just has a problem with getting the words on the page. If I sign on to help, I can get a substantial cut, Davonte's work actually gets finished in a quality way, and the school gets some major attention, too. It's win-win-win." He ticked the wins across his fingers.

"But you're his *teacher*. You're supposed to be teaching him how to write. How is that going to look, with your name on the cover?"

Eric hushed her again, though Davonte was nowhere to be seen. He usually skipped breakfast so he could go running: in that sense, at least, he had some discipline. "My name won't be on the cover. I'll be thanked, the Ranch will be thanked, you'll be thanked—"

"Thank you Marianne, for microwaving my Lean Cuisines. . . ."

"It's good business, Marianne. It makes sense. I talked to Mark, and he thinks so, too. After the meeting last night, Davonte took a cab home and I stuck around with Regina. She ran all these numbers, and she determined that he had the best shot, of any of our students, to make it big."

So that's where he was when she'd looked for him—and not even with Davonte along. At least, Marianne thought, it was a business meeting. Marianne leaned close to Eric. "Why does she care how well our students do? Didn't you say we'd be better off looking at their ability to pay the bills and not even worry about writing talent?"

Eric shook his head. "That isn't what I said. But they're interested because Davonte's success will help us grow the school. It'll help us get more applications, it'll justify raising tuition and open up other markets. Look, you should be happy. I told Regina that you were the one who found him, who argued for admitting him. She said you had real foresight."

"I'm so proud."

"She's also booking a photographer to take some pictures."

"Of the students? Don't you need their permission?"

"Yeah, but mostly of Davonte." Eric lowered his voice. "She and Davonte both pointed out our diversity problem. Maybe some photographs that show a more inclusive environment—"

Marianne felt her face reddening. "That doesn't seem like a top priority for GWGW."

Eric shrugged. "It's kind of obvious—the bigger your applicant pool, the more successful you'll be. Plus the readership of popular Christian literature—the readership of Davonte's book, for example—will be highly diverse."

"And what about diversity scholarships? Fellowships? Did she talk about funding those? Or expanding the advertising beyond Southern Baptist church newsletters?"

Eric didn't answer.

"And Davonte's book," she said. "Don't you mean your book? Why is the coffee here so terrible? How is it possible that I founded a whole school and the most important thing to me is substandard?"

"Coffee is the most important thing to you."

"It's up there."

Eric snorted, then got out his manuscripts for the day and thumbed through them. "I don't know what you're so upset about. I'm the one who's got to write this thing."

"What's it like? I mean, the parts you've read?"

"It's like an AA meeting, with pornography. Bragging about misdeeds, then a bunch of pious blathering. But apparently that's a whole genre now. Regina calls it 'romance and redemption.'"

"Regina," said Marianne, downing the rest of her coffee. "So what's her story?"

"Divorced," said Eric absently. "Two kids. Had 'em when she was really young. Very type A. For fun she bakes competitive gingerbread houses. That's her hobby. She's won, like, three national competitions."

Marianne laughed. She pictured Regina with an X-Acto knife and a tube of frosting, elbowing her kids out of the way. "That's intense. Tom thought you might have the hots for her."

"Tom is an old pervert," said Eric. "Who has the hots for you, by the way."

"Wouldn't that be funny? If you wound up with a GWGW executive, and I wound up with *Tom*?"

"Very funny, Marianne." Eric stacked his dishes and stood. That was how it was with him: one minute, laughing and joking, the next minute you'd gone too far.

"Sorry," she said, grabbing his shirtsleeve. "I promise I won't wind up with Tom."

Eric nodded to show that he forgave her, but didn't make any promises himself.

Meanwhile, unaided by GWGW, the workshops took on lives of their own, their strangenesses multiplying like feral cats under a porch. Lorraine began holding her classes in the sculpture garden, so she could smoke, and her students looked fairly happy to be sitting cross-legged and barefoot on the ground, in between Cain and Abel and Adam and Eve, while she barked instructions at them. Tom now began each of his classes with beachfront tai chi or meditative deep breathing to help soothe the anxieties and feelings of his students. Eric had begun running in the afternoons with Davonte, so they could talk about ideas for the novel. A few times Marianne caught him when he returned from these runs, sweaty and breathless and slightly scandalized. You don't want to know, he told her, when she asked what they'd talked about.

The special classes on publishing and marketing were not scheduled until their next session, in August, but each day Marianne received emails from Regina, many of them including animated PowerPoint résumés of speakers they planned to book. The students' complaints, so vigorous at first, had lessened with each passing day. She was not sure if the complainers were getting used to their teachers' methods and quirks, or losing faith in her ability to intercede on their behalf.

As the lines to her office grew shorter, Marianne waited for the inevitable seriousness and buckling down to take over, for the teachers' strong personalities—at least Tom's and Lorraine's—to win out, for people to reevaluate why they had come and what they hoped to accomplish here. But that wasn't how things went down—or, at least, it didn't happen the way she expected. By the end of the first week, the Ranch had clubs, activities, initiatives, all student-organized—more than Marianne could remember from two years at NYU. There was a running and exercise club founded by Davonte, a knitting and prayer circle that met after supper in the dining room, a sunrise prayer and a sunset prayer. Someone drove into Bradenton to buy lawn games—croquet, badminton, bocce—from the Walmart, and there were after-dinner games nightly. There was a discussion group that was taking on the question of smoking in common areas (some thought it should be banned entirely, while other people thought that was infringing on their God-given liberty). There was a group that convened to discuss biblical allusions in contemporary literature, and another group devoted to the answer (not the question, Marianne noticed) of self-publishing. There was a small group that had met to discuss outreach possibilities—maybe conducting literacy workshops at the prison in Tampa. They had another reading on Saturday night, a boisterous event punctuated by *yes*es and *amen*s and foot-stomping, which Marianne watched from the back of the room.

"I can't wait for tomorrow," Janine told her after the reading. She was the founding member of the Tidy Up club and could be counted on to organize the leftovers, wash the dishes, and put away the chairs efficiently and uncomplainingly. Marianne thought it was too bad that Janine hadn't read any of her own work—Manfred had taken forever to read his three poems, and Davonte read a similarly long, if strangely intelligible,

PG-13 section of his novel—but Janine didn't look disappointed to be on cleanup duty as the readers congratulated one another near the podium.

"What's tomorrow?" asked Marianne, dumping uneaten pretzels into the trash.

Janine frowned. "We're not having a service? I mean, I understood that we were all settling in on the first Sunday, but . . ."

"Oh, *church*," said Marianne. "Church, of course."

"I know there are different denominations," said Janine. "But I think it would be better to have everyone together. We could have a folk service, with music. We have the fellowship group, they could lead us in prayer. And Donald is a very talented singer."

"Right," said Marianne, shaking out the tablecloth. How had she failed to consider that these people would want to have church? "Good idea."

"I'll start telling people," said Janine. "I think a nine o'clock service is a good time, don't you?"

Regina, who'd asked to be contacted with daily summaries, agreed that hosting a church service—a celebration of God, she called it—was a wonderful idea, and Eric congratulated Marianne again for her foresight. "I knew you'd be good at this," he said, thumping her back as she typed up a program in the office. Something about him had perked up recently—he wasn't complaining about his students, even about Davonte. His cheerful bustle reminded her of the manic time before they'd gotten engaged, when he was meeting with agents and strategizing about editors and publishers in his free time. Everything was possible, and every menial task was performed in anticipation of a reward. It was like wrapping presents on Christmas Eve or standing in line at an amusement park—there was bound to be a letdown.

The hastily organized service, held on the beach, seemed to satisfy everyone. Marianne counted, and every student was there, squinting from folding chairs sunk crookedly into the sand. Even Tom attended, bowing his head as Patty Connor, the tearful memoirist from his workshop, led the group in a confident and clear-voiced prayer. Davonte sang, unaccompanied, "His Eye Is on the Sparrow" and "Order My Steps," hymns he must have carried with him since childhood. His voice was so pure and strong that Marianne felt a little swell of pride as beachgoers power-walked behind him, stepping into the surf to avoid disrupting the service while craning their necks to see.

It was wonderful, the students agreed when it was over, carrying their chairs back to the dining hall. They had the rest of the day to read and write, and they talked about how inspired they felt, after the service. Davonte gathered up chairs from some of the older women and carried them in a tall stack, and Tom and Patty hugged.

"Amazing," Sophie La Tour said, linking arms with Marianne and walking back with her to the garden. Marianne hadn't seen her since the session began. She wanted to tell Sophie everything—the feelings she was having for Eric, his romance with Regina, the fears she'd developed about their new funders. But she also wanted to seem successful—to feel successful. "You pulled it off."

"We're so happy it's going well," Marianne said, using the pleasant, cunning neutrality she'd picked up from GWGW. "And your sculptures are a hit—people have already asked me where they can get them." That part wasn't exactly true—they'd asked, a little skeptically, where *she'd* gotten them—but she felt she owed something more to Sophie, who'd done the work for free.

"You can give them my card," Sophie said, after inspecting and approving the garden's reverse chronological layout. She made minor adjustments, turning statues slightly, brushing away pollen, snapping branches that obscured vignettes. "Next Sunday, if you want a bigger crowd, I can put up a notice for my guests."

"Next Sunday, they'll be gone."

"Gone!" Sophie whistled appreciatively.

"Back home, to write. They'll work from home with their teachers. Then come back in late August."

"Now it's your time to write," Sophie said. "And they pay you, all this time." She bent to pull a sapling from the mulch.

"My time," Marianne said. "Yep."

"All from tuition? The reno, the teachers, supplies, your salary?" she asked, straightening and pocketing the weed. "Must be expensive, running this place."

"We've got a little help," Marianne said. "Some investors."

"If you ever want to share the info," Sophie said, "I wouldn't mind some reno help."

"Trust me, you wouldn't want these people," Marianne said quickly. "I'm not sure we want them, to tell you the truth. But here we are."

Sophie opened her mouth, as if she might ask another question, then closed it with an appraising frown. "That's okay," she said finally. "You don't want to say anything, I understand. But it wouldn't be hard to figure it out, you know—if I wanted to. Anyway, you had a nice service, your students seem happy. You should be proud."

Marianne thought she detected a faint note of reproach, or maybe suspicion, in Sophie's tone. She knew Sophie wouldn't approve of GWGW or the compromises she'd made, but wasn't it true that things were going well, that the students were leaving their first session glad they'd come, and maybe even eager to return? Of course she was proud! She was reminded of how she felt on the next-to-last day of the school year, when students in her Brooklyn classes had their dance festival on the blacktop playground. None of it was really her doing—she hadn't done the choreography or the costuming—but she was a part of things, a member of the community, bobbing her head in the sunshine and clapping like everyone else.

She moved through the rest of the day in a detached but not unpleasant fog. Everywhere she looked—in the dining hall or the garden, around the pool or by the picnic tables—there were groups of students trying to figure out God's will, endeavoring to make that will manifest. And they were happy! They said good morning and good afternoon, they told Marianne to *have a blessed day*.

They were always communicating—with each other, with God, with their families via text or email. You could watch any one of them, alone at breakfast or walking along the beach, and see her mouth moving in a kind of permanent, ecstatic prayer. Even the ones whose lips were still, you could tell they were engaged in some kind of godly dialogue. And they were always praising each other—at readings, at prayer sessions, at croquet matches. Their whole existence enacted the kind of expression-reception-praise that writers, in Marianne's experience, became addicted to. It was a wonder, Marianne told Eric, that they wanted to write at all.

On the last morning of the session, Marianne set out a buffet of fruit and cold cereal and coffee, but most of it went untouched. Packed into minivans and station wagons and SUVs, picked up by family members or delivered by cab to the airport, they left, bleary-eyed with hangovers from the punch Marianne concocted again, on their last night. They'd had a pool party and an interminable reading, had posed for digital snapshots outside their rooms, beside the pool, in the sculpture garden. Now they were gone, replaced by cleaning crews, by the sound of vacuuming and leaf blowing and edge trimming.

Marianne had work to do. There were so many vendors to pay—the housekeeping service, three different caterers, paper vendors and electricians and landscapers and computer technicians. There were students, also, who paid their bills in monthly installments, and because Marianne had not known any better back when they were accepted, they each had different pay-by dates, which were constantly being shifted or postponed. She propped the door to her office open and kept expecting to see one of them there, standing in the doorway apologetically, about to complain or make some sort of complaining request. It did not seem possible that twelve days had passed so quickly, and yet it also seemed like the first day, when she'd handed over each student's key, was a very long time ago.

Now was supposed to be the time she used to produce new work, the manuscript time she'd bought with every microwaved Lean Cuisine, with every box of tissues. But already applications for the second cohort, who would begin the following winter, made a tall pile on her desk. Regina had placed advertisements on a couple of prominent websites, and Mark emailed to say that they were now the first hit if you googled "Christian creative writing school."

Why wouldn't we be? Marianne had wondered. Wasn't the Ranch the only Christian writing school in existence?

He hadn't answered, but urged her to think of the guidelines Regina sent when she was reviewing applications (one of the new criteria was "telegenic," which Mark assured her was a less stringent bar than "beautiful"; think of weight loss shows, think of Oprah or Ellen, he said, and just like that they'd started asking everyone for photos). They wanted more people—like Davonte—whose projects had media appeal.

Marianne reviewed the new applications alone. "Don't worry, I trust you," Eric said, when she asked his opinion on a comely writer of confusing, postapocalyptic fiction or a handsome, whiny memoirist. She could tell it wasn't that—not trust but a lack of interest.

Eric arrived with the mail, which now came not in a rubber-banded sheaf but in its own corrugated-plastic bin. He set the bin down and took out his phone. "Look—I got two publisher responses to my query for Davonte."

"You're his *agent* now?"

"Davonte wanted to cut out the middleman," Eric said, tapping quickly. "Though mostly all this project is made of is middlemen, to tell the truth."

Marianne wondered how often Eric was in touch with his own publisher. In recent days Marianne had seen him smiling for no apparent reason, and once, walking from class to the dining hall, she'd heard him whistling. Maybe he'd gotten a good idea for the novel he was working on, she told herself. Maybe an encouraging line from his agent had made its way to his in-box. It could not be simply enthusiasm over a hack writing job that was probably unethical.

"They want to see it," he announced. "Both of them."

"Davonte will be pleased," Marianne said, making her voice as neutral as possible. Through an agreement they'd made with his life coach, Davonte was staying at the Ranch indefinitely, exercising, going to bed early, and badmouthing other R&B artists to Eric.

"Everyone's so busy," Marianne commented, after Eric failed to tell her more. "Accomplishing stuff." It was true: in less than two weeks, Tom had cured himself of sleepwalking, and said he felt so well rested that he wanted to extend his stay. Lorraine had learned to swim. Marianne, for her part, had gotten good enough at typing that she could type as she talked, could find (mostly) the correct keys without looking at her keyboard. "You and Davonte and your book together. Davonte looks so *good*—I mean, he looks more like his old self."

"Things *are* pretty good," Eric said. He sat down at the spare computer, which had been set up for student use, and logged in to his email. "I'm very proud of Davonte. He says he lost ten pounds. But none of those things would have happened without you running the show."

"Ha," said Marianne.

"So what are your plans then? For the break? Think you'll make some more headway on 'The Ugly Bear List'?"

She had just learned how to perform a mail merge and was about to send out the first batch of the next session's rejection letters: *Thank you for your interest in the Genesis Inspirational Writing Ranch* . . . "I had this whole plan of things to do while the classes were in session, but it looks like I hardly did any of it," she said. "I had this idea that the classes would just take care of themselves, that I'd have time, if not to write, then to do research." Her notebook entries, which outlined these plans, read like a series of disobeyed commands from a child: Learn one new thing about an animal each day. Learn how to say good-bye in ten languages. Learn the names of some stars. How easy it would have been to learn those things! But she had not learned any of them, had not even tried.

"That sounds great," said Eric. Over his shoulder, she could see a familiar blue-edged screen, with its cluttered, rapidly scrolling newsfeed. Usually checking Facebook only made him dispirited or annoyed, but Marianne saw him scrolling along as contentedly as a schoolgirl.

"Except I didn't do any of it," she told him. "What's wrong with you? Are you *humming*?"

"Me? I don't think so."

"Well, I want to talk to you about some of the new writers I've picked. Tonight—I thought we could maybe go off campus, get dinner somewhere? We could talk about our books too." She shuffled through a pile of menus she'd collected: Thai, Mexican, seafood.

"Sorry," said Eric, shutting down the computer. "I've got plans tonight."

"Come on," Marianne said. "You don't have to spend every waking moment with Davonte, you know."

"It's not with Davonte," he said. He turned back to face her, crossed his arms. "I don't spend every waking moment with him."

"So where are you going, then?"

He shrugged. "I'm having dinner with Regina."

"Again?" Marianne felt an unexpected, sharp pain in her chest; was this the source of his good mood? "Are you having dinner? Or a dinner meeting?"

"Dinner," Eric said. "We're having dinner."

"How did that happen? Never mind, maybe I don't want to know any more," Marianne said. Twenty-five rejection letters today. She hit Print, but the printer remained silent, and an error message popped up on her screen.

Print, print, print. Error, error, error.

"Fine," she said, her back to Eric. "Tell me. *Why* are you going to dinner with her?"

Eric drew a long breath. "It's just," he began, then stopped. "We talked, after the meeting with Davonte, and I don't know, she's just easy to talk to. We've got things in common."

"Like your interest in competitive gingerbread house construction? Fuck," she said, as a final error message froze her screen. She stood up and called to Tom, who was floating in the pool on an enormous gray shark raft someone had bought for the party, "Tom? Is it true that everything comes down to pussy, in the end? Is that what it's all about?"

Tom gave her the thumbs-up sign.

"Davonte might hear you," Eric reminded her. "And that's not what it's all about, thanks a lot. It's not a date or anything."

"What is it, then? What are your shared interests and experiences?" She squatted to open and close the copier's paper drawer.

"Well, we're both divorced. We both have had certain disappointments in life. Regina's ex-husband took the kids, and—"

"Wait, she doesn't even have custody of her own kids? How does *that* happen, Eric? You have to wonder."

Marianne stood and turned back to face her friend. He hadn't shaved yet today and was wearing a western shirt, one of Marianne's favorites, with a fine gold thread woven into the faded plaid. How long had he owned that shirt? She thought it was perhaps something he'd worn on one of their early dates, those long subway rides to Inwood to look at moldy old tapestries, or out to Queens to eat searingly hot Pakistani food. Back then, Eric would go anywhere with her. It was strange how suddenly and how much she wanted to go to him, to touch him, to ruffle his hair and smooth his collar and feel the warmth of his body. She wanted to sit in his lap and smell him: deodorant and shampoo and something else, like fall leaves. But Eric shook his head, looked down at his feet; he had no idea how she felt, or maybe he didn't care. "I didn't expect you to understand, Marianne. It's not easy to talk about that with someone who hasn't been through it."

Marianne blinked. "Sorry I didn't rush into marriage. I didn't realize it would make me a better conversationalist. If I'd only known."

"See?"

"Sorry, go ahead."

"Regina really loves her kids," Eric continued. "It's hard for her to be away from them. Christine and I had just gotten to the point of talking about having kids when, you know."

"When she cheated on you? Eric, you're lucky you didn't have kids. *Lucky.*"

"Marianne, it's hard to explain it to you. Just because you don't ever plan to get married and have a family doesn't mean it's not right for other people. You act like my marriage is something I escaped."

"Who said I didn't want to get married? Or have kids?" she asked, maybe a little shrilly. "I never said that."

"Sorry," Eric said. "I thought that was something you didn't want."

"No, I might want it. One day. With the right person. I definitely might."

"Oh," said Eric. He frowned as if he didn't believe her, as if she'd expressed an interest in going to some strange or remote country, just for the sake of being adventurous or game. And in some ways that was how Marianne felt. Marriage had always been like a trip to Iceland or Slovenia. She wouldn't say she was *never* going, but she wasn't in a hurry to get there before she went to the sunny, fun Mediterranean countries, like Italy or Spain or Greece. But it didn't mean *never.* "In that case."

"What *else* do you talk about? That can't be all."

"Well," Eric said, running one hand through his appealingly scruffy hair. "She's a marketing strategist, and she has ideas for my career."

"Your *career*," Marianne said. "Like, maybe your next book should be choose-your-own-adventure, or—no—maybe you need to write Jesus into the next one. Definitely."

"Ha ha."

"Eric, are you really saying you are going to take career advice from a Christian diploma mill creator? Seriously? Advice about *writing?*"

Eric stood, in a hurt but dignified way, and made for the door. "She's a fan of my work, if you want to know. She had a copy of *Copper Creek*. She's read it. She had ideas for finding other people to read it, studio people, and isn't that the point? Getting other people to read your work?"

Marianne thought. It had been so long since she'd published a poem or even sent out any submissions that she wasn't sure why she'd written them or why she kept writing them. This was something they'd never agreed on—the point and purpose of writing, the end goal—and she'd always assumed it was because for Eric, he might actually make a living from his books. But maybe the difference was bigger than that. "I don't know," she said. But Eric was gone, and through the hedge Marianne could see that Tom was gone, too, leaving the enormous gray shark raft spinning slowly in the pool.

There was little to learn from the manuscripts, each neatly enclosed in a large manila envelope, bearing postmarks from towns in Florida but also Mississippi, Louisiana, Kentucky, Virginia, even California, and promising new variations on crazy or needy. How did she have so many more to read? How was it that time again?

And what did Eric mean when he said he thought she wasn't interested in marriage or a family? Did it not occur to him that maybe she had not met the right person at the right time in her life? That she had things to do first, before she thought of that?

Did he not realize that it had always been her plan, in fact, to marry *him?*

Marianne took a stack of grubby manuscripts to Davonte's room. Somewhere she'd read that distasteful tasks were better accomplished in company. And it was also true, at least in a superficial, gold record, number-one-hit-song way, that Davonte knew something about heartbreak. That was the subject of half the songs on his first album—heartbroken pleas to be taken seriously by the woman he loved. Her favorite song on that album, "Don't It Hurt?," was addressed to a lover after a long break in their relationship, about both people feeling that they had wasted their best years apart.

He did not answer the door to gentle knocking, did not respond to polite calls of "Donald? Hello?" Marianne thought of leaving him be, catching up with him at dinner, but remembered that she had to go out to pick up more frozen dinners for him, and also some new running-shoe laces that were stretchy, but not too stretchy, and not in any girly colors. She pounded harder.

"Davonte! Davonte Gold! Open up!"

Calling him by his stage name was the best way, Marianne had found, to get a response from Davonte. It triggered some kind of Pavlovian response in him, some need to perform and be recognized for that performance. She heard the loud television muted or turned off, the sound of his feet hitting the carpet, footsteps padding to the door, then nothing. Presumably he was peeping at her through the tiny eyehole, deciding whether to let her in or not. Finally the door opened, just a crack. She could smell incense and marijuana.

"What's up?"

"Davonte, I'm in a bad way," Marianne said, holding the manuscripts against her chest. "Please let me in."

He opened the door just wide enough for her to squeeze through. Marianne was surprised by the tidiness of his room—his suitcase stood empty on the luggage rack, his shirts all hung up in the open closet, his shorts and pants clipped neatly behind them. On the vanity, she saw that his toiletries were lined up. The just-muted television showed vigilant meerkats on the lookout for danger.

She flopped on the double bed closest to the bathroom and sink, setting the pages on the nightstand. Both beds had already been made up, even though she knew the maid had not been by today. Davonte told her that his life coach had encouraged him to do things that reminded him of a certain time in his life, before things had gotten so messed up for him. This included making his own bed—his mother would not abide an unmade bed in her house—but not doing his own food or sundries shopping. "You know you're not supposed to smoke in here."

"You can't burn incense?"

"You know what I mean."

"I was about to go for a run. You want to come running with me?"

"Ugh, no," said Marianne. "I only run when something is chasing me."

"You want me to chase you?"

"Even then, I don't run very fast. I want to ask you about something." Marianne drew a deep breath, then exhaled slowly, hoping the room might provide a subtle contact high. "Do you think I am obviously someone who does not want normal, wholesome things?"

Davonte backed slowly toward the door. "I don't really know you that well, Marianne. I can tell you that I am moving more in the direction of normal things myself, and it's a hard road. But running helps, and so does eating a starvation-level diet. It makes you too tired to want those other things, as fine as those other things might be at the time you are having them. Coach says what you need to do is picture yourself after the food binge, after the partying, after intercourse. He says you need to put yourself in that shame place first."

"*No*," said Marianne. "I'm not giving you some kind of sexual signal here. I'm asking if you think it seems like I don't want to get married and have a family."

Davonte sat on the other bed. Marianne hoped he looked slightly disappointed, but it was hard to tell. His tightly braided cornrows gave his face an earnest, youthful look, and it was easy to read whatever emotion you might seek there. "How am I supposed to know if you want that?"

"Eric said he thought I didn't. But he never asked me!"

"I'm sorry, Marianne," Davonte said. "But I just woke up from my siesta. I have no idea what you're talking about." He found the remote and unmuted the television, then turned the sound way down. The British narrator was talking about the way meerkats care for their young. "They're called kittens. I love that," he said. "I want one."

"I thought you wanted a parrot. To keep yourself from cussing."

"Yeah, a meerkat and a green parrot. And a fox. I heard you could tame foxes, keep 'em in a little crate like a dog." He lay back on his neatly arranged pillows, scuffed off his shoes.

"Davonte, can I ask you something?"

"I guess."

"Do you want to get married? Have a family?"

"All things in good time, Marianne," he said, drawing one knee to his chest, then the other, in a deep stretch. "But I think I told you that I don't like you that way, or at least I tried to indicate it."

"Not to *me*, damn it."

"Well, then, yes, I suppose. It's kind of hard to picture at this point in my life," he said, sitting up and gesturing at the room. "In fact, it is *very* hard to picture. I don't think I could take care of a fox right now, as a matter of fact." He lay back again, pillowing his hands behind his head.

"I don't think you could either."

Davonte began doing some kind of ab move, lifting his legs and holding them straight in the air, then lowering them down to the bed. "But because I am a man, and internationally famous, I don't have to worry about it. I'm lucky I'm not already divorced," he said, steadily raising and lowering his legs. "This is called a pike crunch, Marianne. If you're not gonna go jogging, you might as well do some abdominal work."

"My abs are naturally good," said Marianne. "Not like yours used to be, but they're pretty good."

"If your abs are already naturally good," Davonte said, "there's no reason they can't be great. That's what your man Eric says about my book. It's a good story, and because of who I am I can probably publish it, but why not make it great? Why not win an award? That's the same thing as your abs. They could probably be in one of those yogurt commercials for middle-aged white ladies, but why not try for *Sports Illustrated*?"

Marianne lifted her shirt and looked at her pale, reasonably flat stomach. "You think my abs could be in *Sports Illustrated*?"

"I said they could be in a yogurt commercial," said Davonte. He changed his move to one that crisscrossed the legs. "This is called a scissors crunch."

Marianne began scissoring her legs and found that the exercise quickly became difficult. "So, you think it isn't important to worry about getting married right away?"

"Not for me," he said. "I'm a man. But if you want to get married, and you want some kind of regular marriage, with kids and all that, you have to hustle a little."

"What do you mean?"

"How old are you?"

She blushed, then lied: "Thirty-two." She corrected herself: "Thirty-four."

"My mom had me when she was twenty-two. You could be my mom."

"You're not *twelve*, Davonte. No matter how helpless you act." Marianne was still scissoring.

"But I could be." Marianne wondered if he was still high. "Imagine me, a twelve-year-old you have to take to tae kwon do, to school, to soccer practice. You have to feed me macaroni and cheese on a special plate, with a special spoon, and you have to make me do my homework every night. Is that what you want?"

"How is that any different—"

"Every night. Every day. Eighteen years."

Marianne thought about it. Taking care of other people was certainly annoying and time-consuming, as the past two weeks had demonstrated. "Not really."

"See, but it is what our man Eric wants. He already knows he wants it. He's always wanted it. This is a reverse crunch." He began a new move, thrusting his hips toward the ceiling.

"So, you're saying we're not meant to be together anyway."

"I didn't say that. I'm just saying you don't want the same things."

"What about that woman? Regina Somers?"

Davonte whistled, still thrusting. "She's kind of hot, if you like white women."

"Ugh," Marianne said. She could not bring herself to do the new move and instead continued scissoring. "Why does everyone keep saying that? What makes her so hot?"

"Do you really want me to tell you?"

"No," she admitted. "Eric is going on a date with her. I guess you were there for the first sparks. Maybe you can sing at their wedding."

"I don't do weddings, Marianne," Davonte said.

"I always thought *we* were meant to be. Like, when I first met Eric, he was this earnest guy from North Carolina, and we were around all these bullshitters—excuse me—these *privileged writers*, and we were the ones who saw through it."

Davonte went back to crunches. She wasn't sure if he was paying attention, but continued: "Not that I wanted to marry him or anything, not right away."

"Right," Davonte said. He wasn't crunching anymore, but was hugging his knees to his chest. "That would be the normal, wholesome stuff?"

"Maybe I do want those things," Marianne said.

Davonte was sitting up again, lacing up his shoes. "Let me ask you this," he said. "How long do you think you have to decide?"

As if to prove his point, Davonte did not wait for her to answer. The door closed neatly behind him, and Marianne could hear gravel crunching softly as he jogged away, toward the beach.

Marianne got up to follow him, but found that her legs and abdominal muscles were very sore. Next to the dresser, sitting on the floor beside an endless line of fluorescently soled Nike sneakers, she found, as if it were just another mode of transport, a small pipe, a bag of weed, and some rolling papers. On television, the meerkats were still standing at attention, their short arms resting at their sides, and Marianne felt as if they were keeping watch for her as she rolled a joint, somewhat inexpertly, and lit it with a Bic lighter she found in one of his shoes.

She lay down again, toking Davonte Gold's very strong weed, and reached out to feel the surface of the satiny bedspread with her exquisitely sensitive fingertips. It had been quilted in a diamond pattern with a strong thread that looked like fishing line, and Marianne wondered how this bedspread, which was the same as the bedspreads in all the other rooms, had been chosen, and how long ago that was, and how often it had been washed. It was a bedspread that had been made to last a very long time, and she suddenly appreciated its sturdy ugliness. Marianne lay still and concentrated on feeling its deep seams beneath her legs, her back, her shoulders. On the ceiling was a stain that no one had bothered to spackle or paint over. It looked like a bear slumped over a trash can it was eating from. Marianne could see its black bear mouth and black bear nose.

How long *did* she have, if she wanted the things Eric had so rashly and unfairly accused her of not wanting? Two years? Five? Seven—a very, *very* generous seven years? Certainly if she turned forty and continued to live alone in underfurnished apartments or semiabandoned converted motel rooms, she would have a harder time finding someone who would pledge his troth to her. That was a long time from now, and also a short time. It would be here any minute! Marianne thought, and she smoked the joint down to her fingers. How terrible it was, and how soon. She had known men, on the other hand, who amassed very few goods or skills or real estate and nevertheless managed to marry and procreate long after they were forty. Eric could restart his career a half dozen more times, could lose his hair and get paunchy, and someone would still find it feasible to start a life with him.

Let's say she decided tomorrow, forgave Eric for being a man, professed her love to him, married him, moved back with him to Charlotte. Perhaps the school where he'd worked would hire him again, and maybe they'd also hire Marianne. Maybe even the house that Eric had owned and somewhat fixed up would be back on the market, and with their two jobs they could qualify for a mortgage and buy it again. Maybe he still had the mixer she'd given him. Maybe she'd bake him a cake, take walks with him through their leafy neighborhood, wave to the neighbors, get a dog from the pound. She tried to picture the child they would have, after suitable time practicing with the scruffy obedient dog; she pictured a hairless baby dressed in yellow. She would have to give up poetry in order to take care of the baby—at least for a while—but it would reappear in her life in other forms: the poetry of a washer and dryer in the house, the ordinary, honest poetry of garage door openers and chrome mixers and public television. The poetry of bedtimes and bath times and Play-Doh smells, of Mother Goose and *Goodnight Moon*.

But perhaps it was too late already, and her suitability as a partner and mother had already expired, like the planet's chances of surviving global warming. Nothing else to do but sit and wait for the end, stockpile stores of food and ammunition, figure out how to live off the grid. She'd grow her hair longer and grayer, drink gin and tonics that were all gin and no tonic, spend so much time alone that she lost all sense of appropriate party conversation. She'd stop being invited out other than on the holidays, when she would wear the same tatty clothes she wore now, except it would be many years from now. And unless she somehow (soon!) won the Yale Younger Poets prize or another prestigious and unlikely award, she would not even have Lorraine's opportunities, to fly around the country, filling in or teaching in disreputable programs like this one, collecting a steady accumulation of Delta miles.

Her best option—her only option—was here. The Genesis Inspirational Writing Ranch, the world's first and only low-residency Christian writing school, home of Eric, home of Marianne, home of the ugly bear list.

Part
Three

12

In the last year of her mother's life, when Marianne was seventeen and Ruth was five, Theresa Stuart's line changed. She'd given up painting entirely—the smell of linseed oil and turpentine made her nausea worse—and an illustration style that had been exuberant, detailed, sprawling became spare, as if the line itself were conscious of a finite amount of ink or energy. The line was more fluid, but it took up less space. No more cross-hatching or stippling, those skills her Art I and II students applied clumsily to glass bottles and pewter Confederate-themed belt buckles and deceptively hard to draw deer antlers. Instead she set the pen (never now the erasable, impermanent pencil) on smooth paper and did not pick it up again until the small scene was complete. A lamp on an occasional table. A silver teaspoon resting on a napkin. A mason jar on the kitchen counter. It didn't take much, she told her students, to get your point across. Look how a single line becomes something recognizable—a hand, a sleeping cat, a face.

Marianne's father thought Theresa should stop teaching entirely, as it was never, after all, her life's true goal or purpose. But it's hard to reconnect with your true goal and purpose after drifting so far away from it—especially when you have only so much time left, maybe six or eight months, maybe a year. She kept her advanced afternoon class, Art IV, a small group of serious students, mostly girls, which included Marianne, not a talented artist but a talented *something*, Theresa was always reassuring her. She spent mornings in appointments or chemotherapy, but could be home in time to rest, change, and head to the elementary school, where she took lunch to Ruth and sat with her while she ate it.

It was in chemotherapy that she developed the new style of drawing, which began with a one-handed sketch of an IV infusion pole. The first time she had cancer she'd been pregnant, and she hadn't had chemo then—she'd had the cancer cut out. They watched and waited, then the cancer returned, like a stick the doctors didn't realize was boomerang-shaped, and now she knew the IV pole well, knew waiting rooms, pathology reports, the smarting port. She knew recipes for several marijuana-infused baked goods.

It was amazing to her how this fearsome object, a pole holding bags of fluid, had become so familiar, how with a single gesture she could conjure it not only for herself but for anyone. She'd done the sketch with a fresh Rapidograph pen on good cotton paper—everything she did was archival quality now—and sent it, along with a few others, to the cartoon department at the *New Yorker*. To her surprise—she'd sent drawings meant for the magazine's margins and white spaces for years without a single reply—she received an encouraging note in two weeks, which mentioned not the IV pole but three other drawings: a pair of gardening gloves, a vase, a lady's slipper. The editor said he liked the way Theresa's illustrations evoked the carefree quality of summer—it was the summer fiction issue he imagined for her work, a magazine people read on vacation, or thinking of vacation. The iris was especially good—could she do some more summer flowers, maybe in vases?

The lady's slipper was a spring flower, too fragile to pick. It grew in the deep shade of pine forests near her home, its bulbous translucent-pink flower and fat dark leaves close to the sandy, acidic soil. But she could do tall Hamptons-garden irises too. "Look," she showed her afternoon class, gliding her pen across one of the lady's slipper drawings to lengthen its stem. Marianne, who would soon inherit all of the drawings, the fidgety Rapidographs, the letters back and forth with the editor at the *New Yorker*, watched with a deep archival understanding. How a simple line could not only form a recognizable image, it could also transform that thing into something else.

Transformation and understanding, that's what Marianne was thinking about writing to Janine Gray on a hot Tuesday morning in July. They'd developed an email correspondence during the break in classes—Marianne had initiated it, afraid that Lorraine wouldn't keep up with her students, but she found that she looked forward to Janine's emails, which were sincere and searching, and she tried to put her own sincere and searching thoughts into her replies. Somehow they'd gotten on the topic of character in poetry, and how much you could know the mind of another person. *Impossible.* That was what Marianne was thinking about writing to Janine, because it was what she had been thinking: about Eric, who had grown increasingly distant, and about her mother, who was always both distant and present. She wanted to say more than that, something about the way our preoccupations grew and changed, how our perceptions became part of the truth. But she was missing her mother, and so that's what she wrote in her email—how her mother would always be a kind of mystery to her, dying when Marianne was seventeen and *just about* to ask her things, about sex and love and art. Janine was so lucky to have this time with her daughters, who sounded like lovely and smart young women, and they were lucky to have her too—she would not be a mystery they spent the rest of their lives trying to solve.

She pressed Send, and that was when a new email arrived. She clicked on the link:

Middlesex County, Va. Two local ministers, Darryl and Ruth Boyette, are taking their message of love and life on the road this summer. The couple will leave their flock at Healing Waters Baptist Church to join this summer's Tour of Life, appearing with prominent religious leaders and pro-life advocates across the Southeast to raise money for crisis pregnancy centers.

"We want to share a message about the sanctity and beauty of life," said Darryl Boyette, senior minister at Healing Waters. "This is a message of love for teens in trouble. Well, not in trouble. And not just teens. Anyone expecting a baby."

Ruth Boyette, who has served the church in a counseling and ministerial role for two years, is slated to speak at several major events about her own family background. Boyette's mother was counseled to end her pregnancy when it was discovered that she had breast cancer. "I wouldn't be here if my mother hadn't made that sacrifice, if she had listened to the medical establishment instead of her heart," she said.

Darryl Boyette has been senior minister at Healing Waters for two years. Ruth Boyette began attending services as a teen, and joined the ministry in

2010 after her marriage to Darryl. Her late mother, Theresa Stuart, was a beloved art teacher at Eastern High.

"This isn't about politics, it's about education and helping scared people feel less alone," Ruth said. "Everyone in my family works in education, in one way or another, so it makes sense that I would be an educator too. This is my way of giving back, helping mothers, helping children."

Ruth Boyette's father, Howard Stuart, teaches ethics and philosophy at Rappahannock Community College. Her sister, Marianne Stuart, recently founded the country's first low-residency Christian writing school, near Sarasota, Florida. The Tour of Life is funded by a grant from God's World God's Word, a national faith-based organization involved in education and outreach, and will take the Boyettes to a number of churches and "educational institutions" like her sister's newly founded school. In the Boyettes' absence Healing Waters will be helmed by Associate Pastor Charles Walker, though Darryl and Ruth will have weekly videoconference sessions with congregants throughout their three-week trip. They are expected to return to church in August.

Most articles about Ruth and her church—a BBQ fund-raiser, a homecoming reunion, a new twist on vacation Bible school (VBS All Summer Long!)—were in the free local tabloid, print-only and clipped and mailed to Marianne by their dad, usually without comment. But this one, accompanied by a photograph of Ruth, appeared in a larger, regional paper. Though it was in a section called Faith Notes, it was not written in the gossipy, suspense-driven style the local rag favored (*Guess who is going on a Tour of Life? Have you ever heard of or been on a Tour of Life?*). It was available online and had popped up in Marianne's Google Alerts, set to notify her when any mentions of Marianne Stuart, Eric Osborne, Genesis Inspirational Writing Ranch, or Davonte Gold appeared. So far there'd been dispiritingly little traffic, but this wasn't what she had in mind—her sister putting her own maudlin misunderstanding of their family's history, of Marianne's mother, in front of everyone, or at least the readers of Faith Notes.

Heart pounding, she called Howard, who answered on the third ring.

"Dad! The article—did you see it?"

"Marianne?"

It had always been exasperating to have to announce herself to her own father. "Yes! It's Marianne. Check your email—I just forwarded you this awful article about Ruth's Tour of Life."

"I know about it. I'm picking up the mail for your sister and Darryl while they're gone."

"They're in the paper," Marianne said. "The *Tidewater Review*. Ruth is going to talk about Mom. At antiabortion rallies. At my 'educational institution'—why is that in quotes? Do they think it's not a real school? Dad, did she tell you she was coming here? Did you know that she thinks this?"

"I don't have the full itinerary," Howard said. "Frankly, it sounded a little rushed to me. Fly-by-night. But what do I know? I seem to remember that you invited her to visit."

"To *visit*," Marianne said. "Not to come here and talk about abortion. Not to talk about Mom. And not when school is in session."

"Well, maybe you should call her. I can understand that the timing—"

Marianne began to read the article aloud. She paused after reading Ruth's quote about sacrifice and listening to her heart. "Dad, Mom's cancer was stage 1. They couldn't have known it would come back. She listened to the doctors."

"Your mother was always a good listener. And a careful decision maker."

"It wasn't a choice she made," Marianne said. "Between her own life and a fetus. It wasn't like that. How did Ruth get this idea?"

Howard sighed, and was silent for a minute, maybe more. Marianne waited for him to say that he would call Ruth, go see her, set her straight about Theresa. It wasn't Ruth's fault that she didn't understand their mother; Theresa was sick by the time Ruth was in kindergarten. She was gone before Ruth entered first grade.

"Your mother did have choices," Howard said. "She chose the least aggressive treatment for a variety of reasons. You were young, and chemotherapy is dangerous. She was pregnant. The doctors felt comfortable with her choice. But it was a choice."

"But if she had known—"

"Marianne, losing your mother was traumatic. To you. To your sister. To me. We all suffered, all in our own ways, none of us worse than any other."

Marianne, who had been pacing in her hot office, sat down. It was rare to hear Howard talk about her mother. She wanted him to go on. "We all deal with our traumas in different ways. You believe, as you have the right to believe, that your mother did absolutely everything she could to treat her cancer in its first occurrence. If you believed that she didn't, that would be like thinking that she abandoned you, when you needed her most. Because you did need her. I know that.

"But your sister, she had less time with your mother. Maybe because of that she did suffer the most. Your mother didn't go to ballet recitals for her, or swim lessons, or parent-teacher conferences. She didn't host sleepovers or ground her or do any of that—she was gone. So Ruth thinks about what her mother did for her, and thinking about this sacrifice makes her feel cared for. It's something she needs."

"And she needs to tell other people? About Mom? Doesn't it bother you? That she is twisting our personal history for her own political ends? Or for *Darryl's* political ends? How is this not a political act anyway—aren't churches supposed to stay out of politics?"

"My feelings don't come into it," he said. "Your sister is free to do as she likes, or do as she feels she must. Just as you are. How are things at school? How is Eric?"

She pictured her father sitting at a desk, writing his answers in neat print in the margins—he was nearing the end of his engagement with her. One could only expend so much ink on a student whose argumentation was all over the place. In her own teaching Marianne had frequently felt defeated by student essays, and sometimes fantasized about drawing an X through the entire document and writing "start over" at the end, as Lorraine had once done to one of her poems. Her own go-to comment had been "?".

"School is okay," she said. "Eric is fine. We're not in session now, so it's actually kind of great. But we *will be* in session in August. And if Ruth and Darryl show up—"

"As a matter of fact, I don't think your sister plans to go that far south," Howard said. "But you should call her. Ask her about her plans."

"I will *do that*," Marianne said. "Don't think I won't."

After their phone call ended, Marianne resumed furiously pacing her office. Her first real office—the first room with a door and a desk and papers that did not also include the bed where she slept. It was a mess. Fine, she would clean it. She opened the shades and the window and turned the oscillating fan on high. She threw a bunch of papers the fan knocked onto the floor in the recycling bin. She straightened books on her shelves and stuffed some other papers in a drawer. How selfish of her sister, who was probably younger than any of the Ranch's students, to think she could come here and disrupt their hard-won, expensive time. Time taken away from work and family and home and pets. How devious of Regina—she was sure that she had some hand in this, promoting the Ranch to the Tour of Life, whatever that was. She thought about emailing them both, with a link to the article, and writing only ? in the body of her email.

Soon the office was clean, or at least it seemed clean—Marianne would later have to fish through the recycling bin for bills and letters, and would need to file or recycle the papers stuffed in her desk drawer. The fan oscillated right, then left, stopping briefly at three points in its rotation. Each time the oscillation paused, the fan seemed about to topple over.

Marianne sat down at her newly clean desk and opened the article again on her desktop. She copied it into a new file and printed it. Her mother was progressive, liberal, pro-choice. She'd donated to Planned Parenthood. Choice went both ways—Marianne knew that—and it was possible her mother could support someone else's right to an abortion without choosing it herself. But she was sure that her mother would not have traded her life for a fetus's—even the fetus that eventually became Ruth. She was eleven when her mother told her that she was sick, and also, at the same time, that she was pregnant. For a while Marianne thought the sickness and the pregnancy were the same thing, connected somehow in her mind with her own excruciating and recently arrived periods. No, Theresa explained: she was going to have a surgery, a removal of a tumor in her breast, and then she would be better.

It was harder to remember what her mother had said to her than what she thought after hearing it. How disappointing but inevitable—to be left with the preoccupied, ever-present self when what you desired was the missing other. She could remember feeling worried that her mother's breast would be cut off entirely—as perhaps it should have been—and also about the mechanics of feeding the baby without it. Each time her period rolled around she became convinced again that it was something in her mother's uterus that had made her sick. The doctor visits—to the oncologist, to the obstetrician—got jumbled in Marianne's mind. No one in the house said the word *cancer*, but she knew that was what her mother had, just as she also knew about pregnancy and sex and a woman's always-changing body. She couldn't remember any heated arguments between her parents, no hushed or intense talk of fateful choices. And she was sure that Howard would have had an opinion. Take care of the living first: that's what Howard would have said.

She pulled out her phone, dialed Ruth's number, and got voicemail. "Ruth," she said. "It's Marianne. Call me."

Outside her office window, the surface of the pool was unnervingly placid; the Spanish moss that hung from the oaks was still and ghostly. The classrooms, when she went in every afternoon to run the air-conditioning, felt wrong: clammy with ocean moisture, echoey and dim. Sometimes she thought about what each of the students must be doing at home. A few of them had made Facebook friends with Marianne (what choice did she have but to accept them?). She'd never spent much time on the site—it always made her feel watched and nervous—but lately she found herself scrolling enviously through their pleasantries:

It's a beautiful day!

So grateful for another day!

Or *Writing!* accompanied by a photograph of a desk or a window or a notebook.

She thought especially about Janine, who had not posted a status update since becoming Marianne's friend and wrote to Marianne exactly once a day, usually in the early morning. She imagined whole routines for her: Janine is teaching summer school now, Janine is grocery shopping, Janine is making dinner with her daughters. Janine is writing a poem. It felt a little like taking a sick day from work or school, or the period just after quitting a job, the way you watched the hours pass and imagined what you'd be doing had you not stayed home to watch the hours pass.

Life was lived without you, and you realized that whatever you imagined you'd be doing—whatever luxury or expansiveness the day once held, hours ago—was dissolving, purposeless, invisible.

"How can you stand it in here?" Eric said, when he showed up midmorning. "It must be ninety degrees. That fan doesn't help."

"It does help," she said. "I hate air conditioners. There's something you should read. It's in the printer."

"You should take a trip," he said. He stood looking around—she could tell he was trying to notice what was different—but did not cross the room to pick up the article. "Go somewhere cooler. Go to Montauk. Remember when we went, had lobsters that time? Or go to Maine. I've heard it's nice in the summer."

Marianne did remember going to Montauk with Eric—they'd rented a car and driven out there one weekend in the early fall. The water was too cold for swimming, but the light was clear and golden, especially in the late afternoon when they took a walk through the town. After Eric convinced her that lobsters were just big insects, they'd eaten half-pounders with boiled corn and drawn butter. They'd played minigolf and gone go-kart racing.

"I've heard it's a lot fancier now," Eric told her. "But hey, business is good."

Mark had sent them each bonuses at the end of the first session. Marianne put hers in the bank and did not plan to spend it—who knew if he would take it back, that was her feeling. It felt like a mistake, like when the bank credits you for an extra deposit. They always caught their mistake, didn't they?

"I don't want to go on vacation by myself," she said, but as soon as she said it wished she hadn't. She sounded peevish and self-pitying. "I do remember it. The trip to Montauk. It was one of my favorites."

He sat down at the conference table and began hole-punching Davonte's growing manuscript, then feeding the pages into a binder. Marianne had gotten the hole punch at the local freecycle, and he had to lean on its handle to make it work, section by thin section. "We had some good times," he said, crunching through the pages.

"I thought about it, when you asked me," she said. "When I said yes. That's what I was thinking about. Go-kart racing and minigolf and lobsters."

Eric stopped what he was doing. "And when you said no?"

"It can't all be go-karts and minigolf. That's what I thought."

"No," Eric agreed. This disappointed her—she wanted him to say, *Of course it can! Marriage can be anything you decide.* But instead he went grimly back to punching holes. "I guess it can't."

Marianne walked to the printer and picked up the article—without the photograph, which didn't print, it hardly took up a half page. Maybe no one would notice. Eric had been so cheerful, hopeful since the bonuses arrived.

"My dad asked about you," she said. "I was talking to him about my sister. She may come here. With some sort of GWGW field trip."

"That's great—you wanted her to visit. I bet she'll be really impressed."

"Don't you think it's a little strange—that she is suddenly connected to them, to GWGW?"

Eric shrugged. "They're a pretty big organization. Bigger than I realized at first. But that's not necessarily a bad thing."

"It's a big coincidence."

Eric fitted the last of the manuscript onto the rings and snapped them closed. "Your dad—he liked me, didn't he?"

"Howard is exceptionally hard to read," Marianne said. "He is kind of a hands-off parent. But yes, I think he liked you."

"I always assumed that was what did me in." He smiled as he said it— kindly, forgivingly—then said, "It's okay, Marianne. I'm not mad anymore."

She looked at him.

"We're better as friends. I get it now. It took me a while, even here— when we first got here, I wondered if we could, you know. But I get it now." He shook his head, as if chiding that foolish, romantic self, and Marianne felt not pain but breathless surprise, as if she'd been lightly stomach-punched. "You should go somewhere, really. Work on your book. You should get out of here before the next session."

Eric had his own trip planned, a tour of GWGW's campuses with Regina, and although he kept calling it a business trip, Marianne wondered. Would their paths cross with the Tour of Life? With Ruth? She'd tried not to think about the long car ride to Georgia, the dinners out, the hotel rooms—surely they'd have two rooms—side by side, or even adjoining, in some middling chain. (She's a virgin, Eric had recently confided to Marianne. Not a virgin-virgin, he'd clarified, when she asked how that was possible, but the born-again kind.)

"No, I'll stay," Marianne said. Perhaps demonstrating her dedication would show him that she was different from the girl she'd been in New York. Responsible. Worthy. "Someone has to stay. Someone has to manage all the media attention." She set the article on the small table near the door, but he did not stop to read it.

Ruth did not return Marianne's call, but sent a text instead. *Very busy preparing for this trip! Will call soon!* When Marianne texted back—*Are you coming here?*—she got an auto reply, which she didn't know was possible in a text. Maybe her sister was writing to make it look like an auto reply? *Ruth Boyette is unavailable at the moment but will be back with you soon. Peace and Blessings!*

There were other notices in her Google Alerts—several of the students were bloggers, and the Ranch was mentioned on their various platforms, in generally flattering terms, its name and website passed around like a recommendation for a dentist or a veterinarian. There was also an article about faith and education, and a brief mention in a national news piece about online learning. After Eric posted something on the NYU listserv, Marianne got some emails from her old classmates. The tone of the emails was jokey and teasing—*So you finally did it! Have fun in the Bible Belt!*—but a few people asked if she would keep them in mind for future openings, and attached their CVs.

What really increased their profile, however, was a feature in the Sarasota *Herald-Tribune*. The article ran under a large photograph of the Ranch, which had been taken in a flat, ironic style, like a picture by Diane Arbus or William Eggleston. You could see the cracks in the foundation of the buildings, the weeds that persisted around the sculptures, which still looked naked somehow, despite their painted-on clothes. The wooden sign—Genesis Inspirational Writing Ranch—looked slapdash and temporary instead of modest and unassuming. All that was missing were the students—their cheerful, dowdy clothing, their eager, note-taking postures. The article described the school's structure and business model briefly, but most of the piece was an exposé of the Ranch's connection to GWGW, noted as a "majority stakeholder" in the school. The writer mentioned complaints from GWGW students at other schools to the Better Business Bureau and a class-action lawsuit pending against the organization, brought by a group of sonography students, citing poor training and excessive fees, a breach of contract. GWGW had also contributed funding to a super PAC supporting a controversial amendment establishing the personhood of embryos. Marianne and Eric, named as the school's founders, were referenced as "a pair of New York City writers."

Marianne sat on the steps outside her office, the newspaper bleeding ink onto her bare legs, and thought about what she should do. What did she think would happen when she decided to start the school—when she *agreed* to start the school, which was not even really her idea? Eric was on his tour of GWGW campuses, but Mark was likely in his office. She decided to Skype him on her GWGW-provided tablet, right there from the stoop.

"You're making too much of this," he told her after she explained, holding up the photograph and reading from the article. "Any publicity is good publicity, you've got to remember that."

"Mark, our existing students will not be happy about this," she said. "We've got to write a letter to them. Something."

"Are you kidding me? I bet they'll love that—what was it?—personhood amendment. That's an antiabortion stance. They'll be all over that."

"It's not just antiabortion, it's antiscience, antiwoman. It declares that four cells is the same as you or me."

"I highly doubt that, Marianne."

"And not all of them would support it, Mark. I bet not even half of the students—"

"Marianne, you can pretend that your students are as open-minded as you want, but we have all kinds of data on them. You want me to send it to you?"

"No," she said quickly. "I'd rather you didn't. This was not an issue before GWGW was involved," she said. "They are a for-profit educational conglomerate, that's what the article said."

"Right," said Mark. "And are you enjoying that bonus? Are you happy you can pay your teachers, are you happy we're not already going bankrupt?"

"I'm *not* enjoying my bonus," Marianne said. She held up the tablet and pointed it at the office, the gardens, the empty parking lot. "I am holed up here reading manuscripts, and trying to figure out how this article is not a bad sign about our relationship with an organization I was not crazy about in the first place. How does Frances feel about it?"

"Who?"

"Frances, your great-aunt? Who I have never actually met in person. Who thought of this idea? And funded it?"

"Frances is retired," Mark said. "She's on a fixed income. This school, Marianne, it's her big chance. To have some security, a legacy. Don't you want that for her?"

"Well, of course," Marianne said. It was never clear to her why the phrase *fixed income* implied hardship—it always sounded kind of luxurious, like something you could count on.

"Don't you want her to wind up in a nice home?"

"I thought she was already in a nice home."

"Not if we bankrupt her! Not if we *bleed her dry*. She's one fall away from getting booted to a Medicaid facility."

"I never said we should bleed her dry," Marianne said quietly. "Did she have a fall?"

"Marianne," said Mark, leaning in to his computer screen. "You need to get out more. Go to St. Augustine, go to the Keys. Don't do one of those Everglades tours—too many mosquitoes. Stay somewhere nice. They've got an orchid-flower massage and facial at the Naples Waldorf Astoria that you would love. You want me to send you some links?"

Later that day, Regina called from the road to discuss the article and reassure Marianne that everything was fine.

"There is nothing negative about the school or any of the instructors."

Regina's telephone voice was so low, smooth, and controlled that Marianne had to strain to hear her. "They didn't find a single student to say anything bad about the Ranch. Has anyone called you? Did you talk to anyone before the article came out? Even casually?"

"No," Marianne said. She thought suddenly of the exchange she'd had with Sophie, and Sophie's warning that it wouldn't be hard to figure out the Ranch's funders. But would Sophie contact the newspaper? Marianne thought of Sophie's bumper stickers, the things she'd said in passing about Bible bangers. "I didn't talk to anyone."

"Good," said Regina. "Very few people read the newspaper, after all. Though if they do call you, please refer them to me. Is that okay with you, Marianne?"

"I guess that would be appropriate," she said. "Since most of the suspicious details are about GWGW."

"And you don't remember talking to anyone about GWGW?" Regina asked. "Maybe call the landscapers. The photograph—"

"Can you tell me about the personhood thing, Regina? I mean, what does that have to do with your schools? It's not exactly an issue everyone agrees on." Marianne hesitated to say where she stood on the idea that zygotes and embryos should have the same rights as people, but then a terrifying thought came to her mind. "Wait, our money didn't go to that, did it?"

Regina laughed lightly. "My dear, Genesis Ranch is not exactly contributing to our bottom line. It's rather the other way around, so no— none of your revenue has influenced anything politically. However," she continued, her voice quiet and smooth again, "the association with certain political causes does provide an advantage, financially and strategically."

"But we're not that kind of school," Marianne said. "We're meant to be inspirational, not political. We never advertised any of this to our students. I don't think they want to get mixed up in this."

Regina dismissed her concerns with a quick snort. Marianne could picture her smoothing back her perfect hair with glossy, candy-colored nails, or scrolling through spreadsheets on her tablet. "It's not about the students, though it will help them in the long run," Regina said.

"Representative Tucker has an opportunity to do a lot for our campuses, and that means doing a lot for your students, and I promise you that they are deeply invested, also, in the sanctity of life. So it's win-win. All around."

What was she talking about? Marianne asked to speak to Eric, but was told he was on a campus tour. He was taking notes, Regina said, about some of the features and upgrades they might like to have at the Ranch. She tried to imagine what those would be—internet that didn't cut out with every gulf breeze, perhaps video screens in the classrooms, a new copier and new furniture. A bigger library—it would be nice to have a library instead of the motley collection of weatherworn paperbacks that appeared on and disappeared from the low shelves beneath the window in the dining hall.

But those things weren't necessary. They were no more the school than the hand-painted sign, so plaintive and homely in the newspaper photograph, was an invitation to be inspired. Between Marianne's first and second years at NYU, much of their department had been renovated to look like the banquet room of a Four Seasons—with ornate crown moldings, patterned carpets, arched energy-efficient windows that looked out onto University Place. But her professor, the director of the program, had held on to an office in an older wing. There were exposed, clanking heating pipes, a drafty single-paned window, dingy walls covered with poems, photographs, postcards advertising her students' upcoming books. It always smelled of black tea and orange rinds. When Marianne thought of school—when she allowed herself to go back to a time when her own writing career and adult life seemed possible, even promising— that was where she took herself.

"Would you like me to pass on a message to Eric?" asked Regina.

"Tell him to call me." It surprised her how much it hurt to hear Regina calling Eric by name.

Marianne spent the rest of the day googling Tad Tucker, whose political career she had followed in the pages of the Sarasota *Herald-Tribune*, and whose voice she knew through the popular radio show *Talking to Tad*, which she sometimes listened to in the car. Elected two years ago as a state representative, Tucker had once been a college baseball star, a slugger who washed out in the minor leagues, and had emerged from a muddled business career that sought to capitalize on his waning regional fame. Marianne found references to fast food franchises, batting cage operations, and a for-profit scared-straight-style boys' camp, but he was most known through the radio show. Now that he was a politician, he was officially retired from radio, but he was a guest host so frequently that they'd kept the name. He railed against his opponents, promoted his unconstitutional legislative bills—including fetal personhood—and defended the records of his businesses, which had become the targets, he claimed, of trial lawyers attempting to pay him back for his support of tort reform. On talktotad.net, Marianne listened to clips from the show. The most popular, with more than three hundred thousand views, involved a civil lawsuit brought against one of his batting cage operations. "I mean, let's get real!" the clip began, in Tad's outraged southern drawl. "A kid gets beaned in a batting cage and we gotta get *lawyers litigating*? What's next? Support groups for spelling bee losers? Are we gonna timidly turn to touch football? I'll tell you the same thing I told the family that brought the suit, which is that kid is welcome—free of charge—to attend my Time for Toughness boot camp."

Marianne appreciated Tad's commitment to alliteration, and marveled at the way he used one misfortune to promote another of his businesses, but a quick follow-up search revealed more damning details. The beaned child had been severely concussed, and the trial lawyers found that neither the helmets provided nor the pitching machines met federal safety regulations. Doctors claimed that the child might have brain damage and would need months of physical therapy; in any case, he was in no shape for a Time for Toughness camp, and the family had settled out of court for an undisclosed amount.

Tad had recently achieved some national notice through his vigorous pursuit of antiabortion and school reform bills. He opposed abortion in all cases, and through his personhood bill wanted to officially define life as beginning at conception. He also claimed that Florida's public education system, from kindergarten through university, was wasteful, ineffective, and rife with liberals (who else would accept such low pay but liberals? he radio-ranted). It did not take Marianne long to find out why GWGW was interested in his cause. He wanted to privatize the state's community colleges, making more funding available to training and vocational schools run by private companies. By backing his personhood efforts—investing millions in ad buys and billboards and robocalls and direct mail—GWGW would later ensure a steadier stream of paying high school graduates for its Florida campuses.

But Marianne thought Regina was wrong when she said that the students would not be bothered by the politicizing of their campus. They would see right through Regina's plans and would take a stand for the school they loved—for the rickety folding chairs and long readings, for poetry under the trees and tai chi on the beach. Surely she could count on them for that much.

She logged on to Facebook to check her Ranch feed and saw nothing out of the ordinary—not yet. Davonte had posted a bathroom shot of his scale along with "27 LBS!!!" and had received a flurry of "likes" and positive comments. Janine had sent messages of encouragement to a few classmates. Manfred had made a few cryptic comments about a visit to his mother. Marianne searched for "Tad Tucker," and could see that several students "liked" him—some had even posted to his wall, but Marianne could not see their comments unless she "liked" him as well. Perhaps they were arguing with him, or maybe they lived in his district and needed to plea for some sort of assistance or pet project—

Oops. Hovering over his page on her tablet, Marianne let her finger slip, and now she liked him too.

Horse trading, Eric called it, when he finally called her back. He explained what she had already figured out—that GWGW had calculated that by supporting personhood today, they would feed funding and students to their cosmetology, medical billing, prelaw, and predentistry schools tomorrow. Shifting funds away from public community colleges gave GWGW a huge advantage in recruitment, Eric said, as their schools accepted anyone with a pulse and a student loan.

"I thought nonprofits couldn't donate to political campaigns."

"They're not going to donate to his campaign. They're going to donate five million dollars to an outside group that raises public awareness about *social issues*, not candidates. They're going to pour it into TV ads, right before the election."

"What I am having trouble understanding is how you can so calmly explain it to me, like there's nothing wrong with—"

"I didn't say I agreed, Marianne. I don't agree. Tad Tucker is a pious scumbag and a dirty crook. Whatever advantages GWGW provides, it doesn't make up for association with this guy."

"I mean, embryonic personhood!" Marianne said. "It's not even remotely constitutional. It goes against everything I believe in. And defunding community colleges? I didn't mean for a school we started to take things away from anyone."

"Money from Christians," Eric said quietly. "I think you said you wanted to take that away from them."

"That was different—that was a joke! And you put me up to it."

But he was right. They had cynically and deceptively created these jobs for themselves, almost a year ago, just as GWGW was cynically investing in issues that would lead to better profits. The only difference was the scale of their success.

"Look," Eric said. "I'm talking to the GWGW people, and then I'm talking to Mark. If they won't dissociate themselves from Tucker, I'm getting us out of this. I'll be back by the weekend, and we can figure it all out then. Okay?"

"But your aunt—"

"Frances? What about her?"

"Mark said something about a fall. Did she fall?"

"Not that I know of."

"He said she was one fall away from a Medicare facility—or Medicaid? Basically he said she was poor and old, or about to be poor and old."

Eric laughed softly—at her? At his aunt and her impending homelessness? Marianne could feel her blood pressure spiking. "Mark just worries about money, basically it's all he thinks about. He wants to make sure she's taken care of in her old age. But she wouldn't want this. Not Tad Tucker. I'll take care of it, okay? I promise."

Marianne exhaled, long and slow. Of course Eric was on her side. Of course Eric was coming back to her. A few weeks with an attractive and flattering marketing person could not have changed the man he was, deep down.

13

All afternoon, Marianne waited for the protesters to leave and for Eric to arrive. Dressed in T-shirts, shorts, and sandals the color and shape of baked potatoes, the handful of women looked like a group of eager tourists or museumgoers waiting on an air-conditioned charter bus or a trolley with padded seats. When Marianne first spotted them she assumed they were lost, perhaps looking for the shady marsh walk that was a quarter mile down the road, or maybe for the public beach. It was hot, even for Florida, the past week a consistent punishment of still, humid, hundred-degree days. There was no breeze to rustle the stiff live oak leaves or sway the brittle clumps of Spanish moss.

For twenty minutes they just stood on the sidewalk in front of the Kangaroo gas station across from the Ranch, passing around water bottles and energy bars from a small cooler and squinting into the sun. But then the women must have had some kind of signal, or perhaps they finally verified that the slightly dilapidated motel with no sidewalk in front of it—only a crumbling gravel path—was, in fact, the same Genesis Inspirational Writing Ranch they had read about in the *Herald-Tribune*. A tall woman with sandy-gray hair nodded at the others, and they hoisted handmade signs that read:

GENEI RANCH, COME CLEAN: WHO ARE YOUR FUNDER$?
INSPIRATIONAL WRITING = ANTICHOICE, ANTIWOMAN AGENDA
LIE DOWN WITH DOGS, WAKE UP WITH FLEAS
GENESIS RANCH JOINS WAR ON WOMEN?
and
SARASOTA SAYS SHAME TO SHADY, SHODDY SCHOOL!

Many of the signs featured photographs of Tad Tucker's smiling face, circled and slashed through in red marker.

The street was empty, but the women chanted and bobbed their signs up and down as if for a crowd. "Hey hey! Ho ho! These shady schools have got to go!"

Marianne called Eric right away, but he didn't answer, so she went across the street herself to talk to the protesters. They were actually quite cordial and friendly, and respectfully stopped chanting and set down their signs. Marianne explained that Genesis Inspirational Writing Ranch was not affiliated with Tad Tucker, lamely repeating Regina's line that none of their revenues had directly funded GWGW's donations to Preborn America, the supposedly unaffiliated group behind the pro-Tad ad blitz, whose CEO just happened to be Tad's former chief of staff.

What had Marianne expected in return? That they would say, "Oh, I did not realize that, you're right, sorry for bothering you"? That they would tear up their signs then and there? Apologize for jumping to conclusions, perhaps ask for a business card or an application form? (At Regina's suggestion, she had started carrying both at all times.)

"But *your* funding," said a short, fiftyish woman wearing a visor festooned with buttons and ribbons for NOW, Planned Parenthood, the ACLU, causes that Marianne herself supported. "Your funding is connected to God's World God's Word, is it not?"

Marianne frowned. Should she tell her that in a few days that would all be over? It was tempting, but Eric had cautioned her to keep quiet. When he got here, she decided, she could send him over to speak with them. "We're just a writing school," she said. "We don't make enough money to fund anyone. Trust me."

"We *don't* trust you," said another woman with a deep suntan and an aggressive, nearsighted squint. "We don't trust any of the GWGW schools, which is why we're having protests at each of the five Florida campuses today. My daughter went to one of the GWGW schools, and now she's twenty thousand dollars in debt, unemployed, and living above my garage."

"What school?" Marianne asked. "Not ours?"

"No, not yours," the woman allowed. "A prelaw school. But do your students have jobs and skills? Do they have debt?"

Marianne didn't answer, and the woman continued, with more anger.

"Maybe one day she'll go to a real law school and sue all of you. Or maybe I will."

"We do appreciate that you came and talked to us," said the first woman, accepting the brochures, application, and business card Marianne offered in a conciliatory way. Then she picked up her sign and led her fellow protesters in a fresh, lusty round of chanting.

Marianne went back across the street and, while she considered what to do next, busied herself with watering the hanging ferns and geraniums she'd bought to conceal the main building's cracked stucco walls. It was easy to hear the chanting from where she stood, and she felt conspicuous, so she went inside. She closed the door to her stuffy office, but could hear it still. She checked email on her phone and found a message from Patty Connor, who'd written in Tom's class about her eight miscarriages. *Did you know that the personhood amendment would limit the treatment of my infertility?* Patty wrote. *I'm a pastor's wife and as pro-life as they come, but I oppose this amendment and hate the way it is being used to suggest that I am not a good person, not a good Christian. As an infertile woman, I already struggle with misinformation and societal preconceptions about my disease and its treatment. Tad Tucker's bill just makes things worse for me.*

As you know, it was very difficult for me to share my work and my life story at Genesis Ranch. It took me a while, in Tom's class, to understand that there is a distance between the "I" of my narrator and myself, the writer, and to be able to accept critiques and suggestions. I still have a hard time with that, but I am working on it. How am I supposed to return to class knowing that my actions are being judged this way by my institution? Does this mean that my work will not be read the same way, that I won't be taken seriously? Is this another distancing I will have to work on?

I was very disturbed, furthermore, to see that you "liked" Tad Tucker on Facebook. When I was having such a difficult time at the beginning of the first session, I was ready to pack up and leave. I missed my husband and my home, and frankly Genesis Ranch was not exactly what I expected. But you were kind to me, you sat with me in your office and told me that if I didn't tell my story, who would? You encouraged me to stay, and I was glad that I did.

What am I supposed to think now?

The phone rang, startling Marianne. It was Regina, who had heard somehow about the protesters.

"How many?" she wanted to know.

Marianne turned on the window unit and peeked through the blinds. "Five at first. Now eight?"

"Call me back if it gets out of hand," said Regina, who sounded almost pleased that they had attracted this attention, like a needy girl who'd just been called a name by a boy. "We can always send counterprotesters."

"*No*," said Marianne. "I am trying to get work done. The students arrive in two weeks, and they will not like—"

"This is part of the growth process at many of our campuses," Regina said. "It's a sign of health and vitality, of engagement with the community. What you should do is make a nice gesture. Perhaps you could take them some lemonade?"

Marianne did not respond.

"Marianne," Regina said, in her maddeningly soothing way, "you have to get used to thinking of every obstacle, every stone in your path, as an *opportunity*. Having protesters on our campus means that we are connecting with the public, it means people are paying attention to our goals and our mission, even if they do not agree with them yet. Listen, did you get my notes about the online learning modules?"

Regina had sent Marianne a "profitability matrix" that suggested that their best next step was offering a degree entirely online, even though they were not even accredited—not yet, she always said (*not yet* was Regina's favorite phrase). She wanted to move half of their coursework online as an experiment, and Marianne was not sure how to explain that the "coursework" or "curriculum" her teachers offered depended heavily on in-person participation.

"I looked at it," Marianne said. "Have you spoken with Eric?"

"With Eric?" Regina was puzzled. "Of course! Why?"

"I thought he was coming back today."

"Hmm," said Regina. "I'll tell him to call you."

The next time Marianne went to see the protesters, they had been out there for two hours and were somewhat less congenial. They looked a little wilted, sweat darkening their T-shirts and beading the tops of their lips, but they did not stop their chanting this time.

She wondered when they would leave. The protests she'd been to, mostly against the Iraq War, had definite start and end times. They had not interfered with meals or showering but had been more like exercise: a slow walk through the city with a large group of other people, some shouting, then back on the L train for home. It had been a good feeling, like after going to the gym—not that Marianne went to the gym—the feeling of having accomplished something that you may not have looked forward to but that now was over. Having said *no*, this is not right, I do not agree.

Even before this latest development, it had been some time since Marianne had agreed with the way things were going at the Ranch. She did not agree with the current status of Mark's business arrangement with GWGW, which had somehow resulted in their paychecks being issued by GWGW itself, which Mark swore did not mean they were GWGW employees. Purely for tax purposes, he said. Tom had hit the roof when he saw the globe-cross logo on his first paycheck, but was mollified by the bonus that arrived a week later; Lorraine appreciated the upgrades to business class on her plane tickets. Marianne did not agree with Regina's suggestions to move their curriculum online, did not agree with the "publishing seminars" she had arranged for this second session or the keynote speaker she had invited, at Regina's request: a writer of "Christian erotica" (a genre about which Marianne would have preferred to remain ignorant). And she especially did not agree with Eric's decision to accompany Regina Somers on a so-called business trip and not return when he said he would. No, she did not agree, it was not right, it was not fair, it was not how she had planned for things to go.

She wished she could join the protesters.

"I just want to say," Marianne began, but no one even looked. She began again, in a voice loud enough to match their chanting: "I JUST WANT TO SAY that I am sorry you are so concerned about our associations, and I would be HAPPY TO TALK WITH YOU about them. Okay? SO WOULD YOU PLEASE TALK TO ME? FOR A SECOND?"

Most of Gulf Drive was shaded by craggy-limbed live oaks, but the area around the gas station was all blacktop and cement, and the heat felt as if all of the area's sunlight had been concentrated into that one spot. "Take a water break, y'all," said one of the women Marianne had spoken to earlier, and they gratefully headed for the cooler, which someone had dragged into a tight corner of shade.

The woman removed her visor, wiped back a band of sticky, flattened bangs, then replaced it. "Lena," she said, offering her hand. "What is it you want to talk about?"

"I'm Marianne," she said. "I'm one of the founders of the school. I didn't know anything about GWGW's support of the personhood amendment until yesterday."

"It isn't hard to dig up other dirt on GWGW," said Lena, pointing across the street at the Ranch. "We found dozens of Better Business Bureau complaints in three states, and one of their schools"—here she consulted a folder of photocopied materials, paging through until she found a grainy photocopied picture of what appeared to be a strip mall—"yes, the GWGW Medical Technologies Institute in Alpharetta, Georgia, it is currently under investigation."

"Why?" Marianne reached for the folder, but Lena held it back.

"It's a sonography school, meant to teach people to do sonograms at these medical imaging centers, and all of the classes are online. All of them!" the woman said. She opened the pages to screenshots of the registration forms, which looked like ads for a used car lot: Apply Now! 100% Financing! VISUALIZE a New Future for Yourself! "So when their students actually graduate, with their certificates, they have no hands-on training, no idea what they're doing. They go in to those clinics and do sonograms of people's large intestines. Seems sort of odd, in a so-called pro-life organization, don't you think? They don't even know anything about the life they're looking at?"

"Seems pretty common with that crowd, if you ask me," called a woman standing near the drink cooler.

"They told some people they weren't pregnant at all," another woman said. "But they were."

Marianne considered how to proceed. "Obviously, an online sonogram school is a bad idea," she began. "I am definitely with you there.

But it's not like an online *poetry* school is going to kill someone, or give them harmful information! Besides, our classes aren't all online anyway. They're just low-residency. In fact, we're expecting our students back very soon, and it will be bad for their concentration, very bad for their short residency experience, if they know you're out here protesting. And you're also giving incorrect information, because we do not support the personhood amendment, or Tad Tucker, or anything political."

"Well, when they arrive they can speak to us and decide whom they believe," the woman said.

Marianne went back to the Ranch, got a bottle of white wine from the minifridge in her office, and opened it with a flimsy corkscrew. She took her glass, full to the top and speckled with small bits of cork, and sat down beside the freshly chlorinated pool. She could still hear the maddeningly repetitive chants, but the wine, which she drank in long gulps, helped a little. She pulled out the smartphone she hadn't asked enough questions about. Nothing is free, her dad always said, but she always thought that was pessimistic. She faced away from the street, toward the pool.

Eric was her "in case of emergency contact," so his name appeared first in her contact list, in red. She wondered if she would have to change it if he married again, if she would have to find someone else. She could not imagine who that would be. The phone rang once, then she heard Eric's cheerful recorded voice. "Eric," she said. "It's been a difficult day. There are protesters here who have information about this crazy GWGW sonography school, and I talked to Regina and she didn't seem to have any idea that we didn't want any more to do with this whole personhood debate, or Tad Tucker. Or GWGW." She drew a long, ragged breath. "Call me back," she said.

Marianne turned her pool chair around. Over the fence, beneath the trees, she could see the tops of the protesters' heads as they marched up and down the sidewalk. Hardly a car drove by—this time of year was muggy and vulnerable to hurricanes and tropical storms, and most people preferred to spend it elsewhere. The people who were left were the true locals, elderly people and eccentrics, or the people who made their money during tourist season—chiropractors and Lasik surgeons, dentists available on an emergency basis, Pilates instructors and boutique owners and ice cream purveyors and landscapers. Marianne supposed she was one of them now.

She called Eric's number, then called it again, not leaving messages, just calling, and had moved on to texting when Davonte appeared and sank into a chaise next to her, facing the opposite way.

"It's finished," he said, leaning back.

"What's finished?"

"The book," he said. "The first half anyway. Me and my man Eric got it done."

Was this the reason he hadn't been in touch with her? Was he holed up in a hotel room somewhere, finishing Davonte's manuscript? Was he on the phone with Davonte when she called? And did this mean he'd be back soon?

"It's really good. We start at the peak of Damian's career," Davonte said, holding one hand above his head, as if at the top of a roller coaster. "The tours, the women, the fast living—and then jump forward to his downfall." He swooshed his hand down, then shook his head sadly, truly moved by the trajectory of his roman à clef. "I mean, I cried at that part."

"Congratulations," Marianne said. She remembered the feeling—rereading after finishing a good stretch of writing, allowing yourself to be moved by your own words—though it had been a long time, and she wondered if it was the same if you had someone else writing those words. But then, probably most of Davonte's music involved a great deal of collaboration. It was still his story. She patted his newly muscular arm. "Really, Davonte. You should be proud."

He smiled and shrugged. "You know, more people are recognizing me, too. Since I lost the weight. But you know what? It doesn't bother me, because I know who I am. I'm secure." He thumped his chest, above the heart. "Hey," he said, sitting up and turning back to face the street. "What's all that noise?"

"Protesters," she said.

"Shit," Davonte said, swinging his legs over the side of his chaise like he was about to run away. "How—"

"They're not here for *you*," Marianne said. She was tired. "Not everything is about you."

"Oh," he said. "Good."

He didn't ask any more questions, and Marianne didn't offer any explanations. A Channel 13 News truck had just pulled in to the Kangaroo parking lot, and the chants were growing louder.

14

Janine was in a state. For days she had been unable to concentrate on the revision of a single poem, even though it was almost time to return to the Ranch, and her inability to revise, as Lorraine had assigned, meant that it was impossible to start any new work. This had never been a problem before—poems just materialized, usually at the rate of one or two a day. But it was all dried up in the August heat. She could not remember the last word she'd written or the last cooling drop of rain. Writing in the sunroom was unbearable: even with the air-conditioning at full blast, she baked like a turtle, so she'd moved her notebooks to the kitchen, which had other distractions, like the question of what to make for dinner and the blaring television, tuned to the Weather Channel for days.

Janine was also distracted by the request she'd received that morning for a poem to post to the school website.

Our school is under attack, Regina Somers wrote in an email. *Perhaps you saw the article in the Sarasota* Herald-Tribune? *It was a hack job, Janine, journalistically irresponsible, that suggested that the work that you do in class is not serious or somehow is inferior to work by non-Christian writers. That's why I'm reaching out to a select few students whose writing will showcase the best of the real work that happens at Genesis Inspirational Writing Ranch. I understand from your teachers that you are enormously talented, and I remember from our conversation that you write about the sanctity of life, so I was wondering if you would be willing to share your writing with us, so that we might share it with the world?*

Janine *had* seen the article, after it was posted to Facebook by several of her Ranch friends. She agreed with Regina, and with her fellow students who posted comments, that the whole business was unfair to their school. It had not included interviews with any of the students or teachers, had brought up allegations of political involvement that Janine wasn't sure were true (and if true, she wasn't sure how they were damaging), and included a rather unflattering photograph of the school grounds. In a spirit of solidarity, she'd chosen one of the poems from her Terri Schiavo series and sent it back to Regina with permission to publish, but now Janine wondered if the poem was ready, and she was looking through her collection to see if something else might be better.

Beth sat across from her, staring intently at the television. Janine, who found it difficult to read with the weather people constantly flipping from one set of terrible footage to another—from forest fires in California to a drought in the Southwest to a heat wave in Chicago—worried that it had become an obsession. Janine's take on weather was that it just *was*: there were always fires in California, the Southwest always seemed a little drought-stricken (wasn't that where they had the Dust Bowl?), cities were always too hot in the summer and too cold in the winter. Worrying about the weather felt a little intemperate and godless to her. God made those mountain ranges; if He wanted to burn them up, that was His business. She was even a little afraid her daughter had aligned herself with those climate change alarmists but Beth said no, it wasn't that. She was watching for a tropical storm. She was sure, based on a study of ocean temperatures and wind patterns, that one was about to get cooking. Once it did, all she had to do was guess where it might go.

"If I can just get *ahead* of the storm," Beth said, consulting one of her thick meteorology textbooks while Janine flipped through her poems. On the small kitchen TV, the seven-day forecast appeared against an ocean-blue background: seven fiery suns, temperatures around a hundred every day. "If I can plan ahead, I'll be in place to get my breakthrough story."

Beth had graduated with her associate's degree in June. They'd had a lovely party in the backyard, and Janine had not been made aware of any new tattoos celebrating the accomplishment, thank goodness. Beth was taking some courses in the fall at the university, but she insisted that it wasn't necessary to have a bachelor's degree. What it took to be successful in her field, apparently, was a certain look, a certain resourcefulness and go-getter quality. On days that she left the house for work, Beth wore jewel-colored suits and pumps, even hose. But there were many days that she did not leave the house at all, and wore what were essentially pajamas—thin drawstring pants that dragged the ground, lacy camisoles—as if the effort of dressing up on those other days had exhausted her. She had not once mentioned moving out—and that was fine, completely fine, with Janine, who dreaded the empty nest. She wished sometimes that she could make both of her daughters just two or three or even five years younger.

"I hope by plan ahead you mean you'll tell someone at work about it," Janine said. Beth was a part-time receptionist at Channel 6, but she was convinced that if she got a good video, she could soon be on the weather desk, reporting for Storm Team 6. "I don't want you running off after some storm by yourself."

Beth selected a neon pink highlighter from her pencil case and made a careful, straight mark inside her book. This was the Gray way of studying, which Janine herself had taught her daughters during a brief stint at homeschooling: highlight, underline, and summarize every text and textbook. The idea was to exhaust the text into being understood. Janine's summer packet of poems, dense with Creeley, Levertov, and Rich, was by now thoroughly drenched in pink, yellow, and blue highlighter ink.

"So you won't go by yourself," Janine repeated. "Tropical storms turn into hurricanes."

"That's the idea," Beth said lightly. She was sitting atop a tall stool at what the real estate agent had called "the bar," so many years ago, papers and textbooks spread before her, her laptop charging on the stool next to her, its cord stretched all the way to the back wall. Janine thought Beth was a little careless with the laptop—a graduation gift—but she had learned in many years of kitchen bar conversations to keep any instruction or lecturing or corrections limited to a single topic at a time.

It had been one of the selling points of the house, this kitchen. There was plenty of space for Janine to prep the family meals, with the bar—really just an extended Formica countertop, its off-white color an easily stained mistake—providing a place for her two girls to gather, do homework, tell Janine about their day, receive instruction. She did not realize, at the time, that it would be the place where she would helplessly watch them become both like her and unlike her. Back when they were little, she'd thought herself capable of imparting to her children the traits of her own that she wanted them to have, and teaching them to discard the ones she didn't, in the same way she might show them how to prep vegetables or chicken for a recipe. But Beth had picked up the stubbornness that had never served Janine well, and Christine, who was volunteering at church camp for the fifth week in a row, had adopted Janine's habit of relentless, dull self-sacrifice.

It was a truth Janine was just now arriving at: you had very little control over who your children would become. They would be you, but the worst, most useless parts of you. Last night she'd said as much to Rick, as he was getting into bed, and he had looked at her as if a snake had slithered out of her mouth. It went against everything he believed and worked for, and he had looked both hurt and disgusted before saying, "You know that's not true, honey."

Within minutes he was asleep and snoring, leaving Janine to wonder, when was the last time she had heard her husband call her by her actual name? With Rick it was always *honey, sweetie, babe,* or—worst of all— nothing, just the implied *you.* Janine found that she had been overcome more and more often, since returning from Sarasota, with thoughts and musings like these, and she could barely restrain herself from repeating them. No wonder she couldn't write: who knew what she might say?

"There is nothing a person can do about a storm, Beth," Janine said. She'd put her notebook aside and was now slicing peppers and onions for a ratatouille.

"Mom, someone has to warn people," Beth said. "Meteorology saves lives. Besides, this is my career. I have to take risks in order to advance."

"Risks!" Janine said, waving her knife, one eye suddenly watering. "Isn't life risky enough as it is? Isn't it bad enough to wake up in the morning?"

Beth capped her pink highlighter and uncapped a green one, tested its tip against her finger. "Mom, I don't mean this in a bad way, but you are starting to remind me of Granny, when she was in the home and had Alzheimer's. Remember? How she would say just awful things, how she never liked living in Florida, or about how Haley was on drugs?"

"But those things were true," Janine insisted, wiping her face on a dish towel. "Granny missed Baton Rouge her whole marriage, and your cousin Haley *was* on drugs. Granny never had Alzheimer's, though. She had dementia."

"That's not the point," Beth said. "The point is you don't say those things, those negative things, all the time. Out loud. A normal person doesn't, anyway."

Janine thought of protesting—she did not say negative things *all the time*—but the dish towel she had used was contaminated with onion juice, and both her eyes were now thoroughly crying. Beth was right, it had been hard for her to be normal, to feel normal, after returning from her residency session. Perhaps she would have returned to normal, the mother who gently corrected but mostly just rooted for her children in their every desire, the cheerleader mother she had been, had it not been for the thick packet of poems, or the brief email exchanges—two or more a day—with Lorraine Kominski. BE RADICAL, read the last message she'd received. But how was one to be radical?

"I'm sorry, Mom," Beth said. "Don't cry, Mom."

"I'm not crying," Janine said, rinsing her hands at the sink and patting at her cheeks. "It's okay. I just want you to be safe."

"I will," said Beth. "Don't worry about me. I can take care of myself."

Then Janine just laughed—that was another new development, inappropriate laughter bursting forth uncontrollably—and Beth took her textbook and her laptop into the den. Janine scraped the onions into a saucepan coated in oil, turned the heat down, and left the onions browning while she went to the sunroom to check her email. She had a message from Lorraine, addressed to her whole class:

HELLO ALL. YOU ARE SUPPOSED TO TAKE A WEBINAR TONIGHT AT 6—EASTERN TIME I SUPPOSE. IT IS CALLED "MARKETING YOURSELF IN THE TWENTY-FIRST CENTURY, AN E-BOOK STRATEGY FOR WRITERS." IT WILL BE OF LITTLE VALUE TO YOU, AS YOU ARE POETS. I HOPE YOU ARE STILL POETS, AT LEAST. SEE YOU SOON. L.

Lorraine always wrote in all caps, and always signed her emails with "L," so Janine did the same whenever she wrote back to Lorraine. She had taken a class about email etiquette and had learned that you were supposed to take your cues from your superiors, and always be the last one to write back. So she wrote:

THANK YOU! I LOOK FORWARD TO THE WORKSHOP. I AM STILL A POET EVEN THOUGH IT TROUBLES MY FAMILY MORE AND MORE. IF YOU ARE THE PERSON WHO RECOMMENDED ME TO REGINA SOMERS FOR PUBLISHING WORK ON THE SCHOOL'S WEBSITE, THEN THANK YOU VERY MUCH. J.

She hit Send, and was surprised when a new email popped up almost immediately.

IF YOU ARE TROUBLING YOUR FAMILY IT MEANS YOU ARE DOING IT RIGHT. L. P.S. I DON'T KNOW WHAT YOU ARE TALKING ABOUT REGARDING THE SCHOOL WEBSITE?? WHAT IS THAT ABOUT?

Janine replied,

THERE WAS A BIG TO-DO OVER AN ARTICLE THAT WAS CRITICAL OF THE RANCH, WHICH WAS IN THE SARASOTA PAPER. THEY WANTED SOME SAMPLE WORK AND ASKED ME. I SENT THEM "FROM INSIDE" BUT NOW I THINK THE POEM SEEMS VERY UNFINISHED. I AM ALSO CONCERNED THAT I AM NOT WRITING VERY MUCH AT ALL, JUST THINKING AND EXPRESSING THOUGHTS THAT ARE MAYBE A LITTLE DISTURBING TO MY FAMILY. J.

There was no response right away this time, and Janine went in and stirred the onions—they had browned a little too much—then added the peppers, diced squash, eggplant, and tomatoes, and put a lid on the saucepan. She returned to her computer, hit Refresh, and found another email:

THOUGHTS ARE EVEN BETTER THAN POEMS. DON'T LET ANYONE EVER TALK YOU OUT OF THEM. BUT I AM CONCERNED THAT YOU WOULD BE PUSHED TO SHARE WORK YOU DON'T FEEL IS FINISHED, FOR THE PURPOSES OF THE SCHOOL'S REPUTATION AND PUBLICITY. L.

Janine had also learned that you needed to allow the conversation to wind down, that you should be mindful of your hierarchically superior correspondent's time, but she thought that Lorraine had misunderstood her hesitation as a complaint, so she quickly wrote back:

THANK YOU! IT WAS AN HONOR TO BE ASKED, BUT MAYBE NOTHING WILL COME OF IT? I WILL LET YOU KNOW. J.

The webinar was hosted by God's World God's Word and began with a prerecorded PowerPoint about some of GWGW's other campuses. Janine had taken several webinars with GWGW this summer and was already familiar with the slightly tacky self-promotion, but there were a few campuses she did not recognize. The GWGW School of Social Work, the GWGW High-Tech Career Institute, and the GWGW School of Charter and Home Schooling Administration were all new, housed in modern-looking glass-and-steel buildings, if you could believe the drawings. The accompanying stock photos showed attractive women in business attire, wearing scientific-looking goggles and leaning over attractive, obedient-looking children, respectively.

A pixilated video of the webinar host appeared in the upper left corner at exactly six o'clock. Janine had never had this woman in any of her other webinars and wondered if she knew what she was in for. In fact, Janine realized that none of her webinar teachers taught repeat classes, even though the classes were mostly organized around a similar theme: some way of making money.

"Welcome, writers," said the woman. "My name is Catherine Powell, and I will be your host and your instructor tonight. Would you please all give me the thumbs-up if you can hear me?"

Janine clicked the thumbs-up button, then waited for all of the other students to do the same. She could see their screen names in a little box next to an icon that read "OK," "thumbs up," "?," or "Slow down." Janine had registered herself as JanineG, but many of her classmates had pen names for their internet activity, so it was hard to tell. She thought she recognized Manfred, who appeared to be logged in as WilhelminaD52.

Manfred is that you? she messaged WilheminaD52.

Sure is, sweetheart, he messaged back.

Janine experienced a little passed-note thrill, and typed: This part takes so LONG.

You'd think our comrades would know how to give the thumbs-up by now.

Haha, Janine typed. It reminds me of my life skills classes.

They are seriously in need of some life skills. Have you been on Facebook lately?

Not in a few hours. Why?

You might want to check, when this is done.

"Okay!" said Catherine Powell. "It looks like almost half of you have found the thumbs-up button, so I'm going to move on. Okay! Those of you having private messages, let's turn our attention to the webinar."

Busted, wrote Manfred, but Janine was too obedient to type the question she wanted to ask Manfred—why did she need to check Facebook? Had something else happened? Maybe, she thought, people had seen her poem. But that was vain and unlikely—it was probably more outrage over the newspaper article.

"Let's begin with a survey. How many of you regularly read e-books, that is, books on Kindles, Nooks, iPads, or other e-reading devices? Notice that on the next screen, there's a button to click if you regularly use these devices."

Catherine waved an arrow insistently over the survey question. Janine clicked "no, I do not regularly read e-books yet." Ten question mark icons appeared next to people's names, and three people requested that Catherine Powell slow down.

"Okay, just type your questions on the little screen below, and I will try to answer them," said Catherine Powell.

Does reading on your phone count?

What do you mean by regularly? Every day? Every week?

What Is An E-reader?

CaN it be a regular book or just a book that was published electroniclly?

What are the royalties like for ebooks?

Can you publish an ebook yourself?

Is it true that the government can watch what you are reading if you read online?

ARE POETRY BOOKS PUBLISHED ELECTRONICALLY?

Can you slow down, please?

I saw the Ranch on the news tonight. Can you tell us what happened?

Is it true that the Ranch supports personhood?

Not all of us support the personhood amendment. You can be pro-life without supporting personhood.

You can be Christian and pro-choice.

Life is a GIFT from God!

Are there going to be protesters on campus when we go back?

Several more people registered "?" status. One or two went offline.

"Okay, I am reading your questions," said Catherine Powell, who proceeded to read each question out loud and then give brief answers to each. Yes, reading on your phone counts. By regularly she meant more than twice a year? An e-reader is a device that allows you to read a book electronically. E-books are often published simultaneously with print books, but some books, especially those that are self-published or specialty, are only published in an e-book format. She did not answer the question about the news or personhood or politics or protesters—protesters? Janine supposed that was what Manfred was talking about in his message, and she wondered what Catherine Powell would say to that. "Let's table some of these other questions for later, okay? It looks like, based on the survey, 22 percent of you read e-books regularly. So we have a lot of ground to cover!"

The webinar was only scheduled to last an hour—they never went over the allotted time, Janine noticed—and it was already 6:22. Years ago, Janine had been surprised to have a student teacher assigned to her, a sweet and quiet girl from St. Augustine. Her first lesson, delivered to Life Skills I—a class of hoodlums, non–English speakers, and the mathematically disabled—was on making a soufflé. "What the fuck is a soufflé?" one student wanted to know. The student teacher began a long and overly in-depth answer that included some information about the history of France, and the students asked so many more questions (a favorite way of avoiding work) that by the end of class all anyone had accomplished was the messy cracking of a dozen eggs into his or her mixing bowl. "Look at all them eggs," said one student, whose favorite joke was putting food down his classmates' pants. "Wasteful." The student teacher's next lesson, on pigs in a blanket, had gone much better.

"Let me get to the slides," said Catherine, near the end. She quickly read through a PowerPoint list of guidelines for marketing e-books to readers.

Every book has an audience—you just have to find yours.
Be sure to keep it snappy; people prefer shorter to longer.
Or if it is going to be longer, tantalize them with romance and
   unforgettable characters!
Occult themes are also popular.
Know your market. Who reads the type of book you are writing?
Sell, sell, sell!

Get it? typed Manfred. It spells e-books.
Yes, Janine typed back. The bold letters help.
I'm gonna ask a question now, Manfred wrote.

"Time for one or two more questions," Catherine was saying. "About e-books and marketing. Only those subjects."

Ms. Powell, can you tell us a little about the marketing of poetry? I believe a third of us here are poets.

She mouthed Manfred's question, then said brightly, "Good question! Poetry is a little harder because it doesn't tell the same story—that's not how we think of poetry, anyway, but when you think about it, poetry can tell a story, and that story is the story of your life. For example, think of that little boy with cancer! His book was a best seller and it raised, um, a *lot* of money for other children with cancer! Think about *him* when you are down about your work and its marketability. Inspiring! Wonderful questions, everyone—it was so great to be with you today. Please don't forget to complete the brief survey at the end."

She had already signed off by the time Janine finished typing and proofing her only question:

What if you don't have cancer? What if what you have to say is not about yourself, but about everyone? What if you are signaling through the flames?

Janine had almost finished the questionnaire—nearly as long and tiresome as the webinar itself—when Beth came into the sunroom with her laptop. Today had not been a workday, and all day she had worn a cropped pink camisole and a thin pair of sweatpants that rode her hipbones. When it was time for bed, she would change into something else, but that did not mean, in her mother's eyes, that she had not spent the day in pajamas.

"Look," she said, and opened the laptop so that Janine could see. "Isn't that your school?"

Beth, in her peripatetic weather searching, had stumbled upon on a local Sarasota news channel's site; the screen was frozen on an image of the Ranch. Janine could see the small wooden sign—Genesis Inspirational Writing Ranch—and the familiar white stucco buildings framed behind gnarled live oak limbs.

"What in the world?" Janine said, using an expression of her mother's that sometimes surprised her more than the event she was exclaiming over.

"Watch," Beth said, clicking the Play button.

The camera cut from the image of the Ranch to a shot of a group of people, mostly women, holding protest signs and chanting.

"We're here at the Genesis Inspirational Writing Ranch, a low-residency writing retreat that opened in March. In a few days the Ranch will welcome back its first class of students for a second round of classes. But new questions have arisen over some of the school's political affiliations," said the reporter.

"Genesis Inspirational Writing Ranch receives funding from God's World God's Word, a network of for-profit schools that has not only received *numerous* complaints from the Better Business Bureau," said one of the protesters. "It has also funded a media blitz for a controversial amendment to the state's constitution declaring the personhood of embryos. That's why we're protesting. We're having a day of action against these for-profit schools and their nefarious and secretive political fund-raising."

Janine had seen the commercials, narrated by an urgent and pained female voice, and had received and recycled stacks of glossy postcards. She voted pro-life, would likely vote for this bill—so why did the news story make her heart race? The camera cut to a wide shot of the protesters, then back to the reporter. "The school declined to comment, but we are also joined tonight by Representative Tad Tucker, the sponsor of the controversial personhood amendment."

"Hey," Beth said. "Isn't that the guy Dad used to listen to on the radio?" Janine nodded and held a finger to her lips.

"Hi y'all," Tad Tucker said; his twangy voice was familiar from long rides in Rick's truck, but Janine wasn't sure she'd ever seen him in person. In his rumpled gray suit, he towered over the petite reporter, and the camera caught the sheen of sweat on his smooth brow. "I don't have any fancy signs or slogans, I just wanted to come down to say that I have not received a dime from the Genesis Inspirational Writing Ranch but I admire, very much, what they do. This is a school for Christian writers to work in a nonjudgmental environment, and I feel like the people behind me, what they are about is an *assault* on our Christian values and, yes, on our freedom of speech. Why, the students here are so talented. I read a poem today on the school's website—that's genesis-writing-ranch-dot-com—about Terri Schiavo, God bless her soul, that brought tears to my eyes.

"That's why I'm encouraging our own day of action. Friends, I'm no poet, but I signed up today for a workshop at the school, and I hope you will do the same. This can be *our* day of action, too—supporting freedom of speech and independent thought."

The clip stopped there, and Beth opened a new window and typed in the web address for Genesis Ranch. There, on the front page, was Janine's poem, right next to her endorsement of the school.

"Cool," Beth said. "Mom, you're published."

"Oh my stars," Janine said. That was another of her mother's expressions. She felt faint, the way she had when she learned about the woman who had been married to Terri Schiavo's doctor. She pressed her knuckles into her eye sockets and drew a long breath. "I can't believe it," she said. "I didn't mean—"

"*Talking to Tad* loves you!" Beth said. "This is huge. Dad will be excited. I'm going to link to your poem on Facebook, okay?"

Janine didn't answer. She was thinking about the argument that had started during the webinar, and the starkness of her own poem, alone on the Ranch's website. There had not been any other work. Had the other students objected? And what about the personhood debate? Janine was pro-life, but Patty Connor, one of the memoirists—a minister's wife—had posted that she opposed the amendment for medical reasons. If the amendment passed, according to Patty, she might not be able to have children.

"Mom?" Beth said. "Is that okay?"

"Okay," Janine said weakly. "I guess it's okay."

Her family toasted her with their iced tea glasses at dinner. "To Mom," said Beth. "For standing up for her school."

"And standing up for life," Christine added.

"I'm proud of you, honey," said Rick. "I heard some talk about it on the radio, even."

"On the radio?" Janine asked.

"It's a whole movement, trying to get people to sign up for classes. They're calling it a Day of Inspiration."

Janine was incredulous. "But my class is full. There's no room—"

"One-day classes, I think they said. Or internet classes? I heard it on the radio."

"It's all over Facebook, too," said Christine. "You're going viral."

"Going viral," Janine repeated. She knew what it meant, but the phrase sounded unpleasant, like a tropical disease. She felt a little ill, in fact—tired and achy, her eyes stinging with exhaustion. Janine had spent the afternoon reading links that Patty Connor posted about embryonic personhood, an idea that went way back to the very day of conception to establish the beginning of life. She'd looked at microscopic images of eight- and sixteen-celled embryos and watched a film of the beautiful, translucent cells dividing and dividing. It was amazing to think that every life began that way, that Beth and Christine, even Janine and Rick, had once been tiny clusters of cells, floating unsuspected or hoped-for inside their mothers. The embryo on her screen was certainly *alive*, but it reminded her of a flower or a blackberry more than a baby—something singular and unique, but also mysterious and fragile. She wasn't sure how she felt, politically, about the rights of zygotes (especially considering poor Patty Connor), but she'd written a poem, her first in weeks, and had wept with relief when it was done.

"What if I went with her?" Beth was saying now. "There's a tropical storm forming, and if it develops, it has a possibility of landfall between Naples and Tampa. If nothing else, I could get some footage of the controversy. It would be a great opportunity."

She pulled out her smartphone—another graduation gift—to show Janine an image of the gathering storm: a whorl of white, out in the Caribbean. Janine did not understand how this counted as a reason to go.

"You'll have to ask your mother about that one," said Rick.

Beth looked at her pleadingly.

"Wouldn't Channel 6 miss you? What about school?"

"*Mom*," Beth said. "They want me to develop my talents. They want me to succeed." She said this reproachfully—as if her mother had ever been on some other side! As if she hadn't sacrificed and sacrificed so her girls could succeed. Looking at her two daughters, Janine had the sudden, horrible thought that perhaps a human fascination with zygotes came from their sense of endless, mute possibility, obediently dividing and dividing. This one won't argue, wheedle, act recklessly.

"I wish *I* could go," said Chrissy.

"Yes! Let's all go!" Janine said, standing with her plate, though she hadn't eaten a thing. "Let's all drive straight into a hurricane, straight into hell! Great idea!"

"*Honey*," said Rick, though he didn't get up.

Scraping ratatouille and chicken into the trash, she heard her younger daughter explaining to him: "Don't worry, Dad. Poetry just makes Mom a little crazy."

15

It looked like good news, at first.

The protesters were gone, after their hours of sign waving and tedious chanting. Marianne had come up with a few choice chants herself, but had not had the opportunity to share them. The Channel 13 News van had come and gone, and in the wake of the controversy the Ranch's website received a record number of hits. The low-residency application was downloaded more than four hundred times in a single day, and already the online classes and seminars Marianne had considered canceling for poor enrollment were overflowing.

Up since dawn, Marianne had it all worked out. *These* people—these talk radio listeners, these fetal champions, these Tad Tucker minions— would be the Christians she would fleece. She got out a calculator and did some quick sums, pacing her office with a cup of strong coffee while she considered the ramifications of better cash flow. With their money in hand, she could pay back everything they'd borrowed from GWGW and become independent again. They could build a real library and pay Lorraine and Tom tidy bonuses to make up for any distasteful associations. Maybe she could pay off her own student loans.

"What do you think about scholarships?" she asked Eric, when he called to apologize for his absence. He explained, without answering, that he'd finally finished the first half of Davonte's manuscript, and they were awaiting word from publishers. There was talk of an auction, a six-figure advance.

"Wow, six figures." Marianne blew into the phone, trying to whistle. She did not ask how much of the advance would go to Eric, but she imagined that it would be more than his own two-book deal. "When are you coming back to the Ranch? And what do you think about the scholarship idea?"

"Merit or need-based?"

"Both? One of each? What about the diversity fellowships we talked about?"

Eric cautioned her: she'd been overly optimistic about their numbers before, and there was still a lot of uncertainty. Who knew if the people who downloaded the applications would apply, or if the rate of applications would continue? Plus they'd have to hire someone to read them all, unless she wanted to go blind or crazy doing it herself.

"There's a question on the application—how did you hear about us?" Marianne pointed out. "I'll just look at that."

"And throw them out?" Eric said. She didn't answer. "There's one more thing. Tad Tucker, the man himself, plans to take a class."

"Tell him to get in line, then," she said. "All the webinars and online classes are full. Or did he already register?"

"That's just it," Eric said. "He doesn't want to take an online class. He wants to join a workshop, he wants to come in person."

"You're not asking me to give that man an advantage, are you?" Marianne was not sure she could say "Tad Tucker" without adding "that fucker." And automatic admission certainly would not be fair to the other Day of Inspiration applicants, destined for the paper shredder.

"The thing is, he wants to start right away," Eric said. "He wants to come for this session, actually, with the other students."

"He wants to get here on Monday?"

"Not Monday, actually. He says he can come on Wednesday."

"Well, that's impossible. The classes are full. Plus classes start *Monday*, not Wednesday."

"Not impossible," Eric said judiciously. "My workshop is smaller than the others. He wants to do fiction."

"Why didn't you say so?" said Marianne. "He has plenty of experience *doing* fiction. More than you, even!" When Eric didn't respond, she argued, "Your classroom is tiny. Also, there is the question of balance and community and fairness. And the fact that classes start Monday. No, it is impossible." She sipped her coffee.

"It isn't impossible, Marianne. It's done. He's coming, he's registered. It was part of the deal."

"Part of what deal?"

"The deal you're so excited about—signing up new students, getting out from under GWGW's . . . influence," he said. Then, more firmly: "It's done, Marianne. I will email my students. I will teach him. I will handle it. It's not your concern."

Never in the history of their relationship had Eric been so decisive, so assertive. Even his proposal, she remembered, had been pleading—*please say yes*—and as then, Marianne was too taken aback to argue with him.

"Where are you now?"

"Orlando," he said, without pleasure. "At the School of Hospitality and Travel Services. I'll be back tomorrow."

"Wait," she said, but Eric had already hung up. She was about to dial him back when Davonte came in, breathless, but not from a run. He was still wearing his pajamas, loose drawstring pants printed with cartoon penguins and a thin gray tank that showed off his newly defined delts. "Have you seen the Weather Channel today? Have you read the paper yet, Marianne?"

"Tad Tucker was on the Weather Channel?"

"Who's Tad Tucker?" he said. "I'm talking about the storm. Way out there, but look." He opened a weather map on Marianne's computer and clicked through the spaghetti model possibilities: to New Orleans, to Pensacola, to Tampa. One of them had the storm headed straight for Sarasota. "I'm just glad I got my book done," he said, as if the storm's arrival were a sure thing.

Maybe it was the smugness of his tone, the fact that he was wearing pajamas midmorning, or the definition of his gleaming deltoids, but Marianne exploded.

"Davonte, your book is *not* done! It isn't done, and you didn't get it done, anyway. You had someone else write it for you, which is lazy and dishonest, not to mention a complete waste of the education we are supposedly providing you. The storm is not coming here. Okay? It's not!"

He turned around and blinked, the color rising in his cheeks as if she'd slapped him. She would have liked to slap him, or throw water in his face, or do something else dramatic and hurtful.

"Just thought you'd want to know," he said, closing down the screen and getting up.

"Well, I don't!" Marianne called after him. "I don't want to know!"

He left the door open behind him. Outside it was hot and still, the sky a flat, cloudless blue. Marianne slammed the door shut and sat down at her chair, still warm from Davonte's body. Her email was filled with notifications of new webinar registrations, a few dozen questions from prospective and current students. So many of the subject lines were accompanied by multiple question marks, or the emails themselves marked urgent, that she could not imagine sorting through each confusion, each urgency. There was one from Janine Gray (subject line: POEM?), and Marianne hovered her cursor over the email, but did not click to open it.

16

Janine stood at the check-in table, scanning the list of readings and seminars for something that might be of interest to her daughter. It was the first day of their second session, and all kinds of new seminars were now offered during the afternoon hours they used to spend writing, swimming, or playing croquet. There would be a class tomorrow on "Optimizing the Internet Marketing Experience for Artists" and one on "Expanding Your Circle of Influence." In the days that followed, there would be "Publicity Strategies for the Christian Marketplace," "Capitalizing on Current Events," "Cross-Promotional Tie-Ins," "Giving Your Work Away," and even "Film and Television for Christian Writers." Janine went down the list, starring the ones she thought Beth would like. She starred almost all of them.

The day was cloudless and hot, no sign of a storm, but Beth was back in their darkened shared room, sulkily refreshing her internet weather maps and jotting numbers in a notebook. Janine hadn't expected the Ranch's administrators to agree to Beth's visit. She kept asking, Are you sure it won't be any trouble?, hoping to suggest that it would be. But Marianne had sounded distracted, and she probably was, by the all the attention the school had received. Janine had been distracted herself by the publication of her poem—whenever she got near a computer, she found herself checking to see that her work was still there. Someone had posted it to the Ranch's Facebook page as well, and that was an even more compelling place to visit—every time Janine looked, someone else had "liked" or "shared" it. Janine felt sheepish about all of this, and had even emailed Marianne to ask if someone else's work might be highlighted instead, but she had not received a response. Probably Marianne was too busy, getting ready for all of these seminars. Handing over Janine's familiar key—room 7B—she looked as if she had not slept in days.

Instead of an opening-night reading from one of their professors, they were going to hear a talk on "Politics and Inspiration" by Regina Somers, the woman Janine finally understood was responsible for selecting her poem for publication. Janine remembered meeting her on the very first night at the Ranch, and although she had not gotten much out of Regina's webinar on "Growing Your Audience through Christian Tumblr and Pinterest Sites," she felt that in general the woman projected an image of competence, enthusiasm, and encouragement to all the writers at the Ranch. She had a good handshake, she looked you in the eye, and her hair was always perfect. Her webinars frequently used acronyms and other types of mnemonics, a tactic Janine herself had used in classrooms over the years (though she finally had to toss her old HOME EC poster, which spelled out classroom rules, when someone defaced it to read HO EC), and she slowed down just enough to answer questions but not so much that Janine got bored. Janine thought that with her smooth presentation style and professional demeanor, Regina would be a good role model for her daughter, and decided she would insist that Beth join them for the presentation.

She hadn't yet seen anyone from her class, not even Lorraine, with whom she had been corresponding with greater and greater frequency. BE BOLD, Lorraine had told her. DON'T MAKE EXCUSES FOR WHO YOU ARE. DON'T APOLOGIZE.

BE RADICAL.

She had spent the whole summer puzzling over this idea of how to be radical, and wondered if Regina's seminar might offer some other clue. Wasn't it radical to take Terri Schiavo as her subject, to try to imagine the poems that came from her locked-in mind?

WHAT ELSE? Lorraine had wanted to know, when Janine sent her some drafts in May.

Janine had interpreted this to mean that she was telling the story too narrowly, and tried writing from the point of view, then, of Terri's mother and father. Writing those poems, she'd cried for days, imagining herself and Rick in that situation. She'd thought the poems were good, maybe better than the ones she'd sent with her application, but Lorraine had not liked them.

OF COURSE HER PARENTS ARE SAD, Lorraine wrote in an email. LIFE IS SAD. BUT THIS IS PITY. THIS IS SCHMALTZ. START OVER. ALLOW DOUBT TO COME IN. WHAT IF TERRI WANTED TO DIE?

I THINK SHE WANTED TO LIVE! Janine insisted.

WHAT IF SHE WANTED BOTH? Lorraine wrote. WHO HASN'T WANTED BOTH, EVEN WITHOUT THE PROBLEMS OF COMMUNICATION, COGNITION, AND SELF-CARE? YOU MUST ALLOW HER SOME COMPLEXITY, JANINE. IF YOU ARE GOING TO INVITE YOURSELF INTO SOMEONE'S MIND, YOU HAVE TO ACCEPT THAT IT'S MESSY IN THERE.

It amazed Janine that she had been able to take advice from this woman, who had lived a different life than Janine could even imagine—a woman who still smoked like a chimney and did not seem familiar with or at least was not bound by social norms, a woman who talked openly about wanting to die. Yet Janine sensed that she was right about poetry, if nothing else, that she saw clear through to the problem, how what you were trying to say did not fit the way that you were saying it. After initial resistance Janine had started a new set of poems to go with Terri's, this time from the point of view of the police officer who guarded her after they removed her feeding tubes, and she had worked on them all June and the beginning of July. She had not shown them to Lorraine yet, but had instead gotten stuck in the revisions of her original poems, and then on the terrible pressure of having one of those poems (virtually unchanged from her submission) out there, for anyone to read, on the Ranch's website.

I HAVE WRITER'S BLOCK, she admitted yesterday. REVISER'S BLOCK?

THAT IS A MYTH, Lorraine wrote back, mystifyingly, and sent her a long and somewhat confusingly line-broken poem, "Asphodel, That Greeny Flower." Janine printed the poem and highlighted the lines about heaven and hell, dutifully made a note to herself to read the *Iliad*, to look up the references she didn't understand. But one part made her heart beat faster: "It is difficult / to get the news from poems / yet men die miserably every day / for lack / of what is found there." Janine had found these words profound—they made her see desert wars, and her husband's shouting news programs, and the stark white walls of a hospital. She'd looked up the poet and learned that he had also been a doctor—not the kind to leave a patient to die a thirsty death, but the old-fashioned kind who carried a doctor's bag and made house calls. She read everything Lorraine sent her, two and three and four times over, but the lines about the news had stuck with her, and she'd recited them in her head on the long drive while Beth alternately texted and slept. *It is difficult to get the news from poems yet men die miserably every day for lack of what is found there.*

"We are at a profound moment in our history," Regina told them from the podium. Because of the excessive heat, they'd moved the outdoor event into the dining hall, and Regina had to raise her voice above the noise of the air-conditioning. Janine thought the crowd looked a little thin; she did not see Manfred yet, or any of the teachers. There were empty seats on either side of Beth and Janine. "It's a time of political and cultural upheaval as well as a time of revolutionized communication," Regina went on. "You can leave this lecture tonight, go back to your room, and share your writing with someone on the other side of the world. That has never been possible before. Think about it! You have a chance to directly influence people with your *beliefs* and your *values.*"

Janine looked sidelong at Beth and smiled encouragingly; though Beth was not a writer, she was a communicator, an influencer. Behind Regina, on a large portable whiteboard, someone had written POLITICS, vertically, in large block letters. Janine rustled through her bag and brought out her notebook, dutifully copying the word neatly down the left margin.

"*People* have a short attention span," Regina said, writing out the word in a perfect cursive hand. "That is a proven fact. But what are they inundated with, from all sides? Politics. On television, on the radio, around the dinner table. At church! It has invaded our lives. Would you do this for me? Turn to your neighbors and tell them about your three most recent engagements with the world of politics. Make a list for me."

"What did I miss?" said Manfred, taking the seat on the other side of Beth. He leaned forward to squeeze Janine's shoulder.

"Manfred!" Janine exclaimed. "This is my daughter, Beth."

Beth pointed at Janine's empty page. "Dad and Fox News, put that down. We're writing a list of the ways we've experienced politics recently."

"Ah," said Manfred, and Janine wondered if the reference to the cable channel shocked him. "I got pulled over on the way here."

"How about your poem?" said Beth.

"My poem isn't political," Janine said. "Manfred, were you speeding?"

"It was on *Talking to Tad*," Beth insisted, taking her mother's pen and notebook and writing it down. "Getting pulled over isn't political. Not if you're white."

Manfred gave her an appraising look.

"Okay," Regina said. "I'm hearing some excellent and fascinating contributions. Some of it is about our own campus, the way we have been pulled into the political dialogue. How many of you were concerned to see that there were protesters on your campus?"

Janine raised her hand and looked around to see all of the other hands in the room up, too—even Regina's.

"*I* was concerned," said Regina. "I thought, this campus is a place where people come to get inspired by big ideas, not to debate the issues of the day. But then I realized something. Those issues that people are interested in"—she tapped the board—"those *are* big ideas, and the interest they have represents an *Opportunity* to get your message across." She turned and wrote *Opportunity* on the board.

"If you can connect with what is happening in your state, in the country, and use it in your writing, you have many platforms, not just the traditional book-sales platforms. *Leverage* your message across these platforms, and that will generate *Interest* from stakeholders, which will then generate interest in readers. And then—"

"Totalitarianism? Tyranny? Tragedy?" Manfred guessed at the next word under his breath. Beth giggled, and Janine shushed him.

"*Tell your story*," said Regina, neatly looping the words across the board, "in a way that connects both with what you want to say and with the political landscape, and you will not only be creating art, you will be winning hearts and minds, and most importantly, making an impact on the culture. Let me give you an example."

Regina capped her marker and leaned on the podium. She drew a long breath, like she were about to share something difficult, or profound, or personal. "Let's say you are the author of a romance series. How many of you read romances?"

A few tentative hands went up. "Be honest," she chided, raising her own hand. A few more people joined her. "I'll admit, I read them. But sometimes I think they're not that wholesome, you know? Or realistic?" She pulled out a fat paperback and held it up for everyone to see. "This book? It's about a woman whose husband leaves her, but then she finds love with her gardener. How many of you have gardeners?"

One silver-haired woman sitting near the center of the room raised her hand.

"Would you want to find love with your *gardener*?" Regina called to her, making a face.

"That is a personal question," the woman said, crossing her arms.

"Is that Lilian?" Manfred asked, craning forward. "It is!"

"Wouldn't it be better—more inspiring—if the woman and her husband worked it out? If they got back together?"

Lilian snorted.

"Okay, what's your problem with that? The husband, he's old news, right? He watches too much television, he snores?"

"Among other things," she said.

"What if he starts, I don't know, running, and he gets in shape, and he learns some kind of lesson about how he's treated her?" Regina asked, tapping the marker against her stockinged knee as she worked out the most boring romance Janine had ever heard of. "What if he does all that, while realizing that the gardener has designs on his wife, and then he takes up gardening, and she loves roses, so he puts in rosebushes for her? Can you see where I'm going with this, politically?"

The students shook their heads.

"Interracial dating?" someone tried.

Regina turned back to the board. "I'm going to skip down to the *S*." She wrote, *Subtle, but not too subtle.*

"That's the key! This series would be about defense of marriage, the sanctity of marriage, but you don't want to hit somebody over the head with that. You could start out kind of subtly, with this couple, then gradually show everyone else in the community, how important marriage is, the way it holds them all together. Your message: marriage is hot! Think about a sexy gay man, really buff, works out every day, but his heart is full of despair because he know his lifestyle hurts God?

"Imagine the woman he meets at church, where he's trying to turn things around, trying to banish these thoughts. She is so beautiful and pure that he realizes that his former life is all folly and narcissism. Imagine telling their love story."

She filled in the last two letters.

Imagine the stories that people have been afraid to tell.

Cancer is also a good story line.

"That was quite a performance," Manfred said, when the presentation was over and they stood around the snack table, eating stale crackers, sweaty cheese, and M&M's.

Janine was reluctant to criticize. Regina had come up to her, after the lecture, and told her how much the poem's publication on the website meant to her, and suggested that she might want Janine to read at a special event she was planning. Janine did not care for public speaking of any kind, but she was still glowing with Regina's praise. "You missed the first part," she said. "That part was important."

"I'm sure," Manfred said. "But have you noticed how many webinars they have us taking?"

"The registration fees are killing me!" said another woman, grabbing a handful of candy. "Every time I turn around. Don't you think?"

"Honey, nothing in life is free," said Manfred, looking meaningfully at the candy.

"They make you pay for those extra classes?" Beth asked. "They could have used the money to get better snacks."

"Oh," said Janine, who didn't like to talk about money.

The next morning, Beth was exultant over some changes in the wind. She was already awake and sitting at the room's only desk, the computer screen reflecting a moonish glow on her face, when Janine's alarm went off at seven.

"They just named it," Beth said. "Helen. It's a named storm."

Janine blinked in the dark room—Beth had pointedly drawn the heavy curtains last night, though Janine preferred to let in a little sunlight to make waking up easier. She imagined a cool wind whipping through the mangroves and sea oats, dark clouds moving fast across the sky.

"That's good," she said sleepily. She sat up. "I guess."

Janine showered and changed—quickly, half-hidden by the bathroom door, for she was shy in the presence of her daughter's perfect body—into the sturdy, comfortable clothes she would have worn during the back-to-school rush: capri pants and a T-shirt, sandals with cushioned insoles. She combed her wet hair, decided against blow-drying, patted sunscreen onto her cheeks.

"If it keeps heading this way, they might be evacuating by Friday," Beth said. "I may need you to help me with the camera I brought."

"Bethy, I have class all week," Janine said. "I'm sure we won't be evacuating."

"*We* won't be," Beth said ominously, but when Janine peeked outside— it was already muggy and hot—she saw another sunny, cloudless day, no reason to worry. A little part of her was disappointed on Beth's behalf, but it was true that she had been looking forward to the residency since April. "Come to breakfast," she said. "You didn't meet all my friends last night. They're serving pancakes."

"I have an energy bar," Beth said, clacking away at her keyboard. "Thanks."

Workshop was buzzing with talk not about the storm, but about Tad Tucker—rumor was that he planned to arrive on Wednesday for the fiction workshop. Janine took a seat between Maggie and Manfred, both looking bleary-eyed and sleepy. Janine wondered if Maggie had patched things up with her husband, if Manfred was on or off the wagon. Three students had not shown up; Janine could think of a hundred reasons why, but people were speculating that it was concern over the Ranch's recent controversies.

"He doesn't *look* like much of a writer," Lilian sniffed, twisting a diamond tennis bracelet around her thin, tanned wrist.

"How much do any of us look like writers?" Maggie asked.

Lilian patted her smooth bob; clearly she thought she looked writerly, or at least cultured.

Maggie shrugged. "I look like a soccer mom. I drive a minivan. I *am* a soccer mom."

"Lorraine looks like a writer," Janine said. She had decided that Lilian was harmless, even pitiable, just a rich and lonely woman, some doctor's former trophy wife. "Or at least she looks the way I pictured writers looking."

"And she keeps time like one," said Lilian. "Tad Tucker is a crook. My husband's colleague treated the boy who was injured at one of his batting cages. He has permanent brain damage, that's what I heard."

"At least he got treatment," said Janine quietly. She couldn't help herself. "My husband used to listen to Tad Tucker on the radio. I don't think he's so bad."

"He's a right-wing nut," said Lilian. "Didn't you see Patty's Facebook posts?"

Janine looked at Maggie, who shrugged. "I'm not a Tad Tucker fan myself," Maggie said.

"We all had to apply," Manfred sniffed.

"Did you see that the protesters are back this morning?" asked Julia, the woman with the knitting. A long red scarf trailed from her lap to the floor; she kept her eyes on what the needles were doing, so it was hard to read how she felt about Tad Tucker or the protesters. Janine wondered if obscuring your feelings about a topic was one of the benefits of knitting.

Had anyone heard about Tucker's connection to GWGW? someone asked. That was sure an interesting story, someone else replied. What about the online sonography school? Had anyone talked to the protesters, who were back, and sitting just steps away from the office? No, no one had approached the protesters, though it was odd the way they had set up their lawn chairs facing the Ranch, as if they were waiting for a show. Better to ignore them than to try to get involved, to find out what they want. They all agreed that it was a blessing that Tad Tucker was a fiction writer and not a poet, that their own workshop would not be affected by any scandal. Was he staying on campus? Probably not, they decided. Too low-rent for somebody like that.

Lorraine arrived at 10:15—she was punctual in her lateness, Janine had noticed—and handed around a survey. "I don't understand why they need to know these things," she said, pacing the front of the room as the class answered questions about their television habits, their favorite movies, their household incomes and education levels, which internet provider they used, and how they felt about the webinars they had taken.

Lilian was still finishing her survey when Lorraine snatched it away. "It doesn't matter," she said, shuffling it into her pile. "Did you all take the web classes?"

They murmured unenthusiastic assent.

Maggie raised her hand. "Why didn't you teach any of the webinars, Ms. Kominski?"

"I would have no idea how to do that," Lorraine said. "The topics were all beyond my area of expertise."

"They didn't seem to be about writing," Janine offered. "They were more about business topics. How to earn a living."

"This is all nonsense. Come on, we're going for a walk. Bring a chair if you don't like sitting on the ground."

She led them to the lawn shaded by twisted old oaks. No one, not even the immaculately attired Lilian, dragged along a chair. No one spoke. Along the roadway, crape myrtles dropped the last of their bright pink blossoms, and through their pale, dry branches you could see the protesters sitting in the merciless sun.

"See them?" Lorraine said, not even bothering to lower her voice. She crouched, her long skirt dragging the mulch beneath the crape myrtles. Her students crept next to her and kneeled or crouched as they were best able. If the protesters took notice of them, they did not let on. "Here they are in the blazing heat, holding up their signs not because camera crews are here, not because they think we'll come out and pay attention to them, but because something compels them to do it. Maybe the news cameras will be back tomorrow, maybe not. Maybe someone will listen to them, take some of their literature, or maybe they will be completely misunderstood. No one is going to give them money, they can be sure of that." She stood, with effort. "That's poetry."

Then she turned around and went back inside, not looking behind to see whether they would follow. Janine was right behind her. The mildly air-conditioned room felt much cooler after the outside heat, and

Lorraine was already announcing the order in which they'd be work-shopped as the last of them filed in. First she wanted them to make some revisions on the poems she'd selected to talk about, and she walked around the room, dropping heavily marked papers at each of their places, like an annoyed waiter delivering bread or sodas to impatient diners.

"She learned our names," Manfred whispered, as a paper fluttered to his hands. He sounded pleased, though his poem was marked through with lines, crosses, and angry-looking arrows.

Janine gasped as her own poem came to rest in front of her. "Last Day," it was called, and every line was struck through with blue felt tip—except for two, in the center, which now looked both lonely and burdened, like the survivors of a disaster. It was a poem she'd spent weeks on.

"Leave your revisions in my office by the morning, and I'll get them to you at workshop. We'll do exercises tomorrow, and we'll be work-shopping the first of you by Wednesday. You have today to work," she announced. "That will give you a good reason to skip the seminars they have planned."

She nodded at them and left, in her usually hurried and fumbling way, like she was afraid some of them might chase after her.

"She left me five lines," said Manfred, after some of the others had left. "That's an improvement for me, though I won't say they are my fa-vorite lines."

"She didn't cross out any of my lines," Maggie said. "But she did write 'start over' at the bottom. And circled it. Oh well."

"I have two lines left," Janine said quietly, still staring at her blud-geoned poem. Lorraine had critiqued her work before, had sent notes and emails exhorting her to be strong or radical, but this felt more personal, to have her writing marked through—obliterated, banished—with the stroke of a pen. She felt sick to her stomach, thinking of the connection she had assumed existed between herself and her teacher. "Two."

"It's better than 'start over,'" Maggie said.

"I think I'd rather start over."

Janine tried to write in her room, opening the curtains wide to let in light, but Beth's things were strewn across every surface; even the air, humid from her late-morning shower and permeated with the smell of coconut shampoo, was full of her. She shouldn't have brought her here, should have insisted that this was her time away, that it was something she needed. Even Rick said as much: You sure you want to take her? But Janine was helpless in the face of criticism from her daughters, the suggestion that she might not want what was best for them. Beth had known that and used it against her.

Where were these mean thoughts coming from? She did not want to think them, not about her own daughter. What was wrong with her?

Janine took her spiral notebook, with the two acceptable lines copied into it, outside, but that was no good either—everywhere she looked she saw a poet. Thinking about other people writing poems did not motivate Janine but instead made her feel nervous and self-conscious and competitive. She wondered how many good poems could be written on a single day, at a single school. Two? Three? Maybe none, she thought, looking at her classmates. She started walking toward the Kangaroo; Beth said this morning that she needed tampons, which was better than Beth not needing tampons, but still. Sometimes Janine thought she'd done too much for her girls; their expectations of her were too high.

The protesters were in their same spots, camped out on lawn chairs with their signs propped against their knees. Close up, Janine could see that some of them had marked the letters on their signs in pencil before going over the lines with permanent marker, and had written their slogans along ruled guidelines, also marked in pencil. POETRY or PROFIT? read one of the signs that Janine could see. She thought about her poem, which when she last looked (just this morning), was still on the Ranch's web page. It wasn't making any money—Janine had no idea how many times anyone had looked at it, even—but someone had added links: to the Wikipedia page about Terri Schiavo, to the foundation her parents had established in her name, and, somewhat disturbingly, to the *Talking to Tad* radio show.

The protesters did not look up at as Janine skirted around their long, silent line, but kept their eyes trained on the school. In the Kangaroo, she bought tampons and seven bottles of water, then carried the heavy bag of water back to the protesters. She walked in front of them, then went down the line, pulling the water bottles from the thin plastic bag and handing them over without speaking. Thank you, they each said. At the end of the row there was a woman wearing a visor decorated with metal buttons and peering through a pair of binoculars.

"Is he in there?" she asked.

"Who?"

"Tad Tucker," said the woman, letting the binoculars rest on a string around her neck and looking up at Janine. "Today's the first day of classes, isn't it?"

"It is," Janine confirmed. "But I haven't seen him. I heard that he's coming on Wednesday."

"You hear that?" the woman called down the line. "Some inspiration!"

"Wednesday!" said another woman. "No wonder it's so quiet today."

"I'm not sure, though," Janine said, afraid she'd said too much. "Who knows if he's coming at all. May I sit down?"

The woman inched her chair over enough that Janine had a small patch of grass to sit on and resumed looking through her binoculars. "You're a student here? What do you think about a politician using your school for political gain?"

"Maybe he just wants to write," Janine said.

"Then why isn't he here?" The woman looked again through her binoculars, as if he might be hiding behind the bushes somewhere.

Two years ago, Janine's school offered yoga to the teachers once a week as part of a stress-reduction initiative. Janine had not learned much more in class than the proper way of sitting in the lotus position, but she had looked forward to each class, especially the silence at the end, when the teacher would ring a small bell and they would sit with their eyes closed as sound reverberated in their chests. She'd been disappointed when her principal cut the funding, but had never attended a yoga class on her own after that.

Now she sat lotus style, her spine as straight as she could make it, her feet tucked against her thighs. Lorraine had said that this was poetry, sitting without expectation. She tried yoga breaths, taking deep bellyfuls of humid air then exhaling slowly, and hoped she didn't look silly. She thought about the poem she wanted to write, about the security guard's experience of watching Terri. It had been so awful to think about—guarding someone who was dying, guarding her from the people who wanted to save her—that it had been difficult to express what he might have felt. In the poem, the speaker forced himself to think about other things—going to his son's T-ball game, grilling steak for dinner, the smell of his wife's hair. The pleasures of being alive. But that had left her nowhere to go, using his voice, except guilt. He hadn't faced Terri's impending death and what it would mean. Janine hadn't made him. That was why Lorraine crossed out most of her lines.

Janine longed for her pen and notebook, which she'd left back in her room. She began to get that feeling, a sort of pent-up but not unpleasant sensation, that always signified that a poem was coming. It was similar to the way she sometimes felt before initiating intimacy with Rick—something that seldom happened anymore but used to about once a month, during the fertile part of her cycle. The poem feeling was similar in the way that the desire surprised her, the way it seemed to come from nowhere, from everywhere. Also in its fragility.

"You okay?" asked the woman next to her. She offered Janine some of her water, but Janine shook her head.

"I'm okay," she said, standing. "Just tired. I have to do some rewriting."

The woman nodded, unsurprised and unimpressed. "Storm might be here by then, anyway," she said. "That'd turn all his plans upside down, wouldn't it? Have you been watching the weather?"

"My daughter studies meteorology," Janine began, then stopped herself. She knew if started talking about her children, she would lose her momentum, her desire. "I'm sorry. I have to go."

17

Tad Tucker arrived in a black Suburban, parked directly in front of the office, and left it running. He was accompanied by the same two polo-shirted GWGW assistants, Christopher and Matt, who had first appeared with Regina. She was already on campus when they arrived, waiting on the steps in a bright pink skirt suit and holding a bucket-sized Styrofoam cup of sweet tea.

Marianne kept the storm door propped open so she could watch from her desk. She'd thought—she'd hoped—that the incipient tropical storm, which was in fact headed in their very direction, would have been enough to keep Tad Tucker away from campus and focused on more pressing matters. *Wouldn't miss it!* he'd texted them all last night. *See you around 1:00.* Sophie had sent a text—*Lots of cancellations here—you?*—and Marianne had considered canceling classes, rescheduling the whole session, but Regina, ever the optimist, encouraged her to wait and see.

"Representative Tucker," Regina said, handing him the tea as he came up the steps. "So good to have you on campus."

He took a long sip through the straw before answering her. "Good to be here," he said, clapping Regina on the shoulder. Gray-blue smoke clouded their ankles. Marianne peered out the door and into the cavernous Suburban—no Ruth, she was relieved to see. No Darryl. "Nice spot, but I was glad to have Chris and Matt for directions. You don't have much of a sign."

"Regina? Could you please close the door?" Marianne asked. The office was filling with Tad Tucker's exhaust.

"Sorry 'bout that," said Tad Tucker. He tossed his keys to Chris, pointed to a nearby spot where he could park, and opened the door, which Marianne realized, for the first time, was a smaller, nonstandard size. He had to duck to fit inside. "So you must be one of the founders of this fine institution."

"Guilty as charged," Marianne said. " You know, with your penchant for alliteration, I'm surprised you're not a poet."

"My penchant for what, honey?"

"Oh, Marianne is one of our poets," Regina said. "You know how they are! Always trying to swell their ranks!"

"I see you've got protesters across the street. Not too many, though," he added, peering through the blinds.

"I imagine there will be more later," Regina assured him. "It's early."

"All right," he said, taking one last look. "Let's get this show on the road."

Marianne led them down the path to the fiction cabana, where ten students barely fit and where the raftered ceiling would barely clear Tad's six-and-a-half-foot frame. Tad kept stopping so that Matt could take his photograph, and by the time they made it to the classroom he was sweating profusely. Marianne had tried to persuade the two other workshop leaders, whose classrooms were larger and better air-conditioned, to switch for the day with Eric, but Tom refused on behalf of both of them. "We don't want that guy in our spaces," he told her. "We might not have had any say in allowing him here, but that doesn't mean we have to accommodate you."

"I didn't have any say in it either," Marianne argued. She was surprised that Tom blamed her and not Eric, but she was also surprised that he'd returned to campus at all. "It wasn't my idea. But one day, that's it, and it's over."

"You're in charge, aren't you?" Tom asked, and she hadn't known how to answer.

Class had already started when she opened the door. Someone had thought to remove the table and gather the metal folding chairs in a circle.

"Welcome," said Eric, nearly knocking over his chair to get to the door. "We're so glad to have you, Representative Tucker."

Half the class stood, eagerly extending their hands, as Tucker walked in. The other half stayed awkwardly seated, wearing tight smiles. Davonte, whose newly polished manuscript had been bumped so they could workshop Tad's story, sat with his arms folded across his chest.

"Davonte Gold," said Tad, extending his hand, then balling it slowly into a fist. "I loved *Hurt Songs*, brother. Great album."

Davonte nodded, but did not fist-bump Tad Tucker.

"Well, it's very crowded in here, so I'll see you all at the reading later," said Regina, backing out of the doorway. "Marianne?"

"Marianne wanted to observe the workshop," said Eric, widening his eyes at Marianne.

Marianne had expressed no such desire, but she knew the look Eric was giving her, had given it herself to teachers and administrators when faced with a particularly volatile class. For a moment she felt sorry for Eric, dressed in his lame GWGW polo, badly in need of a haircut and a shave. When his book first came out, he'd interviewed for a job at Sarah Lawrence, and she pictured the stately room he might have taught in, the sturdy, genteel furnishings, the well-prepared young students he might have had there. "I did," she said, taking a seat in the corner and waving good-bye to Regina.

"I just want to start by saying that it's a privilege to be in this class with you, to spend this Day of Inspiration with you," said Tad, taking the empty two seats next to Eric. "It was so inspiring to be able to share one of my big passions in life with you." He looked genuinely pleased and excited to be there. Marianne had not read his story, and Eric had only shaken his head when she asked him about it.

"Actually, you don't talk during this part," said Davonte. "That's one of our rules we learned on the first day, back in March. You just listen and take notes."

"Great," Tad said, opening his leather portfolio and taking out a gold pen. "That's what politicians need to do more of, in my opinion. Listen and—"

"No talking at all," said Davonte firmly. "Just listening. Am I right, Eric?"

"Well," Eric said, looking down at his notes. "Why don't we start by sharing some of the things we admired about Representative Tucker's—"

"Tad," said Tad. Davonte gave him a stern look. "Sorry!" he said.

"About Tad's work," Eric said.

The room was quiet. Some people looked at the manuscript, searching for the parts that they liked. Others looked at the walls, the ceiling, as if the virtues of Tad's story might be found there. What had he written about? A gruesome late-term abortion? A science fiction piece about vengeful, sentient zygotes? Marianne leaned forward in her seat.

Finally Louis, the one-world-government novelist, said, "I was surprised, actually, that Tad wrote a story about baseball. I was thinking that this would be, I don't know, a kind of political piece. But it was about baseball. I like baseball."

The other students nodded, grateful for the opportunity to approve baseball.

"Writing about baseball has an excellent literary tradition," said Eric. "Philip Roth, Bernard Malamud, DeLillo—"

Tad's pen raced across the page as more people offered positive thoughts about baseball.

"Didn't the story feel sort of . . . familiar to you, though?" someone asked.

"Yeah," said Davonte, leaning forward. "The cocky guy that misses and misses and strikes out? I kept thinking, I heard this somewhere before. Don't talk, man," he said, pointing at Tad. "You gotta wait."

"Davonte, Tad is our guest," Eric chided.

"I thought you said he was a student," Davonte said. "Same as us."

"Let's stick to the work."

"I will admit, I guess, that I wanted it to be more political," Louis said, turning the manuscript pages and frowning. "I wanted there to be more at stake. I wanted it to be about something bigger."

"There is something at stake," Davonte said. "The pitch. Will he strike out or not?"

"It's interesting, the way he's compressed time," someone else offered.

"It's 'Casey at the Bat'!" interjected another student. "That's why it's so familiar."

Tad's face reddened and his fancy pen slowed as he realized that the students did not mean familiar in a good way. "But—" he said.

"No talking!" said Davonte and Louis at once.

"You'll have your chance, don't worry," Eric said. "Why don't we think about the ways Tad could expand the story, given what we have here."

"He could hit the ball instead of striking out," Davonte said.

"The story could take place over the entire game."

"He could have something else on his mind? Maybe an internal conflict?"

"What do we really know about this batter, anyway? Could we have some backstory?"

Tad Tucker had stopped writing entirely. The slight flush in his cheeks had become a fiery red that engulfed his head, from his wide neck to his shiny bald spot. Apparently he had not counted on constructive criticism.

"These sound like excellent, very well considered suggestions," said Eric. "Though of course it will be up to Tad to decide what to do."

When it was finally time for Tad Tucker to talk, he looked about to explode.

"Well, I just want to thank you all for sharing your suggestions. They're very interesting. Maybe if any of you decide to write a story about baseball you can use them," he said. "I'm happy with my ending. Sometimes when you go up to bat, it's the bottom of the ninth, and you're the best player on the team, you still don't hit the ball. It happens in 'Casey at the Bat,' and it happens here, because it's one of the tough truths of life."

"I think Davonte was just trying to broaden the landscape of narrative choices," offered Eric. "Since it's a first draft."

"Well, I know when to leave well enough alone. You can't just spend your life tweaking every word of a story to see if it comes out different. Well, maybe some of you can. I learned to write on a deadline, and I wrote this on a deadline."

"That's a talent," Eric noted.

"And it wound up on the front page of the sports section of the *Hurricane*."

"Oh," said Eric. "You wrote this in college. Well, you're a busy man, Representative Tucker. It really was great that you took the time to . . ."

"Retype it," said Louis.

"Well," said Marianne, after workshop was over and she was left alone with Eric. "Tad Tucker doesn't like criticism. Go figure."

"Nobody likes to be criticized, Marianne," Eric said, packing papers into his messenger bag. "The class basically accused him of plagiarizing a children's poem."

"It sounded like a terrible story."

"It was," he said, shaking his head. "It was a terrible story. But they've written some stinkers themselves."

"As bad as that?"

"No," he admitted.

"On the bright side," she said, "it looks like you've taught them something. Louis seems to have made progress, for example. And they didn't bring Ruth—I mean, I didn't think she'd show up without telling me, but it's been so long since I've heard from her." The day would be over soon; nothing horrible had happened. This was what passed for elation for her, these days. Nothing horrible. One foot in front of the other.

"How did it come to this, Marianne? In a couple of hours, we're hosting a fetal personhood–themed reading. We've invited members of the press. How are we going to keep our pictures—our names—out of the paper?"

"The reading is personhood-themed? The press is coming? I told Janine—I told her—that it was just a small reading, just like a normal Friday-afternoon reading, with her peers and one external person, Tad Tucker, who is just there to listen. Will there be cameras?"

Eric hung his head. "There will be cameras."

"But Tad isn't speaking?"

"He wants to say just a few words—"

"Shit, Eric. I *promised* her. She came to me last night, not sure if she should do it or not and I convinced her—against my better judgment—that it would be fine. She was afraid that some of the other students would see her as pandering to a political cause. She doesn't want her work to be read like that. You promised me, Eric. You promised that it wouldn't go like this."

"I'm sorry," Eric said. "You're right. Just a few more days—"

"The students *know*, Eric. They know that GWGW has invested in all of those fetus billboards and commercials and postcards. I mean, it's in the news!

"Damn you!" she said, making for the door. "I trusted you! I thought, Eric won't let me down. Eric knows the score. I was so stupid!"

"I'm sorry," he said. "But you were the one with all the plans—to pay back our loans, to build a library and offer scholarships. How did you think—"

"Not like this! I never said like this!" Marianne paused in the doorway. "I can't believe I was falling back in love with you," she said, before running up the hill.

The dining hall, arranged for the reading with the salad bar pulled into the kitchen, the round tables pushed against the north wall, was packed. Usually GWGW's students filled up five rows of chairs, but today there were people standing along the south walls, leaning beneath the gilt-framed pictures. A camera crew was running extension cords into the kitchen, and Regina was talking to the catering staff and pointing at the loud HVAC vents. Marianne spotted Lorraine sitting in the back, marking papers with a red felt-tip pen.

"Lorraine," she whispered, crouching behind her. "Do you think there's time to cancel?"

Lorraine didn't look up. "I don't think so, Marianne. I think the die is cast, as they say. This happening is happening."

"I told Janine there wouldn't be press."

"I'm sure she's seen the cameras," Lorraine remarked. "Janine will be fine. She's tough. Tougher than you were."

"Where is she?"

"Up front," said Lorraine, marking through someone's poem with a fat *X*. "We had a cigarette. She'll be fine."

Marianne stood and scanned the front row, where she saw Janine's familiar mousy brown bob bent over some papers. A pretty young woman rubbed her back. Davonte was doing squats.

Regina strode down the aisle in a pink flash. "There's your friend," said Lorraine. "Better take your seat."

"Welcome, everyone, and thank you—so very much—for your support," Regina began, her voice quiet and halting. "As you know, we have faced enormous criticism of the work that we do here." She gripped the sides of the podium. "Important work, but frightening, threatening to some people."

Marianne looked around her, expecting to see people rolling their eyes, or at least looking away from the phony, almost tearful Regina, but the audience watched her expectantly. She paused for a long moment before going on.

"That's why I'm so happy and so grateful to see you all here at the Genesis Inspirational Writing Ranch, a partner campus of God's World God's Word," she said, appearing to blink the tears away. "And I'm so very thrilled that many of you will be joining us in online classes and seminars. But I want to first recognize the students who have been inspired by the school since March! Please stand!"

The Ranch's students stood and waved sheepishly, while everyone clapped. Please do not recognize the teachers, Marianne silently commanded. Do not.

"And the teachers!" Regina said. "Oh, they are so modest, they won't even stand. But I want to recognize"—here she looked at her list—"Eric Osborne, novelist; Tom Marshall, memoirist and journalist; and Lorraine Kominski, poet."

Relieved to be forgotten, Marianne leaned back as Regina introduced Davonte as a reformed, world-renowned star and novelist. He read a short scene in which his protagonist, Damian Silver, convinces a woman not to abort his child, and even choked himself up a little, by the end. He sat down to generous applause.

Janine received a longer, even more effusive introduction from Regina Somers. "Just think!" she said. "A year ago, Janine Gray had not shown her work to anyone outside her family. Now her work has been read by thousands of people!"

Janine's face was flushed as she made her way slowly to the podium, and Marianne could see that her hands trembled as she held the pages of her work. "I wanted to say before I started that I am grateful to Lorraine Kominski, who has taught me so much about poetry, and to my fellow writers, who have made all kinds of sacrifices to be here. I also want to thank Marianne Stuart, who believed in me from the beginning. Marianne, I would not be here—none of us would be here—if it weren't for you."

Students and guests craned their necks to look at Marianne, who slunk down a little in her seat. Janine read Ferlinghetti's "Poetry as Insurgent Art," then turned to her own work. Her voice was clear and even and just slow enough, full of feeling for the words. Lorraine smiled and closed her eyes to listen, but Marianne could barely hear her, she was so intent on intercepting Tad Tucker, who stood and clapped as Janine finished, starting a standing ovation that cascaded through the hall.

Marianne jogged down the center aisle. She was faster than Tad, and made it to the microphone first. "Thank you, Representative Tucker, but I can't let you—"

He was still clapping manfully as he made his way to the podium and cleared his throat. "I want to talk to you about freedom. Freedom of speech. Freedom of thought. Educational freedom. And before all those, the freedom to be a person," he began. Patty Connor got up and walked out. Stricken, Janine kept her eyes on Marianne as she edged back to her seat.

"But before I get into that, I want to acknowledge another person, crucial to this school's founding." Marianne thought he would talk about Frances, quickly thought of what she would say, if prompted, about this woman she'd never met. *An artist! Who wanted a place for others to find inspiration!* Tad threw an arm around her shoulder and yanked her close to him. "That's this gal right here, Marianne Stuart, and Janine is right— none of us would be here without her. She had the whole idea to begin with, years before it was any kind of possibility. I want to confess that I was skeptical at first—what could some New York City poet know about *our* culture, *our values*? But I've gotten to know Miss Stuart, and, well, I'm the first to admit when I'm wrong."

There was some pointed coughing. Marianne tried to lean toward the microphone—Thank you! What an evening! Let's all have some punch!—but Tad's grip on her shoulder held her fast.

"First off, she's a Virginia gal. Second, I've learned about her family, a good family with roots in the church," he continued, hugging Marianne closer. He smelled of a noxiously sweet aftershave, and she craned her face away from his jacket. He let her go and stepped back, grabbing the microphone and whisking the cord behind him. "Do you know, Marianne, that we have a surprise for you tonight?"

Marianne shook her head imperceptibly, then watched as Tad gestured to Regina. "A reunion!" he continued. "A family reunion, of two beautiful and hardworking Christian sisters."

And there was Ruth, emerging from the kitchen in a navy skirt suit, her hair pulled back tightly, her pale, makeup-less face implacably serene. She *did* look beautiful—in a vaguely corporate-Madonna way—but also scared and slightly tottering in her navy heels and tan hose. Marianne reached to take the mic from Tad, but he turned away, toward the audience and Ruth, who stepped shyly onto the dais, aided by Regina.

"This gal here is Mrs. Ruth Boyette, wife to Darryl Boyette, minister of Healing Waters Baptist Church, and sister to Miss Marianne Stuart—"

The audience clapped their approval.

"Ruth," Marianne whispered as her sister approached for a quick, light hug. "Why didn't you call me? What are you doing here?"

"—is a big part of what we're calling the Tour of Life," Tad continued. "Which is something I want to invite all of you to join, about the sanctity of life, the power that we have to protect the powerless. That's why she's come here, to talk with you about your power, and to congratulate all of you, and also her sister for making this space where you have the freedom to exercise that power. Isn't that right, Ruth?"

Ruth nodded, and Tad replaced the microphone in its stand. Ruth leaned in slowly. "I'm here to tell you all a story." She paused, and Marianne could see that her shyness—the unsteady, slow walk, the determined composure—was something she had practiced. She was not scared. She was, in a way that Marianne would never be, at home here.

"It's a sad story, in a lot of ways," Ruth continued. "My mother—" she looked back at Marianne with a sorrowful expression. "*Our* mother died when I was in kindergarten. She had breast cancer, and she was a warrior." Ruth paused again.

"But her fierceness started long before she got sick. I would not be here before you today, in fact, if our mother had not chosen life—"

The audience seemed to be holding their breath. This could not go on. Was Marianne going to let Tad Tucker and her baby sister take over, *ruin*, whatever was left of what she had built? With a fantasy concocted about a time she couldn't remember?

She reached around Ruth and pulled the microphone from the stand, roughly, then stepped away and glared warningly at Tad and Ruth.

"None of us would be here without our mothers," Marianne snapped, a little more harshly than she meant. "Mothers are wonderful, I think we can all agree, we owe them every gratitude. But our mother was an artist, like all of you, and she isn't here to speak for herself or her experience or her . . . choices. This evening is after all about our students and *their* work, and we want to thank them, especially Donald and Janine. What wonderful, inspiring readings they gave!"

Some people stood, clapping heartily, while others looked around in confusion. She saw Sophie La Tour at the back of the hall, arms crossed and frowning. Davonte bowed his head as neighbors back-patted him. Janine left in a hurry, poem clutched to her chest, before anyone could reach her.

A great success, Regina called the Day of Inspiration, after Tad Tucker and his entourage drove away. Scrolling through messages on her tablet, she predicted that, once the story went live, they'd be able to open even more classes. "Of course, we'll probably need to hire additional instructors, but think of all the free publicity we just got. Did you hear the excellent plug Tad gave the work you are doing here—not to mention independent, online education?" she asked. "Though I have to say it's a shame that you didn't let Ruth give her talk. She has become *such* a powerful speaker on this tour. You should have seen the standing ovation she got at our Institute of Christian Game Design and Videography."

Ruth sat in a folding chair, massaging her left foot. She looked more like the self that Marianne knew: petulant, barely out of her teens, a pretend adult. Some of her hair had escaped from its bun, and her cheeks were flushed to her temples. "It's hot in here," she said. "Don't you air-condition this place?"

"We turn it down between events and dinner, to save energy," Marianne said. She was loudly dragging tables across the room, getting seating ready for dinner, and starting to sweat herself. "That's part of what we consider being good Christians, being good stewards of the Earth. But I can turn the air on if it's important to you."

Ruth narrowed her eyes, scuffed her pump defiantly back onto her foot. "You don't believe any of this. Regina, she doesn't believe in any of this."

"Hmmm," said Regina, still scrolling through her messages.

Marianne made the slashing motion across her neck, and Ruth smiled wickedly. "Marianne and my dad—they *never* come to Healing Waters. They never went to church, never took me to church, after Mom died." When Regina said nothing, Ruth continued: "She is *atheist*, Regina. She told me that, when I was a kid. Ask her a question about the Bible! Any question, a little bit hard, I guarantee you—"

"Do you really have some kind of planted memories of Mom going to church, Ruth?" Marianne asked. "I mean, because that's what they would be. False memories, except with Granny at Christmas and Easter. Which was before you were born, by the way."

"Because she was sick! Because of me, right? You think it was because of me, which is why you won't ever let me talk about her."

"Because you don't know what you're talking about, Ruth!" Marianne slammed a chair against the edge of the table nearest Ruth, watched her sister wince.

Suddenly Marianne was very tired. She had not meant to yell. She took a deep breath and did a count of tables as she exhaled. Seven more to set up. "You should have called me. You should have told me you were coming. Regina, *you* should have told me—"

Regina placed her tablet inside her leather tote and hooked the tote over her shoulder. She buttoned her pink blazer and squared her shoulders. "I don't have a sister, but I always wanted one," she said, her voice measured and strangely soft. "I'm an only child, actually. I understand that disagreements come up at emotional times like this. But emotions are good, right? For poets, and for feeders of the flock? As for Marianne's Bible knowledge, I'm not stupid. I'm not *unaware* of where she comes from . . . spiritually. But that doesn't mean you're not each doing good work. Important work. Though perhaps you need some time apart. The Tour of Life continues, right, Ruth?"

Ruth nodded and stood, following Regina without looking back. Like looking back would freeze her, turn her into a pillar of salt. Marianne knew that much, mostly from college, or maybe reggae songs, but weren't those also legitimate ways of garnering knowledge?

She didn't watch Regina and Ruth leave, either, though she heard the heavy door shut behind them. She needed the ten more tables in place, napkins restocked, silverware in bins, iced tea cups stacked upside down, Muzak playing softly, the thermostat cranked down to seventy. Ketchup and salt and pepper and sugar and Sweet'n Low centered on every table.

Where she came from—spiritually! How did Ruth follow that woman? How did she not see that Regina didn't even care what she believed?

Just as she was refilling the last ceramic dish with pink sweetener packets, Eric arrived.

"Sorry I'm late," he said, reaching for the bag she gripped under her arm. "Let me help."

Marianne pushed the table at him, hard, and walked out.

In her office, she opened a bottle of wine, then sat down at her desk. She had not returned an email in days. She'd left everything to Eric, and he hadn't delivered on a single promise.

You're in charge, aren't you? Tom had asked.

None of us would be here if it weren't for you, Janine had said.

Marianne opened her email, poured a glass of wine, and waited. Today alone, she'd received a hundred new messages—from students, from applicants, from curious parties. She scanned her unread mail and found one from Martin Rice, of the Sarasota *Herald-Tribune*. The subject line read "Interview for Tomorrow's Paper?"

Marianne opened it, found his number, and dialed. "Martin Rice? Yes, this is Marianne Stuart, from Genesis Ranch. I got your message. I'm free to talk."

18

Later Marianne would realize that she'd done things out of order, that she should have gone first to see Frances, or talked to Mark, or even Eric. Maybe one of these people could have talked her down, warned her against going to the press. Or maybe she should have called Sophie— who hadn't waited to speak to her after the reading, and who Marianne suspected of calling the reporter in the first place. Instead she'd dialed Ruth's number, but couldn't decide if she would yell or apologize, so she hung up before her sister answered. Like she'd answer anyway, Marianne thought while finishing most of a bottle of wine and shakily driving Eric's car to the coffee shop suggested by the reporter, Martin Rice, who looked much younger than she pictured. Perhaps it was his youth and eagerness—he seemed so *interested* in everything she had to say, so rigorously observant—that made her talk.

It had been easy to get away. Everyone at the Ranch was at dinner, gossiping or fretting about the Day of Inspiration. Day of Desperation, she told Martin Rice. He just nodded and wrote in his notebook, his recording device a fulcrum between them. The coffee he offered churned in Marianne's stomach, but she drank it anyway, like medicine.

"Let's go back a little," Martin suggested. "To the beginning of the school."

"It all went wrong when GWGW got involved," Marianne said. "God's World God's Word—you know them?"

He nodded.

"They offered us all of this funding, and all of these services, and it sounded okay for a while—well, maybe not okay, but necessary, just to keep the school running, to pay our teachers. I didn't know the whole story—I didn't know they were connected to this crazy personhood bill, or the way their support of Tad Tucker and personhood was just a way to get something else they wanted."

"Which was?"

Marianne took a swig of coffee. This was her moment, her chance to deal a real blow to Regina and everyone else at GWGW. "Phasing out Florida's community college system. They're spending five million dollars on Tad Tucker's campaign, just so they can shut down public community colleges. So they can swoop in with their . . . Christian medical billing schools. Christian prelaw academies. Christian sonography schools."

"Christian writing schools?"

Marianne shook her head so vigorously it hurt. "We had no idea. We are independent—*were* independent—before they started funding us."

"Why did you need their help? Why did you take their money?

Marianne tried to explain about the cost of everything, about Mark, but everything she said opened up a new question. How did she know Mark? How did it all get started? Why here, why now? What inspired her to start the school?

"I didn't start it," she told him, sitting up a little straighter in her chair. "I served as its first director."

He took out his phone and read from the school's website, which had somehow been changed overnight. There was a bio of Marianne under "About Our Teachers"—she was right at the top. But instead of listing her education and experience and publications, the bio described her as the school's founder, a Virginia native who dreamed of starting a school for inspirational writing after graduating with her MFA (it did not say from where). At the end, a slew of corporate words: *partnership* and *synergy* and *opportunity*. Martin looked at Marianne and frowned, like he was very confused. Was the school not her idea?

Well, it was, she said, but not in a serious way. She had the idea that it could work, she said, and would be popular and profitable, but it was actually Frances Ketterling who wanted the school to open. Marianne told him everything she knew about Eric's aunt, how she had the same dream, but was serious about it. She paid for the school to open. She paid Marianne to be here. It was a job, she told him.

"If she paid, then why did you need to go to GWGW for money?"

Marianne sighed—this was the hardest part to explain, the part she herself didn't understand. "Running a school has so many expenses—all the fees and permits and salaries." She struggled for a metaphor that would sound convincing. "We were caught a little flat-footed when we realized . . . how much everything would cost."

"Don't you collect tuition?"

"Tuition helps," she allowed. "But, take my graduate school, it wasn't providing everything I got there on my tuition alone. Though I guess I don't see why not. The point is, most schools have this big endowment! We were just starting out!"

Martin Rice asked if she had a business plan. He wanted to see numbers, which Marianne didn't think to bring—in fact she didn't even have them, had never had them, though she didn't tell him that. Instead she told him that Frances was getting older, and what would happen if she fell, and he looked confused again, frowning at his notebook for a long time while she went on about retirement communities and assisted living and skilled nursing. Why didn't she have those numbers?

"If you weren't serious about it, why did you serve as the school's director?"

That was the time, Marianne later realized, when she could have lied. Could have embossed, embroidered, embellished, burnished, polished, smoothed. In her growing anger—at Eric, at Mark, at Regina and everyone at GWGW—it didn't even occur to her. She opened her mouth and told him about not having full-time work, about coming down here, reading applications on the beach. She talked about the terrible vampire stories and ridiculous memoirs, the endlessness of it all, how she'd wanted time to work on her *own* book.

"Your book," Martin Rice repeated. He looked back at her bio. "Poetry? What's it called?"

"'The Ugly Bear List,'" she said, again without thinking. "This was my chance to finish it—and also get some inspiration." She told him about the book's concept, the shit list that changes you, the bears in your mind, and how she started the book around the time of the Tea Party's insurgency, but had stalled out in her anger and helplessness. Her realization that no one and nothing ever gets off the list, that it just gets longer and longer until you realize you've spent half your life and brainpower simply keeping track of things you don't trust, things you fear, things you hate. "I thought, maybe this will help me understand them. But then, they were actually really different than I imagined—all these complicated and smart and interesting people. I realized, the real ugly bear list was made up of people like Regina Somers and Tad Tucker. The manipulators, the profiteers."

He nodded and took indecipherable notes. She kept talking, trying to make him understand.

"Are you a Christian, Marianne?"

"No," she said.

"Are you a Buddhist?"

She shook her head.

"Would you describe yourself as spiritual but not religious?"

"I'm not that either. Whatever that is."

He frowned at his notebook. "Do you believe in God, or any other higher power?"

"No. I do not."

"Then why start a faith-based writing school?"

She said something incoherent about the power of writing to heal, to help, to make things better in your life.

"Do you believe that?" he asked.

"I don't know," she said. "I don't think so."

"Why then?"

"Why?" she repeated.

"Why are you talking to me? You know you'll probably be fired."

That idea—the idea that the school could go on, without her, that it could go on at all after everything she'd said—had not occurred to Marianne. She sat there dumbly, staring at the dregs of coffee sludge and sugar at the bottom of her cup.

"Okay," he said, looking through his notes. "Tell me more about this . . . ugly bear list. Can you explain that again?"

She got another cup of coffee, dumped in three packets of sugar, loaded it up with milk. Cool coffee, Ruth had called it, when Marianne made it for her as a treat. It was something their mother made for Marianne.

Marianne felt the last wave of intoxication wash over her, then recede. She sat back down. She told him that the ugly bear list was her mother's idea, inherited from her grandmother, a kind of private push-back against the forces of hypocrisy and false piety. She said she'd been depressed since her mother died—she didn't know why she said that, but as soon as she said it, she knew it was true. How long ago was that? he wanted to know. A long time, she said, counting on her fingers under the table. Seventeen years.

"Wait," Martin Rice said. "Wasn't that what Muhammad Ali called Sonny Liston? 'You big, ugly bear'—he was taunting him, you know, like he did. Ugly Bear Liston. Ugly bear list. Your mother or grandmother must have gotten it from the papers." He sounded pleased, like Marianne had returned to him a pleasant memory, though he looked barely out of college.

"Oh," said Marianne. "I didn't—"

"Your mother—" He paged through his notes. "She was pro-life?"

Marianne took a deep breath, tried not to think about the knockout she wished she could deliver this kid, who didn't seem to understand anything she'd told him. She forced herself to imagine that Ruth was listening, said that her mother's life was complicated, and that she loved her children, and that her personal decisions were beside the point.

"Okay," said Martin Rice. "I think I've got what I need."

"But I haven't told you about Janine," Marianne said. "Her poetry, how I think it's good. I haven't told you—"

He turned off his recorder, closed his notebook, checked the time on his phone. "You've given me a lot," he said. "I understand that you didn't mean for things to go this way."

"Wait," she said as he stood. "How did you find out about us? Who gave you my email?"

"I can't tell you that," he said, like it was the most obvious thing in the world.

Marianne watched him leave, the notebook and recorder tucked into a messenger bag, then drove herself to the Largo Shores Club. It was getting late, the sky so inky it was hard to tell what was encroaching storm and what was night. The wind was picking up; she felt it buffeting the sides of her little car. Eric's little car. The parking lot was nearly empty, but so many spots were marked handicapped that she still had to park far from the entrance.

The Largo Shores Club was nothing like the home where Marianne's granny lived. Its lobby had leather furniture, lamps instead of overhead fluorescents, and real paintings on the walls—no ugly motel prints or crucifixes or no-smoking signs.

Hello? Marianne said at the front desk. Hello? she said to no one. She peeped over the front ledge to see that the surface of the desk was covered in papers and unsorted mail. It looked like it had been abandoned in a hurry, or else used by a number of people who didn't have to sit there. She heard the sounds of people talking and laughing from a back room and followed them.

Hello? she said again, opening a heavy wooden door to a large and echoing recreation room, with four Ping-Pong tables manned by a half dozen deeply tanned seniors in coordinated active wear. No one noticed her.

"I'm looking for Frances Ketterling?" Marianne said. "She lives here?"

A woman wearing a pink sport visor and matching pink wristbands, who'd just landed a winning shot, knew where she was. "Frances is taking in the orchids!" she said. "Before the storm! I'll show you."

On the long walk to find Frances, the woman talked about the various features of the Largo Shores Club, gushing as if she were selling Marianne a timeshare. Swimming, tennis, competitive bocce, conversational French and Italian: it was for active seniors, she said, and also people with a certain kind of refinement. She looked at Marianne appraisingly as she said this—Marianne wondered a little anxiously if she would pass muster. Something about the phrases "conversational French and Italian" and "taking in the orchids" sounded deeply appealing to her.

Finally they found a woman carrying an armload of orchids in terracotta pots. The flowers trembled precariously on their stalks, and the whole collection seemed about to topple out of her arms, but she would not let them take any. She was shorter and stouter than the woman with the visor, and wearing an expensive-looking linen tunic. You have to wait until the very last moment to take in orchids, she was saying. They benefited from the prestorm humidity.

"I'm Marianne Stuart. From Genesis Ranch? I need to talk to you. Could I help you carry the orchids?"

"No," she said, this woman whose property Marianne had inhabited, whose school she'd run for more than a year. Marianne could not be trusted to carry her orchids, but she could follow her and open the doors. So she did that, back and forth from the patio into the carpeted hall and an even nicer dining room, where she set them on a long bare table. Finally they were done, and after counting the plants she looked at Marianne and seemed to realize who she was.

"I'm sorry," she said. "I'm just preoccupied." She waved her hand in the direction of the now cleared-out patio.

"Please," Marianne said, "sit down."

She did, and Marianne sat across from her, looking over the still somehow trembling orchids. Marianne told her everything—how the Ranch had spiraled out of her control, into the hands of GWGW and Tad Tucker and Regina Somers. She'd left too many decisions to Mark and Eric. It was no longer the place Frances envisioned, and she was ready to resign. Marianne told her about the new exploitative marketing efforts, and the conversation she'd felt forced to have with Martin Rice, and how there would probably be an exposé in the paper. The enormity of what she'd done suddenly crashed around her in a terrible kind of hangover.

Frances reached across the table, pushing the tremulous orchids aside. Her palms were warm and smooth. Her eyes were the clear blue of the gulf on a sunny day.

"My idea was a bookstore," Frances said. "I was getting older, and tired of running a hotel, and I thought—I know, a bookstore. With an inspirational bent—a place where people of religious and spiritual feeling could come together to buy books, and maybe have readings and events. But the bank turned me down for financing—they said bookstores were dying—and when I called Mark to help me put together a business plan, he remembered an idea Eric told him about, an idea for a school."

"So it was Mark's idea," Marianne said.

"No," she said. "It was Eric's. Eric talked his brother into starting the school. Eric was in love with you."

"We were engaged," Marianne said. "That was a long time ago."

"He was in love when he started the school," Frances insisted. "I've been married six times, and I know what it looks like when a man is in love. He wanted to win you back. This was why he started the school."

"Oh no," Marianne said. It felt good—and also terrible—to be told, to have it confirmed, that Eric still loved her. Good because she loved him too, and terrible because she had just ruined everything.

"But he didn't tell me!" she said. "He lied!"

"He lied to me too," Frances said. Her voice was resigned and patient, the voice of someone long used to lying men. "At first I was angry. I mean, this is my *retirement*! But then I thought—maybe it will work? Maybe I'll dance at your wedding and kiss your babies. Don't you want that?"

Marianne started to cry.

"Here," Frances said. She picked up one of the smaller orchids, with tiny orange-and-purple flowers, and handed it to Marianne. "You should have this. For your office."

"I don't think I'll have an office anymore," Marianne sniffed. "Aren't you and your friends evacuating soon?"

"Of course not," Frances said, straightening in her chair. "I don't abandon ship, and I don't accept your resignation."

Marianne took the orchid and left. By the time she got back to the Ranch, it had already lost two of its five flowers.

The wind had died down again, and it was dark enough to make her way back to her room without anyone noticing. Or maybe she could escape, join the lucky evacuees slowly inching their way up I-75 in advance of Tropical Storm Helen. She imagined herself in the stolen car, music playing, nothing to do but drive north—away, away.

19

By Saturday the storm was officially classified a hurricane, with landfall predicted for Monday night, but Marianne was not among its evacuees. Neither was Janine, whose daughter had lucked into a reporting gig and had taken their car, or Tom, who had nowhere else to go, or Davonte, whose manager/coach was suddenly unreachable. On Saturday afternoon Lorraine rode with a small group of students to Tampa, where they'd booked flights back to where they came from—New York and Amarillo and Chattanooga and other less vulnerable destinations. Most people drove, following the marked evacuation route to join the traffic jams Marianne had fantasized about, but no one offered her a ride.

At the Ranch, none of the remaining students—not Janine, not Davonte, not even Manfred—was speaking to Marianne after reading Martin Rice's exposé in the Thursday paper and receiving a long email from Regina expressing disappointment in Marianne's leadership and doubt about her mental health. Students avoided her, as if her mental instability or her atheism, or some combination of the two, might be catching, and on Friday she'd been fired, over the telephone, by Mark.

"I'm sorry," he told her. He did not mention a severance, but suggested that they could possibly still use her as a reader of applications.

"That's okay," she said lightly. She pictured her voice like a pale balloon, escaping, then bumping against the ceiling. "I'll pack my things and be gone before the storm."

"You can stay through the storm."

"Ha," she'd said. "That doesn't seem advisable. Or likely."

"But where will you go?"

She hadn't counted on a lack of transportation. Now she busied herself with packing while all around her the usual storm preparations went on without her: securing the lawn furniture, boarding up windows. Janine went shopping for water and nonperishables while Eric and Tom argued about the best way to nail up plywood, and Davonte desperately tried to get in touch with his manager.

Many of the students hadn't wanted to leave; that was the surprising part. When evacuation was first suggested as a possibility, an idea spread around the Ranch that the students could stay, helping to prepare their school for the storm's landfall by writing and praying. God would protect them, they surmised. They would weather the storm like Noah in his boat and would be able to finish their second session in a memorable and probably quite inspiring way. They imagined themselves feverishly finishing seven-hundred-page novels, arriving at the closing insights of their memoirs, being struck by bolts—figurative bolts—of inspiration for long sequences of poems.

Regina thought this was a brilliant idea, initially. "It is time to take a STAND," she said in a second email to students. "The recent negative press should only make our resolve, our faith, more durable." She changed her mind after getting some strongly worded advice from her insurance company, and Eric broke the news to the students at Friday morning's breakfast, asking them to pray for the Ranch from home, to keep writing, to check their email for updates. He did not mention the article or Marianne, and no one asked.

She was finding it hard to pack. She'd had to beg for boxes from the Kangaroo, and now she could not remember which supplies, which staplers and pens and notebooks, she'd bought with her own money. Should she even bother? But what would she do without a stapler? Without pens and notebooks and folders? It seemed that everything in the office was indispensable; she'd have to take it all. Then there was the question of books—where were the books she'd lent to the makeshift library? How could she leave without her Rich and Merwin, her Lowell and Levertov?

But when she checked, they'd all been returned, as if by their very association with her they'd lost all usefulness. Marianne got a box, and set about packing them. She didn't know where she was taking them, or how. She didn't have an apartment; she didn't have a car. She had no job, and no prospects for a job. Eric wasn't speaking to her.

She thought of Sophie, smugly drinking wine at the Manatee—was she leaving? Though Martin Rice had refused to divulge his sources, she was sure now that Sophie was involved. Sophie owed her *something*—an explanation, a place to stay, a ride to safety.

She started toward the Manatee Inn with her box of books balanced on a rolling suitcase, but turned around before she got to the sidewalk. Eric could mail her books to her—that was the least *he* could do, after tricking her into founding a sham institution of higher learning, and then selling it to an even shadier operation. For love, Frances said! Marianne left the books next to her orchid, which had dropped two more flowers, and lifted the suitcase by its handle.

"Didn't think I'd see you again," Sophie said when she arrived. She smelled like turpentine and whiskey, and held the door wide open.

Marianne looked around the cottage, protected from the storm by the main building, which sat between it and the water. Sophie had her storm shutters closed, yellow candles flickering, Loretta Lynn on the turntable. A new painting leaned half-finished on its easel. "You're not evacuating?"

"We don't evacuate," Sophie said. "We're the captains. We go down with the ship."

"My ship is sunk. You should know that."

"I read the paper. I'm sorry. You'll survive it, though." She poured whiskey into a jelly jar and handed it to Marianne, then turned back to her easel.

"Nope," Marianne said, and took a bracing sip. "I'm done. And you didn't just read the paper—you must have called Martin Rice. Maybe you called the protesters too."

Sophie continued painting—a snowy egret in a dark pool of water. "Did you think you could keep it a secret?" Marianne didn't answer, and Sophie continued. "You were drowning, kid. I saw it on your face, when Tad Tucker was waving you and your students around like he owned you. I mean, do you even know what that man is about?"

"Of course I do," Marianne said. "I mean, *now* I do—we were in the process of extricating—"

"Bullshit," Sophie said. "I did you a favor."

"I have no job! And nowhere to live! And everyone at the Ranch hates me! Understandably, but still—"

"Then why did you talk?" Sophie's brush scratched violently against the canvas, but her voice was calm. Maybe it was the smell of turpentine or the maddeningly patient questioning, but Marianne was reminded of teenage fights with her mother before she got sick. Sophie was right: Marianne didn't have to meet with Martin Rice. She could have referred his email to Regina, who would have rebuffed him handily.

"I don't know," she said. "I was drunk. Sort of."

"You do know," Sophie said. "What you did was brave." She turned to look at Marianne.

"You could have told me first."

"You could have told your students first. You had a lot of chances. A lot of warnings. The protesters—"

"You put them up to it?"

Sophie shook her head. "I have friends, and maybe I let something slip. It's a small community, I told you that from the start. And there are reasons for people to be fighting this organization you got yourself mixed up in."

She went back to painting moonlight on the water, around the egret's legs. Her gestures turned gentle, almost tender.

"You'll start over," Sophie said. "You're young. And Christians—they're supposed to be good at forgiveness. Real Christians anyway."

"I want to leave, Sophie. I want to evacuate."

"What about your ex? Is he still there?"

Marianne nodded. "Some of the students too. I'm not like you—I'm a serial ship-abandoner. I bail out. I did it to my sister after my mom died, I did it to Eric after he proposed, and now I'm abandoning the Ranch."

"You have unfinished business there," Sophie said. The wind was picking up. Sophie stabbed her brush into its glass and took off her smock. Marianne wondered if she'd finish the painting, or if she considered it finished now. "You need to go back, before it gets worse."

"Maybe I could stay here?"

"People are still in your inn, your school, whatever you want to call it. You opened the doors to them. Think if they need something and you're not there. What if something happens and you're gone—how will you feel then?"

It was true. Janine was there, and Davonte, and even Tom—she was responsible for all of them. She'd personally chosen them, invited them, made coming to the Ranch seem like something worthwhile, something to change their lives for the better. She drained the rest of her glass.

Sophie opened her door and peered outside, then came back to her workstation and blew out the candles, picked up the needle in the middle of "Fist City." "I'll drive you," she said. "I think I'm gonna head inland."

"What about going down with the ship?"

"My guests are gone, the Manatee will be fine. Or it won't be. But you should gather your folks and make a plan."

They rode in silence, and when Marianne got out, she didn't thank Sophie. She felt like a child being returned to the scene of a crime, to apologize, come clean. She gripped her suitcase obediently and carried it through the storm's stinging raindrops, all the way to her door.

She turned and waved. Sophie drove away, into the pale and greenish dusk. Marianne opened the door to her room. A hurricane was coming; there was that. She hoped it would swallow her up.

When Janine first read the newspaper article, she wanted to disappear. How had she let herself be used that way? How could she have given money and time to such scam artists? What would Rick think, and her daughters, when they found out? How foolish she'd been to think that she was being celebrated for her talent, when all Marianne wanted to do was use her. For money she could understand: everyone needed money, and of course school wasn't free. But the idea that Janine's own beliefs would be fodder for Marianne's book—that she was being mocked—it was as bad as anything she'd felt during the worst of Terri Schiavo's ordeal. Janine skipped class on Thursday, something she'd never done in her life, and locked herself in her room. She couldn't stand to look at anyone.

But then the storm came closer, and closer, and Beth got a call from the Weather Channel. Manfred came by with a sandwich, and Eric Osborne apologized to her, and Lorraine brought her some cigarettes. Regina sent her several emails (she didn't write back), as well as one group email suggesting that Marianne might, in fact, be crazy. Janine wondered if that could be true. She had not seen her since the reading. She wasn't sure what she'd say if she did.

Janine didn't have any choice but to stay and help everyone get ready.

It would be fine, Eric assured them, just a Category 1. He'd seen plenty of storms during his childhood, when he used to visit his aunt in Tampa. It would be fun, he said. They'd take precautions.

The safest places on the Ranch, Eric told them, were the dormitory rooms that ringed the parking lot—they were farthest from shore, with inland-facing windows, and were on a slightly higher incline than the rest of the Ranch. For added security, Eric and Tom nailed up plywood, moving efficiently down the cracked cement walkway with a mouthful of nails, while Janine brought in grocery bags bulging with canned food and white bread and peanut butter. They each chose a separate room, but as soon as the first hard drops of rain hit the roof and the initial gusts of wind creaked the tree limbs and the plywood, Donald and Eric and Tom gathered in Janine's room, where they'd stashed the provisions. Janine sat at the foot of the bed, switching between the local news and the Weather Channel, searching for a glimpse of her daughter. Donald calmed his nerves by eating peanut butter sandwiches and reading gossip websites on his laptop. Tom worried about his motorcycle, which he'd wheeled into the gardening shed, and read a book about Afghanistan's opium trade. Eric couldn't sit still, kept going out into the storm and reporting back to them every few minutes.

"Wind's getting gustier," Eric said, dripping rain. He picked up his phone and texted someone. "Soon it'll be hard to stand up."

"Oh," said Janine, thinking of Beth. "I hate to think of her out there by herself."

"I've never heard of anything happening to a weather reporter," Eric said. "Ever."

"What about those storm chasers?" Donald asked.

"That's for tornadoes," Eric said. "A hurricane is different. More predictable."

"Tell that to the Katrina victims," Donald said.

"In *comparison*."

"There she is!" Janine said. She turned the volume way up. Beth stood near a pier as waves crashed behind her in a gray sea. She held the microphone with one hand and kept her hood up with the other as rain lashed her parka. She had a pleasing on-camera voice—loud enough to compete with the sound of the storm and the surf, but not panicked. "The normally bustling streets of Sarasota are unrecognizable today as tourists and residents alike have evacuated Helen, likely to make landfall as a Category 1 storm later tonight," she said. "Behind me the Venice fishing pier is being battered by wind and waves, but we have not had any reports of damage yet."

"The Weather Channel," Tom said. "Big time."

"Oh," said Janine, wiping away tears. "Look at her."

"My mom watches the Weather Channel all day," said Donald. "She leaves it on *steady*, programs in wherever I am so she can keep track. She's probably got it on right now. I gotta tell her I know a Weather Channel star. I'm gonna email her."

"I should call Rick," Janine said, reaching for her phone. She punched in the numbers with shaking fingers, held it up to her ear. On television, they cut away from Beth. Janine wondered if what she'd said was true—if residents were also evacuating, or if that was just meant to make the report more exciting. It did seem quiet along their stretch of the key, all the businesses closed down. Even the gas station was darkened and empty, though no one had bothered to board it up.

"Eric, the internet's out," Donald called.

"That happens," Eric said. "In a hurricane. Probably won't be back until tomorrow."

"Shit," said Donald. "Can you fix it?"

"*No*," said Eric, looking at his phone. "I'm not getting a good signal either."

"Honey?" Janine held her hand over one ear. "*Watch the Weather Channel*. We're safe here, just riding out the storm, plenty of food, good company. Love you!"

She snapped her phone shut. The lights flickered.

"Stay on," Janine pleaded.

"Don't do this to us, Helen," Donald commanded the ceiling. He closed and unplugged his laptop.

Then it was dark.

It was very dark, and very quiet except for the sound of rain battering the roof.

Janine reached for her handbag. She pulled out a keychain flashlight and aimed it around the room, over Donald's and Eric's and Tom's faces.

"I told you we needed to leave some spaces to see out of," Tom said. He pulled his flip phone out and waved it around the boarded-up window. "It's totally blocked. It's like a tomb in here. I can't take it."

"I'll get the candles," Janine said. "We bought flashlights too, and batteries. You should save your battery, just in case. We can take the boards down tomorrow, you'll see."

"You've done this before," Donald said. "That's good."

"Marianne is all by herself over there," Tom said. "Somebody want to go check on her?"

"I could go," Eric offered.

Janine didn't comment. It was lonely and a little strange, being the only woman in the room, but she didn't think she could stand to go through a hurricane with Marianne, to sit on a bed with her and hold her hand and reassure her. She'd been arguing in her head with Marianne ever since she read the newspaper article, though she hadn't spoken a word to her. In her mind, Marianne sat at a desk in Janine's classroom, her hands folded meekly, while Janine interrogated her. Why did you go to the newspaper, and not to us first? Do you really have so little respect for us?

Janine lit two candles and placed them on the dresser, just below the mirror, where they flickered with an amber light. "I filled the bathtub and the sink," she said. "Just in case."

"Just in case what?" Donald asked.

"For drinking or flushing."

"I'm not drinking bathwater, no offense," he said, moving to claim a bottle of water.

"It isn't bathwater. No one is going to take a bath in it," Janine explained.

"It touched bath. That makes it *bath*water."

"It's hot in here," Tom said. "Stuffy."

"I could open the door," Eric said. "Just a crack."

They agreed—just a crack, just enough to let some fresh air in.

"But be careful," Janine said.

"It's just like a really long thunderstorm," Eric said.

Eric went to the door, with Tom behind him, and opened it a crack, then halfway. Janine and Donald followed Tom, hoping for a cooling gust of wind. Outside, the light was gray and eerie, hourless, and they could see rain bouncing where it hit the pavement. It looked like someone was throwing bucket after bucket of water into an already drenching rainstorm. Rain overflowed the gutters and poured off every side of the roof. Wind tossed the palm fronds and creaked the long oak branches. Somewhere they couldn't see, a tree limb snapped and crashed. Small branches, driven by the wind, thumped the roof loudly.

"I'm gonna move my bike before it gets any worse," Tom said. "A big limb could smash that shed flat."

"Or it could fall on you," Janine said.

"Where are you gonna move it, anyway?" Eric said.

"To my room," he said. "I want to be able to see it."

"Tom, you can't put a motorcycle in your room," Eric reasoned. "It won't fit through the door."

"Fine, gimme the keys to the dining hall, I'll put it in there."

"I don't think it's safe to go out," said Janine. "You can always replace a motorcycle."

"It's fine, " Eric said. "I'll go with him. It's not too bad, I've seen worse. The power will be back tomorrow, the next day tops."

Janine could see that he was enjoying this, being the experienced one among them, though how many years ago was it that he was last here? Ten years ago? Fifteen? Beth had told her that storms were getting worse because of global warming—stronger, more unpredictable—and it seemed to Janine that this was true. Though she also wondered if there was just more coverage of storms, television programs you could watch twenty-four hours a day, like Donald's mom. Eric pulled on his raincoat. Tom flipped up the collar on his jean jacket.

"Pay attention out there," Donald called as they shouldered their way into the storm. "We should put something about a hurricane in my novel."

Janine looked at her phone. "I'm getting a text. It's Lilian, from class. She wants to know if we have any extra rooms. We do, don't we?" Janine scrolled through the message. "She says she didn't evacuate, she was afraid her husband would sneak in and change the locks on the condo. But now she says no one else in her condo is around, and she's lonely. I should tell her to come, right?"

"Tell her to bring more bottled water," Donald said.

Janine typed a response, then knelt next to the bed and clasped her hands.

"I thought you said we'd be fine," Donald said. Janine closed her eyes more tightly and continued praying.

"We all need strength," she said finally, standing up.

Lilian arrived in her silver Mercedes with several bags of fancy non-perishable groceries, a large cooler full of ice, a battery-powered radio, battery-powered lamps, and two suitcases full of clothes and toiletries. It took several trips into the storm to bring everything inside, and everyone got soaked. Lilian stayed rather dry in her yellow anorak, standing under the eaves and calling out encouragement and instructions.

"A hurricane party!" she announced, once they were inside Janine's room. Immediately the room's smell changed, from peanut buttery and mildly sweaty to expensive and perfumed. Janine thought of those women who were so bossy they altered the schedule of your menstrual period—it was all done through smells, wasn't it?

"I haven't been to one of these in years. I would have invited y'all to my place but then I thought this would be more fun, like camping." Lilian lighted one of her travel lamps and set it next to the candle, where it glowed with a medicinal white light that canceled the flickering candles. "And look! I found these notebooks at a back-to-school sale when I was out shopping. I got one for each of us." She reached into one of her grocery bags and handed around speckled composition books, the pages tightly stitched into the spine.

"Thank you," they said, holding the notebooks like schoolchildren and eyeing the bags of groceries, packed tightly with sea-salted taro chips, cans of smoked almonds, and imported chocolates. Lilian positioned a second lamp on the nightstand between the room's two beds but did not offer any food.

"Some roads were already closed by the time I was driving over. This could be a big one," she told them, shucking off her shoes and getting into Janine's bed. Janine still sat at the foot, holding her notebook. Lilian stacked all the pillows behind her and propped her notebook against her knees. In the antiseptic light, her powdered face looked pale and ghost-like, her penciled eyebrows vaguely menacing. "I hope my husband does come back to the condo. I hope he makes a wrong turn and gets washed out to sea. Do you know since class was canceled I've written five poems?"

"Congratulations," Janine said. She hadn't written a word since Thursday morning. "That's really a lot of poems."

"These newest ones are through the eyes of his Russian bride-to-be—did I tell you he's decided, apparently, on the Russian? That man *never* changes his password on anything. The poems detail the realizations she has about his faults."

"Hey, Lilian, mind if I pass around some snacks?" Donald didn't wait for her answer but moved for the bags.

"Oh, sure," she said. "There's wine, too."

Janine opened the wine, which had a twist cap, and poured it generously into the small paper cups she found tucked among the snacks. She passed a cup to Donald, then Lilian, and left two out for Eric and Tom, who should have been back by now, she thought.

"I'm taking these chips down to Marianne," said Donald, pulling on Lilian's raincoat. "I feel bad for her, all alone. She's next door, right?"

"Two doors down," Janine said. "But come right back, so we don't worry."

"That was such a great reading you gave," Lilian said, after he'd left. "Both you and Donald were great. I was impressed."

"Thanks," Janine said. She wasn't sure if Lilian understood the context of her poem, but it didn't matter. "Now I wish I hadn't given it, of course."

"Why?"

"Well, because of the newspaper article," Janine said quietly. "And Tad Tucker being there, giving a speech. I don't agree with everything he says—"

"Tad Tucker didn't write your work for you, did he?"

"No," Janine said.

"He didn't change what you wrote, or how you read it?"

"No."

"And he isn't keeping you from writing now?"

"No," Janine said. The wine wasn't bad, she thought. She hoped there were more bottles. "I guess not."

Small debris pinged, then thudded above them.

"I don't know about you, but I just feel like I have so much to say," Lilian said. "It's like somebody has been tamping me down all my life, and now it's my time. Nobody's gonna stop me, you know what I mean?"

Janine nodded, though she knew it was too dim for Lilian to see her. Janine did not drink, did not even keep alcohol in her house (Rick stored six-packs of beer in the garage fridge), but there were exceptions to every rule: at weddings, she toasted the bride and groom, and at hurricane parties, she consumed whatever was offered until the storm was over. You had to drink to get through the waiting, the wondering, the thrashing wind and rain, the hours without electricity or contact with someone you loved. You had to drink to get through the doubts about a God who would do such a thing as send a hurricane right to you, a storm that might destroy your house or kill your family, your neighbors. And on top of that, a God who would make a member of that very family a weather reporter! You had to wonder about a God like that.

Everyone had those doubts, she'd wanted to tell Marianne, but the words stuck in her throat. *I haven't believed in God*, Marianne had said in the interview. *Not for a long time.*

But what if everything Marianne said was true? What if Lorraine didn't care whether she was radical or not, but was only looking for a paycheck? All those webinars—each time, she'd paid the administrative fee willingly, propping her debit card against her keyboard and typing in the numbers—what if they'd just been a scam, a way of collecting money and information? It was true that she hadn't learned much from them. It was true that they'd asked a lot of personal, irrelevant questions at the end. Lilian opened a second bottle, and Janine held out her cup for more.

Just then, Donald opened the door, and somewhere a tree limb came down with a great crack. He jumped over the threshold, slammed the door behind him.

"You didn't invite her back?" Janine said.

"She wouldn't come," Donald said. "She went looking for Eric and Tom. I told her not to, but she said she'd be okay."

"Why can't people just stay inside?" said Lilian.

Selfish, muttered Janine. She was sorry she'd let anyone leave the room. It had been hours since she'd heard from Beth. She would be fine—of course she'd be fine, Janine saw her live on the Weather Channel—but that did not loosen the tight, sickly knot of worry Janine felt in her stomach. She sipped and sipped Lilian's red wine, which tasted like wet leaves and cherries, and listened to Donald's fears: the thin roof would cave in, they would suffocate in the heat, they would drown or be crushed. Janine reassured him each time—that seemed to be what he was looking for—but privately she wondered. From the sounds of things—creaking and moaning and crashing, several leaks already dripping from the ceiling—either the storm was especially bad, or their shelter especially flimsy. Humbly—for wasn't realism a form of humility?—Janine prayed it was one thing or the other, but not both.

Please not both, she prayed. In the beginning of the night, she had been praying for her children's safety, for Beth in her weather van and Rick and Chrissy at home, but suddenly it occurred to her that where she was—in a converted motel, feet from the shore—was possibly the most dangerous place of all. That *she* could die, leaving her children motherless and her husband a widower, was not something that she ever thought about. That she could die at a Christian writing school that was not even founded by an actual Christian suddenly seemed very possible. She wished desperately to be back in her old life, writing poems that no one would ever read, making dinner, washing dishes. Doing laundry: in the close, humid room, she wanted nothing more than the orderliness of her laundry room. She'd been vain to apply for school, to waste the money on something that would never help her family, that only made her cross and impatient with them, that made her want to be alone.

"I'm going to look outside," Janine said. She stood, and told herself the dizziness she felt was from the heat, the claustrophobia. "Selfish!" she said again, this time loud enough for Lilian and Donald to hear.

"She's in love with him," Donald said. "That's all."

"Who?" said Lilian.

"Marianne. She loves Eric. That's why she's gone after him."

Someone knocked clumsily, and Janine lurched for the door—it would be Marianne, she told herself, back with Eric and Tom, all of them soaked and relieved and back to believing in God again.

She opened the door, was met with nothing but cooler air, a metallic smell, the sound of wind shuddering the eaves. "Marianne?" she called. Looking down, Janine saw the source of the knocking sound: a garden statue, tipped over on her side, had washed up against the sill. Upright, her arms were outstretched in a fleeing posture, but lying on her side she appeared to be swimming, her face contorted in an expression somewhere between delight and fear. Janine crouched down to move her from the doorway and was surprised that she was not made of stone at all, but of some cheap composite material that had been painted to look like stone. She was easy to lift with one hand.

The parking lot coursed with water, the edge of a flood lapping the concrete walkway outside the door. Peering through the rain, Janine could make out the shapes of other statues floating along, headed down the sloping lawn toward the beach. The entire campus appeared to be in the midst of a large, ever-expanding lake, with a current that ran to the gulf.

"Oh no," said Janine. "Oh *no*."

The weight of her voice was enough to summon Lilian and Donald, who now stood next to her in the doorway.

"My *car*," Lilian said. "I should have parked up the hill. But see, the water isn't over the walkway, it isn't above my tires."

"But what if it rises?" Donald asked. "What if it comes up from the beach? What if it floods us?"

"It won't," Lilian insisted. "It never has."

"But Marianne—if she went to find Eric and Tom, she's out in the storm now." The thought of her out there, unsaved and drowning, gave Janine a pain in her chest. No one deserved to die alone in a storm.

Donald grabbed her arm. "Janine, don't you go too."

She stepped out onto the walkway, without even a jacket, and immediately felt the wind pulling her, wrapping around her legs and arms and torso like a living thing. She pictured herself toppled into the flood with the statues, floating out to sea, and flattened her back against the wall. She inched along, the plywood over the window rough against her T-shirt, rain splashing water onto her feet and her shins, until she reached the end of the walkway.

"Janine!"

She turned slightly at the sound of her name, afraid to step away from the wall, and saw her friend behind her. "Donald!" she yelled back, but her voice was small compared to the wind.

"I'm coming with you," he said. He grabbed her hand, and she clutched his tightly.

If someone had told Janine that one day she would be holding hands in the dark with an entertainer of questionable reputation while hurricane-driven wind and rain lashed her legs, she would not have believed him. But she could not imagine letting go, no more than she could imagine abandoning Marianne to the storm.

They fought their way into the wind, passing dormitories and class-rooms where days before people had been worrying over the tiniest things: who was cooking dinner at home, why was the internet out again, what had someone really meant by a critique? Janine remembered the two lines Lorraine had not crossed out in her poem, how pitiful and lonely and disaster-stricken they'd looked on the marked-up page, but now the lines themselves were gone—she couldn't remember a single word.

20

It was raining hard when Marianne left her room, with heavy wind and patches of lightning overhead. She called for Eric and Tom, but if someone answered she didn't hear him. She looked up at the sky; maybe the rain was slowing. How long was a hurricane supposed to last, anyway? Whatever time it was, it was not supposed to be dark like this, black clouds moving fast against a slate-gray sky.

And her feet—they weren't supposed to be so wet, so heavy from the few minutes she'd spent running, aiming her flashlight to check each building she passed. Empty, empty, but so far she did not see any roof damage or downed trees, and she could see that everything would be better when the storm was over. Everything could be fixed, everything could be righted. When she found Eric they'd take off her shoes and wring out her socks. They'd talk about what to do next.

But where was he? Aiming her flashlight toward the empty beach, she saw that the gulf was nearer than it usually was, swallowing the mangroves with great black gulps. And how was it that the gulf approached from two sides—in front of her and behind her, from the west *and* the east, water pouring down from the parking lot in a great river, running over her shoes and up her ankles?

The water slipped up her calves, so cold she gasped. It hit behind her knees, knocking her over, and as she tumbled down the suddenly steep hill, under and over the water, scraping her legs and elbows and palms and head against gravel and sand and tree branches. This must have been how her mother felt when the cancer returned, when she knew that she would die. Shocked and betrayed and angry and helpless and sorry, so sorry to be leaving. She felt herself letting go. It's over, she thought. What now?

21

Dear Ms. Somers,

I would like to respectfully withdraw from the Genesis Inspirational Writing Ranch.

I tried calling to talk to you, but I just got a recording directing me to your website, and then when I tried to type what I wanted to say in the "contact us" box it was too long, so I hope this letter finds you. I suppose you all are busy with the rebuilding or reorganizing, so I won't take much of your time. I want to explain why I don't think I'm fit to continue at the school, but also to say how much I appreciate everything you tried to do for me. It was an honor to see my work posted online and to receive the Tad Tucker "Inspiration" scholarship, and I mean that more sincerely and more deeply than it sounds. The idea that anyone thought I had something to say and that anyone would want to read it has meant a great deal to me.

You are probably thinking that the protests and the article and my feelings about the reading are the reason I'm leaving, but that isn't it. The main reason I am leaving and think you should give the scholarship to somebody else is what happened after the storm, not before. It was what happened after the storm that made me rethink things, that made me realize that Marianne Stuart was right to go to the papers, if wrong in the way she started the school.

I want to cancel the interview that you have scheduled for me with ABC News. When you told me about it, I was still too surprised to tell you what I thought, to tell you no definitively. You know that feeling you get, when something seems so wrong that you don't even feel that it could possibly be about you? You leave your body and go . . . somewhere else?

I know it would be better to tell you this over the phone, but like I said, I tried, and I'll send this overnight so you have some notice. I will make a written statement of what happened, though, so you can have it for your records and for insurance purposes and for my records, too. I hope that will be good enough.

On August the fifteenth a hurricane was predicted to hit the coast of Sarasota. It made a sharp and surprising turn, so we weren't exactly expecting it, and there was trouble getting out for some of the students. I had the means of evacuation, but my daughter, who studies meteorology, had an opportunity to do reporting for the Weather Channel and I agreed to stay with her. In any case, I wasn't the only one: Marianne Stuart, Donald Goldston (Davonte Gold), Tom Marshall, and Eric Osborne all stayed at the Ranch. Some of us had experience in storms and some of us had no choice and none of us thought it would be as bad as it turned out. We had plenty of food and water, and we boarded up all the windows and did normal storm-preparation chores.

We lost power about six thirty, and shortly after that, Lilian Avery arrived with more provisions. She was excited to have a hurricane party.

Everybody came to my room, except for Marianne. We had not spoken since her interview with the paper. In my room the rest of us talked, we played cards, we drank wine; she may have heard us through the thin walls. The storm didn't sound too bad at that point, just lots and lots of rain. Eric had told me earlier that the rooms we were in never flooded, so I thought we were safe.

I don't mean to blame him, but I don't see why he and Tom had to go out in the storm over a *motorcycle*. If they hadn't done that, Marianne wouldn't have gone out after them, and Donald and I wouldn't have had to go out after her.

I understand that I keep veering away from the facts, the story, throwing in my commentary. I'm not a prose writer or a reporter. I'm a poet, so feelings come into it for me, and the story doesn't always take a straight line. But I will try.

Donald and I decided Marianne went in the direction of the fiction classroom, where there was a garden shed, so we went that way. We kept as close to the buildings as we could to cut down on the wind. I had my flashlight and could see, once I passed the dormitories, that the water was rising fast. The gulf was eating up the shoreline, coming up past the mangroves, and water was just pouring down the banks. I thought that if Marianne was

anywhere else on campus she'd be okay, but if she'd come down here looking for Tom and Eric she'd be in danger of drowning, literally getting washed
out to sea.

I lost my flashlight somehow, but I didn't feel afraid for my life, as you
wrote in one of your press pieces. I was a swimmer in high school, I've always been a good swimmer, and I knew that I would be okay. I felt God with
me and Donald, keeping us safe. It was a powerful feeling, as strong as I've
ever had in church or prayer.

Somehow, even without a flashlight and with all the clouds and the rain,
there was a reflection on the water, and that gave us enough light to see
Marianne clinging to the side of the shed, her arms and legs wrapped around
a post, her eyes shut tight, like that would help hold her where she was.

The story I listened to you tell me—even though you weren't there—
was that Donald swam across the washed-out gully to reach her, pulled her
down, and swam her back to me. That is not what happened. The truth is
that the current was way too swift, and full of fast-moving debris: tree limbs,
trash, pieces of metal peeled off from roofs. Donald and I tried wading into
it, but the water was still rising, and it just about pulled us under.

"Marianne," I yelled to her. I yelled and I yelled, just her name, for about a
minute, but she couldn't hear. That's when Donald started yelling—he is a performer, and he has a good strong voice. He sang her name across the water.

Finally she opened her eyes, and I saw something there, but not helplessness—something fiercer than that. The water was up to her waist. The wind
was so strong, it had started taking down more trees. Donald yelled to ask if
she was okay, but she didn't answer.

I pointed up and she nodded, that look still in her eyes, and started to
climb. She hauled herself up that post inch by inch, until she could reach
the shed roof. The water helped her a little, rising as it was, floating her. She
had to lean sideways to grip the side of the shed's roof and pull herself over
and on top. When she climbed on top, she just lay there flat for a minute. She
must have been exhausted.

She couldn't stay there—we knew that, and she must have known it too,
because she sat up and looked back at us, as if we could tell her what to do.
The shed was wobbling with the force of the water all around it. Tom's motorcycle was clanking around, bashing at the walls.

Then a big limb came down in the rushing water; it just rolled down the hill. Donald and I had to scramble to get out of its way. It was a half-rotten live oak limb, gnarled and twisted. The leaf ends caught in the mangroves, and the broken end, maybe a foot thick, caught the side of the shed.

The water changed then. The limb was so big it acted like a dam, and the current was faster and stronger before the limb, and slower after. It was clear that the force of that strong water would take the shed down, then everything—the posts and roof, the oak limb, and Marianne—would be washed out to sea.

She saw this, understood it at the same time I did.

"You're gonna have to jump," Donald yelled. The rain had let up a little, but the wind was worse than ever, and the raindrops stung like needles. I didn't know how strong a swimmer she was. It was possible she could still get swept out, but it seemed like her only chance. I suppose I could have gone after her, like you said, but I didn't. You want to say that I'm a hero, but all I did was yell and point. I kept thinking about my daughters, how much I missed them, how much I wanted to see them again.

Marianne jumped, grabbing for the limb, and got one arm across it. She clung to it on the calmer gulf side, pulled herself along, bit by bit, the rough bark scraping her bare arms, her neck, her cheek. Those were the scrapes she had when you saw her. Donald helped her up when she made it across.

She was delirious. She kept calling Donald Eric, and asking about her sister, but she was strong enough to stand—no one carried her, though she leaned on Donald. The rain wasn't as bad then, but the water was still rising. We were all the way to the dining hall before we could walk without a current pulling at our ankles. That's where we found Eric and Tom, sitting inside at one of the tables in the dark, eating those little boxes of cereal from the breakfast buffet like a couple of teenage boys while the water came up over the steps and through the doorway. There I go again with my editorializing.

We told them about the flood. I was sort of holding on to Marianne then—she'd gotten scraped up and her clothes were torn and she was dazed. I sat her down in a chair. Eric had parked the van in the Kangaroo lot, which was higher up, and we decided to get everybody together and evacuate. That was one smart thing he did, moving that van.

Lilian meanwhile was yelling that the water was coming into the rooms. We couldn't find any rope, but there were long-handled mops in the dining hall, so Tom and Donald grabbed those and held them out while Lilian scrambled over her car and into the rising waters. It wasn't deep but it was swift, and if you weren't ready it could knock you off your feet. One at a time, they grabbed the mop handle and Donald pulled them in, passed them to Tom. We scrambled for the van. We got out of there.

I understand that the Ranch was badly damaged in the flood, and that you are moving to a new location, partnering up with a school of social media, or something like that. It sounds nice, and the possibility of more online classes sounds convenient too. I just don't think it's for me.

Partly, to be honest, this is because I can see that you are already re-writing my story. Take the ABC News interview with me and Donald: why just us? We are two people out of six, and while some of them (your staff members) did not make the best decisions, everybody was part of that experience, and we made it through together. And Donald did not save Marianne, not the way you described it. Though he might remember things differently and might be interested in the opportunity, it isn't the truth. I don't blame him—I understand that, as a novelist and an entertainer, he may have a different relationship to the truth—but I am not comfortable with that. What really happened is complicated and messy. Like you told me, if you want to sell a story it has to be simple.

Thank you again for what you tried to do for me. I'm sorry that I'm not up for it, but I'm not.

Please don't put any more words in my mouth. I am working on a book of poems, and I can tell that it will be slow going. But when it's done, every word will be my own.

Sincerely,
Janine Gray

22

"Hallelujah!" Janine said to Marianne after they made it up the hill. She kissed Marianne's forehead, whispered that it didn't matter, the things Marianne said and did; she was alive and God loved her. Marianne said nothing, but allowed herself to be half carried into the passenger van that Lilian had waiting for them on the street. In the backseat Janine covered her with a raincoat and let Marianne rest her head on her lap like a child. The rain pounded the ceiling and splashed the windows. Marianne shut her eyes tight; it felt so good to be covered, prone, silent. She was hoping she might have a bad concussion, brain damage, something to free her from dealing with everything that had to be done. Why had she held on? Why hadn't she let go? It would have been easy to drown, but she could feel the soreness in her arms and legs, bruised and scratched with the effort of clinging.

They made it to Ocala, found a seedy motel with a single vacancy. Tom thought this was funny and began calling them—Tom, Davonte, Eric, Marianne, Janine, and Lilian—the Motel 6. "Hey," he said, "at least it has hot water and electricity."

They took turns in the shower. Marianne went last, standing under a jet of lukewarm water. She ran a sliver of soap over the dirt-encrusted scrapes on her shins and inside her arms, pulled leaves and twigs from her hair. When the water ran mostly clear she turned it off, stepped onto the soggy bath mat, pulled her torn dress back on, wrung and knotted her hair at the nape of her neck.

The room glowed with charging devices, the only valuables they had had time to grab. No one talked much, not to each other. Everyone was texting and making phone calls—Janine to her husband and her daughter (Beth was fine, triumphant actually), Eric to Regina and Mark, Lilian and Davonte to their families. Tom acted like the whole thing was no big deal—no cell phones in Panama or Nicaragua, et cetera—but Marianne suspected he didn't have anyone wondering where he was. She called her father, who wasn't aware of the storm's severity, and Ruth, whose phone went to voicemail. She texted with Sophie, who had made it to a friend's house.

"Hey," Eric said, touching her shoulder after they turned off the lights. "Let's take a walk." Marianne's heart pounded as she followed him down the dingy carpeted hallway and through the heavy exit doors. It was barely raining in Ocala; it was hard to believe the sky could be calm again. It was late, past one o'clock, but the parking lot lights burned bright as day.

"You should have told me," Marianne said. "You brought me here on false pretenses. Frances told me—she told me everything."

"I thought you knew," he said. "I was going to tell you."

"Which was it? You thought I knew, or you were going to say something? It can't be both!"

"It is both. I wanted to talk to you about it, to clear the air, but I also was sure that you knew. When we talked about it, it seemed like you knew."

"I didn't know. I almost died."

"Why didn't you stay in the room? What were you thinking?"

"I was looking for you," she said. "I was going to save you! Why didn't you come back?"

"It was raining too hard! Tree limbs were falling! Even Tom saw that we couldn't make it to the shed! Any reasonable person could see that it wasn't safe!"

"I am not a reasonable person! You know this about me!"

"I know," he said finally, defeat in his voice, maybe even remorse. "I'm sorry. That's the difference between us."

"It is," Marianne agreed. She could tell they felt differently about what they were agreeing to, felt the admission diminished the other person. What it meant was: they could not be together. What it meant was: she'd been wrong about him.

It took three days to get back to the Ranch, there was so much damage to the roads. All the classrooms and dormitories were flooded, the water line halfway up the walls, and there were big tree limbs everywhere. Lilian found a small, hand-sewn notebook, the pages splayed and water-logged. "Dear Ruth," she read, "Here I am, trapped in a motel with my ugly bear list. Serves me right."

Everybody knew it was Marianne's, but they were so glad to be alive they weren't even mad—they thought it was funny, no hard feelings, back to business as usual. No one talked about her newspaper admissions, the fact that the school was founded dishonestly, although Eric and Regina were already on damage control, offering reassurances and refunds and scholarships. No one blamed Marianne outright, not Eric, not Regina, not Lilian or Davonte or Janine. But the Christians among them—Marianne guessed that was everybody but Eric—could not miss the message that God destroyed what she built, that her arrogance was being punished. She knew, once they got away from their own mortality, that their forgiveness would be temporary.

And it was.

So she went home—not to New York, but to Virginia. Her father knew, by then, about the scandal and the storm, but he didn't ask many questions, and they fell into a mostly silent routine: up at dawn, coffee, a long walk, more coffee, work. Marianne felt a little bereft, watching him grade the stack of papers that was always on the dining table, a little naked without her own admissions folders to cart around. She read; she worked on poems; she sent texts and emails to Ruth, all unanswered.

When would Ruth see her? she asked Howard one morning on their walk. She couldn't shut her out forever—could she?

Marianne had to jog to keep up with her dad's pace. "I almost died," she said.

"Maybe you need to reach out again," he said, slowing slightly, "in a different way. I've been doing some gardening at the church. Maybe there's something you can do. Something to help."

Finally Ruth agreed to a meeting brokered by Howard—Marianne could help put together the new nursery and playroom at her church. Marianne showed up early, but her sister was already there, struggling to open a box with dull scissors. "Here, let me," Marianne said, slicing open the box with her house key. On the side of the box was a photo of the finished play set—Noah's Ark, modern but unmistakable, made of smooth bentwood. "You don't have to put that together," Ruth said.

"Because of the flood?" Marianne said. "Or the Bible? Or maybe you think I'll screw it up." She reached inside to find the assembly instructions, opened a lengthy booklet written in German and pictographs. "Which I probably will."

"Sorry," Ruth said. "I'm sure you can handle it."

"You can ask," Marianne said. "About what happened. It's okay."

"Well," said Ruth. "You can tell me."

"I didn't mean for things to go the way they did," Marianne said.

"Which things? The part where you humiliated me in front of everyone at your school? The part where you went to the press and talked about how it was all a con? Or, let me see, the part where you recklessly endangered people's lives?"

Marianne wanted to argue—it was her school, and Ruth and Tad humiliated her—but remembered what Howard told her, she was here to help, maybe to listen. "I didn't want to hurt anyone," she said quietly. "I didn't mean to endanger anyone's life."

"Did you really just want to punish people, for believing? And take their money?"

"*No*," Marianne said.

"But you did take their money."

"I think I just wanted a change, I wanted to see if I could go back in time a little. Some of the experience was actually good. For me, and for the writers. I think."

"I'm sorry that things didn't work out with Eric. You loved him."

Marianne sighed and turned the booklet in her hands upside down. Here was the thing about coming home to family: even after years spent mostly apart, Ruth and Howard knew her better than anybody, and it felt good to be understood by people who would still let her in. That was how she'd once felt about Eric.

Their breakup, or whatever it was, still hurt, but the dull ache in her chest lessened a little every day. "It wasn't meant to be," Marianne said. "I think things should work out quickly if they're going to work out. You should *know*. Like Mom and Dad. Or you and Darryl."

Ruth smiled, and it struck Marianne how easy it was to please her sister, to make her happy: like anyone, she needed to be seen, to have her choices recognized and supported. She stood, and Marianne thought that she would hug her, but instead she retrieved something from her purse—a series of abstract black-and-white images in a long roll. Marianne gasped when she realized what it was.

"Eleven weeks," Ruth said. "That's from eight weeks, so you can't see much."

"It's beautiful!" Marianne said, not looking up from the fuzzy, television-static image. She wasn't sure what was baby, and what was Ruth. "Dad knows?"

"You're the first person we've told."

Marianne sat down amid the boxes, still holding the sonogram. Ruth unbuttoned her pants and sat down next to her.

"I found out not long before we went on the Tour of Life. My first sonogram was at one of GWGW's schools."

"Not this one," Marianne said quickly.

Ruth shook her head. "We were at this sonography school in Alpharetta, on the way back from the Ranch. I'd had a blood test by then, and Darryl said, why don't we ask them for an ultrasound? He was really proud and excited. It seemed like an okay idea to me, but when they got started, they looked worried. The sonographer couldn't find anything. Darryl took me to the hospital in Atlanta, and they found the baby, and the heartbeat, and everything was fine. But I was so scared—the whole ride there, in that awful traffic, I thought I had miscarried. I thought it was my fault—for traveling, for putting myself in a stressful situation."

"Oh Ruth, I had no idea—"

Ruth shook her head. "But that wasn't what was happening. I was fine. And it would have been one thing if it had been a student, a new student, but it was a *teacher* who did my ultrasound. We went home after that."

Marianne reached to take Ruth's hand, but Ruth crossed her arms. "I was so mad at you, Marianne."

"But you waited to tell me first," Marianne said quietly. "Why, if you're so mad at me?"

"You don't get it. I *look up to you*, Marianne."

"I'm sorry. I really am. If I could take it back, all of it, I would. But the baby's okay? My niece? Or my nephew?"

Ruth nodded, a little teary, and Marianne said she'd be right back—she needed to get something from the car.

Marianne had brought something for Ruth too—she had enlarged some of the sketches she'd saved from their mother, and bought simple pine frames for them, for the church nursery. Roadside daisies, a lady's slipper in the woods, a frog on a lily pad. She came back with an armload and held them up, one by one. She told Ruth about the lady's slippers, how an editor had confused them with irises. She left out the part about their mother's willingness to play along.

"The children will love these," Ruth said, standing and rubbing her back.

"Mom would be happy for you," Marianne said. "She'd be really proud." Marianne held the lady's slipper against the wall, at eye level.

"Lower," Ruth said. "We want the kids to see them."

Marianne told her, again, how their mother in her last months had lunch with Ruth every day, how they both picked her up after school and sometimes early, walking to the playground so Ruth could swing—she was obsessed with swinging, as high as she could. That was the time of these drawings.

"Tell me another," Ruth said, one hand on her stomach, after Marianne finished each story. And just when she thought she'd exhausted her store of memories—it was a long time ago—her mind, miraculously, presented another.

"Maybe I'll stay," she told her father at dinner. "I could get a job at the community college. We could be coworkers."

"They're not hiring. Only firing, unfortunately."

"Somewhere else then—in Williamsburg or Richmond. I could get a car."

"You can't stay here," Howard said. He softened when he saw her stricken face. "I mean you can stay with me as long as you like, but it wouldn't be good for you to live here."

"I don't have anywhere to go," she told him. "I lost my job."

"I remember you had a job before you went down to Florida," he said.

"I remember they wanted to hire you—that elementary school? You'll get bored here, Marianne. You'll never meet anyone. Trust me."

"But what about the baby?"

"I'll buy your tickets. Before the baby's born and after."

"You're that eager to get rid of me? After I almost drowned?"

"You need to go back to your life," he told her.

He was right—it was as if she'd lost her path. She needed to go back to the place she'd been before she got lost.

So she called around, made some appointments in New York, bought a train ticket and packed a suitcase. She called Mark, guilt and fear churning in her stomach, and asked him for a reference. He didn't sound angry or even surprised to hear from her. He caught her up on the latest news.

The Ranch was reopened on an existing GWGW campus, an Orlando-based school of mass communications and social media. Mark and his partners had, in his words, exited the investment opportunity. It was unclear how much his share of the take would be, but he said he'd set some aside for Eric and Marianne: a finder's fee, he called it. Eric was rewarded with a full-time GWGW job, with a real salary and benefits and a 401(k). He and Regina had just left for a trip to the British Isles—no hurricanes there, after all. He was taking her to the James Joyce House of the Dead, to Frank O'Connor's birthplace. Real romantic stuff, Mark told Marianne. She could tell he was trying to spare her feelings.

After reading Lorraine's student evaluations, they kept her on as poetry faculty. Tom said he'd had enough—he picked up a visiting writer gig in California. Frances was happy, for her part, to collect the insurance money. "Nobody lost out," Mark said. "Except, well, maybe you."

"What about the students?"

"We're overenrolled! They love the Ranch."

"No—the individual students. Like, what about Patty? And Davonte? And Janine Gray?"

"Davonte's doing great—didn't you see him on *Good Morning America*? I don't know about everybody else, but we were very generous with the people who went through the storm."

"Mark, did we have to do it this way? Did you have to have GWGW's help?"

He snorted. "Nobody gets anywhere on their own, Marianne. Not anywhere worthwhile."

Marianne thought that this was most truthful thing she'd ever heard Mark say.

"Can I call them? Email them?"

"Who—GWGW? I don't think—"

"No, Mark. The students."

"Marianne, like I said, I'm glad to give you a glowing reference. I'm glad to send the money—it's enough to get you into a new apartment, get you on your feet again. But don't you think it would be better to make a clean break? Start over? That's what I'm thinking would be best for everyone."

She gave him her dad's address and hung up. In her suitcase she'd packed the new clothes she'd bought, some notebooks, the snow globe from her mother. The water in the globe was now half-evaporated; it looked like there'd been a flood.

I love you, Janine had said, planting a kiss on her forehead. I forgive you.

23

Marianne's favorite time of day: four o'clock in the afternoon, blue-gray light filtering through her classroom's grimy windows, new tempera paintings hanging from the ceiling or drying on the racks near the radiator. Everything put back in order: the math manipulatives in their bins, books reshelved, brushes washed, paint jars lidded and rinsed. Desks wiped down, papers stickered with glitter stars. Halls quiet. Time to leave.

Today it snowed, one of those wet, early-December snows that usually stops as quickly as it starts. But the snow kept falling into the afternoon, and when twenty-five restless first-graders wouldn't turn their gaze from the windows, couldn't focus on the too-complicated fractions lesson, Marianne leaned toward them conspiratorially and whispered, "Do you want to hear the best words ever written about snow?"

"Yes!" they mostly screamed.

And she recited the last stanza of Wallace Stevens's "Thirteen Ways of Looking at a Blackbird."

"Ms. Stuart, how do you know that, without looking at a paper?" Sabrina, a favorite, asked without raising her hand.

None of Marianne's students were particularly good at raising their hands, but they all loved poetry. Marianne recited it again:

> *It was evening all afternoon.*
> *It was snowing*
> *And it was going to snow.*
> *The blackbird sat*
> *In the cedar-limbs.*

"That's called reciting," she said. "If you say something enough, it gets stuck in your brain. It's the same as learning a song. Want to hear the rest?"

They did, and spent the afternoon working on their own poems, inventing the spelling or dictating their lines to Marianne, who copied them in a large hand onto gray loose-leaf. Thirteen Ways of Looking at P.S. 150. Thirteen Ways of Looking at Ms. Stuart. Fifteen Ways of Looking at My Shoes. Ten Ways of Looking at a Subway Rat.

Marianne has been teaching under a provisional license since September, when she moved back to the city and enrolled, using the money Mark sent, in a teacher certification program. Usually she has one good teaching idea a day, one moment when all the students are actually paying attention not because she threatened them or raised her voice or was on the verge of crying but because of her own enthusiasm and energy. Hardly any of these ideas have been planned ahead of time, and most of them are what the principal calls "off task." Her class celebration after Obama's reelection, their Panama City pen pal project, the time they wandered the halls with rulers, measuring doorways, floor tiles, the water fountain: this was not what they were supposed to be doing at the time. And certainly the principal would have noticed this off-task poetry writing, but it was snowing, and half the teachers hadn't even come to work, and because of that there were kids from the second grade crowding Marianne's classroom, and now they all know some of the words to a famous poem.

> *It was evening all afternoon.*
> *It was snowing*
> *And it was going to snow.*

Thick flakes cover her hair and coat and backpack as she makes her way to the elevated train stop, largely deserted. She is headed to the city—a shorter commute than back to her neighborhood, but still an hour's train ride, maybe more with weather delays.

Are you sure you can make it? Janine texted her, earlier that day.

Yes, she texted back. *You?*

Of course!

Marianne is nervous about seeing Janine, and she wouldn't mind canceling their date at a coffee shop, well known for its eight-dollar hot cocoa, near her Midtown hotel. But she isn't going to be the one to back out—not after Janine made the flight from Florida. She is here with her daughter—Beth has an interview with the local NBC affiliate—and wants to see Marianne in person.

They'd started talking again not long ago. Marianne heard that Janine had not returned to school, and she was worried. So she called, she emailed, she texted. Finally, in late October, Janine wrote back— there was a hurricane set to make landfall in New York; would Marianne take shelter, please? Marianne was struck by how reckless she still must seem, how careless of her own life, when that wasn't how she felt at all. Not that there was much she could do about Sandy, other than wait in her fourth-floor apartment for the water to recede and the power to be restored. *Things are fine*, she texted after the worst was over. *I'm safe.*

Praise God! Janine replied, followed by a long email about how she thought, after their storm, that she'd give up poetry forever. It worked for a while—she was made department chair at school, and Beth was applying for jobs in faraway places; her husband's job was busy, and her younger daughter was raising money for orphans. They turned the writing room her husband built for her into an entertainment room, with a big-screen TV and surround sound, and at night they watched reality programs: *Ice Road Truckers, Pawn Stars, America's Got Talent*. But she said she just felt empty and unanchored, like a part of her was missing or dead.

Marianne wrote back to her right away. You are a poet, she told Janine, and that is something you just can't help, like a disease or a birth defect, but if you accept it, it can make things better, can at least help you understand things. She sent a poem she'd written about Ruth and asked Janine if she wanted to exchange work—not a teacher-student relationship, nothing formal. Just an even exchange. Work for work, thoughts for thoughts.

So they write, they email, they talk on the phone. Sometimes they Skype after school in the very classrooms that have exhausted them, or else at home, after supper. Marianne sits at her kitchen table and Janine sits in a closet she's rigged up for writing, much better, she says, than the big glass room her husband built. They talk about poetry—Janine has become a big reader of the Beats, but also the Black Arts writers and the Imagists. Marianne has been reading old favorites: Plath and Sexton and

Dickinson, Rilke and Neruda and Szymborska and Levertov and Rich and Olds. They have arguments about writing. Janine doesn't understand how Marianne can write if she doesn't believe in God, and Marianne doesn't understand why she would write if she does. What's the point, they both wonder? Neither one can explain it to the other.

But in person, that's different, Marianne thinks, when her train finally screeches to its stop. It's possible Janine has saved some recriminations for this meeting—why wouldn't she? Or else they'll be awkwardly silent around the things that have gone unsaid: how Marianne could have started an entire school under false pretenses, why she allowed Janine and her work to be used by GWGW, why she went to the press and not to her students.

She gets up anyway, climbs the stairs, and walks through stinging sideways-blown snow to the coffee shop crowded with tourists clutching shopping bags. Christmas music playing. A quick scan around the over-warm room—maybe Janine isn't here, she thinks—but then she recognizes her friend, seated with two mugs at a small table near the window.

"You made it!" Janine cries, standing. She embraces Marianne, even though her heavy coat is wet with snow. "The line was so long, I got you some too. I hope it's still warm."

"How was Beth's interview?"

"Fingers crossed, but I think it went well. That's an amazing thing to come out of the storm—the Weather Channel footage has brought in so many opportunities."

"That's great, Janine. She deserves it." Marianne sips the intensely sweet, thick cocoa.

"Do you think she'd be okay? If she lived here? She's never lived away from home. And New York City . . ."

"She'll love it," Marianne says. "She's tough and smart. She'll do great, and the storm—" Marianne doesn't know why she's bringing up Sandy, when it has taken such enormous effort not to read a message into this second, destructive storm. But that doesn't mean it isn't on Janine's mind. "We don't usually have weather like that. If we do, I'll help—she can call me anytime. Or maybe I'll call her?" She says this last part as lightly as she can.

Janine shakes her head in wonderment. "You see? So many blessings.

I'm reminded all the time that God has a plan for every trial He puts in front of us."

"It was definitely a trial, wasn't it?" Marianne hopes she is opening up a place for Janine to let her have it.

"Look," Janine says, reaching into her bag. She brings out Davonte's book, *Shelter from da Storm*, and slides it toward Marianne. "I went to a reading at our Barnes & Noble and got it autographed for you. Did you know there's a whole character inspired by me? I think you're in it too."

"Thank you." Marianne already has a copy, sent by Eric, whose name is prominently featured in the acknowledgments pages. She has yet to read it.

"Did you know he actually wrote most of it himself?" Janine asks. "He decided, halfway through, that he actually *liked* writing. Plus he told me he didn't think Eric had a very good handle on the redemption part."

Marianne laughs. "That's probably accurate," she says, running her fingers over the glossy book jacket. "I'm glad he did it on his own. Eric didn't tell me that."

"Do you still talk to him?"

"Not much."

Janine tells her how if she just lived in Panama City, she'd have so many single men to introduce her to—good men from church, and a couple of guys in a writing group she found online. They've started meeting once a month, reading their work aloud. Marianne feels a little stab of jealousy over the fact that Janine has a writing group without her.

"Do you talk about school—the Ranch? Do they know about it?"

"That's behind me," Janine says firmly. "It wasn't what I expected, or maybe even what I hoped, but it wasn't all bad. I think that it was God's plan. I hope you believe me."

Marianne nods.

"I took your advice," Janine says. "I sent those poems to Terri Schiavo's parents, telling them I wouldn't publish another one or even keep writing about their daughter if they didn't want me to. I was so worried, waiting to hear back—maybe I wouldn't hear anything, I thought, and that would be the worst. But they wrote back, a really nice note. They *thanked* me. So I wanted to thank you. Because I've been writing more."

Janine reaches across the table, takes Marianne's hand in hers, squeezes. "You know, you deserve good things too. You deserve to finish your book and call it anything you like. That's what Terri's parents told me. And it's what I wanted to tell you."

Marianne sits back, a little stunned, but does not let go of Janine's hand. On her computer, the folder of poems—slowly but steadily growing—is still named "The Ugly Bear List," but she thinks of that title as temporary, a placeholder until she finds something better. It may be a while before she finishes this book, but she's not in a hurry.

"Thank you," Marianne says. She doesn't know what else to say, so she starts naming the good things in her life. "I'm so glad to see you. I had a good teaching day today. And my sister called last week—I missed the gender reveal party, but she's having a girl."

"A girl!" Janine squeals. People at nearby tables turn to look at them, and Marianne realizes that they probably think it's her news, this baby girl. But that's okay—it is her news, isn't it?

"And good teaching days," Janine says. "You have to hang on to those. It's such a dream to be here—can you believe this is my first time in New York? And it snows? Think you'll get out of school tomorrow?"

Marianne looks outside, where fine white flakes dance and swirl, illuminated by the streetlights and the headlights of slow-moving traffic. It's close to her own childhood image of the city, the one she learned about in the books she read with her mother. But school here is never closed, and she knows which kids will be there tomorrow, sleepy-eyed and warming themselves by the radiator. She'll read *The Snowy Day* with them, do cut-paper collage, heat paper cups of chocolate milk in the microwave.

"Probably not," she says. "But that's okay."

"Every day is a gift," Janine says. "A gift from God."

Marianne doesn't believe that, but she is glad to be alive. For months now, at random times of day, gratitude has washed over her in waves—for Janine's friendship, for her father and Ruth and the baby. For the warmth of sun on her face in December, a child leaning against her knees at story time. The lift of finishing a poem or starting a new one. She hopes it lasts.

Riding the subway home, she allows herself to remember the feeling, as she went underwater, of desperately wanting to live. She remembers letting go, then being knocked into a post and grabbing hold before climbing onto the flimsy shed roof. She doesn't know how Davonte or Janine had the courage to wait for her in the rising waters, or how she had the courage to jump.

Tonight there will be an early holiday party in her building—they put off the condo sale, and no one, except Marianne, even bothered to move out. Still, her neighbors have been gone so much on their own various journeys that they hardly noticed she was away for a whole year. She'll put off her lesson plans, get dressed up, drink bourbon cocktails that burn her throat pleasantly.

Marianne! Her neighbors will say. What have you been up to?

And she'll be tempted to tell them everything. She can picture herself making light of it all, exaggerating for effect, portraying herself as the victim or the hero. It's just the kind of story they'd be into.

But then she'll think about Janine, and she'll feel guilty. She's resolved not to betray anyone again, and not to lie.

Maybe she'll say she had a teaching job down in Florida.

Maybe, just to mess with them, she'll tell them she got saved.

Acknowledgments

Thank you, Katie Dublinski, for your vast patience as I worked on this novel, and your wisdom and thoughtfulness as you helped me shape it. Thank you, in fact, to everyone at Graywolf—especially Fiona McCrae, Susannah Sharpless, Marisa Atkinson, Caroline Nitz, and Casey O'Neil. And to Kimberly Glyder for another beautiful cover! I continue to feel so proud and lucky to be a member of the Graywolf family.

And thank you to my other wolfpack—my many friends at North Carolina State University. I'm especially grateful to Wilton Barnhardt for his sharp notes and ideas, and to John Kessel, Shervon Cassim, Dorianne Laux, and Eduardo Corral for being such excellent colleagues. Thanks to my students for asking after the novel, and for being so inspiring in the classroom and beyond.

Thank you to Dan Kois, Meaghan Mulholland, Krista Bremer, and Jon Mozes for your enormously helpful feedback and encouragement.

Thank you to Jill McCorkle, who supported and cheered this book from its beginning.

And to Maria Massie, my wonderful agent.

I'm also grateful to the National Endowment for the Arts, the North Carolina Arts Council, the Durham Arts Council, the Sewanee Writers' Conference, the Squaw Valley Writers' Conference, and the Orion Environmental Writers' Conference, for support and inspiration while I worked on the book. And also to Edna "Diddie" Parrish, for your Florida hospitality.

Finally, I'm grateful to my family for your steadfast support—to Buttons and Terry Boggs, who have always believed that you can live a good and useful life as an artist.

To Beatrice and Harriet, who each arrived at just the right time.

And to Richard—I'm so lucky to have you as a first, best, and last reader, and a partner in all things.

Belle Boggs is the author of *The Art of Waiting: On Fertility, Medicine, and Motherhood* and *Mattaponi Queen*, a collection of linked stories set along Virginia's Mattaponi River. *The Art of Waiting* was a finalist for the PEN/Diamonstein-Spielvogel Award for the Art of the Essay and was named a best book of the year by *Kirkus, Publishers Weekly*, the *Globe and Mail, Buzzfeed*, and *O, the Oprah Magazine*. *Mattaponi Queen* won the Bakeless Prize and the Library of Virginia Literary Award and was a finalist for the 2010 Frank O'Connor International Short Story Award. Boggs has received fellowships from the National Endowment for the Arts, the North Carolina Arts Council, and the Bread Loaf and Sewanee writers' conferences, and her stories and essays have appeared in *Ploughshares*, the *Paris Review, Harper's, Orion, Guernica*, and other publications. She teaches in the MFA program at North Carolina State University.

The text of *The Gulf* is set in Arno Pro.
Book design by Rachel Holscher.
Composition by Bookmobile Design and Digital Publisher Services, Minneapolis, Minnesota.
Manufactured by Versa Press on acid-free, 30 percent post-consumer wastepaper.